The Vi

The
Viper
of Milan

Marjorie Bowen

Elliott & Thompson
London

CONTENTS

CONTENTS

Introductory Note

Perhaps it is only in childhood that books have any deep influence on our lives. In later life we admire, we are entertained, we may modify some views we already hold, but we are more likely to find in books merely a confirmation of what is in our minds already.

When – perhaps I was fourteen by that time – I took Miss Marjorie Bowen's *The Viper of Milan* from the library shelf, the future for better or worse really struck. From that moment I began to write. All other possible futures slid away: the potential civil servant, the don, the clerk had to look for other incarnations. Imitation after imitation of Miss Bowen's magnificent novel went into exercise books – stories of sixteenth-century Italy or twelfth-century England marked with enormous brutality and a despairing romanticism. It was as if I had been supplied once and for all with a subject.

Why? On the surface *The Viper of Milan* is only the story of a war between Gian Galeazzo Visconti, Duke of Milan, and Mastino della Scala, Duke of Verona, told with zest and cunning and an amazing pictorial sense. Why did it creep in and colour and explain the terrible living world of the stone stairs and the never quiet dormitory? It was no good in that real world to dream that one would ever be a Sir Henry Curtis of *King Solomon's Mines*, but della Scala who at last turned from an honesty that never paid and betrayed his friends and died dishonoured and a failure even at treachery – it was easier for a child to escape behind his mask. As for Visconti, with his beauty, his patience and his genius for evil, I had watched him pass by many a time in his black Sunday suit smelling of mothballs. His name was Carter. He exercised terror from a distance like a snowcloud over the young fields. Goodness has only once found a perfect incarnation in a human body and never will again, but evil can always find a home there. Human nature is not black and white but black and grey. I read all that in *The Viper of Milan* and I looked round and I saw that it was so.

There was another theme I found there. At the end of *The Viper of Milan* – you will remember if you have once read it – comes the great scene of complete success – della Scala is dead, Ferrara, Verona, Novara, Mantua have all fallen, the messengers pour in with news of fresh victories, the whole world outside is cracking up, and Visconti sits and jokes in the wine light. I was not on the classical side or I would have discovered, I suppose, in Greek literature instead of in Miss Bowen's novel the sense of doom that lies over success – the feeling that the pendulum is about to swing. That too made sense; one looked around and saw the doomed everywhere – the champion runner who one day would sag over the tape; the head of the school who would atone, poor devil, during forty dreary undistinguished years; the scholar… and when success began to touch oneself too, however mildly, one could only pray that failure would not be held off for too long.

One had lived for fourteen years in a wild jungle country without a map, but now the paths had been traced and naturally one had to follow them. But I think it was Miss Bowen's apparent zest that made me want to write. One could not read her without believing that to write was to live and to enjoy.

Graham Greene

To my Mother

Author's Note

This story should be read as a fantasy, the theme of which is Italy of the late Middle Ages. The various potentates mentioned and places described belong to the author's imagination. The names of some of the characters will be found in the History books, but the names only.

'Lovely in the midst of crime,
    And yet unlovely through excess of guilt,
He dazzled through that dim-lit time,
    And noble blood for a vain shadow split.'

I

GIAN GALEAZZO MARIA VISCONTI

It is a day in early summer, as beautiful as such days were in the Southern lands of 500 years ago. It is Italy steeped in golden sunlight which lies like a haze over the spreading view; the year 1360, when cities were beautiful and nature all-pervading. Here is Lombardy, spread like a garden in the hollow of the hills, ringed about with the purple Apennines, covered with flowers, white, yellow, purple and pink. This wide road, one of the finest in Italy, winds from Milan to Brescia, its whole length through chestnut woods and plains covered with flowering myrtle. Primroses in great clusters border its sides, and from the midst of their delicate blooms spring the slender stems of poplar-trees; these are red-gold, bursting into bloom against a tender sky; tufts of young green; clumps of wild violets.

But for all its unspoiled beauty, the road was one of common use, for Milan was within hail. Villas, the summer dwellings of its wealthy peers, stood back among the trees, surrounded by magnificent grounds. Behind them beautiful open country spread into the blue distance, fragrant and glorious with budding trees. And cold and magnificent the great city itself, with its huge walls and gates, crowned and emphasized the landscape's beauty. The lines of hundreds of turrets and spires, bold and delicate, leaped up against the sky. And paramount, catching the eye with colour, weighing on the mind with meaning, were the city's banners. They floated from the gates and the highest buildings, half a score of them, all with the same device. Far off could that device be read: a green viper on a silver ground: the emblazonment of the Visconti.

From afar the city was a vision of stately splendour, and the low dwellings clustered round about her walls, in the shadow of the palaces, appeared to the nearing traveller but a touch added of the picturesque. A close survey, however, revealed semi-ruined huts; in their foul neglect and unsightliness, a blot upon the scene. They were homes of peasants, who, tattered and miserable, starved and unwashed, seemed their fitting occupants. Here comes a band of them slowly dragging along the road toward Milan, men, women, and children, leading a few rough-haired mules, laden with scanty country produce. It was poor stuff; and a poor living they made at it. The wealthy grew their own fruit and vegetables, the poorer could not afford to buy. Crushed by hopeless oppression into a perpetual dull acceptance, the crowd trudged along, with shuffling feet and bent heads, unheeding the beauty and the sunshine, unnoticing the glory of the spring, with dull faces from which all the soul had been stamped out, and 'fear' writ large across the blank.

Every movement showed them slaves, every line in their bent figures told they lived under a rule of terror, too potent for them to dare even to raise their eyes to question. A stream of grey and brown monotony along the glorious road, decked with the fairest beauty of fair Italy, these miserable peasants were strangely out of keeping, both with the radiant blossoming country and the magnificent city they drew near.

Keeping close behind them walked a young man and a boy, better attired than the others, yet travel-worn and weary-looking. The delicate cast of their features bespoke them of another part of Italy, as did the soft Latin tongue in which they held their whispering excited conversation. The elder, whom his companion called Tomaso, was a fair-haired youth of about nineteen; the other, like enough to be a relative, a mere child of ten or twelve. The sun was growing hot, and their stout cloaks of dull red serge were flung back, showing their leathern doublets, to which the elder boy wore attached a great pouch of undressed skin, which evidently bore their day's provisions.

Suddenly, when Milan, clear and grey, was distant barely half a mile, the group of wretched figures was roused from its shuffling apathy: and the terror latent in their aspect leaped into life and motion.

Swept back by the others, the two Florentines gazed in amazement to learn the cause of this panic. In the distance, brilliant between the dark stone of the gateway of the city, fluttered a banner, blazoned with the same device as those that blew above the walls. The peasants' eyes, sharpened by fear, were quicker than Tomaso's: it was some seconds before he could discern that the banner fluttered from the canopy of a splendid coach, magnificent in gold and scarlet, issuing from the sombre shadow into the sunshine of the road; and as it drew nearer, he looked with pleasure not unmixed with wonder at the rich gildings, fine silk, the beauty of the four black horses, the size and magnificent liveries of the huge negroes who walked at their heads. To him it was an interesting sight, an incident of his travels. But to the Milanese peasants it was the symbol of the dread power that ruled Lombardy with a grip of blood, the device that kept Milan, the wealthiest, proudest city in the north, cringing in silent slavery; the banner that had waved from city after city, added by force or treachery to the dominions of Milan; the banner of Gian Galeazzo Maria Visconti, Duke.

With trembling hands and muttered threats to their slow beasts, the hinds dragged their burdens to the roadside, forcing the children back into the hedges; leaving clear the way. Cowering and awestruck, in fascinated expectation, they stared, toward that oncoming banner, and at the horseman who rode behind.

Still at the same measured pace the coach advanced; a cumbrous structure, swung high on massive gilded wheels, and open under an embroidered canopy of scarlet silk. At the head of each black horse walked a negro, richly dressed in scarlet and gold. The trappings of the steeds were dazzling, in stamped leather and metal.

But this splendour of array the peasant folk of Lombardy were used to; it was not that which made them crouch as if they would ask the earth to hide them, shiver and shudder yet farther back as if the soft green bank could save them.

In the coach sat two, a man and a woman, but both so old and shrivelled that the distinguishing characteristics of their sex were well-nigh lost. Both were richly clad in furs, and half-hidden in satin cushions, nothing of the old man visible but his wrinkled face, grey beard, and, loaded with rings, thin yellow hands, the fingers of which were clutching nervously at his heavy silken robe. The woman, painted and bedizened under a large red wig, weighed down by a gown of cloth of gold, and with pearls around her neck, wrung her hands together, and whispered incoherently below her breath. Both had sunk together among the cushions in an attitude of despair, the man looking steadily in front of him with white face, the woman casting terror-stricken eyes over the wretched spectators in a mute appeal for help, if even from them.

Behind them rode the single horseman who had struck the terror. His pace was leisurely, his horse's bridle held by a pale-faced man with long red hair, of a stealthy bearing, crushed and mean-looking, but resplendent in a jewelled dress. The rider himself slight and handsome, about thirty, plainly attired in green, gave at a first glance, small token of the spell he exercised. He rode with ease and surety: in one hand a half-rolled parchment from which he read aloud in a soft voice, in the other a long whip with which he flicked and teased the occupants of the carriage.

The coach and its occupants, the solitary rider, and the red-haired man, were the whole of the procession.

At the rider's side hung a single dagger, the others were unarmed, yet the crowd trembled under a spell of fear as if half Italy had backed that man. No one gave sign of feeling, no one moved, though the wretched couple looked around keenly and eagerly, with the helpless misery of those who have fallen below everything save fear, and will stoop to ask help of the lowest. And the Visconti banner floated out dreamily upon the light spring breeze, and the rider rode at ease and read from the parchment with a smiling face.

Suddenly the old man rose, and threw out his hands with a wild gesture toward the crouching peasants. His frantic cry was stifled on his lips, and a cut from the whip sent him back to his seat with a snarl of impotent fury. The woman sobbed aloud, but sat still, for the tease of the whip followed their slightest movements, though the horseman seemed to heed nothing but the parchment from which he read.

> 'Beautiful the Tuscan flowers grew
> Around the Florentine –'

The soft lines died away on his smiling lips: he raised his eyes and looked straight at the old man, who, at the words, had turned in his seat and was gazing over his shoulder with an intensity of hate.

But on the pause there followed a cold laugh as the old man winced, faltered, and dropped his eyes from that charmed and steady gaze. Again the whip circled round them, and the calm voice continued:

> 'But straight and firm the poplars grew
> The Lombard ranks between.

The woman gazed around at the crowd, desperate in hopeless misery. Hopeless indeed. Not a finger was raised, not a word uttered, though, men alone, they numbered more than fifty.

> 'Perchance thou wouldst not dare to turn
> And draw the veil from off that face,
> Fearing what secrets thou might'st learn
> Both for thine own and her disgrace,'

read the horseman, and the cavalcade passed on its heavy way, and the faint hope that had leaped to life within the wretched victims, at sight of human eyes upon them, died within them.

But on the outside of the crowd, Tomaso and Vittore,

kneeling with the rest, as that banner drew near, now stirred uneasily, and, as the coach came abreast, the woman made a convulsive movement with her hands. The elder sprang to his feet and stepped forward impulsively. At sight of him in the roadway the horseman drew rein, and the terror-stricken crowd watched breathless, while the youth advanced boldly to his stirrup, hot words upon his lips, defiance in his eyes. The red-haired man at the bridle crouched, but before the lad could speak, the rider, leaning forward, struck him a blow full across the face.

There was no need for a second. With a scream of pain, Tomaso fell back, and then, as if noticing them for the first time, the horseman sent his glance on the crowd. No sound or movement: they cowered beneath his eyes in deprecating silence.

'Drive on,' he said, and the dreary procession started again, winding through the sun and shadow toward Brescia.

So great was the spell upon the peasants, that though the wounded boy lay moaning in the road not a man, scarce a child among them, stirred from his place till the banner of the Viper was a silver speck in the distance.

Then with shaking hands the youth was dragged into the ditch amid a babble of blame and fear. Vittore, rising from his stricken comrade, gazed into the distance with horror-stricken eyes.

'Who was it,' he whispered at last to the woman near him. 'Who was it.'

She turned a dull face from the scattered vegetables she was gathering together.

'Who art thou that thou knowest not,' she asked.

'I come from Florence,' said the lad quickly, 'travelling to Verona.'

'To Verona! Thou art not on thy way to Verona here.'

'I know it, but the company we travelled with was bound for Milan. Three days ago we missed them, and thought to find them in the city where we looked to spend the night, but now –'

He glanced at his companion and could scarce refrain from weeping.

'To Verona!' said an old peasant, turning sharply at the name. 'To Verona!'

The child dropped again to his knees beside Tomaso.

'Yes,' he said, over his shoulder. 'My cousin – he is done to death, I fear me – and I were travelling by way of Milan to della Scala's court –'

He broke off, and wrung his hands. 'Oh, help me, some one; Tomaso is dying!'

With a certain dull humanity, kindness it could scarcely be called that was so inert and full of apathy, one or two of them gave what help they could.

'Thou art from Florence!' said the old man again. 'Aye, indeed, I *know* thou art from Florence, for thy mate here to have had daring. Why camest thou from *Florence* to anywhere by way of Milan.'

For even to the dull mind of the peasantry, Florence, who alone of the cities of Italy had preserved her liberty, seemed a country of the free, a republic of equality.

'Tomaso's father sent for him to come to him in della Scala's court, and as last year my father was slain in the wars with Venice, since then I have resided with my cousin – and so accompany him – having naught else to do!'

The boy looked up bewildered; he was half-dazed with this sudden misfortune.

'We go to Verona!' he repeated. 'We have food and a little money – if only this had not happened!'

He turned to his prostrate cousin and burst into tears.

The woman looked at him with pity: the old peasant shrugged his shoulders.

'Thy cousin was over-bold! As well face the evil one –' he mumbled and crossed himself, 'as step into the path of the –' he stopped abruptly and cast uneasy glances around him.

'And that,' cried the boy, his tears arrested, 'that man on horseback.'

'That was the Visconti! Aye! Gian Galeazzo Maria, Duke of Milan!'

The lad gazed down the road with interest and new terror.

'The Duke of Milan! He who lately warred with Florence!' he cried breathlessly.

'Aye, and beat her!' There was a touch of pride in the answer, for the peasant was of Milan. But the boy did not notice the remark, he was too absorbed in terrified conjecture.

'And they in the carriage –,' he whispered.

A silence fell. The crowd shuffled away from him, and turned their faces to the city. Used to scenes of horror as they were, the cavalcade that had just passed them seemed, even to their half hearts, to have chilled the sunlight with its terror.

A young woman suddenly snatched her child up from the ground and strained it to her, in a passion of distress.

'Oh, Luigi, Luigi, my little child, it was his father and mother, his father and mother!'

She grasped the old man's arm. 'Marked you how she looked at me,' she cried.

The peasant checked her outbreak, but looked down the road with gloomy eyes.

'They will never return from Brescia,' he said; 'they must be near seventy – old for such an end. However, hush thee, woman, 'tis no affair of ours!' Several anxious voices echoed him.

'Why should we care!' said one, ''tis a Visconti the less to crush us.'

And Vittore saw the whole band turning off, pushing, driving, and urging their beasts along. He dragged at his still senseless companion in a sudden panic.

'Help me!' he said. 'We would go on; I dare not stay alone.'

The old man laughed harshly.

'Where will you go to? Are we to drag you into Milan to be whipped to death for harbouring you; and Verona is in the hands of the Visconti – his last and greatest victory!'

'But my uncle – della Scala's court!' cried the boy distractedly. The old man drew himself up in his rags and spoke with a mixture of pride and awe.

'Mastino della Scala perished in the flames of his burning palace; his wife is a prisoner, yonder in Milan, in the Visconti's hands. Thou hast not much to look for from della Scala's court,' he said.

'Hold thy peace! Hold thy peace!' cried angry voices. 'What hast thou to do with such as he,' and the old man, whose better intelligence made him a source of danger to the others, was dragged away.

'But thou wilt not leave me here,' said Vittore, in distress. 'Where shall I go? What shall I do.' But the peasant folk were not much moved by his misfortunes, too much used to scenes like this.

'We risk our necks by staying by thee,' growled one dark-browed man. 'As for thy companion, it is his own mad doing. He is dead, and we may be dead this time tomorrow, and kicked into the ditch like him.'

Even the woman listened blankly to his entreaties, and the throng sullenly departed on its way.

'Any moment a soldier of the Visconti may come by, or the Visconti himself may return, then anyone found tending one of his victims will be in sorry plight.' This, mumbled out with curses at the delay, was their only answer.

The peasants of Lombardy lived in the shadow of an awful name. Gian Galeazzo Maria Visconti knew fear of neither God nor man, neither pity nor remorse.

The young Florentine sank down upon the grass, and looked after the retreating train in mute distress. To seek for help would mean to leave his cousin, and he could not move him. Tomaso lay in a deep swoon, for the blow had driven him back upon a stone. Terribly wounded about the face, Tomaso added to his young cousin's distress by his ghastly appearance, his head bound in rough bandages, torn from Vittore's clothing, and now darkly stained with blood. The boy wrung his hands and looked up and down the road – no one in sight.

It was just after the victory in the long-standing wars between the cities; Verona had fallen into the Visconti's hands; interchange of traffic was for the time laid low; the road was likely to be deserted, and for hours none passed.

The boy dragged Tomaso's head and shoulders as far into the shade as he could manage, remoistened the bandages about his head, and tried to force down his throat some of the food and drink they carried. But the youth muttered between clenched teeth, and lay with wide-staring eyes, inert and unresponsive. His consciousness had returned, but he was delirious with fever. As the day wore on, new and sickening terror seized on Vittore. The Visconti would return to Milan! Hiding his face in his hands, he sobbed aloud. Since the bright dawn of the morning, what a change in prospects! Della Scala's court a ruin, and Tomaso's father – his uncle, the only parent he had left now – what of him! And Tomaso too! He must sit there and see him die beside him. As the noontide waned, he had fallen again into stupor, and the boy looked at his changed face distractedly.

'He is dead!' he cried, 'I know he is dead!' But he dared not leave him; besides, Milan held a terror, and he would scarcely dare to enter it. Perhaps when the peasants returned they might have pity on them; if not – again his sobs filled up the lonely outlook. The long hours dragged by; a horseman passed, a mercenary laden with some plunder from Verona; he did not even turn in his saddle. A few peasants slowly came back from Milan, seeking their huts around the neighbouring villas. But they were as deaf to his cries as before; he could come with them if he liked; but the other – he was dead and killed by the Visconti; let him lie there. And now Vittore was in despair; the sun was beginning to drop behind the trees, the delicate stems of the poplars stretched in long blue shadows, the faint golden light lay across the primroses, making them fairylike. Suddenly a step aroused him. Some one along the road. He started to his feet, and there, still in the distance, but rapidly approaching, was the figure of a traveller, his shadow thrown before him, his face set toward Milan.

II

'Francisco'

A gleam of hope sent Vittore forward. Here was some-one who, alone and on foot, must know the perils of travel, and might be kind-hearted; though, with Tomaso dead, what even pity could do for him he scarcely knew. Then again the boy's heart failed him. Perhaps this was no more than some wandering robber. He paused, drew back, and the traveller came on not noticing him, his gaze fixed keenly on the distant city.

By the roadside some boulders, half-hidden in violets and golden with moss, offered a seat, and half-stumbling over them, the stranger abruptly withdrew his eyes from Milan and saw for the first time the boy who from a few paces off was timorously observing him.

He was a powerful mean of gigantic size, clothed in coarse leather, undressed, patched, slashed, and travel-worn. His legs were bound with straw and thongs of skin, the feet encased in rough wooden shoes stuffed with grass.

A battered leathern cap covered his head, and from his shoulder hung a ragged scarlet cloak. A dagger and a sword were stuck in his belt, a leather pouch hung at his side. The man's face and bearing belied his dress. He was not handsome, and a peculiar effect was given to his expression by the half-shut brown eyes, but he had a grave and stately bearing, and as he bestowed a searching gaze upon Vittore, the boy felt renewed encouragement.

'Sir,' cried the lad advancing, 'I am in great distress. My cousin lies there dead, or dying. Help me to get him to some shelter.'

'I am a stranger here,' replied the traveller, 'and have no shelter for myself tonight.'

His accent, like his bearing, again belied his dress. He spoke in the refined Tuscan tongue, the language of the better classes, and to Vittore, who was gently nurtured, more familiar than the rough dialect of Lombardy, which he and Tomaso could only barely comprehend.

'But what I can find for myself,' he added, 'thou art welcome to share. Where is thy cousin.'

Vittore pointed to the recumbent figure half-hidden in the bank; the man glanced across, then around him. The sun was almost set, a whole flock of delicate little pink clouds lay trembling over Milan, its noble outline already half in shadow.

'It will be dark soon,' he said, 'and perchance –' he broke off abruptly. 'Thy cousin, didst thou say? – what has happened to him? Wounded in some roadside fray.'

He rose as he spoke and crossed over to the fallen boy. 'And what are you two doing travelling alone,' he demanded sternly.

'Alas, messer, we were going to Verona.'

'To Verona, by way of Milan.'

'We had no choice. The company we travelled with were bound hither, but three days ago we missed them, and came on here alone, lest perhaps they had preceded us. But for this accident we thought to pass the night in Milan – but now, what shall we do? And we hear that Verona has been taken!'

The stranger was bending over Tomaso, and Vittore did not see his face.

'How did this happen,' he asked presently, touching the mark upon Tomaso's face. And Vittore told him.

The stranger was quiet a long breath.

'So this is *Visconti's* doing,' he said at last. 'Thy cousin is a brave lad.'

And he fell again into a silence which Vittore dared not break, while under the stranger's care Tomaso opened his eyes, and feebly muttered and tried to rise. But the other bade him wait a while, and turned to Vittore again.

'And which way did Visconti ride,' he asked.

The boy pointed. 'The peasants said it was toward Brescia.'

'And he has not yet re-entered Milan.'

'No, messer.' By now Vittore felt and showed respect.

'Then we will not enter Milan either,' said the stranger, 'since Visconti has not.'

The boy gazed on him, struck by his tone, and Tomaso's eyes, half-closing, re-opened and fixed themselves upon the stranger's face.

'Messer, you hate Visconti,' whispered Vittore.

The man laughed shortly. 'There are many in Lombardy who hate Visconti,' he said. 'Perhaps I not less than others. Boy,' he added, with sudden intensity, 'I have only two things to live for: one is to tell Visconti to his face what one man's hatred is.'

And leaving them half-terrified, he strode into the road, and shading his eyes looked long and searchingly away from Milan; but the dusk was settling fast, and there was not a soul in sight, not a sound.

Presently, with an air of relief, born of new-sprung resolution, the stranger returned to the expectant boys.

Revived by his tendance and by the cool evening air, Tomaso was helped upon his feet. Vittore clasped his hands in joy to see him move again.

'Messer, how shall we thank thee!' he exclaimed.

'Call me Francisco,' said the traveller. 'Thou wert journeying to Verona, didst thou say? What kinsman hast thou there.'

'My father,' whispered Tomaso feebly, 'Giorgio Ligozzi.' Leaning against the stranger, indeed half-carried by him, Tomaso felt him start. 'Thou knewest him, messer.'

'He was put high in favour at della Scala's court, and sent for us to share his fortune,' put in Vittore eagerly.

'Ah,' said Francisco, 'della Scala's court has perished. I am from Verona. I saw it burned.'

Tomaso's head sank dizzily upon his helper's shoulder. Vittore's young heart swelled, then seemed to break within him. He choked back his sobs.

'And della Scala – and my uncle: did they perish too.'

'Who can tell,' replied the stranger sternly. 'Who shall say who perished or who not on such a night as that on which Verona fell.'

'But della Scala's wife, the Duchess is yonder, prisoner in Milan.'

'And that proves, thou thinkest, della Scala must be dead! Maybe; who knows? All the same, thou art a brave lad and a gallant for the thought.'

He paused to rest Tomaso on the boulders that had been his seat. 'And for that speech of thine I'll tell thee something, boy. I am the Visconti's foe. For the sake of della Scala, whom I knew, for the sake of Verona, where I lived, for the sake of something dearer to a man than life, I am sworn to hunt him down – and now, no more. We will see to shelter.'

Resting Tomaso's head against his knee, Francisco turned a trained and searching gaze about him.

To the right, on some thickly wooded, slightly rising

ground, could be discerned the unmistakable outline of a great wall, built to a monstrous height, no doubt the boundary of a villa of unusual size and magnificence. Beneath the wall, half-hidden by a grove of chestnuts, was the usual cluster of huts: the dwellings of the hinds and vassals of the villa's noble owner. But no smoke trailed upward, nor did any sign of life strike upon the ear.

'We will try those huts yonder,' said Francisco. 'They are far enough from the road for security, yet not too far to hamper any return hither. They seem deserted, but even if inhabited, they are scarce likely to refuse me shelter for a wounded boy.'

And Vittore, looking at his size and stern appearance, thankfully agreed with him. Almost carrying Tomaso, Francisco led the way, and quickly reached a footpath which, after many twistings, brought them out into a turf-grown opening around three sides of which the cottages were built. The fourth was the wall enclosing the grounds, and along it, bordering a ditch, ran a pleasant path which, as they subsequently discovered, led to a small stream, artificially extended, where it passed the villa, to a lake of some not inconsiderable size.

But, as Francisco had surmised, the whole place stood empty and deserted, though it could not have been long since the faggots had blazed on the open hearths. Signs of occupation were too recent.

The wayfarers gazed about them wonderingly. It was a place of charm. The fast-grown grass was thick with flowers; and a wooden bucket hung idly from its chain above the wooden runnel.

Supporting Tomaso, Francisco turned into the nearest hut, and noted it was better fashioned and better fitted than many of the like. A low doorway admitted into the long divisions of the space, each lit by small square openings in the walls. The light by now had faded, and save that it was empty of life, little else would have been discernible, but a portion of the roof had been broken away, as if by some pikeman's reckless thrust, and through the gap some of the sweet spring dusk showed them faintly their surroundings. A few stools, a wooden table, roughly hewn, a broken earthenware bowl, and a rudely painted crucifix, half-torn from the wall, completed the furniture.

'They fled in haste,' said Francisco grimly. 'Has Visconti been here too.'

'See,' cried Vittore, and he picked up from his feet a silver goblet.

The other turned from where he had laid Tomaso and took it from him eagerly.

The piece was heavily chased, bearing a raised shield wrought with the German eagle and lettering 'C.S.'

'German,' he said. 'Plunder. Possibly from the villa. This may account for its desertion. Yes – no doubt: the owner of the villa has crossed Visconti's path.'

And his teeth ground over the name as he set the goblet on the table, where it gleamed with a faint ghostly light.

'Sleep,' he said presently to Vittore. 'Eat this and then sleep. Thou canst do so with safety.'

The boy, glancing up into his face, believed him, and was soon lost to everything in the deep sleep of utter weariness of mind and body. Francisco bent above Tomaso and gave him wine to swallow, and set water by his side. The youth caught the hand that tended him and kissed it.

'I am grateful,' he murmured. 'Tomorrow I shall be well.'

'Aye, get better,' said Francisco. 'Thou mayst be of some service if thou wilt. Nay,' he added, checking Tomaso's feeble but eager impulse, 'I know not yet what I can do myself. But we have a cause in common,' and he smiled faintly. 'And now sleep. You sought della Scala's court. I will not desert thee.'

Taking his tattered cloak from his shoulders, he laid it over him, and Tomaso lay back on the ready spread couch of heather, and watched peacefully.

There was no light in the hut, but the moonshine began to show across the open doorway. Francisco pulled a stool to the table, and sitting, drew out his dagger and carefully examined it, then laid it ready. He felt in his wallet as if to reassure himself of something, and then Tomaso saw him slip something on his hand – it gleamed: a ring!

'Who is he,' thought the youth, not sure he gazed upon reality. 'Who is he.'

Then he dozed unwittingly, and, waking with a start, saw the moonlight streaming through the broken roof, the faint stars, and near him Vittore sleeping. The goblet still shone upon the crazy table, but the hut door had been closed and, save for themselves, the place was empty.

* * *

Francisco stepped out into the spring night, fire beating at his temples: *Visconti was abroad!*

The moon, half-shrouded in a misty vapour, was rising above the fragrant chestnuts, and brilliant in the semi-dark, like flame behind a veil, the clumps of wallflowers gave out intoxicating scent.

Francisco noticed them, and thought grimly they were the colour of blood just dry.

The spell of the moon and of the hour lay on everything; a weird ghostliness seemed to step among the trees; a sighing came from the great bushes in the garden of the villa: *'Visconti is abroad!'*

Francisco touched his dagger and went forward. Across his path two white moths fluttered, white by day, now silver purple, illusive and mysterious. To the man's fevered mood they seemed an omen; souls of the dead allowed to take farewell of earth; and with straining eyes he watched them float away and up, and out of sight. Who had perchance just died?

Francisco's giant sinews tightened. He went forward swiftly to the road, and strained his eyes and ears along its silver length.

Nothing to be heard! Nothing to be seen! Had he lost his chance, had the Duke re-entered Milan? Or had he gone too far to return that night? He sat upon the boulders where he had rested previously, his face turned toward Brescia, his hand upon his dagger.

The soft air was strengthening into a gentle wind; the poplar leaves were dancing, and darkening clouds began to drive across the moon. But the man heeded nothing the changing; light or dark, what matter once Visconti had crossed his path? Long he waited. Not a sound save the dancing of the leaves, the rising wind, the soft noises of the night. At length Francisco leaped to his feet, and his breath came short and fast. He could hear something. The wind was against him. He lay down; he put his ear to the ground; then he leaped to his feet again, transformed. It was unmistakable, though still far off; the thud of horse's flying feet.

Francisco waited.

With each second the wind rose; the clouds raced and

gathered, and darkened half the sky, and the man, straining every nerve, thought at first it was the wind he heard mingling with the trample of the oncoming hoofs. Then he knew it for screams of fury and wild shouting. 'It is the Visconti,' he said, and involuntarily his tense arm sank and his muscles loosened; those mad shrieks could freeze the marrow.

Nearer came the onset, trampling horse and yelling rider; and Francisco set himself anew.

'He rides with his own soul for company,' he muttered grimly.

Now the furious cries came clearly, terrible, inhuman; and in another moment, horse and rider were in view.

'Yes, Visconti.'

Standing in the stirrups, he lashed at the foaming horse in a blind rage and horror. His cap was gone, and hair and cloak were blown about him. He shouted wildly, cursed and shrieked.

For a breath Francisco paused. This could be no human rider; well was it known in Lombardy that the Visconti trafficked with the fiend, and this must be he; and the man shrank and turned his eyes, lest he should see his damning face.

But the next instant his courage and his purpose had returned. The horse was upon him. Swift as thought, Francisco leaped and clutched the bridle in a hand of steel.

But the mad impetus defeated him. He was dragged forward like a reed; only his own great strength for the moment saved him. And now his wild shouts were added to the rider's. He struck upward with his dagger; he tore blindly.

'Do you not know me, Visconti,' he called. 'Do you not know me.'

But his dagger was dashed from him. The horse's foam blinded him as it sprang desperately on. He heard Visconti's demon scream, and as the earth whirled round with him, caught one fleeting glimpse of the white, distorted, hated face – then, he was prone upon the ground, and Visconti, spurring on his way, looked back upon him with triumphant yells.

'Fly fly!' he screamed, 'they are after us, but we escape them. Fly!'

The dawn was showing when Francisco, spent with the passion of failure rather than from any hurt, came slowly back and picked his dagger from the road. Not far from it he saw a parchment roll tossed from Visconti's doublet in that frantic forward lunge – Visconti who had safely disappeared within the walls of Milan!

Francisco picked up the roll.

It was inscribed with poetry and patched with blood.

III

THE HOSTAGE OF THE D'ESTES

'A hundred thousand florins – and no more, even if they refuse the bargain.'

It was the Visconti that spoke. In a small dark room in the Visconti palace, he and the pale-faced, red-haired man, who had held the bridle of his horse two days before in the procession that had wended toward Brescia, were seated opposite to one another at the table; between them a pile of papers over which the secretary bowed his shoulders.

'The demand is a hundred and fifty, my lord,' he said, his voice meek, his eyes furtive.

'They said two hundred to begin with,' was the curt answer. 'A hundred thousand florins, or I go elsewhere.'

The secretary's pen flew nervously across the parchment, filling it with a cramped, mean writing that trailed unevenly along the page. Visconti's secretary wrote a characteristic hand. Visconti leaned back in his chair, watching him in silence.

The room was small and circular, hung with leather stamped in gold, and furnished plainly even to bareness. A narrow lancet window, placed low in the wall, admitted a subdued light, which fell upon the only spot of colour in the room, the suit of turquoise blue the secretary wore.

'A hundred thousand florins, to be paid in gold,' repeated Visconti; 'and no more, Giannotto.'

He rose and began to pace the room. Long habit and constant contact had not lessened the secretary's fear of

Visconti, nor mitigated the hate, none the less intensi-
fied for being for ever concealed under the mask of
cringing servility. But in Giannotto's dislike there was
nothing noble; it was merely mean hate of a sordid soul
that grudged the success of the bold crimes itself could
never dare to undertake. Had the secretary been in
Visconti's place, there would have been as vile a tyrant,
of equal cruelty and far less courage.

The Duke moved to the window and stood there in
observation awhile, then turning, spoke to Giannotto
with a smile. His eyes were a beautiful grey, open wide,
and just now lighting up a pensive, pleasant face. But the
secretary knew it too under a different guise.

'My sister's alliance with the Duke of Orleans gratifies
my ambition, Giannotto,' he said, 'and is well worth a
hundred thousand florins. So far the Valois have never
married out of royal houses.'

'Yet they consider themselves honoured by this match,
my lord,' said the secretary.

'They consider themselves well paid,' returned
Visconti. 'Now, if I can find a daughter of the
Plantagenets for brother Tisio, behold us firmly placed
among the dynasties of Europe!'

Early in the fourteenth century, but no more than a
meagre fifty years ago, before the last Visconti culminat-
ed the evil of his race, Matteo Visconti, Gian Galeazzo's
grandfather, had first firmly established his family as
lords of Milan, supplanting their rival the Torriani, who
had long reigned as magistrates-in-chief, and under
Martin della Torre risen to some eminence. Every year of
the fifty since then had seen some increase of territory,
some fresh acquisition of power, till with his last overthrow of della Scala, the seizure of Verona, and the mur-

der of his father, already miserably deposed, Gian Galeazzo had planted himself upon a level with kings.

Almost the whole of Lombardy was under his sway, and that sway extended from Vercelli in Piedmont to Feltre and Belluno. Florence, lately leagued against him in support of his deposed father, had been beaten in battle after battle and was glad to escape, shorn of her fairest possessions, and cherishing only her liberty.

All this Giannotto knew. Della Scala, Duke of Verona, had owned fair lands and wide, Verona, Brescia, all now in Visconti's hands. The secretary wondered, as he thought, how long it would be before the triumphant Gian threw away the mere rag of respect, the mere mockery of a title which bound him to the Empire, and became King of Lombardy in name as well as power.

'And thou thyself, my lord,' he said. 'Thou wilt marry a Valois to thy sister! Who will be thy bride.'

Visconti smiled. 'These marriages are for ambition. Dost thou think I shall marry for ambition? No, Giannotto, I have placed myself above the need of that. The alliances that make the Visconti one with the kings of Europe are for Valentine and Tisio; I shall marry –'

'For love, my lord,' ventured the secretary, with a hint of sarcasm.

'Whom I please,' said Visconti. 'Which is not what Valentine is doing,' he added with a smile.

'She may give trouble yet, my lord.'

Visconti frowned. He thought of Conrad von Schulembourg, the brilliant young German noble, who had been a favourite with him and all his court and had won the heart of Valentine Visconti; no favourite of his now. 'As for my lady sister,' he said, 'let her dare turn her eyes save where I bid her.'

His own grew ominous, and Giannotto shuffled uneasily.

A noise without broke the sudden silence of reflection. Visconti, responding at once to what it meant, glanced a moment from the window where he still stood, then swept down to the head of the table. He leaned across to Giannotto, not that he valued any response that he could offer – Visconti's secretary was no more to him than the chair on which he sat, valued solely for his skill in letters – but his triumph had to have its vent. 'Hark!' he cried. 'Listen to it, Giannotto! The wealth of Verona is pouring into Milan! The spoils of Verona, Giannotto, the treasures from Mastino della Scala's palace!'

Giannotto winced before Visconti's passionate joy.

''Twas a man I hated, Giannotto – I would he had lived to feel it. The only man I ever *hated*, because the only man I ever feared, the only man who ever dared to despise me! But he has fallen, he is dead, his wife is in my power, and in his fall he has placed me higher than my highest hopes.'

Carried away by his transports, he seized Giannotto by the arm and dragged him to the window.

The secretary gazed into the courtyard, where a group of soldiers and servants were busy conveying statues, gilt and silver plate, rich tapestry, glass, china, and arms, from carts and mules into the narrow doorways that led into the grim interior of the palace. They were presided over by a major-domo in a black gown, who called out directions in a shrill voice. To one side a few unhappy men, of note enough to have been spared, watched in grim silence the unlading of the spoils that came from the sacking of their palaces. The great gates stood at their widest, and through them wound a long train of soldiers, some driving before them groups of prisoners, tightly chained together, others galloping in laden with plunder of all kinds, art treasures, blackened as if by fire, banners and suits of armour.

'Ah, Giannotto, look,' cried Visconti, '*della Scala's* collection, *della Scala's* jewels. How my treasury will be enriched! Only one thing mars it, that he should not be here to see!'

He turned from the window. Giannotto followed, cringing.

'Still, thou hast his wife, my lord,' he said. Gian's eyes flashed afresh.

'Isotta d'Este – ah!'

He leaned back against the wall in silence. A certain winter morning, five years ago, rose clearly before him; a massive castle, frowning from the rocks above Ferrara, and on its steps a fair girl who stood there and laughed to see him ride away back to Milan, his offers of the Visconti's friendship scorned and flung in his face by her proud family, the haughty Estes. Visconti's face grew dark as he remembered her; almost more than della Scala, her dead husband, did he hate Isotta, della Scala's wife. And she was in his power. Greatly would it have soothed him to know her death was in his powers too, but the lust of ambition was greater with this man even than the lust of pride or hate.

Isotta d'Este was a valuable hostage to be used against her family, should they think of avenging their fallen kinsman.

'Where hast thou finally placed her, my lord,' asked Giannotto, with his stealthy glance. The Duke started from his reverie.

'In the West Tower,' he smiled. 'Every day I go to gaze on the room that holds her to make sure it is not a dream; to see and feel with my eyes and my own hands that her prison is doubly sure. If Isotta d'Este should now escape me – but she will not!'

He crossed the room to leave it, but paused at the door.

'Be watchful, Giannotto, the Princess Valentine may try to leave the palace. I have spies on her every movement; still, thine eyes upon her also will do no harm – to *me*!'

He laughed an instant. A rustle of the hangings and he was gone. Giannotto sat on silently, looking in front of him. His thoughts were with Valentine Visconti, Gian's unhappy sister, whom he had been told to watch; from her they travelled to the German Count, who, five days ago, had left the palace.

'I wonder if she loved him,' he mused. 'I do not think she did. Dear God, she did not need to wait to love a man, her life was not such that she could pick and choose her way of escaping from it. Conrad offered one and she was ready to take it – now – *five days ago!* Yes – Count Conrad is dead, and she will marry the Duke of Orleans! Ah, well! The German was a fool, he deserved no better fate than a fool! I do not think she'll break her heart if she can find some other way.'

He returned to his papers, pausing now and then to glance toward the door, as if to keep himself on the alert for the Duke's noiseless entry.

But Gian had bent his steps elsewhere. Plainly dressed, he passed almost unnoticed across an inner courtyard to a dark angle of a wall where a secret door anew admitted him. The whole Visconti palace was a sombre and gloomy place; men crept about it on their tiptoe, glancing fearfully around them, afraid of their own shadows. Visconti smiled to himself at sight of fear; he loved to be feared, to hold lives in the hollow of his hand, and play with them and death.

The door let him into a long narrow passage flagged with stone, and lit by diamond-shaped holes left in the walls; the air was damp and chill, and Visconti drew his cloak around him. Unlocking a second door, he ascended a flight of stone steps, pitch dark, from which he emerged into a large circular chamber with a thick pillar in the middle from which the groined ceiling sprang. Save table and high-backed chairs of blackened wood, there was no furniture. This chamber was the outer guard-room of the prison wing, and a gloomy-faced man leaned against the pillar, his eyes fixed upon the opening door. It could be no other than the Visconti entering thus, and he crouched almost to the ground.

'What is thy guard,' said Visconti.

'Twenty men in each guard-room, my lord, and each one picked for size and trustworthiness, and I myself keep watch upon the doors. Escape is impossible.'

'By so much the more that thy head will answer for it.'

As he spoke, Visconti flung wide one of a ring of doors opening from the chamber, and stepped into a posse of soldiers. No one spoke. Glancing keenly to the right and left, Visconti passed through their ranks into the room beyond – a small apartment, dim lit and hung with arras. An old woman sat at a tapestry frame with her back to the door, but at Visconti's entrance she rose, as at something expected, and sank in a deep obeisance.

Gian Maria closed the door behind him.

'How is she,' he said. 'How does she bear her change of prison.'

The old woman glanced toward an inner door, massive and iron-clamped.

'When I am with her, my lord, she sits in silence, her eyes for ever on her missal; indeed she has not spoken since we brought her here; but when she is alone, she weeps, I have heard her through the door; she weeps passionately, and calls wildly upon her husband to save her.'

'I would I had him, to stand him gagged against the door to hear her,' said the Duke.

'By the look of her she will die of it,' continued the old woman. 'But if I know anything of prisoners, and I have seen a few, thou wilt never break her spirit, my lord.'

'She *must* be more humbled now,' he said to himself. 'She *must* turn and implore me for pity.'

The huge doors creaked and swung on its hinges, and he stood at the top of two low stone steps, looking down into Isotta's prison. It was little better than a dungeon of stone, lofty but dark, with one window deep set, high out of reach, and thickly barred. The walls were hung with faded tapestry, the gloomy, sad-looking folds drooping like torn, captured standards. A huge chest of sombre blackness leaned against the wall; above it hung a horn lantern, which after dark gave all the light that was obtained. For the rest, a few high-backed chairs stood stiffly about the room. In his black dress Visconti, pausing at the head of the steps, seemed part of its gloom. His wide-open grey eyes looked straight across, at the solitary occupant.

Isotta sat in one of the huge black chairs, her delicate hands resting on the faded crimson velvet of the arms, her feet on a wooden footstool. She was of a fair and noble appearance, but her face was marred by sorrow and her eyes red from many tears. Her pale yellow hair was drawn under a white veil. Her long grey dress clung close about her slender figure. On her knee rested a little book, and on this she kept her eyes. Not by so much as a flutter of her hand did she show she knew of the Visconti's presence.

He waited, raging inwardly, but words would not come easily to break that silence. At last he slowly descended into the room, his eyes still on her face.

She never stirred, nor raised her own. With his noiseless tread, Visconti paced around the chamber, raising the arras, and testing with his dagger every block of stone. It was a superfluous precaution; any attempt to escape would have been simple madness, and Isotta d'Este was not likely to give way to frenzy. Still it was joy to be sure and doubly sure that she was safe. Every inch was inspected, every crevice searched. Meanwhile from time to time he observed her keenly. But she seemed not to know her solitude was broken, save that once, when he passed her, she swept in the train of her gown, as she might have done had a leper come too near. A simple thing, but it goaded him, and for a moment she was near her death; rage almost overcoming prudence. But as he stood behind her chair, half-inclined to strike, he noticed on her hand a ring. His expression changed; he smiled; his hand dropped down. The ring was of pearl, cut with the arms of della Scala, and worn on the third finger of her left hand; her wedding ring.

Visconti smiled again. Stooping, he raised her hand, and – 'Will she bear this in silence,' was his thought. For a moment it seemed as if she might not. The delicate fingers stiffened and half-closed, then, as if remembering anew, she left her hand passive in Visconti's hold, and only by a faint quiver told she knew the ring had been withdrawn. The despoiled hand fell back again on to the velvet arm, her eyes were fixed immovably upon her book, and Visconti, turning away to the door, silent as he came, looked back at her, incredulous of such control. She was sitting straight and slender, her delicate head poised high, but – ah yes, he thought it must be so! – he noted with delight that her breast heaved and the firm line of her mouth trembled ever so slightly. For a second he stood thus, a ray of the pale prison light caught by the ring he held, then the door clattered and shook back into its bolts, and he was gone.

IV

VALENTINE

Swiftly as he had come, Visconti returned to the palace, and the banqueting hall beyond. He stepped in silently, and softly let the curtains fall behind him.

The room was of enormous size, and overawed the gaze. The four large entries, one in each wall, were curtained alike with gloomy purple. The ceiling was domed and of immense height, showing a dim tracery of carved wood, from which hung golden chains, suspending jewelled lamps. The high and narrow windows were wrought with painted saints, splendid in colouring. From domed ceiling to panelled floor the walls were carved with men, women, saints, martyrs, flowers and birds wrought together, in simple-minded joyousness of design, executed with the delicate workmanship of Niccolo Pisano's school. Silk arras, hung from carved gold rods, here and there concealed the carving. A carpet, the work of two men's lives, delicate in purple, brown and gold, spread across the centre, where long low tables of walnut wood, rich and dark, could seat two hundred guests. Purple velvet chairs were set about in the corners, and the light streaming through the coloured window saints fell in gold and green across an ivory footstool inlaid with jewels.

As Visconti entered, the hall was empty, yet he stepped stealthily, as if he felt eyes watching him. Seating himself in the window recess, he waited, and presently, as if at an unuttered summons, the curtains at the far end of the room were rustled apart, and a lady entered. She was Valentine Visconti, Gian's sister. Her dress was of red and brown, embroidered with gold, her tawny hair piled high under a golden net upon her well-set head. She had the clear, colourless skin and the wide red lips of the fair-haired Italians, their rich presence; she was of a fine carriage, not easy to overlook; she might have been ten years younger than her brother; she was as tall and as stately.

She looked straight toward the window where Visconti sat.

Gian returned her gaze, not changing his position. Valentine drew nearer.

'Why hast thou set spies upon me,' she demanded.

'Why didst thou try to fly Milan with Count Conrad,' he returned. 'I was foolish not to spy on thee before.'

Her grey eyes glinted.

'I tried to escape from a life that was grown intolerable,' she cried, 'and I will try yet again!'

Visconti smiled.

'My sister, thou art much too precious; I shall not let thee go. Thou art worth a great deal to me. Through thee our family will be united to the Royal House of France. My sister, thy husband will be the Duke of Orleans, and not a German fool.'

But Valentine was also a Visconti: she advanced with blazing eyes.

'I will not marry to serve thy ambitions; I will not help to steady thee upon the throne. Mark me, Gian, sooner than wed a Prince whom thou hast chosen, I will drag thy name into the mire, and sit in rags at thy palace gates.'

'Only thou hast not the choice,' he answered pleasantly. Her anger rose the more as she felt her helplessness.

'I will not marry the Duke!' she cried. 'I will not walk up to the altar.'

'Thou canst be carried,' said Visconti.

She moved up and down, twisting her hands in an agony of impotence.

'I will appeal to the Duke of Orleans himself!' she cried.

'A bridegroom who is bought for a hundred thousand florins!' sneered her brother. 'And how will thy appeal reach him? Come, my sister, be calm, the Duke will make as good a husband as Count Conrad. Bethink thyself, thou mayst live to be crowned Queen of France. Wilt thou not thank me then, that I saved thee from a German count.'

Valentine fell to weeping.

'What has become of him,' she sobbed, 'the only human being who ever turned to me in pity. The only one who ever cared for me. What has become of him.'

'What becomes of a fool when he crosses the path of a Visconti,' asked her brother calmly.

Valentine lifted her head.

'He is dead, then,' she said.

'It matters not to thee. Thy husband will be the Duke of Orleans, and thou art a prisoner in the palace till he takes thee from it.'

She caught at the arras; Visconti left her, and reached the door, his figure a shadow among the shadows.

The girl rushed forward with a cry. 'Gian!' she called.

He paused, his hand upon the curtain, and looked back at her.

'Gian!' she repeated, and stood still gasping, her hand upon her breast. The stiff folds of her dress gleamed richly in the subdued light that fell upon her from the painted window. 'I know thee for what thou art,' she said; 'there are only three of us left, only three. Where are our parents, Gian.'

'They were stricken down at Brescia,' and Visconti took a quick step toward her.

'They are dead,' she breathed, 'and they died as our brothers died, Filippo and Matteo –'

'Did they so! Then take warning by it,' and Gian, coming stealthily still nearer, turned a look on her. Valentine quailed, as Francisco well-nigh had done; the hot words of remorse and rebellion died away unuttered, and she hid her face, her high spirit cowed again into a bitter weeping.

Visconti left her noiselessly.

V

THE PAINTER'S DAUGHTER

Three days had passed since that futile midnight encounter, and Francisco had found no means to enter Milan.

He stood on the banks of the water looking moodily toward the city, watching the figure of Vittore, who trudged along the meadows – his errand to procure provisions.

The three still sheltered in the ruins, to which no owner had returned, nor had any signs of life or occupancy broken the silence within the villa's all-encircling walls. Now, as he watched Vittore out of sight – the boy looking back often to renew his courage – Franciso's brow was furrowed, and his eyes heavy with sleeplessness. The stream, clear, deep and sparkling, here ran darkened with the shadow of the willows that bent over it their long bluish leaves. A path, thickly bordered with reeds, ran beside the water to the head of the small lake into which the stream flowed, whence it continued, a scarcely discernible footway, toward the city.

Behind Francisco, separated from him only by the fosse, was the wall of the villa, and, Vittore being lost to view, Francisco withdrew his gaze, always roaming restlessly in quest of something that should aid him, and glanced along it curiously. His eyes rested on a great tuft of yellow lichen, brilliant with scarlet spikes; it was so huge and spreading he could not but stare at it. From the lichen his gaze travelled slowly upward, but not a foothold could he see. Spreading above the wall the topmost boughs of a gigantic yew showed a clear-cut black against the sky, and on the broad, fan-like surface brooded a pair of doves, pink, grey and white. The beauty of the scene, its calmness and repose, exasperated the man's inaction. He stamped on the little flowers at his feet, then, with a bitter curse at his folly, threw himself upon the grass to watch for Vittore's return, and ponder, for ever ponder, on his purpose. Suddenly there shot into sight upon the stream a little boat, with high curling prow and gaily painted sides. A blue sail was furled above it, and it was impelled lightly forward by a delicate pair of oars. The grounds of the villa formed a promontory, and coming around the brow of it the boat broke upon his gaze and was within hail at one and the same moment. It came rapidly nearer, and the stranger's first impulse was to hide himself from these unexpected and unwelcome intruders; but there was no time; as he rose he was observed, but the genial hand-wave and the merry laughter reassured him. These were simple pleasure-seekers. He reseated himself, and the boat came on.

The rower was a dark-haired man of middle age, clothed in a plain brown robe. Lean and vivacious, eager-eyed, he appeared one of those people who are always talking and moving; even seated and rowing he gave the impression of restlessness; of the good humour common to the people too. His companion was a young girl dressed in a simple blue gown. She was a delicate blonde, very young, very slender; the curls of her amber hair were blown across a round dimpled face; eyes of a dancing blue; a sweet small mouth curled in laughter, a fine chin and throat, a slack young figure. This was her principal characteristic, the floating yellow hair like a veil about her.

Coming abreast of Francisco, the man paused on his oars with a friendly greeting.

'Good day, messer,' he called. 'So thou hast found our secret haunt. Graziosa and I had thought this place our own,' and as he spoke he waved his hand around him at the water.

The boat rocked now alongside the path, and Francisco courteously approached.

'I am a stranger here,' he said.

The other glanced at him anew, and with the awakening of a little friendly wonder.

'A stranger? Ah, the, this is new to thee – this most beautiful part of Italy. I assure thee,' he continued excitedly, 'I have been through the fairest parts of Tuscany, I have wandered about Naples, but never have I seen such colours, such lights as here!' Again he waved his all-inclusive hand. 'Thou, messer, as a stranger, must see how wonderfully fair it is.'

He paddled the boat nearer among the reeds in his eagerness to obtain new sympathy.

'I have not been used to judge lands by their beauty,' returned Francisco. 'Yet methinks I have seen spots as beautiful and easier to hold in time of need.'

The other twisted his mouth in contempt. The girl leaned forward, laughing. 'You forget, father,' she said, 'everyone is not a painter.'

But the little man, as if he had found a sudden mission, secured the boat, and, still in silence, stepped ashore, helping his daughter to follow him. Francisco, preoccupied and mistrustful, saw this with uneasiness, and would gladly have withdrawn. Moreover, the smiling face of the happy girl was an added sting to a burning thought.

The enthusiast, however, had no idea of giving up a possible convert, and swept aside the other's protestations while he commenced pointing out the beauties of the yellow lichen against the villa wall, the sight of which had restored all his good humour.

'See!' he exclaimed. 'How bright it is! See the contrast of the yew – so brilliant, yet so in harmony, so – you do not paint,'

'No,' said Francisco between grimness and scorn. 'Do I look as if I did.'

The artist glanced anew at his huge frame and tattered attire, and mentally decided he did not.

'Ah, then, thou dost not understand,' he said; 'but I, I *am* a painter. Agnolo Vistarnini is my name, messer, a student of Taddeo Gaddi.' He swept off his leather cap with an air of profound respect.

'Ah, he could paint! I am far behind him, messer, but I can see! I can see! Which thou canst not,' he added with superb pity.

'Graziosa,' he called, turning to his daughter, 'we will stay here awhile.'

And seating himself on the bank, he produced from his wallet a panel of wood, polished and carefully planed, upon which he began to draw the outline of a corner of the scene, using a dark brown pigment.

Francisco fell again to brooding while the painter chattered on, dividing his attention between the panel and his daughter, who was wandering up the stream, filling with flowers a flat basket.

'Thou see'st yonder my daughter, messer,' he said, pointing to the slender figure in blue. He blew a kiss in her direction. 'She is the model for my angels –'

'And the model for thy devils?' asked Francisco suddenly.

Vistarnini started and looked around at the speaker.

'Devils! Messer!' He crossed himself. 'God forbid there should be a model for such found anywhere,' he said.

'Yet methinks thou hast in thy city yonder,' said Francisco with a bitter smile, 'one who well might sit for the fiend himself: Visconti.'

'The Duke? Ah, my friend, hush, hush, thou art a stranger, take care! Even in this lonely spot such words are far from safe. Who art thou, messer, who dost not live in Milan and yet speakest with such a look of the Visconti.'

'Do not all who know the Visconti speak with such a look of him.'

The painter gazed at him in silence.

'But thou askest for my name,' continued the other. 'I am Francisco di Coldra, one who has suffered much from the Visconti.'

'In the sack of Verona, perhaps,' asked Agnolo after a pause.

'The sack of Verona was some time ago. The prisoners have been in Milan twenty days!'

These words were inscrutable, and the little painter did not even try to understand them; but they kindled a memory that would not be repressed.

'Ah, and what a night that was,' he cried, 'when the Duke re-entered Milan with them! Since I do not hurt thee by the recollection, messer, let me tell thee, it was a splendid sight, that night the Duke returned. I live a quiet life, as an artist may do, even in Milan. I know little, I care little for the wars of princes. They tell me the Visconti's crimes outnumber the stars; but, messer, his shadow has not fallen across *my* house, and what one does not see one does not fear – but when he returned from Verona, that was a sight, messer. It was late. Our house overlooks the western gate, and all day long the messengers had come and sped, bringing the news the Duke was here. Towards evening – we leaning from the window as did everyone – Alberic da Salluzzo comes galloping to the walls – red-hot upon some report that the Visconti has been slain – to look to the arming of the citizens. Even as we strain from the window, following the flash of his plumes – back he comes in madder haste – the Visconti is alive! The people shout and yell, and some cry 'tis not the Visconti's army on the road, but della Scala's. Meanwhile a mob, with Napoleone della Torre at their head, begins to agitate, to threaten riot. With a strong hand Alberic puts them down – the streets are cleared, Graziosa and I on the balcony, all is dark, silent, save now and then the clink of the armour of the sentries on the walls. I am too excited for sleep, messer, all so hushed, so subdued, waiting, waiting. All at once it comes. Oh, the rattle, the roar! The great gates clatter back, the streets fill with crowds no man can keep back. The victorious army pelts through them; two men on every horse, great flaring torches throwing their yellow light on the torn banners and the wild faces of the soldiers, and then the cannon, leaping over the rough stones, drawn by the smoke-blackened gunners, all tearing, rushing through the street, a mass of light and shade, wonderful, wonderful! In the midst, the Visconti, the ragged light streaming over his battered armour, and Isotta d'Este, guarded between two soldiers, swaying on her black horse, and above all the shouts of the frenzied triumph of the Milanese... Ah!'

Agnolo paused now for want of breath, and glanced at his companion.

But Francisco offered no response. His face was turned away, and his hands were clenched. The little painter had a vague sense of having allowed a mere artist's enthusiasm to carry him too far into a dangerous theme.

'Ah, well,' he continued in a deprecating tone, 'a splendid sight truly, and one to fire the blood, but I am a man of peace, and I greatly grieve della Scala should have perished. He was a noble prince.'

The stranger rose abruptly.

'Do not speak of della Scala,' he said harshly. 'I love to hear his name as little as Visconti's. His was the crime of failure.'

'Failure! Who would not have failed,' said Agnolo gently, for he thought he spoke to one who must have lost his all in the sacked town. 'I know little of such things, but 'twas here and there asserted he fell by craft as well as force, and he was a great soldier and an honourable man, Messer Francisco.'

'He had all the virtues, doubtless,' said Francisco, 'and lost Verona.'

'And his life!' replied the painter. 'Ah, well, these things are grievous! The saints protect my daughter from all share in them,' and he glanced affectionately toward Graziosa, returning through the grey-green willows with lilies in her hands.

'For my pictures,' said the painter, pointing to them. 'I am painting an altar-piece – for the lunettes. I shall have Graziosa as St. Catherine, and Ambrogio (her betrothed, messer) as St. Michael. These flowers will make the border.'

He took some as he spoke, and began arranging them in wreaths. Francisco would scarcely have heeded the speaker's words, save that his glance was caught almost involuntarily by the girl's sweet blush at mention of her lover's name.

'Thy betrothed,' he murmured, interested a moment in the happiness that was such a contrast to his own feeling. 'And does he paint too.'

Graziosa looked up with sparkling eyes.

'Beautifully,' she said eagerly. 'He is at work now in the Church of Sant' Apollinare in Brescia. We have not seen his painting, the journey is too long; but some of the panel bits he has shown us, and they are noble.'

Francisco smiled faintly at her outspokenness, and her father laughed good-humouredly.

'Thou must not listen to her,' he said. 'She overrates his painting. He paints well, truly, but cold! ah, so cold; no spirit in it! He will sit for hours thinking how the fold of a robe should fall. I, however, have seen Taddeo Gaddi paint! The angels would seem to flow from his brush as if he gave no thought to them!' But Graziosa turned a smiling face from the boat she was unmooring.

'His altar-piece will draw all Lombardy,' she cried.

'Say rather that his altar-piece draws him away from thee,' laughed the painter, 'and thou wilt be nearer to the truth. The altar-piece has all his time; thou but a few meagre hours a week! Still, they love each other, messer, and are happy, so we never care whether Ambrogio paints well or ill.' Graziosa seated herself under the blue sail, and looked up with radiant eyes.

'I am very happy,' she laughed softly, 'so never mind whether he paint the best or the second best in Italy.'

The painter grasped the oars and pushed out into the stream: 'Good-bye,' he called, and Graziosa waved a hand; then something in the stranger's aspect made the little painter pause again.

'Gladly would we offer our poor hospitality, messer,' he said, 'only the gates are sternly barred to any stranger...' But Graziosa, glancing also at the strong, commanding figure, and the stern set face, checked her father's impulse.

'We are too humble, father,' she said gently, 'but if there were any service we could render, any message –? We live at the sign of *Lo Scudo*, the armourer's, near to the western gate.'

'I will remember it,' said Francisco simply.

Graziosa drew her blue cloth hood about her smiling face, and, with gentle strokes from the painter's paddle, the boat disappeared.

When Francisco found himself alone again, momentary misgiving seized him that he had lost an opportunity.

Could these folk have been of service? They were of a sort unknown to him; courtiers, soldiers, burghers, merchants, with all such he was at home, but these plebeians of kindly nature and good speech, of humble rank and careless happiness, were new to him. The painter's talk of his craft had had no meaning for Francisco, it had passed from his mind for craziness; but the girl had said they dwelt near the western gate – could they perchance have been of service? But presently he dismissed the notion; they were too simple for his purpose.

Raging in the pain of rekindled memory and present helplessness, Francisco paced to and fro, waiting for Vittore's figure in the distance.

Suddenly his eyes rested again on the great clump of yellow lichen, and he stopped, arrested.

In the midst of it he had seen something that interested him, something very much its colour, but not quite its kind.

He approached, and thrusting his hand in among the great tufts, touched the rusty iron of a disused bolt. There was a door here, then, that led into the grounds of the deserted villa!

Francisco's heart beat strongly.

From the finding of the silver goblet in the ruined hut, he had associated with the Visconti's name the darkened dwelling and its silent grounds. There was none to question, for there was none of whom he dared inquire; but more than once Francisco had thought of trying to enforce an entrance, only to find, however, that by whomsoever abandoned, ingress to the villa had been left well nigh impossible. But here was an entrance that had been overlooked, and it was not to be wondered at, for the rusty bolt could have been discerned only by eyes as keen as his, and the door belonging was completely hidden by close-growing ivy, too frail to climb by, but the most effectual of all concealments. Tearing up the lichen from its roots, Francisco set to work upon the ivy. The delicate, rope-like strands clung with their black filaments like fingers bewitched, and little had been accomplished when Francisco, taking cautious survey around him, saw Vittore returning across the meadows. Concealing what he was about, Francisco waited till the lad came up, flushed and triumphant from a successful errand.

'What news going in the city,' asked Francisco.

'All is quiet. One of the soldiers snatched a leek from me, another bade me tell my sister he was still unwed. They jested finely, but I should not like them to have turned to questioning me. They were so many, and so finely armed.'

'And the money? Didst thou need to change the pieces that I gave thee.'

'Yes, messer, I had not enough! They said it was Veronese.'

'Nothing new to them in Milan now – the money of the Veronese,' said Francisco, with a flashing glance toward the ramparts.

'They told me 'twas no longer taken; that the Duke was having it recast. But a bystander reached forward, and gave me a piece of Milanese. He said that he would keep my piece; it bore the della Scala arms, he said, and was a curiosity.'

Francisco muttered something that the lad did not catch.

'Well, thou hast faced the soldiers and the market now,' he said aloud, 'and art safe for other journeys, as I promised thee. Go on to the hut, and give thyself food and Tomaso. Keep close and answer none. I will be with thee presently.'

The boy went on obediently. These two days with his rescuer had taught him and Tomaso both that what Francisco said he meant, and his word was their law already. But Francisco needed stronger allies.

With some half-formed thought that the villa might conceal one, he now returned to his attack upon the ivy, and after many a wrench and cut and struggle, the garden door stood bare enough to use. It was stained, discoloured, locked and immovable.

But this was nothing to Franciso; with his dagger he cut the woodwork around the lock, removed it, and thrusting his hand and arm well through the breach, with no great difficulty withdrew the upper and lower bolts. With knee and shoulder then he pressed inward, driving against the weeds and growths that choked it, and presently had forced an aperture that would admit him.

After a cautious glance along the meadow path, fortunately for his purpose little used, he replaced the loose strands of ivy as far as he was able, and slipping through, pushed the door back into its place, filling up the broken lock with green.

He was in a garden of great beauty. The yew-tree overhead shaded a patch of velvety green starred with daisies. Before him a straight path led to a marble seat and a belt of cypress trees.

The ring-doves cooed blissfully; the flowering trees stirred; there was no other sound save the distant one of faintly splashing water. Treading softly, Francisco set forward in the direction in which he knew the villa lay.

VI

THE RESCUE OF COUNT VON SCHULEMBOURG

The house, a low, graceful building of white marble, was approached by a broad flight of steps, flanked by a balustrade almost hidden in early roses, which trailed in great clusters over it and along the velvet turf. Fronting it was a great fountain, and a wide avenue of yew-trees, patched with sunshine, led up to the façade.

To right and left spread turf-grown paths, edged with orange and lemon trees, and sweet with the scent of the citron and myrtle; around their roots grew violets, primroses, daffodils; and behind, beyond, on all sides, were grass and walks and trees, a sea of moving green.

The place was profoundly quiet. The statues, placed here and there, looked out from the foliage smiling; the dainty seats of coloured stone were empty, innocent of satin skirt or ruffled cloak. There was no sign of the recent care of man; no wild things stirred; beside the basins of the fountains lay two peacocks, dead. The villa doors were open, showing something of the long corridor that traversed the lower floor, but silent as the scene without. The stillness was unnatural; the beauty of the place, the two dead gorgeous birds, the open doors and lovely sunshine, made an impression that appalled.

The day was long past noon when, through the dim corridor, there was the faint flutter of garments. Some one was slowly moving. The sunbeam's slanting ray struck through the doorway on a strange, haggard-looking figure: a man. He was wasted, bent, and shrunken; his limbs tottering under him. Where his blue velvet cloak fell back, it showed a splendid suit of black and gold, embroidered and decked out with ribbons, but the splendour hung upon a hollow frame: a skeleton. Long locks of pale gold hair heightened the ghastly hollowness of the pinched face. Conrad von Schulembourg was paying with this form of death for the favour of Valentine Visconti. As her brother's favourite, he had thought it safe to lift his eyes to her; being something of a gallant fool, very gay to face danger, very incredulous of its ever coming to him in this hideous shape. He was not quick to read character, especially Visconti's character. Could Gian Visconti have seen his victim now, even he might have started, for it is hard to imagine what men who die of hunger look like.

The trees, softly moving, made pleasant light and shade; the myrtle blossoms blew and sailed in little clouds of mauve, while the sweet-smelling leaves of the citron hung their rich clusters over opening lilies. Conrad, dragging himself across the grass, with straining eyes and parted lips, thought only of the water in the fountain, and saw only those two dead birds. Poisoned! Visconti had forestalled all chances.

The Count had scarcely strength for any definite purpose of self-help. He craved water, and turned to drag himself away in search of some he might dare drink. Ere long, he knew not how, he reached it; a little hollow fringed with fern, in its centre a calm and placid pool, the trees mirrored in its peaceful surface. Count Conrad fell beside it, gazing longingly. A statue of a wood-god, the sunlight yellow in the hollow eyes, leaned from among the bushes, and mocked him with its smile.

Another effort and he had reached the stone. The water was so cool, so clear, so pure and still, it seemed impossible that it should harm him. He reached his hand out, then convulsively resisting the impulse, drew it back, and sank again upon the grass. At a flutter of white from the boughs near, Count Conrad lifted his eyes, and saw a dove that flew past him to rest upon the rim; he watched it eagerly. The bird preened itself, shook its feathers daintily, stooped and drank. Conrad drew himself a little nearer. Suddenly with a cry the bird whirled up into the air, beat its wings together vainly, and fell back into the water, dead! Poisoned! All the water poisoned! Desperation giving him a moment's strength, Count Conrad rose and regarded the dead dove with greedy eyes, but steeling himself against the impulse to devour his own death, he crawled on with the vague thought to reach the gate. Some instinct of remembrance guiding his stumbling steps, he came upon it. It was twice his height, and all its elaborate tracery offered no single aperture through which a child could thrust his hand. Sick and blind he clung to it; he tried to shout, to scream, his voice died in his throat. In helpless rage, his wild face pressed against the iron, his eyes starting, his tongue lolling out of his dry mouth, he gripped and shook the lock.

Two children running by, stopped, gazed, came nearer, and then at what they saw, fled, screaming. No one else approached. The world seemed empty. Twilight began to fall. Then in his half-delirium Count Conrad thought again of the dead bird, and laughed wolfishly to himself, making with tottering steps back toward the hollow. To search coherently for food or drink or succour was now beyond his power. Presently again he sank across the grass and lay there crying like a child, whimpering and whispering. Once or twice he made an effort, snatched at the long grass, fell back again, and lay now in silence.

After a time, but while it was still light, he seemed to wake as from a trance, and saw a figure moving down the glade toward him. Was he still living? He could scarcely tell. Was this Visconti come again to mock him? The thought spurred the man, though dying, almost to strive to rise and meet his fate standing. But sky, grass, trees, and stone reeled about him in a chaos of green and blue. He strove to speak, but his tongue refused. The dark figure came nearer, stopped beside him, stooped and spoke, but Count Conrad did not see nor heed. He lay, a woeful spectacle, as if dead indeed.

He awoke, as he thought never to wake again, with moistened lips, and water on his forehead, and a face that was not Visconti's bending over him; a dark face with strange brown eyes that looked at him with sombre interest.

'Thou comest from the Duke,' gasped Conrad. Francisco shook his head.

'I am no emissary of Visconti.'

'Then thou comest to save me,' whispered Conrad eagerly, hope dawning in his eyes.

'I will save thee if I can,' replied Francisco. 'Thou art alone.'

Conrad moved his head. He was too weak for more. Then a sudden thought shot horror into his face, and he struggled to a sitting posture.

'The water!' he gasped out. 'The water – from that fountain – thou gavest me to drink of that.'

Francisco followed in surprise the direction of his glance. 'No,' he said. 'I had it with me; 'twas water and wine too.

'Oh!' Conrad sank back. 'The water is poisoned – all –'

'Poisoned – Visconti's doing!' said Francisco.

'How didst thou get in,' whispered Conrad feebly. 'Visconti barred all entrances.'

'I found one unknown to any; canst thou, with my help, walk there.'

'I think – I can walk – to safety,' was the answer, and the love of life lending him strength, he staggered to his feet, and helped by Francisco and invigorated by the wine, made slowly forward.

But they had not taken many steps before Francisco well perceived he had rescued a man past helping himself, well-nigh past any help from others.

With a sigh Conrad sank speechless into his arms.

Francisco looked around him. He had come far from the entrance he had forced, and Conrad, plainly starved and emaciated as he was, was still a man full grown. To leave him and to return to Tomaso would be too dangerous. The place must be under observation. But to seek safety himself and abandon the helpless man was not a thought to occur to Francisco, though, hampered by his dead weight, he would be at any pursuer's mercy, or fall a prey to any ambush; so with stout words of encouragement, and forcing more wine through his lips, he lifted the Count to his shoulder and made as rapidly as he was able to the door beside the lichen. It was a breathless journey, but at last, and unmolested, Francisco gained the wall and laid his burden down. Reconnoitring without, he saw no sign of danger, and, glad of the oncoming dusk, dragged up the man and laid him, at least free, outside the door. The cool air blowing from the water, a few drops more wine, in which Francisco soaked some crumbs of bread he found within his wallet, enabled the rescued man again to move.

It was an easy matter now to bring Vittore and Tomaso, who would not be left, and between them Conrad, too spent to put questions, was carried to their shelter and laid on the rough heather couch in the hut, from which one of his own vassals had not long been driven; a poor asylum enough, but one for which he only too gladly exchanged the deadly splendour of his own magnificent abode.

'Who is he,' asked Tomaso, in timid surprise. For the first time since their knowledge of him Francisco laughed, and without bitterness.

'One of Visconti's victims! It is some poor satisfaction to have rescued two,' he said. 'I know nothing of him except that it is plainly to be seen he is some person of distinction. We will nurse him to the best of our skill. Tomaso, he may be of use –'

Then suddenly Francisco's humour changed. He glanced around him at the boy, the youth, scarcely recovered from his fever, the ghastly figure on the ground over which he bent, and fury shook him. Of what use anything against Visconti? 'Oh, terrible to be so helpless!' he cried passionately. 'We will leave this place. I break my heart in vain against the walls of Milan. I will to Ferrara, to della Scala's kinsfolk there.'

'And they will aid thee,' asked Tomaso trembling.

Francisco smiled, but this time grimly. 'I can but try,' he said. 'Della Scala was once known and trusted there. And in no case can we stay here!' He pointed down at Conrad. 'The place will not be safe for us, let Visconti once discover his victim has escaped him. We will depart to Ferrara, and fall upon Visconti while he is unsuspecting that I – that anyone lives still to animate the Estes against him...'

An hour or two later, while Vittore and Tomaso slept, Francisco keeping watch beside him, Conrad woke from a light doze and felt that he had hold on life again. He tried to murmur thanks to his preserver, but the other checked him.

'Thou art not of Italy,' he said

'I am Conrad von Schulembourg.'

'Conrad von Schulembourg!' echoed Francisco in surprise. 'Visconti's trusted friend!'

'The trusted friend of him who fastened me within my villa yonder to die a lingering death of hunger, or of poisoned food.' The drops started on his forehead, he gasped for breath.

Francisco soothed and tended him.

'Think not of it; get well,' he said, as he had said to Tomaso. 'Live and help rid the world of the Visconti. He would have thee die a dog's death. Is not life dear to thee.'

'Yes, I will live,' said Conrad, 'and I will take revenge both for my own wrongs and for a woman's sake.'

Francisco turned quickly and looked at him keenly.

'A woman's sake! Thy motive is the same as mine: I too am living for a woman's sake.'

Then, at the other's questioning stare, Francisco continued more quietly:

'I am from Verona, Count; that will tell thee much. I belonged to della Scala's court, and barely escaped with life from the sacking of the town. Thou see'st I can for that and other matters more than equal thee in hatred of Visconti.'

He rose and moving toward the door, looked out.

'Oh, I am impatient!' he cried passionately, 'to be riding toward Ferrara!'

VII

GRAZIOSA'S BRACELET

Tisio Visconti, mounted on a white palfrey, rode slowly through streets of Milan, a lean figure, with a foolish face and vacant eyes.

For the elder Visconti was half-crazed, a fact to which perhaps he owed his life, Gian Galeazzo not fearing his poor disordered intellect enough to deprive him of aught, save his birthright – the sovereignty of Milan.

One or two men-at-arms in splendid livery rode behind him, and as he passed the people bowed humbly, respecting him solely as the Duke's brother, for Tisio was powerless for good or ill. Some few there were who pitied him.

About the streets of Milan he was a far more familiar figure than his brother, who was seldom seen, but of whose unscrupulous power Tisio was the living symbol.

Complete liberty was allowed him; still the soldiers behind were rather guards than servants, and charged to see he did not leave the gates. Dropping his loose reins on the palfrey's neck, Tisio Visconti looked around him with lack-lustre eyes and a dull smile. He was riding through the long, narrow streets, cobbled and overhung with high straight houses, that led to the western gate.

Through this gate his father lately, his brothers months ago, had been driven to their deaths; his father, infamously, his mother beside him, in the full light of day to Brescia; his brothers, secretly, at dead of night, to Brescia also, whence they returned no more.

Yet to Tisio the gate and street had no memory or

meaning; he looked ahead of him at the green trees beyond, and his eyes lit up. It was to see them he came. To him the world outside Milan was paradise; sometimes the soul within him rose and chafed at his dull captivity, and then he longed passionately for those green fields and trees, which he knew only from within the city gates.

The street was empty now; it was noontide, the hour Tisio preferred, when there were few abroad. The sun was hot, its rays flashing on the pikes of the sentinels who paced the walls; and Tisio's followers wiped their brows and chafed. But he gazed with wistful eyes, unheeding, into the beauty and the calm, the green and the gold. The sentry took no heed of him; so many times he had done the same; ridden to the gates, waited, looking eagerly through, then patiently returned to the gloom of the Visconti palace.

Either side the massive entrance lay houses, low, of grey stone, enclosed in square courtyards, entered by doors deep set in the thick walls.

From one of these, as Tisio turned, a girl emerged in a scarlet robe. She carried a bunch of lilies, on her arm hung the basket that betokened her errand. She and the little group of horsemen were the only life in the silent, sunny street. Tisio's eyes lit upon her, and he smiled. Like all the Visconti, there was poetry mingled with his madness, and the sight of beauty touched even his crazy brain.

The girl, starting when she saw the horsemen, paused, as if to retire, her hand on the door, her brilliant robe gorgeous against the background of grey wall. The colour, and the sunshine falling over her golden hair, made a picture Tisio was not slow to see; his eyes fixed upon her eagerly; he drew up his horse and turned to the page who, spy and attendant in one, invariably accompanied him.

'I would speak to her,' he said, with the eagerness of a child. The girl, seeing she attracted notice, turned, frightened and confused, to make good her escape, but the page, riding up, stopped her authoritatively, but with a reassuring smile.

''Tis the Lord Tisio Visconti, lady; fear nothing; he would only speak with thee,' he said.

But the girl's alarm increased at the mentiom of that dreaded name.

'He mistakes me for another, sir,' she said. 'I have never so much as seen even the Duke himself.'

'My lord would speak with thee,' repeated the page. 'He is not the Duke, but it is the Duke's pleasure that he be obeyed in matters such as this. Come, maiden, there is no need to fear: it is an honour.'

He turned his rein again, and, indeed, not daring to refuse, the girl followed and stood timidly by Tisio's side. He looked at her long and eagerly, at her scarlet dress, her sunny hair, the white and green lilies in her hands. Still he did not speak, and she raised her head and looked around questioningly and fearful. But the page only smiled: the men-at-arms sat silent and indifferent.

'Thou art very beautiful,' said Tisio at last. 'What is thy name? Whose daughter art thou.'

'Graziosa Vistarnini, my lord; Agnolo Vistarnini is my father. He is a painter.'

But Tisio's eyes grew vacant, and his gaze wandered to the lilies.

'Did they come from yonder,' he asked, and pointed beyond the gate.

'No, my lord. From a friend's garden. My father thinks to paint them.'

Still Tisio did not heed her answer; he laughed foolishly.

'I may go,' asked Graziosa timidly. 'I may go, my lord,'

He bent from the saddle and lifted from her shoulder a long lock of her curling hair, and stroked it, dropping it with a sigh.

'Give me these,' he said, pointing to the lilies; 'all the flowers I know grow in Gian's garden – Gian is the Duke of Milan.'

And at his words, and the tone in which he spoke them, Graziosa's pity overcame her fear.

In silence, tears in her eyes, she handed him the flowers. He took them eagerly, but before she could withdraw her hand, he grasped her arm with a childish exclamation and touched the bracelet of fine workmanship she wore upon the wrist.

'I will have this too,' he said, laughing with satisfaction: but the girl drew her arm back sharply and turned to go.

Tisio fumed. 'The bracelet,' he said peevishly, and the page motioned her harshly to remain.

Graziosa turned to him in confusion and distress.

'I cannot give it him,' she said, the tears starting. 'I entreat thee, sir, ask him to let me go.'

But the page intimated to her warningly she had best make no to-do. There was only one law for the citizens of Milan: that was the tyranny of the Visconti; let the one who encountered it only in the capricious whim of the crazy Tisio be thankful.

'Hold it good fortune, it is naught but a bauble he demands,' said the page. 'Give him the bracelet; he will drop it, forgotten, tomorrow. Ask for me one day at the palace. I will restore it. But give it now, before he grows angry. Thou hadst better.'

Tisio's face was darkening.

'Make haste, make haste,' cried the page impatiently, 'or it will be thou and thy bracelet both that will be carried off.'

'My betrothed gave it to me,' she murmured. 'I cannot part with it.'

'I will have it,' repeated Tisio imperiously, with outstretched hand. Graziosa's helpless tears were flowing; slowly she unclasped the bracelet; the page took her treasure with an easy air, handed it to his master, and turned the horses' heads toward home.

'Thou wilt be none the worse,' he laughed, as they rode away. Tisio, absorbed in his new toy, gave her neither look nor thought, for jewels, gold ornaments of rare design, were the craze of this Visconti's diseased brain.

Graziosa pressed her bare arm to her lips, and looked after them, the tears of vexation streaming down. She thought of Ambrogio, the painter-lover, whose gift it was: what would he say to find her bracelet gone?

'Oh, if only Ambrogio had been here,' she cried, 'he would not have let the Duke himself take it from me – but I – what could I do? – if only he is not angry that I let it go.'

She had not much faith in the page's words; besides, how dare she venture to the Visconti's palace? Her tears flowed afresh; she picked up the poor discarded lilies, all her pleasure gone. In the distance she could see Tisio, still handling the bracelet with delight, and she half-smiled, even through her tears, at so strange and pitiful a thing. 'It makes the poor crazy lord happy,' she said softly, 'but it breaks *my* heart to lose it,' She watched Tisio disappear; then, her loss a certainty, she turned with reluctant feet upon her errand.

Meanwhile Tisio, absorbed in his new spoil, rode toward the palace.

The projecting gables of the houses sent clear-cut shadows across his path; the strong noonday sun blended the city into brilliant light and shade, broken only by the vivid colour of the drapery fluttering at some unshaded window, or the sudden flash of pigeons' wings against the golden air.

As they neared the great gate of the palace, a group of horsemen, galloping noisily ahead of them, dashed into the vast courtyard and drew rein with a fine clatter at the entrance steps.

Tisio, following, raised his head, and looked dully at them – a band of his brother's soldiers, hired mercenaries; it was usual enough to meet them both within and without the Visconti's abode. As he was dismounting, the leader of the band addressed him familiarly.

'My lord hears thee not, sir,' said the page, 'his thoughts are with his spoils.'

The soldier laughed with a grimace.

It was the freedom of one whose services are valuable enough, even when well paid, to permit him to bear himself with small respect to his employers. For the mercenaries were a power; the transfer of their services could ruin states and lose towns, and even Visconti had to pay them well and concede licence to their leaders; for upon them, to a great extent, his sovereignty rested, and Alberic da Salluzzo could take more liberties than any. He was a famous captain, noted for his skill in wars and turbulence in peace, a man with no country and no honour, endowed with dauntless courage and endurance, of vast rapacity and of all the cruelty his age allowed.

Making no way for Tisio, and motioning curtly to his men, he strode up the stairs, a stalwart figure, overdressed in splendid armour, and swung into the ante-chamber of the Visconti's audience-room. It was deserted. Alberic, astonished, paused on the threshold, looking round in amazement for the crowd – courtiers, servants, seekers, soldiers – wont to fill it.

Opposite was the closed door of the Visconti's room, but even Alberic dared not knock there unannounced. He was turning away to seek enlightenment, when a dark form he had passed unnoticed in the distant shadows of the great room rose, and he recoguized, as it advanced, the secretary's stooping figure.

'What has happened here,' demanded the soldier.

'Is there need to ask,' answered Giannotto. 'The Duke has had the room cleared. He will see no one.' Alberic half-laughed, and shrugged his shoulders.

'The madness is on him at Count von Schulembourg's escape. Is that it,' he asked. 'But art even thou excluded,' he continued in surprise, for Giannotto was the one man who could come and go unannounced, unbidden, the one man who knew Visconti's secrets.

The secretary smiled, the slow smile that men's lips learned in the Visconti palace.

'It is best for the Duke to be alone, and for me that he should be,' he said. 'The news that Count Conrad has escaped hath galled him much; it came at a bad moment too, following on those parchments twice found within the grounds' – he paused. 'Thou wert sent to find the writer, or the one who put them there; art thou successful.'

Alberic shook his head. 'I return as I went. Beyond finding that doorway forced in the wall, messer secretary, there is no token whatsoever of how the Count escaped. But after so long a fast, messer,' Alberic showed his teeth, 'it is not likely that it was alone.'

'The one who aided him is he who inscribed those parchments.'

''Twould seem so,' answered Alberic. 'We have searched anew among the huts from which we drove Count Conrad's German dogs; on the threshold of the largest there was – this.'

He drew out of his breast a parchment, a long narrow strip, scrawled across in irregular writing, and handed it to Giannotto.

'What does it say,' he asked.

Giannotto glanced at it hastily, his eyes on the Duke's door.

He read, 'Della Scala lives!'

The captain whistled softly. 'Now, thou may'st hand that to the Duke instead of me,' he said.

Giannotto searched the writing keenly. 'Della Scala cannot live; 'tis some trick of the Torriani.'

Alberic laughed harshly. 'Whate'er it be, I say *thou* shalt have the pleasure of showing it the Duke!'

'Nay, thou must speak of thy own failures, friend. Besides, the Duke will need thee for his further orders. Count Conrad must be found, alive or dead!'

'Was it his ghost attacked the walls last night,' asked Alberic; and not wholly did he speak in jest.

The secretary cast uneasy looks across his shoulder at the ominously shut door.

'It angered Visconti strangely,' he whispered. 'But it was a handful of madmen. Wandering robbers from the hills! They were four at most, and they tried to scale the walls of Milan!' He smiled in scorn.

'And yet,' said Alberic, 'they were almost on the ramparts ere they were discovered, and when they were pursued fled back into the night silently, nor could we find whence they came, nor any trace of them.'

'However that may be,' said Giannotto, 'the Duke hath dismissed even me, and the delivery of this parchment had best wait till his black fit has left him.'

He raised the arras from the entrance that opened on the stairway, and passed out of sight along the corridor, leaving Alberic standing in the unguarded entrance of the deserted audience-room, undecided, the parchment in his hand.

But he did not stand there long alone. One or two servants stole back to their places, afraid to stay away; and presently, with slow steps and vacant smile, there passed by him Tisio Visconti, followed by the page who never left him.

'Thou, my lord,' cried Alberic. 'Now, how would it be if I ask him to hand this parchment over,' and he turned with a swaggering laugh to the page.

The page shook his head, not comprehending. Tisio, unheeding seated himself in one of the great chairs, Graziosa's bracelet still between his fingers.

'I will wait no longer,' cried Alberic suddenly; 'let the Duke summon me.'

But the next moment Alberic's swagger dropped, and he swung his plumed hat low to the lady who, unattended, stole across the threshold.

It was Valentine Visconti.

Her breast was heaving; suppressed excitement showed in every movement; it was not difficult for Alberic to read she had heard of Count Conrad's rescue.

With a motion of the hand she bade him wait, and turned to her brother, huddled in his chair, gazing blankly at the floor.

'Tisio!' she said, and her tone was very gentle. 'What dost thou here.'

He looked up, and his dull face lit at sight of her.

'I wait for Gian,' he said simply.

Valentine shuddered. 'What wouldst thou see him for, Tisio.'

He smiled, and held out the bracelet. 'To show him this.'

The tears rushed to Valentine's eyes but she remembered the captain and turned to him.

'Thou carryest something here to give the Duke,' she asked.

'Another parchment, lady,' said the captain. 'But I fear my lord is in no humour for its contents.'

Valentine's eyes sparkled brightly. 'Thou has not the courage to present it.'

'I confess, lady, I am waiting till I am obliged to,' answered Alberic.

Valentine held out her hand. 'Give me the paper; I will give it to my brother!'

The captain hesitated.

'Since thou hast not the courage,' she added almost with a laugh. All Gian's orders had not availed to prevent some whisper reaching Valentine of his evil humour and the cause of it: Conrad's escape, the threatening parchments; the hint that della Scala lived. Alberic, glancing at her, saw a triumph and a malice in the lady's glance that made him doubly feel he did not care just then to await Visconti's coming. But still he hesitated; the Duke might vent on him his fury with his sister.

'This business will not wait,' cried Valentine, 'give me the parchment to deliver, or knock at yonder door and hand it to the Duke yourself.'

But the captain of the mercenaries bent low, shook his head with a significant gesture, and, handing over the fatal missive, bowed himself away. Valentine turned again to Tisio's page.

'Take thy lord away,' she said. 'The Duke may not be best pleased to see him here'.

But Tisio would not go. Valentine, bending over him, stroked his hands tenderly, then breaking from him, leaned against the wall in sudden woe.

'All of us crazed,' she cried bitterly. 'All of us, surely; wretched people that we are!'

Then, at the sight of the parchment she held, her former mood returned. Conrad was alive! He had vowed devotion. He would return to her rescue. She would live to be free; to come and go outside the Visconti palace, outside Milan, out yonder in the world. She leaned back against the arras a moment, dizzy at the thought of so much joy, and her courage rose high, her eyes danced.

'The Duke must have this parchment,' she said; 'and since Alberic da Salluzzo does not care to seek an audience for it, why, Tisio, thou shalt see me give it. The Duke loves not an interruption when he is angry,' she added, with a soft laugh. 'But 'tis my duty to show him this.'

And she advanced toward the ominously closed door.

The page looked uneasy. He had no wish to face Visconti in his fury. Yet well he knew he dared not leave his charge.

Valentine tapped at the door with gentle fingers.

'Gian!' she called.

'Lady, this is madness!' cried the page, startled into speech.

She looked over her shoulder.

'I am also a Visconti, boy,' she said. 'Why should I fear the Duke.'

'Gian!' she called again, her beautiful head close to the dark panels. 'I have something here of great moment. Why let everyone know thou art so moved? Gian! Thou makest thyself a mock; dost thou *fear* Count Conrad, that his escape moves thee so.'

A pause: then with a smile Valentine stepped back a pace or two into the chamber.

'The Duke comes!' she said, and the page turned pale.

The inner door opened as smoothly as silently, and Visconti stood there looking at the trio. He was dressed in purple velvet, but his doublet was tumbled, the fine lace frills at his wrists wore torn to rags, his eyes strained wide open, and for a moment, as it was with any who encountered it, his expression gave his sister pause. But again she remembered Conrad lived, and she held out the parchment. 'I thought it well to give you this,' she said.

Gian advanced and took it in silence. But those torn ruffles, that disordered doublet, had their meanings, and the look in those wide eyes, as he turned them on her, quelled the mockery in hers, in spite of herself.

'Begone!' he said, 'and do not usurp another's office again. Leave me.'

'With thine own thoughts, brother,' she said softly, facing him.

'Be careful,' he answered; 'thou shouldst know my

humours, and that 'tis dangerous to cross them. Remember it only suits my purpose that thou shouldst live!'

At this Tisio, as if half-comprehending the threat, rose, and his brother's eyes fell on him.

'Thou too! What dost thou about my doors? Hast thou come too to dare me with thy folly.'

His eyes blazed, his hands worked. Tisio, dazed and affrighted, let fall Graziosa's bracelet.

The page stooped to recover it.

'What hast thou there,' cried Visconti with sudden change of tone; and the page, quivering for his life, handed the bracelet on bent knee. Visconti studied it one second, then, with a sound of fury that sent the boy crouching back against the wall, control left him. His eyes lighted on Tisio, and in maniacal fury he seized him by the shoulder and shook him as though he were a rag.

'How camest thou by this,' he yelled. 'How came this bracelet in the Visconti's palace? Answer me!'

Tisio whimpered, but had no reply, till, with a shout, Visconti flung him from him with such force that, save for Valentine, he would have fallen; then he turned upon the page who knelt by, trembling.

'Answer me!' he cried furiously. 'Answer! Where got the fool this.' He held the bracelet out. And the sight of those torn ruffles around his long white hands made the boy's hair rise.

'Indeed, my lord,' he gasped, 'a girl, whom my Lord Tisio – met by the western gate –'

'Gave it him!' shrieked Visconti. 'Ah, the three of you shall pay dearly for this hour's trifling with me!'

'My lord took it,' cried the page, half-wild with terror. 'He took it, my lord; she wept to give it.'

'She wept to give it,' said Visconti slowly.

There was a pause. When he spoke again, his tone was calmer.

'Then he shall be slain for taking it,' he said, flashing a look on Tisio, who, huddled in the chair, moaned with distress as he leaned against his sister.

'Shame! Calm thyself!' cried Valentine. 'What has Tisio done? Is this the first ornament he has liked and taken? Have they not orders to let him have his pleasure.'

'Mark me,' returned Visconti. 'Take care thou dost not make my dislike overrule my ambition – the pair of you hold your lives solely at my pleasure?'

He turned to the page.

'Go, and take thy fool with thee, and keep from my sight.'

With a white face the wretched page rose and helped Tisio to his feet. At a whisper from his sister he went meekly, Visconti's mad eyes on him the while.

A terrible silence fell.

Valentine steadied herself against the arras. She was thankful to see Tisio go – alive. To ask why the jewel Tisio had fondled had so angered Gian was beyond her daring. 'He is possessed,' she murmured to herself.

With an unpleasant laugh Visconti turned to her.

'Didst thou urge him to flaunt me with this,' he asked. 'Flaunt thee,' said Valentine. 'How should I know a toy like that could rouse such fury.'

The Duke looked at her keenly, and crushed the bracelet together in his hand.

'As I say, thou darest me far because thou art worth something to my plans – but I have the power, and I keep it.'

She was silent, and he turned to pass back into his own room.

But at the same moment Giannotto spoke. He had entered unobserved, and drew near his master with an obsequious movement.

But Visconti met him with a snarl.

'I will see no one! Did I not say so? Take care, Giannotto, lest I see *thee* too often.'

The secretary paled, but kept his composure. He had learned that to shrink before Visconti only served to arouse him the more.

'I would merely say, my lord,' he remarked, 'Alberic da Salluzzo awaits further orders.'

'Hath he found the Count,' flashed Visconti.

'My lord, no; nor trace of him, unless these parchments be one.'

'Thou hast another there?'

Giannotto, bowing low, handed Visconti a packet. His head was bent, his eyes downcast, and the smile that flickered over his thin lips unseen.

'This, my lord, was brought in by one of Alberic's men – found an hour since outside the gates of Count Conrad's villa.'

It was sealed, and inscribed with the Visconti's name.

Visconti seized it, and Giannotto, stepping back, watched furtively his furious face.

Gian looked at the packet. There was no attempt to disguise the writing. It was the same as that upon the parchment Valentine had given him with its brief threat: 'Della Scala lives,' and the seal of it was the Ladder of the Scaligeri. Long Visconti fingered it in silence, then remembering he was not alone, glanced wrathfully up to see that Valentine was watching him with a faint smile of scorn, and that Giannotto, for all his downcast head, waited with eyes keen with expectation. But Visconti curbed himself. To have the mastery of others he must keep the mastery of himself.

'Giannotto,' he said, and the secretary started as if a whip had touched him, 'thou wilt see to it that da Salluzzo searches Milan and all Lombardy – that he spares neither treasure nor blood – and that he brings to me dead, or living, Count Conrad von Schulembourg, and the writer of these parchments.'

With an obeisance Giannotto went, in silence, and Visconti slowly broke the seal of the packet. Then he turned to Valentine.

'Art thou waiting to see if it contains a message from thy Conrad?' he said fiercely. 'Have no fear! Thou shalt see his head ere night.'

She shuddered before the taunt, and turned to leave him.

It was always the same; let her meet Visconti with never so high courage, she left him quelled, discomfitted, dismayed.

'Go!' shouted Visconti, in sudden fury, and she stayed no longer to question or defy.

Carrying the half-opened packet and the parchment, Visconti re-entered his private room. It was dark and silent; no sound from within or without broke its deserted gloom.

He was alone, nor was he likely to be disturbed. Seating himself, not without a furtive glance over his shoulder, he looked at the writing again, the writing and the seal, then opened the packet.

A roll of parchment, close writ, strangely stained in places a reddish brown, fell with a rattle on the floor. Visconti started back, he stared at it, uttered a hoarse sound, stooped and picked it up. The parchment was

inscribed with poetry. Here and there among the stains
a line was readable.

'Perchance thou wouldst not dare to turn –'

His glance caught the words. He looked around with
wild eyes.

A huge, black bureau, fitted with many drawers, stood
in one corner of the room. Visconti, the parchment in his
shaking fingers, went to it, still with glances around, and
drew out drawer after drawer, till he had found the thing
he sought. It was among neat piles of parchments, anno-
tated in Giannotto's hand.

Visconti turned them over hastily, till he came upon a
document hung with the seals of Verona, a cartel of defiance, neatly endorsed in a clerkly hand, and signed in
large, bold writing, 'Mastino della Scala.'

Eagerly he turned to the cover of the packet, and laid
the two writings side by side. They were the same.

Visconti leaned against the black chest, breathing
heavily, his face not good to look on in its white devilry.

'He lives! Della Scala lives!' he cried, and struck at himself in his rage. Then his gaze came back to the blood-
stained parchment crumpled in his hand.

'And this –? And this – where got he this? The parchment that I read from on the road that day; the parchment that I thought was left at Brescia, in that –'

The words died away on his lips. In a sudden paroxysm
of something more than fury, Visconti drove it down
among the others within the drawer, and locked and
double-locked it in.

The day was fading; in that dull chamber the light fled
early and entered late. Visconti glanced again stealthily

at the dark arras, faint in the dusk. He strained his ears listening; the air was full of voices, far away, pleading for the most part, yet some so near and threatening, Visconti held his ears. They died away as they had come, but to Visconti the silence was more terrible.

'Giannotto!' he called. 'Lights! It grows dark –'

He listened; he heard those sighs again, then suddenly the sound of flying feet, hurrying, hurrying; with a scream of horror Visconti rushed up the steps calling wildly for lights.

The huge door swung open at his desperate push, then, falling to behind him, shook the tapestry; as it fell into place again a long sighing filled the empty room.

VIII

FOR A LADY'S GIFT

Tomaso Ligozzi sat in a corner of the ruined hut, with enthralled face, listening to Count Conrad, who lounged against the wooden table opposite. It was five days since Conrad's rescue. He had made a recovery the more rapid that no leech had been there to meddle with him. Left to the simplest nursing, the barest needful nourishment, and the vigour of his own constitution, Conrad had rallied, till now, in almost full health, no trace was left of the hollow-faced, emaciated figure Francisco had carried into safety.

The morning after the rescue, it was decided that the hut was no longer a safe shelter; and, carefully destroying all traces of their habitation, the three, under Francisco's leadership, helping Conrad between them, betook themselves to a thicket near. There, in his solitary prowlings to and fro, Francisco had discovered a deep cave underneath a sand-bank, the entrance well overgrown with boughs and bushes. Here, not without discomfort, they hid till Conrad should be fit to travel, and comforted themselves for the wretched exchange when they heard the shouts of Alberic's men.

Francisco was disappointed in his new ally. Count Conrad showed a levity, a forgetfulness of injury, that chimed badly with his own deep purposes. Tomaso was his chief reliance; his plan was to secure horses by fair means or foul, and, as soon as Conrad could sit the saddle, to depart for Ferrara. So far Francisco's stealthy and cautious manoeuvres to possess himself of what he needed had been unsuccessful; but at last he had come upon the track of something possible, and today, with Vittore to help him, he had departed to bring back with him the horses for their flight.

Twice between dawn and noon had Alberic's men scoured their neighbourhood. Two, indeed, had come so near the hiding-place that their talk was plain. They spoke of the parchment found the day before and of the Visconti's fury.

It seemed fairly sure that for many hours at least the soldiery would not return, as they could scarce confine their search to the one spot only; so, before Francisco's departure, it was arranged between him and Tomaso that their rendezvous at sundown should be the ruined hut where they had first had shelter, there being no means of horsemen treading the thick brushwood around the sand-cave, and the hut affording opportunities of space and movement.

After a weary day and the second visit of the search party, which alarmed them as to the heat of Visconti's pursuit, but reassured them also as to returning to the hut, Tomaso and Conrad reached it an hour before sundown and prepared to wait.

At first keenly anxious, straining for every sound, as time went on, unconsciously they grew more at ease, and Conrad beguiled Tomaso with his talk.

At last, with a sudden sigh, Conrad broke off; and lapsed into silence. Tomaso sat alert, looking through the open door.

'Francisco is long,' said Conrad after a while.

He was dressed in the leather doublet of a peasant, coarse and plain, yet very different from the rough attire Francisco wore. He was very handsome, of a sunny, pleasant expression, a quality rarely found among the Italians of Lombardy; and today, although prepared for flight, his blond curls were as carefully arranged as though he still shone at the court of Milan.

'Messer Francisco is long,' he remarked again, and Tomaso turned with a start.

'He has doubtless met with unexpected difficulty, lord,' he said with some reproach. 'Horses must be found – somewhere – for our journey tonight. Every hour we stay here is dangerous.'

'My heart misgives me that I did not accompany him,' said Conrad; 'we should all four have kept together.'

'Doubtless too many would have hampered him,' was the reply.

Tomaso did not add, as he might have done, that Francisco had his doubts of Conrad's discretion, and had left Tomaso charged to see he committed no rashness in his absence.

'Thinkest thou he will get the horses,' continued the Count, twirling his curls through his fingers. 'Let us hope he will try naught so mad as that attempt on the walls of Milan we made two days ago! The saints preserve us! But I thought it was all over with us! That was a fine race – tearing through the dark with Visconti's soldiers at our heels!'

Tomaso was hurt at the flippant tone that reflected on Francisco's judgment.

'It was a gallant attempt,' he said, 'and all but succeeded; once within the town, we might have done much.'

'And so might Visconti,' remarked Conrad airily. 'Thou art young, Tomaso, or thou wouldst see how worse than useless was such a mad escapade.'

'Something had to be done,' returned Tomaso, 'this inaction was maddening Messer Francisco.'

Conrad smiled and changed the subject.

'Who *is* this Francisco, thinkest thou,' he asked. 'For a mere servitor at della Scala's court, he bears a mighty hatred to Visconti.'

'He served the Prince, and lost his master and his all in the sack of Verona. It is not strange he should wish to revenge della Scala's wrongs and his own.'

'I think him of better birth and station than he claims,' said the Count judicially. 'He has the bearing of one gently born.'

'I take him for what he calls himself,' the boy replied. 'I owe him my life. I would die to serve him, nor would I question him.'

'But would remind me that I owe him something too,' laughed Conrad. 'When the time comes to show it, I shall not prove ungrateful.'

He seated himself on the table, and idly swinging his legs, looked around the hut with lazy distaste and seemed to think of dozing.

'Remember we travel tonight, my lord,' said Tomaso, annoyed at such indifference.

'If our good friend gets the horses.'

'There is no "if," unless we wish to perish,' flashed Tomaso. 'If Francisco gets no horses, we must from here on foot.'

'I do not oppose it. Rather than be taken into Milan, I will travel on foot in any other direction till I drop,' laughed the Count.

'Thou takest it lightly, my lord,' said Tomaso. 'Thou dost not seem as eager for revenge as thou wert. Think of the death Visconti doomed thee to. Thou hast great wrongs to right – wilt thou not return to Milan to avenge them? Or wilt thou ride away and forget.'

The laugh faded from Count Conrad's face, and his eyes flashed.

'No, Tomaso, I shall not forget,' he said; 'too well do I recall that night when I crept down the palace steps with my Lady Valentine. Visconti met us; parted us; ah, when I think of her face! – she was forced back to the horror of her life again: I, carried off to die of slow starvation in my own villa. Yes, yes; if his wrongs are like mine, Francisco did well the other night when we dashed on Milan; such wrongs put madness into one. Think of it, Tomaso; bound, gagged, half-crazed at the misfortune, I was hurried hither, secretly, at night, to be left to a dog's death in my own villa. Death was what I expected, but I nerved myself to meet it as a noble should. There is a long low room in yonder villa, with narrow windows I could scarce get my hand through – all of stone, and meant for cool in summer heat; into this I was forced, unbound, left with mock ceremony, and the door locked upon me. Ah! the sound of that key, Tomaso; they seemed to turn it in my heart, for I guessed its meaning. I had heard too often of Visconti's letting his prisoners die of hunger, and, as I listened to the soldiers' footsteps fading in the distance, the cold horror of the truth seized my heart. At first it seemed impossible that I could starve in my own dwelling. I mocked my fears; I could force, I could break the window! I laugh now at my own absurdities. I could do neither, I could do nothing! Terrible hours followed, Tomaso, terrible hours and ter-rible days. Still I would not own the truth, and still, as no one came, I knew it to be true! I thought of the Lady Valentine, and wondered what her fate might be. I thought of Germany, and wept to think I should never see it more! Then one evening, as I lay, I think, half-senseless, I heard the key turn in the lock, and Visconti entered, followed by Giannotto; two white hounds slunk at his heels: well I remember. Dear Lord! I was fallen so low in my misery, I fell at his feet and begged for mercy, for pity, or speedy death! And he – smiled on me, and bade Giannotto bring food!

'I cursed myself for my weakness, but could have kissed his feet. Then what happened I hardly know. As in a dream I saw Giannotto lay a tempting feast; a banquet for one or two, such as I and Visconti had often shared together! I blessed him with uplifted hands! When all was set, he turned to me, still smiling:

'"Thou askest for food," he said: "I would not refuse thy last request, Count Conrad."

'And he flung one of the hounds a piece of meat: it ate and died! Without a word they turned and left me, the feast still spread, the dead hound by the table. Then methinks I lost my wits, and went mad with rage and agony. When my ravings ceased, I found myself, my hands upon the food, it almost at my lips. But I resisted; I set it from me; and then my eyes wandered round the room in blank despair. I saw – the key still in the lock! I thought it was a vision, a trick of Satan. I crawled toward the door: I dragged myself along. It was no vision: they had gone and left me free!' Conrad paused; Tomaso, an absorbed listener, drew a deep breath.

'What did it mean, lord,' he asked.

'Ask me not, Tomaso,' answered Conrad with a lighter air. 'They were so certain I should eat and die, it made them careless, or Giannotto had a throb of pity. Many kindnesses the knave has had from me. I know not what it was; such things will happen. I have heard of them when in my native land from prisoners of war. But all I knew and cared for was that I was free! At first, indeed, it seemed to promise little good. I crept, I know not how, into the garden into the air: the sky was overhead: it gave me strength: let me but get to the water and I would live.... As by a miracle I reached the fountain.' Again Conrad paused, shuddering at remembrance of his anguish.

'The fountain,' repeated Tomaso, absorbed in the relation.

'The fountains were poisoned, boy; you know it; it boots not talking of it; it is all past and done with, and I live, a sound, free man, thanks to our brave Veronese; though in sooth how he could have saved me, had he not been a giant, I leave to my good angel to think out;' and Conrad laughed.

Tomaso looked surprised. He could not understand how Conrad could so easily shake off his hatred of Visconti, save when the thought was forced on him.

A silence fell which Conrad was again the first to break.

'The Lady Valentine,' he said, following his own train of thought, rather than addressing his companion, 'does she ever think of me.'

Tomaso inwardly wondered how much he thought of her. Save when telling his tale to Francisco, this was the only time he had named her. It seemed as if his sufferings and his love alike were to lie lightly on his mind.

'They say in Milan Lady Valentine is to marry the Duke of Orleans,' Tomaso ventured presently.

'They say!' echoed Conrad with scorn. 'The Frenchman is not even yet in Italy. Much may have happened ere he is.'

Tomaso rose and looked from the doorway anxiously.

'It is close on sundown,' he said, 'it is time Francisco came.'

'It is intolerably wearisome,' yawned Conrad. 'I would had gone with our friend – 'twould have been more enlivening than this.'

Tomaso's face ill concealed his scorn.

''Tis a matter of life and death, Count Conrad; even now the soldiers may at any time return.'

With a pleasant smile von Schulembourg leaped from the table.

'Pardon me, if I vex thee with my seeming careless-ness,' he said, with the charm of manner that could always win him friends. 'I owe too large a debt to all of you, to be really so heedless as I seem; but methinks there is no single thing –'

'Save keep ourselves in readiness, my lord,' said Tomaso. 'Francisco charged us to be so disposed that we could leap into the saddle without a breath's delay.'

'I remember,' said Count Conrad, lapsing again into an idle mood. 'Methinks our Veronese deliverer issues com-mands as if well used to it.'

The youth made no reply; he was gazing eagerly along the chestnut-bordered path, sorely impatient for Francisco's return.

'Canst thou play chess?' asked Conrad suddenly. Tomaso looked around at him in surprise. Did the German noble jest?

Von Schulembourg was again seated on the table, admiring his shapely hand, which he held against the light.

'Play chess?' repeated Tomaso. 'No, my lord.'

Count Conrad crossed his legs daintily and sighed.

'It were a splendid chance to teach thee – had we but the men. Thou hast read old romance, boy? And must remember how the knights and ladies play at chess? 'Tis a royal game.'

He sighed again, and glanced with disdain down at his leather doublet.

'Yet 'twere strange to play chess in this garb,' he added, and kicked the table with his heels in discontent.

Silence again fell, Tomaso still at the door, unheeding of the Count's complaints, watching anxiously through the gathering dusk.

'By heaven, boy!' Conrad exclaimed suddenly. 'Till this moment I had forgot it. Lady Valentine's gift – thinking of the chessmen brought it to my mind. I swore never to leave it – with my life! And 'tis behind me in the villa.'

'Behind thee, lord,' cried Tomaso, bewildered and startled at his excited tones. 'Where? What?'

Conrad was on his feet, his eyes sparkling with excitement.

'At the villa,' he cried. 'I know where it is, I will go and fetch it.'

'My lord, consider what thou say'st,' and Tomaso barred the door with outstretched arms. 'We promised Francisco we would not leave the hut – to attempt the villa would be simple madness!'

'Why, boy, the villa is close by,' laughed Conrad, 'and Francisco may not be back for hours most like; he may hang back till dark. Meanwhile am I to twirl my thumbs in here, and Lady Valentine's love-gift calling to me from beyond that wall? Out of my way, Tomaso. The dagger may be useful, and 'tis beautiful: a handle carved out of a single stone. Lady Valentine will not forgive my losing it!'

'The Lady Valentine will forgive the loss of a dagger, lord, when thou helpest to rescue her from Milan,' Tomaso said curtly. 'But what use to seek her gift and give thyself again into the Visconti's power?'

'Tush, Visconti! Visconti!... I have heard the name enough,' returned Count Conrad. 'I intend to have my lady's gift – it suits neither my honour nor my affection to leave it there to be some mercenary's plunder; and the chessmen too, boy! The set the Emperor gave – ah! you would love them – silver and ivory – I will bring them too. They will while away more weary hours such as these. What was I thinking of to leave them there so long!'

'At any moment Francisco may return, and without thee here time will be lost; moreover, his orders were that we await him.'

At Tomaso's words, Conrad raised his arched eyebrows.

'Order? To thee, maybe; thou art a boy, and of humble station. I am von Schulembourg: orders scarcely tally with that name.'

He drew his mantle over his despised doublet, and stepped to the door, putting Tomaso aside and not heeding his entreaties.

'Calm thyself, I shall be back long before the grim Veronese!' he said airily. 'Were there light enough, there would be time to learn the game before he comes again.'

'I will learn from no one who so little knows his duty,' cried Tomaso in hot wrath.

But it was as impossible to anger Conrad as to stop him, and with a smile on his lips and a good-humoured wave of his hand, he was gone.

Gone, absolutely gone, out of sight, into the heart of

danger and at the crucial moment, for a set of chessmen
and for a lady's love-gift.

After an undecided pause of utter vexation, Tomaso
could not resist the impulse to start in pursuit after him.
But Count Conrad was fleet of foot; he had disappeared,
and Tomaso dared follow no farther, for Francisco might
return at any moment, and to find them both gone
would make bad worse.

And scarcely had he re-entered the hut when he heard
the sound of horses ridden cautiously, and in a few
moments more Francisco turned into the open.

He was mounted, Vittore in front of him, on a powerful black horse, and leading two others, and his face was
animated with his triumph.

'Thou see'st,' he said, 'we are well provided, though it
has taken me all day. Now, to mount, without pause.
Where is the Count?'

'The Count,' faltered Tomaso, half-crying with vexation, 'the Count –'

'Well, what of him?' said Francisco, pausing keenly.

'He has gone back to the villa – to fetch something.
Oh, Messer Francisco, prevent him I could not – he left
but now –'

'Gone back to the villa!' cried Francisco. 'Did he rave?
Is he in his senses?'

Tomaso wrung his hands.

'He went to fetch a dagger he remembered and some
chessmen.'

With a cry of rage Francisco flung himself from his saddle. 'Methinks I left a fool to guard a fool,' he said. 'Did
I not tell thee to see Count Conrad kept from folly? Our
lives are on it.'

Tomaso paled at his displeasure, and faltered out a

recital of what had happened, but Francisco cut him short.

'The thing has happened,' he said sternly, 'and may cost us dear, but mine the fault to trust the foreign coxcomb.' Never had the two boys seen him so moved, and they shrank into silence.

Francisco fumed with anger. 'We will ride without him,' he said at length; but even while he bade Tomaso mount, and saw to his own girths, he paused irresolute, and Tomaso was thankful. He did not like to think of the gay Conrad left to meet his fate alone. He ventured to speak.

'The dagger was a lady's gift,' he said, 'the Lady Valentine's. He could not bear to leave it.'

'He will be wishing that he had,' said Francisco brusquely; but his face softened, and he added presently: 'He must be brought back, we cannot wait, and 'tis too dangerous to abandon him – for him and for ourselves.'

He flung the reins to Tomaso, and lifted Vittore to the ground.

'Stretch thy legs the while,' he said.

'Shall I go, messer?' asked the boy.

'He will come quicker at my bidding,' said Francisco grimly. 'Keep open eyes,' he added, 'the soldiers must come by the road if come again they do. Hold thither at once and spy, and then return and wait us here. Tether the horses carefully and water them. They cost me something.' He pointed to his roughly bandaged arm.

Half wild with remorseful vexation, Tomaso watched Francisco go the way the Count had gone, till his tall figure was lost to view. Then he and Vittore surveyed each other with anxious eyes.

'Oh, cousin!' cried the boy, 'we have had a fearful day!'

'Thou wert fortunate,' returned the other bitterly; 'Francisco is not vexed with thee.'

But Vittore, full of his tale, was eager rather for a listener than himself to give sympathy.

'Till noon we found nothing,' he said. 'Francisco hung around the farmhouses, but there were naught but sorry jades in every stable that we peered into, every one we tried, Tomaso, and so we roamed farther and farther across the plains –'

'But how didst thou ever get such steeds as these,' asked Tomaso, looking admiringly at the splendid animals, well groomed and well fed, fresh and vigorous.

'We took them,' said Vittore proudly. 'We came upon a camp of soldiers with horses and to spare, and Francisco asked them would they trade with him, and offered money, but they jeered and shouted and drove us off. Then Francisco stood before me while I crept up to those three and loosened their halters. The soldiers drank and sang; some lay and snored; they thought that we were gone, then suddenly –' his voice sank with excitement.

'What happened,' asked Tomaso with interest. 'I am glad that thou didst show thyself a brave lad, Vittore; what happened.'

'They saw us; three of them rushed out; there was a fight, and Francisco won.'

'Won? Against three?' cried Tomaso.

'He scattered them like the wind,' said Vittore. 'I know not how. He is a giant. He flung me on this black horse here; he mounted, I had the halters of the others in my hand. We rushed away. Of one he broke the head, I think, with his thick staff, and had his arm hit hard, but 'tis not hurt, he says. Some followed awhile, but they drank too deep; we left them like men dazed and mad, some falling by the road. It was a great business, cousin, but I felt no fear; Francisco is a brave, brave man.'

'He is a leader of men, methinks,' said Tomaso gravely. 'I little doubt the Count is right; he is more than he appears. Now we will leave the horses here behind these chestnuts, and step toward the road and reconnoitre.'

IX

THE RETURN OF THE DEAD

Gripping Vittore's hand, Tomaso looked cautiously up and down the road.

Crouching back in among the wayside trees, they commanded unseen a view of any who might come or go; and though the days faded fast, it was still light enough to see many paces off.

'No soldiery about tonight,' whispered Tomaso; 'they have ridden farther afield. We will go back, Vittore.'

They had turned to retrace their steps when Vittore clutched his cousin's hand yet tighter, and suppressed an exclamation.

'Look!' he whispered, 'a horseman coming toward Milan.'

Tomaso looked round nervously, and saw a single rider approaching swiftly, but casting searching glances around.

As the boys watched, mistrustfully waiting, still in hiding, to see him safely pass, to their dismay he slackened pace, and finally drew rein altogether and looked eagerly in their direction.

'Not a movement,' breathed Tomaso, and Vittore crouched in silent fright.

None the less, motionless as they thought themselves, some slight movement betrayed them, for the rider dismounted, advanced toward their hiding-place, and softly spoke.

'Who is there? I am a friend,' he said.

'He is a Florentine,' whispered Vittore joyfully; but

Tomaso leaned against the tree in silence, and even through the gathering dusk, as the younger boy looked up, he saw that he was pale and trembling.

'Canst thou direct me?' said the stranger. 'I can pay thee for thy services.'

'Answer him, Tomaso,' Vittore whispered eagerly; 'he is a Florentine, he will not hurt us.'

Tomaso made a step forward. 'It is someone we know,' he said chokingly, 'or my brain is playing me strange tricks.'

As he spoke, he put aside the branches that hid them, and stepped forward. The stranger had guessed their hiding-place unerringly; he stood close by, his horse's bridle across his arm. He was a slight, roughly-dressed, but well-formed man of middle age, light in colour and of strong yet delicate features.

'Thou needst not fear me,' he began with a smile; then, as the two figures drew nearer, he paused, and in his turn, grew pale and trembled.

Tomaso, tossing his hair back from his face, with parted lips, stepped close, followed by Vittore.

'Father! Thou dost not know me!'

'Son! Tomaso!' cried the traveller. He seized him by the shoulders with trembling hands, and scanned eagerly his face.

'Tomaso!' and his voice was shrill with feeling. 'Tomaso at last!'

They had not met for many months and years – two at least; the father, absent at a distant court, serving where chance had led him, for fame and fortune; the son, growing from boyhood into man in distant Florence.

Since Verona fell, Tomaso had mourned his father as dead, and he, in his turn, had wandered far, searching for the pair who had started out to find him.

With stifled sobs of joy, Tomaso clung about his father's neck, and was clasped to him in frenzied pleasure.

'They said thou wert dead, Father!' broke out the youth at last. 'I never thought to see thy face again.'

'I thought the same of thee, my son,' returned Ligozzi tenderly. 'I have been searching for traces of thee long and wearily. I thought thou must have perished on thy long journey, having found out Verona had fallen. But is this Vittore?' He drew to him paternally the boy who, so far, had watched the scene with wide-eyed curiosity.

'And now, what art thou doing – and where staying?'

As if he feared to lose him, Tomaso held his father tightly by the sleeve, over which the bridle had been slipped, and Vittore clinging to the other hand, they drew him forward between them to the place from which they had come.

'I am glad thou art not dead,' said Vittore; 'Tomaso grieved for thee sorely, and so did I.'

Tomaso laughed happily. 'Grieve! Aye, did we! But now we can rejoice.'

'But why this haste,' Ligozzi asked, 'where dost thou hurry me.'

'Back, Father, whence we came, for I was left in trust. It is a path thy horse can follow, and I will tell thee what has happened as we go.'

Ligozzi followed without further question, too full of joy for speech, and taking so much pleasure in that it was his son who spoke as for the moment not to heed too keenly what he said.

But when Tomaso, beginning, boy-fashion, with the last, and not the first, came to mention of the Visconti's blow, Ligozzi roused to fury.

'Methought I saw a scar across thy face,' he said, 'yet in this light I could not see too well. It is only one more wrong to set against the Visconti's name, one deed the more to be avenged.'

Tomaso took the clenched hand and covered it with kisses. 'I can forgive him now,' he said, 'since thou wert not slain when Verona fell.'

''Twas no fault of the Visconti's that any living soul escaped,' returned his father. 'Still, go on with thy tale, Tomaso; who is this Francisco, that thou nam'st so oft.'

Tomaso, eager and suddenly light of heart, told all he knew, and ere his recital ended they had reached the open, and found everything as they had left it, the horses safe, nothing seemingly disturbed.

'Francisco will be pleased at a helper such as thou, Father,' said Tomaso proudly; 'thou wilt be of more service in his venture than the German Count.'

'And when this Francisco returns presently, the plan is that we set forth at once for Ferrara,' asked Ligozzi.

'And meanwhile rest, Father, and I will bring thee food. We have already eaten.'

'I, too, my son,' answered Ligozzi; but he seated himself on one of the rough wooden stools and watched Tomaso affectionately, as he brought the poor horn lantern from the wall. He lit and set it on the table, where it cast a straggling and wretched light.

'Francisco is surely overlong,' he said; 'suppose the soldiers think to search again on their way home from some outlying district.'

'Then there will be another fight,' said Vittore, 'but Francisco will get the best of it.'

Ligozzi laughed.

'I owe this Francisco much,' he said; 'he must be a brave man, and his care saved you both. From Verona, didst thou say?'

'From Verona, Father. He said he knew thee, thy name; he is di Coldra; he knew thee, he has said, and the della Scala also!'

At della Scala's name Ligozzi's eyes filled with tears, and his voice trembled when he spoke.

'*I* at least knew della Scala well,' he said, 'and loved him too.'

He paused. 'Next to thee, Tomaso,' he continued sadly, 'his memory has filled my heart during these weary weeks. I, hoped, hope against hope, he might have escaped even as I did, but there comes no sign he lives.'

'Then thou didst not see him perish,' asked Tomaso softly.

'On that fearful night on which Verona fell,' answered Ligozzi, 'della Scala himself defended the gates, fighting like a lion. But he was betrayed, Tomaso, by a dastard in his pay, and the Visconti's soldiers poured in through the breach, secretly, and seized the palace, the Duke unwitting till it was too late and the palace flaming. I had to carry him the news; may I never have to do the like again. The palace was a sheet of fire, the Duchess was within, and the Visconti's soldiers swarming. The Prince rushed like a madman through the streets, a little group of us behind him. Too late! The Duchess was too great a prize, the miscreants had lost no time, and she was gone. A tale had reached the Duke while he still struck about him frantically that Gian Visconti himself had led the onset, and was still within the precincts with his prisoner. But it was a trap, Tomaso, set by a traitor. Della Scala, rushing where the pikeman pointed, was led beneath a burning stairway. It crashed in. I was behind the Duke; a beam struck me down, I thought among the dead, but some friars found me and brought me back to life; of della Scala they knew nothing.' He paused, and hid his eyes a moment in his hands.

'Thou didst care greatly?' said Tomaso, after a painful silence.

'He was a noble prince,' replied his father. 'I owe him everything; he made a friend of me, and I ever found him brave and generous, as strong as gentle, and most honourable – and he loved the Duchess, aye, he loved her. The Duchess still lives, a prisoner in Milan, but della Scala –'

He sighed deeply, and rose as if to put from him the memory of the tragedy.

'But to return to thy deliverer,' he said, 'one Francisco di Coldra, thou say'st; he claims I know him. What manner of a man is he?'

As he spoke he moved with Tomaso to the door, and looked out into the dark. What kept Francisco and the Count?

'He is tall and strong,' replied Tomaso, 'with thick brown hair and heavy eyes; a handsome face, I think it, Father, stern and sad. He is worn – as if from sickness. The Count thinks him better than he gives out; I know not.'

Ligozzi was silent; his figure alone was visible.

'Seeing the case is as thou say'st, Tomaso,' he remarked at last, 'every moment of delay is dangerous, and thy friend is long.'

Tomaso stepped into the open, and, to ease his impatience, brought forward the horses.

'I think they come,' he cried joyfully in another moment. 'It seems a dream, Father, that thou shouldst be here to meet Francisco.'

Ligozzi was still strangely silent. He drew back within

the doorway. Hurried footsteps were heard, the crackling of fallen boughs, the swish of the flowering grass. Ligozzi saw a tall figure looming toward them through the dusk, a slighter one beside him.

Tomaso, from where he stood, eager and excited by the horses, cried out to them. Ligozzi, still farther back, bent down to Vittore, who stood beside him; seen by the dim light of the horn lantern, his face was strangely agitated.

'Has this Francisco half-closed eyes, and a ready, pleasant smile?' he asked.

Vittore looked up in surprise.

'He has such eyes,' he answered. 'I have not ever seen him smile like that. Thou didst know him then, my uncle?'

'Yes,' Ligozzi answered brokenly. 'I think – I remember him – at della Scala's court.'

But here Tomaso, calling on him, re-entered the hut, followed by Francisco, whose stately presence seemed to make the mean place smaller still.

'My father,' said the boy joyfully; 'my father, saved from the taking of Verona, and come a long way in search of us!'

Francisco fell back, uttering a stifled exclamation; the anger cleared from his brow. He looked keenly at the figure in the shadow.

'Ligozzi!' he exclaimed, with shining eyes. 'Ligozzi lives!'

'It was a miracle, was it not?' said Tomaso eagerly. 'He has come to join us. He owes thee thanks, Messer Francisco, as do we.'

And all this time his father had not spoken. Tomaso wondered at it, and now, when Ligozzi came forward shrinkingly, Francisco raised his hand as if to keep him back, or warn him, or restrain.

'No thanks are needed,' he said quickly. 'I am Francisco di Coldra, from Verona, and ever ready to serve those whom Visconti hates!'

Ligozzi stood bare-headed, as if dazed.

Francisco spoke again, with meaning. 'Thy travel hath confused thee, sir,' he said; 'thou thinkest thou art still at the Duke of Verona's court, that thou standest thus humble?'

At this, Ligozzi roused himself. 'Tomaso has told me –' he began. But again Francisco stopped him.

'We must to horse!' he cried. 'To horse! Too much time has already been shamelessly wasted,' and he strode out, motioning to them to follow.

By the horses stood Conrad von Schulembourg, bringing them one by one under review, in the scanty gleam of light afforded by the lantern, and that flickered upon them through the space that answered for a window.

'A roan!' he cried gaily. 'I ever loved a roan charger. I will have this one, Francisco.' He spoke airily, as if ten minutes since Francisco had not lashed him with his tongue, and threatened him even with death, should his foolhardiness endanger them again.

'Thou wilt ride the black,' said Francisco coldly.

'Because I love the roan,' asked the other with a laugh.

'Because I say so,' returned Francisco.

A mocking answer rose to Conrad's lips, but it was never spoken. With a gesture, Francisco motioned him to silence. He turned and listened.

'Horses! And coming hither!' he said. 'Soldiers!'

The others, grouped close by, ready to mount, stopped paralysed – yes, Francisco's ears had caught the sound aright, the tramp of horsemen, and coming upon them from the road.

Escape with horses any other way there was none, though Conrad madly urged they should mount and fly.

But Francisco turned on him threateningly.

'Am I to run thee through?' he said; 'these horses mean more to me than thy life, or my own. Where shall we ride? Into the water? No, go back into the hut.' He turned to Ligozzi. 'Aid me tether these beasts where they may be unnoticed. These men perchance are only riding through.'

It was done in silence and with expedition. The soldiers' voices were now plain, and the jangle of their arms.

'Come, Ligozzi,' said Francisco, 'thou and I will play at being soldiers, and see how we can overcome Visconti's men. 'Tis a game that thou and I have played before.'

He drew his dagger as he spoke, and stepped back with Ligozzi into the hut. The door was closed. Francisco glanced around. By the table stood Conrad, showing even at that moment the silver and ivory chessmen, which he slipped out of his doublet one at a time, and passed them before Vittore's now wandering, now fascinated gaze.

Ligozzi and Tomaso stood beside their leader, one on either hand. Tomaso's face was white; the Visconti's scar showed plainly; his breast throbbed with excitement. Ligozzi's gaze was riveted upon Francisco.

A sudden babble of voices outside told the soldiers were in the open. A voice cried: 'Halt!'

But ere this Francisco had put out the light. They stood in darkness.

'I know that voice,' said Francisco at Ligozzi's ear;

'Alberic da Salluzzo. When last I heard it 'twas in Verona, at the burning of the palace. Dost remember?'

Ligozzi nodded. They held their daggers ready. No one stirred. Count Conrad thrust his chessmen back into his doublet. He regretted Francisco had dragged him so furiously away before he had time to find Lady Valentine's dagger with the emerald. It could have been of service now.

There was a lull outside. The soldiers had dismounted, but the captain kept his seat. The horses champed, threw up their heads, and clanked their trappings; but as he talked with the men told off to hold them Alberic's swaggering tones were plainly audible.

Suddenly a shout arose.

'They have found the horses,' said Francisco.

Alberic flung himself from the saddle. They could hear that. Torchlight suddenly flared across the opening, high up in the wall, and more faintly through the broken roof. There was a sudden blow upon the door Francisco's giant frame was barricading.

'Who is within here?' cried a harsh voice. 'Open!' and there came another blow.

But it scarce had fallen when Francisco, so swiftly no one could foresee his intention, stepped aside and let the door fly open as if the blow had forced it. On the threshold stood Alberic da Salluzzo, resplendent in jewelled armour and waving plumes. In the smoking torchlight, badly held, it seemed as if the place he looked into were empty.

'Who harbours here?' he said, and stepped across the threshold. 'Bring thy torch here, Guilliamo.'

But Francisco was swift. The door was shut before the soldier heard, and Francisco set once more his giant frame against it. In an instant, by the breathing of the men near him, da Salluzzo knew he had been trapped. He turned to escape, he was about to call but a hand of iron closed round his throat. In the dim light the place seemed full of threatening forms.

He was trapped indeed! Half-strangling, he ground his teeth at his folly more than his plight, and struggled to get his dagger, but his hands were caught.

In vain he struggled; he was a powerful man, but he who held him was more powerful. In vain he tried to cry aloud to those without; his voice was gripped within his throat. Slowly but irresistibly he was forced back against the farther wall, with a strength he thought could not be man's.

In a moment more, the soldiers without, nonplussed, but only for an instant, by their captain's disappearance, broke in the door. They could scarce believe their senses. Da Salluzzo lay dead upon the floor, and over him there towered a tall figure. They saw naught else. These men had fought with Alberic at the sacking of Verona; they knew that form, they had seen that face before. By their torches' smoky glare it seemed unearthly, and the eyes to flame, the form to fill the hut.

'Come and fetch your captain!' cried Francisco. But at the voice, at the look of his wild face as he advanced, they dropped their torches and scrambled back across the threshold panic-struck.

'Mastino della Scala!' they cried, 'Mastino della Scala!' And dropping the lights they fled in terror.

X

THE TURQUOISE GLOVES

Della Scala is alive!

The news flew like fire around Milan, rousing even the indifferent to some interest. The rumours then were true? Della Scala was alive? In the market-place, in the streets, in the houses it was discussed – the name of della Scala was on every lip. But in the Visconti palace it was not spoken. Silent, sombre as ever, the castle frowned over its beautiful gardens, and only by the companies of horse that spurred out of its side gates to fortify still more strongly the nine cities once held by della Scala and now the Visconti's, only by this could it be told how much the news meant to the man within.

Giannotto, walking softly through the corridors, paused and looked out into the garden.

Something had caught his keen eye, and he watched, hidden by the curtain of purple silk.

A sea of flowers lay spread beneath him, while beyond a more formal part of the grounds, crowned with white terraces and set with cypress-trees, rose clear against the sapphire sky. To the right lay Isotta d'Este's prison, the western tower, a massive building of huge strength, encircled on three sides with a moat, and guarded by soldiers.

Giannotto's eyes glanced from the silver banner that hung above, lifeless in the summer air, to the soldiers at their posts below.

There was an entrance to the tower near to the palace, guarded, but little used, half-hidden by myrtle that had filled up the dried moat and climbed up the wall; and, as

Giannotto still watched, the figure he had seen enter there, hooded and cloaked, passed out again hurriedly, sped between the sentries, who studiously took no heed, and was soon lost to sight along the winding paths.

The movement was quick, the figure gone almost as soon as noticed; a casual observer would have taken little heed, but Giannotto's eyes were trained, and he knew the figure for whose it was: Valentine Visconti.

'She must have bribed high,' he thought. 'High indeed. Why should she visit the prison of Isotta d'Este?' He followed her figure across the garden with curious, suspicious thoughts.

'She is daring,' he mused, 'and foolish. Did she think no one's eyes could be on her, when Visconti has spies who are to watch her every movement?'

He turned back into the corridor, twisting the ends of his scarlet robe between his fingers, and smiling to himself.

The secretary was in a better humour than his master; that Mastino della Scala should live to vex Visconti, that he should have snatched von Schulembourg, one of his dearest victims, back from underneath his very hand, pleased Giannotto, as did anything that annoyed Visconti, save when his master's rage was such that his secretary felt its working.

The Duke he knew to be alone. The brief audience he accorded was long over. Visconti had no friends; they, who must, sought him in the morning in the audience-room. For the rest, like the others of his tainted race, he lived alone.

He paused outside Visconti's door, and the secretaary smoothed a smile from his face, and, tapping lightly, entered with a silent, cringing movement.

The chamber was dark, although it was full noonday. Visconti had no love for the sunlight, and even the narrow windows were obscured and shrouded in dark purple.

The walls were panelled in carved wood, but, apart from the stiff chairs, the sole furniture of the apartment was a long low chest, set open, and showing silver goblets and curious bottles and glasses twisted into strange shapes, and coloured. At the farther end were two doors close together, and between them sat Visconti, huddled up against the wall, gazing at the floor with strained, wide-open eyes.

Giannotto, entering softly, noticed in his hand a bracelet, fashioned as a snake, emerald green, of striking workmanship.

'A messenger from the Bologna embassy, my lord,' he said, closing the door behind him, 'has entreated me to ask thy attention for them.'

Visconti looked up quickly, and put out of sight the bracelet with a snap of anger.

'What, do the Bolognese trouble me?' he said fiercely.

'They only follow the example of the Pavians, my lord,' returned the secretary smoothly. 'They would have thy mediation between the rival factions in their state.'

'My mediation! Pavia asked it, as thou say'st, and so did Bergamo; yet do the twain who then appealed to me reign in either city now? The Bolognese are foolish,' said Visconti.

Giannotto shrugged his shoulders. 'That need not trouble thee, my lord. Bologna is a wealthy town. Thy lordship will think of it.'

The secretary's eyes were on the ground. Gian Galeazzo slipped his bracelet into his doublet and rose.

'Aye, I will think of it,' he said, 'but for the moment

there are more precious things to do even than using the Bolognese against themselves.'

Giannotto waited. The Duke paced to and fro a moment, then broke into the subject next his heart.

'Thinkest thou della Scala will outwit me?' he said eagerly. 'Thinkest thou that if he do reach Ferrara he will rouse the Estes to action?'

'He had two good hours' start,' returned Giannotto, 'and the road to Ferrara offers many chances.'

'And those men – who let him escape them? Do they still live?'

'Aye, my lord. They are valuable. It is enough that Alberic da Salluzzo has been lost to us –'

'They shall yet hang for it,' said Visconti.

With rapid steps he returned to his seat, flung himself into it, clutching the arms with vice-like grip.

'He cannot do anything, Giannotto,' he said. 'He cannot rouse the Estes – against me! No; when della Scala ruled nine cities, and his revenue was equalled only by the kings of France – I stripped him, I routed him. And now!' he smiled and his eyes widened, 'he is a beggar. Perhaps it is not so ill that he lives to know it. It is a better revenge than any I could have devised, della Scala a beggar, a hanger-on at his kinsman's court, deafening his ears with unwelcome prayers, sinking into contempt before the people who once owned him lord!'

Giannotto was silent. He could not imagine Mastino della Scala a beggar at any prince's court.

But Visconti, blinded and absorbed by hatred, continued unheedingly:

'Carrara also, the Duke of Padua, is too necessary to the Estes. They cannot stand without him. Will he, thinkest thou, ever be won over to side with Mastino?

No, Giannotto, I do not fear him. Let della Scala live robbed of all – and with Count Conrad as an ally!'

'Shall we then dismiss him, my lord?' ventured Giannotto smoothly; 'he who is not worth fearing is not worth considering.'

He seated himself at the low table as he spoke, his watchful eyes on Visconti, and drew some papers from the flat bag at his side.

The Duke returned no answer. In truth he heard not what was said, but leaned back in his chair and fell to thinking. The secretary, looking at his brooding face, shuddered a little at what his master's thoughts might be. He wondered also as to that green bracelet Visconti had concealed.

The silence grew oppressive, and Giannotto moved uneasily. He loved not to sit alone with Visconti when he fell into these musings.

The Duke roused himself.

'Ah,' he said, breaking suddenly into a passion of declaim.

'A god can do no more than say, "I have succeeded – in all I have undertaken, I have succeeded!" And I can say as much. I have succeeded. I looked on life and took from it what I wanted, the fairest and the finest things that offered; and the price – others paid it. Truly, I have succeeded!'

Giannotto shrank back at Visconti's outburst, and made no answer.

But the Duke had forgotten him. He was but uttering his thoughts aloud.

'Five years ago,' he said exultingly, 'I rode outside the gates of Verona and challenged della Scala to single combat. He sent his lackey out with a refusal, and in my heart

I said: "I will bring that man so low that life shall hold nothing so sweet to him as the thought of meeting me in single fight!" I have succeeded! Isotta d'Este looked past me and laughed, and I said, "She shall live to feel her life within my hand." In that also I have succeeded!

'And three years ago, only three years ago, I stood within this very room, four lives between me and the throne of Milan – four lives, all craft – and two young. But I – I the youngest, took my fate and theirs into my hand. I said: "It is for me to reign in Milan – I am the Duke." In that I have succeeded!'

He paused, with dilating eyes and parted lips, intoxicated with pride.

'This ambition is his madness,' thought Giannotto; but he still was silent.

'In another thing,' continued Visconti, and his voice was changed: he breathed softly, and his eyes sparked pleasantly. 'Last May-day I saw the people in the fields, pulling flowers; I knew they were what poets call happy. Among them were two girls, one dark, one fair, and she with the dark hair had her betrothed beside her. They were happy among the happy, they loved each other – and I rode unseen. The may was thick and white, I watched them through the flowers and vowed: "I too will be happy, even as they are happy, though I am Visconti; I will be loved for myself alone; that fair-haired girl shall care for me as her companion for her lover – life shall give me that as well!"'

And he rose, triumphant, smiling, resting his hand on the arras that hid the door behind him.

The secretary gazed upon him fascinated.

Lifting the arras, he paused again, and looked back with a smile that transformed his face.

'In that too have I succeeded!' he said melodiously; and, opening the narrow door, he was gone, as always, noiselessly.

The secretary shook himself.

'Why does he unburden his soul to me?' he murmured. 'Does he think, because I sit silent, I have no ears, no memory – that I shall forget? "In that too have I succeeded!" Aye, thou hast it all thine own way, Visconti, so far.'

With a slight shrug of the shoulders Giannotto fell to writing.

When his pages were finished, he put them into his bag for the Duke to sign, and grumbling at his absence, stayed, but dared not follow. Presently he decided to take his own dismissal.

As he rose to go he remembered Valentine Visconti, flying through the garden after her secret visit, and he considered if she could bribe him to silence heavily enough to make it worth his while to venture an encounter with her.

Visconti did not stint his sister for money, and she might pay well. Still, dare he let her know he spied?

Then his thoughts went to Isotta d'Este, and he wondered, with some interest, what her fate would be.

In open day Isotta d'Este had been captured; all Europe knew she was his prisoner; Tuscany and the Empire already looked with interest on the Duke of Milan's growing power, and that Duke a usurper. Visconti had to step warily.

Still busy with his thoughts, the secretary had reached the door, when it opened and the ancient Luisa, Isotta's prison attendant and spy, entered, glancing expectantly around.

Giannotto looked at her slowly; he hated her – indeed, he hated most people, but her in particular, for she equalled him in servile cunning and surpassed him in greed.

'I would see the Duke,' she said, looking at him mistrustfully.

'Thou canst not see him,' returned the secretary, 'for he is not here.'

But old Luisa seated herself calmly on one of the black-backed chairs. 'I will not take thy word for what I can or cannot do,' she said. 'I have important tidings for his ear alone.'

Giannotto longingly wondered if it were possible to win her news from her and share in the reward.

'I will get thy news in to the Duke,' he said. 'Trust it to me, and I will see he does not forget who brought it, but 'tis impossible to see him now.'

Luisa smiled.

'I would be my own news-bearer,' she said, and made no movement to go.

'Visconti is in his laboratory,' said Giannotto angrily. 'Whatever thy news, art thou so mad as to think of following him there? Wilt thou not trust it to me?' he added more gently.

She shook her head placidly.

'Have thy way,' sneered Giannotto. 'Stay and see the Duke, and be dismissed for having left thy post, and remember there are more eyes on the western tower than thou knowest.'

The old woman looked uneasy, but stubbornly kept her place. And seizing his bag and papers, Giannotto was gone, and the heavy door closed behind him before she could know what was going to happen.

'Giannotto!' she cried in alarm. 'Listen a moment –'
And she ran and pushed at the door.

Giannotto opened it a little and showed his smiling,
crafty face.

'Wilt thou give me the news or wait till the Duke
leaves his laboratory and finds thou hast been absent
from thy post an hour, perchance more?'

'Take it then,' said Luisa with a cry of vexation. 'But I
will repay thee, Giannotto.'

She thrust into his hands a piece of parchment.

'It was left with me by the Lady Valentine to give Isotta
d'Este. Now, make what else of it thou canst,' and Luisa
shuffled past him, terror overmastering greed. To be
locked within that chamber to await the Visconti was
what she had not heart for. Moreover, she could tell the
Duke another time – and he would listen – how
Giannotto had forestalled her.

She shuttled off, and Giannotto in triumph re-entered
the chamber. He read the parchment, one of many: 'Della
Scala lives.'

'And the Lady Valentine conveys it to Isotta d'Este's
prison,' mused Giannotto. 'Now, shall I tell my lord that
piece of news or no?'

He regarded the two doors, between which Visconti's
chair was set, and gently tried them: one was locked, the
other opened to the touch. He dared investigate no further, and returning to his chair, sat down to wait. The
minutes dragged on, and he fumed with impatience.

Visconti's laboratory was not altogether a secret
place. Giannotto had helped him in his experiments;
there was an assistant who tended the fires. But no one
followed the Duke into it unbidden.

But, as time went on, Giannotto debated with himself

that he would venture. Visconti was long. What was he doing? It was an opportunity to spy. If caught, the secretary could plead anxiety as to his master's safety. Summoning his courage, Giannotto rose and crept to the unlocked door and softly pushed it back.

It opened on a flight of stairs, black marble, carpeted in gold, the high walls hung with tapestry in red.

The steps were few in number, before they twisted abruptly out of sight. Round the bend floated a thin wisp of grey smoke.

Giannotto slowly and cautiously mounted. At the bend the steps still continued, twisting again.

It was very silent, very still, only the lazy floating wreath of smoke moving. Giannotto came within sight of a door, ajar. He marvelled at it. It was thus Conrad von Schulemebourg had escaped – through an unlocked door. Visconti trusted overmuch to the terror of his name.

Giannotto slowly and cautiously pushed it a little further open. It showed him the outer laboratory, a long low room of grey stone, and lit by a large window set back a man's height in the wall.

Hanging over a clear charcoal fire, burning in a pan, was an elaborate silver pot, seeming to quiver in the vapour that shimmered off the fire underneath.

Around it on the floor stood glasses, vases, jars and goblets, glass, china and gold.

Save this, the vault-like chamber was void of furniture; only on the stove near the window lay a pile of things, curiously mixed. They held Giannotto's eyes. They were not in the laboratory when he worked there.

A man's doublet of white satin, a scent bottle, a spray of roses, a mask, a poniard, two scarfs intertwisted, and, sparkling on an inlaid tray, a massive ring – he knew it, he had seen it on Isotta's hand – her wedding ring; all this thrown among two birds and a hound, stiff and dead.

Giannotto started a step back. Then his eyes fell on the window-seat, and even he could scarce suppress a cry.

For Visconti stood there, erect and motionless, so motionless and so one with the stone beside him, Giannotto had not known him there. From head to foot he was clad in grey. In his right hand he held a pair of gloves, turquoise blue, magnificently worked in pearls, and in the other a small phial filled with a yellow, slow-moving liquid. This he held high against the light, which fell strong and cold upon his upturned face and thick, curling red hair, and Giannotto gazed, fascinated, on the gleam of his teeth as he smiled with a slow satisfaction. Giannotto had seen enough. His heart beat quickly. He drew the door to again, and crept back down the steps unobserved, gaining the outer chamber, trembling; and there for a moment fell upon his knees, as if in thanks for a most merciful escape. His thanks were not without their reason. Hardly was the secretary in his chair again, when a light footfall sounded and Visconti entered.

For one moment Giannotto thrilled with terror, but a covert glance at the Duke's face reassured him.

'I have this to give you, my lord,' he began at once. 'It was left in the Lady Isotta's prison.

Visconti took the parchment.

'By whom left there?' he asked.

'I know not, my lord,' said Giannotto. 'Luisa brought it, but dared not leave her post.'

His own narrow escape of a moment since had tied up Giannotto's tongue.

'It will not be hard to discover,' said Visconti. 'Some one who did not bribe Luisa high enough.'

'Della Scala lives,' he read again.

'Let the Lady Isotta have it,' he said. 'It may keep her alive. It looks to me that she may die, Giannotto, of the bad air and the confinement,' and he smiled. 'I would certainly not have her death. Give her the parchment,' And he handed the parchment back, dismissing Giannotto with the gesture.

Clearly Visconti was in a mood that held neither comment nor reward, but one the secretary was glad to escape from so easily. With a deep obeisance he departed.

'Who bribes the woman to comfort Isotta d'Este? The soldiers are to be trusted,' mused Visconti. 'Once I know I will remember it.'

He drew from his doublet the velvet gloves of turquoise hue and laid them on the table.

They were beautiful in their perfect workmanship, huge gauntlets fringed with pearl and gold and tasselled at the points with rubies. On the back was a rich design also in pearl and gold, and they were lined with white satin, covered in fine silk lace.

Truly they were a work of art. Visconti raised them delicately by the tassels and looked long at their rich blue, admiringly, and with a curious expression.

XI

MASTINO DELLA SCALA

In the council chamber of the Estes' summer palace at Ferrara were gathered the heads of the reigning families of Lombardy.

At a long table, set across one end of the apartment, two men were seated talking to one another in low voices. They were Ippolito d'Este and Giacomo Carrara, Duke of Padua. D'Este, a stern, grey-haired man of fifty or so, with keen eyes and a hard mouth, was talking rapidly, tapping the while his fingers nervously upon the table.

Carrara, florid, pleasant-mannered, with brilliant black eyes, black hair, and a ready smile, leaned forward and listened, observing him keenly. Opposite them, but the length of the table away, a lady with tired eyes and a patient mouth leaned back in her chair, motionless, watching the trees seen through the window.

She was Julia Gonzaga, the representative in this gathering in the name of her infant nephew, of the city of Mantua and its domains, the head of the fourth and last great family of Lombardy who dared to raise a hand against the encroachments and the power of Visconti.

But if at this end of the chamber the only sound was low converse, all subdued and quiet, at the farther end gay voices and bursts of laughter broke the stillness.

For seated in the broad window-seat, toying with a sprig of myrtle, was Count Conrad, brilliant and light-hearted, clad in the last extreme of fashion, resplendent in primrose velvet and mauve silk, with long scalloped sleeves that swept the ground.

Around his waist was a gold belt suspending, by a jew-elled chain, an orange stuck with cloves and enclosed in a case of silver filigree.

Count Conrad also wore ear-rings, pearl drops that shimmered through his blond curls, and on each wrist a bracelet; yet even this effeminacy could not altogether destroy a certain manliness that was the Count's, in spite of an almost seeming wish to disallow it.

Beside him, half-leaning through the window, was a youth of twenty, of that brilliant beauty too bright to last.

He too was dressed more like an idle courtier of the Valois court than a fighting noble of the free cities, and the rare charm of his face was marred by the spoiled affectation of his manner.

'Another war!' laughed Conrad. 'I have done naught but fight since I left Germany. I am on the sick list.'

'Not when the war is of thine own seeking,' said Vincenzo.

'Because thou needs must fall in love with the Visconti's sister – as if there were not others as fair and far safer to woo!'

Conrad crossed his legs and glanced critically at the taper points of his gold shoes.

''Tis not my wooing of Visconti's sister has caused war,' he replied. 'Thy brother-in-law –'

'I beseech thee,' cried Vincenzo petulantly, 'leave me some little rest from mention of his name and wrongs! Ever since you rode into Ferrara some six days ago, there has been naught else talked of but Mastino, Mastino's wrongs, what we must do for Mastino – till I fair weary at the name!'

'You would not risk your all to glut his vengeance?'

remarked the Count. 'None the less his wife is your sister, and a d'Este.'

'No need for the heroics he makes over her, even so. Visconti will not hurt her, yet we must be hurried into war for it, forsooth!'

'I owe della Scala my life,' returned Conrad airily. 'I should be the last to speak; still, my wrongs are as many and as deep. I love the Lady Valentine. *I* have lost my land and my jewels, my house and servants, yet I am quite ready to settle in some other part of Italy – and forget Visconti. *I* do not go about trying to entice other people into *my* quarrels.'

He sniffed at his orange as he spoke, and breaking off the end of the myrtle, stuck it in his belt.

Vincenzo's beautiful eyes flashed. 'Art thou a poltroon then?' he cried scornfully. 'Loved I a lady and she were kept from me, I would not rest while a stone of the palace that held her remained one on the other.'

Conrad raised his eyebrows, startled at the sudden change of front.

'Then you should understand Mastino,' he said.

'I hate Mastino. He is wearisome,' cried Vincenzo, pettishly. 'Still, I do not love a laggard.'

Conrad's reply was checked. Ippolito d'Este had arisen and was calling them to join him. Reluctantly they rose, Vincenzo with a yawn of distaste, and approached the table.

Ippolito frowned at Vincenzo's face.

'You would spend all your time in idleness, it seems,' he said. 'Have you no interest then in our decision as to the aid della Scala asks?'

Vincenzo dropped into his seat, seemingly rebuked. 'Aid, my fathe?,' he said. 'I knew not it was aid della Scala asked, methought 'twas all!'

'My proposal is an army,' said Giacomo smoothly. 'A small army. Let us see what success della Scala has with a small army. Our all *is* much to ask.'

'What say you to that?' asked Ippolito of his son.

'With all my heart,' returned Vincenzo. 'An army small or large, so long as it rids us of his gloomy face about court.'

'Thou art an insolent boy,' interrupted his father sternly. 'At thy sister's wedding thou wert proud that Mastino della Scala stooped to pat thee on the head. The Duke of Verona was once as much greater than we, Vincenzo, as we are higher than a footman. It goes not with nobility nor with honour to slight the fallen.'

Vincenzo blushed under his father's rebuke and sat silent. But Giacomo, always ready to smooth things over, turned to the Duchess of Mantua.

'And you,' he said. 'You, lady, what think you of trusting della Scala with an army?'

Julia Gonzaga smiled a little wearily.

'Where is he, to speak for himself?' she asked.

'We are waiting for him,' Ippolito replied. 'He said he would be with us. He is late,' he added testily.

'Doubtless the hour has escaped him,' put in Giacomo pleasantly. 'The Duke of Verona will not fail us.'

'He will disappoint us – if he turns up,' said Vincenzo under his breath. But Conrad caught the whisper and choked with a suppressed laugh – not that the remark was funny, but that Count von Schulembourg was foolish. Ippolito's stern eyes were turned on him.

'Is this a council of war?' he asked, 'or a gathering of –'

'A council of war,' interposed Conrad hastily, with his most winning smile.

But d'Este looked on him with mistrust; he had no love for the light-hearted German.

Still Mastino came not, and Giacomo moved with a great show of patience and forbearance.

''Tis scarcely the way to treat with us,' he said.

''Tis treatment good enough for those who bear it,' breathed Vincenzo, and Conrad sniffed his orange. Ippolito's brow grew dark; he struck a gong beside him, and a page appeared.

'Tell my lord of Verona we wait for him,' He turned to the others. ''Tis agreed,' he said quickly, 'that we furnish della Scala with a small army – to be contributed between us.'

Carrara moved in silent assent; on Julia Gonzaga's face a faint scorn showed.

A silence fell, broken only by the tapping of d'Este's fingers on the polished table.

Then at the farther end of the chamber two pages drew apart the scarlet curtains and Mastino della Scala entered. Conrad, glancing up, wondered how even for a moment he could have mistaken him for aught but what he was, so noble and stately was his bearing.

Conrad and the d'Estes moved at his entrance, but slightly, and kept their eyes upon him as he walked to the head of the table and there took his place.

Though by far the plainest in attire, his simple leather doublet in marked contrast with Conrad's display and Vincenzo's fashion, he took the head of the council, naturally and unquestioned. So much of the glory of his former greatness still remained to him.

'And are your councils ended?' he asked. 'I would hasten you, my lords. Still further delay, and Visconti will be first in the field.'

He paused, and took his seat in the large black chair, looking keenly at their faces.

For a moment no one answered, then Giacomo leaned forward with a deprecating smile.

'My lord of Verona,' he said smoothly, 'you ask us to venture everything – and give us five days in which to decide – surely you are not surprised our answer is not quite ready?'

Mastino della Scala bit his lip to keep back an angry reply. 'Five hours were enough in such a case as this, my lord,' he said quietly.

Now d'Este spoke hastily. 'We have come to a resolution, Mastino – one in which we all agree,' and he looked questioningly around upon the others. No one answered, and, taking silence for consent, Ippolito continued:

'We will aid thee, Mastino, I and Carrara, and the Duchess of Mantua –'

He paused a little nervously, and Giacomo kept his bright black eyes on Mastino's face.

'My lord of Ferrara says rightly,' he put in smoothly. 'I will second him.'

The note of condescension in the Duke of Padua's voice stung della Scala sharply; it was only with an effort he controlled himself.

'With what will you aid me?' he asked calmly.

Still d'Este hesitated, for his proposal was mean even in his own eyes, but Giacomo answered for him in even tones: 'We will aid you with an army of ten thousand men, Lord della Scala, to be recruited from Padua, Mantua, and Ferrara; well armed and –'

But della Scala had risen.

'Spare thyself a catalogue of their virtue, my lord of

Padua,' he said. 'For I refuse thy offer – one well worthy of a Carrara!'

Giacomo paled with anger; his merchant descent was a sore point, and Mastino's words struck home.

'Refuse!' exclaimed Ippolito. 'Ten thousand men!' Della Scala glanced at him with scorn.

'Ten thousand men!' he echoed. 'Yes, I refuse ten thousand men. I thought thou once lovedst me, d'Este, and wert too much of a soldier to dishonour me by such a proposal.'

'We can make it more –' began Ippolito.

'Dost thou not think I can see through this?' interrupted Mastino bitterly. 'This offer is but given to get rid of me – a safer way of dismissing me from the court that once cringed to entertain me than a plain refusal. Ten thousand men! I thought better of thee, d'Este.'

'Then fifty thousand,' replied Ippolito stung by the reproach.

'A royal number,' put in Conrad, but della Scala turned on them in fury.

'No!' he cried. 'Not fifty nor a hundred thousand men, to make sport for Visconti's leisure hours – Visconti who holds nine towns of mine alone, Visconti who is leagued with France and has the Empire at his heels, Visconti who has gained Bergamo, Lodi, and Bologna and has half the mercenaries of Italy in his pay! No, d'Este, I have been too great for that. Since you so forget what I have been, and who my wife is – I will leave thee, nor trouble thy peace for men thou caust not give ungrudgingly. And thou, Carrara, I will leave thee – in thy blind folly, to wait for Visconti's eye to fall on thee; all thy prudence will not save thee then. Meanwhile, I will try in the towns of Tuscany if there be men left in Italy to face a tyrant!'

They sat silent beneath his wrath and he turned to go,

but paused and looked back to them with a glance they could not meet.

'Only hear this before I go,' he said passionately; 'there is one thing thy faint-heartedness shall not touch, one thing I will achieve without thy aid, though thy meanness leaves me, and that is, at any cost, the freedom' – his voice trembled – 'of Isotta, my wife. I will free her,' he continued sternly. 'Before you all I mean it; she shall be saved, even if mine honour goes to do it.'

And he turned away, but Count Conrad rose, roused out of himself by the excitement Mastino had inspired.

'I will follow thee,' he cried.

'What wouldst thou have, Mastino?' cried Ippolito after him, half-distraught. 'What wouldst thou have?'

Della Scala turned in the middle of the chamber, magnificent in his wrath and pain. 'All,' he said proudly. 'All thou canst give, and above all, thy trust. I am no boy to be put off with a few soldiers. I need Modena, Ferrara, Padua, every town of Lombardy that is in thy hands; all thy money, all thy troops, everything thou canst give – and then I will crush Visconti. When I fell it was through most foul treachery. I will league with no half-hearted friends again.'

And again he turned to leave, this time Conrad at his heels, when a soft voice arrested him, Julia Gonzaga's.

'I have this to say before thou leavest us, della Scala,' she said. 'All I have, Mantua and its lands, is at thy disposal, and I am proud so great a captain as my lord of Verona should command my men.'

Mastino turned, his eyes sparkling with joy.

'My greatest thanks for thy gift, lady,' he said, 'and still more for the gracious manner of thy giving,' And before he could say more Vincenzo rose impulsively.

'Shall we be outdone by a woman!' he cried, his beautiful face flushed. 'It goes not with our honour, Father, we should leave Mantua to fight Visconti!'

Ippolito no less was roused.

He stepped toward Mastino and held out his hand.

'I ask thy pardon for too much wariness,' he said with a faint smile. 'I am as proud now as ever of my relationship to thee, and everything within my hands is thine to use as thou wilt against Visconti.' Mastino grasped his hand convulsively.

'Thou shalt not repent it,' he said, his generous soul melting at once. 'While I live thou shalt not repent.'

Meanwhile Giacomo Carrara's prudent brain had rapidly concluded it would be most to his advantage, at least for the moment, to side openly with della Scala, even in this wholesale fashion.

'I too am of the same mind,' he said pleasantly and frankly. 'All I have is thine, della Scala.'

'Then in a few days I will march on Verona!' cried Mastino, 'and with thy generous aid I shall recover it! My heart is too full. I cannot speak my thanks,' he continued, 'but by my honour and my sword I swear, thou, d'Este, thou, Carrara, and thou, lady, you shall never regret your trust in me.'

XII

GRAZIOSA'S LOVER

In the courtyard of the painter Agnolo's house in Milan, the sunshine fell strong and golden, sparkling on the fountain that rose in the centre from its rough stone basin, and throwing the waxen blossoms of the chestnut into brilliant relief against the sapphire sky.

The courtyard was of stone. Around three sides ran the wall, one with its door into the street; opposite was a large garden, entered by an archway, the wicket in which stood always ajar.

The fourth side of the quadrangle was formed by the dwelling-house, which stood with its back to the ivied walls, itself a long, low building, the upper half of which, jutting above the lower, was supported on pillars of carved stone.

Around the bottom wall ran a wide border of plants, some climbing, others heavy with brilliant blossoms, trailing along the ground, and in the cool, blue shadows in the recess formed by the projecting story were large pots of spreading ferns, vivid green, mingled with the spikes of bright scarlet flowers.

The basin of the fountain in the centre was velvet green with moss, and over the limpid water there spread the flat leaves of water-lilies. Above the wall rose the sweet-smelling chestnuts, spreading their fan-like foliage and snowy blossoms, tier upon tier, against the brilliant sky, and through the low arch, trellised with roses, the garden stretched, a bewildering mass of colour, white, mauve, yellow, pink, blue and red, into the soft distance, a swaying mass of trees. It was late after-noon, and the shadows were lengthening, as out of the house, the door of which stood open, came the little painter. He stepped into the sunshine, mopping his face and shaking his clothes.

From head to foot he was a mass of green slime, his doublet torn, his hands scratched, his face hot and per-spiring. After a few vain attempts to remove the dirt that clung to him, he looked around with a rueful counte-nance.

'Graziosa!' he called. 'Graziosa!'

The lattice of an upper window was thrown open, and Graziosa looked out.

At sight of her father she laughed. 'Hast thou been down thy passage again, Father?' she called from the window.

Agnolo made a wry face good-humouredly. 'That I have,' he returned, 'and fell into a pond at the other end.'

'The other end!' echoed his daughter. 'Then you got through?'

Vistarnini rubbed his damaged hands together with satisfaction. 'Aye,' he said with a smile, 'after tearing my clothes, fighting briars, stepping on toads, stifling with dust, and pitching on my face in the dark, I –'

'Fell into a pond!' laughed Graziosa.

'Got to the other end,' cried the little painter. 'Got to the other end!' Graziosa disappeared from the window, and came running into the courtyard, a slender figure in scarlet.

'Got to the other end,' repeated Vistarnini breathlessly. 'A noble underground passage, Graziosa, that is what we have discovered, large enough to admit an army if need were, and with a concealed opening, leading out through a cave to the midst of –'

'A pond,' suggested Graziosa with a glance at his garments.

'A wood – the pond was a mere accessory; a wood, some two miles beyond the town.'

'Then since this end is reached from our house, we are the only ones who can gain access to it.' said Graziosa.

'We are,' returned the painter proudly. 'And, Graziosa, we will remain so.'

'Thou mean'st thou wilt tell no one?' asked his daughter.

'No; it will be very useful. I hate to be for ever passing the gate, giving accounts of myself to every saucy soldier. In time of need, should there be a war then perchance we can speak of it.'

'I think we should speak of it now,' said Graziosa thoughtfully. 'I think we should tell the Duke.'

'Tell the weathercock!' said Vistarnini. 'I tell thee it will be useful; the tolls nearly ruin me – and now I can bring everything I buy outside in through the secret passage.

''Tis scarce honest, Father.'

Agnolo laughed.

'I discovered it,' he said. 'No one knew of it, and the Duke can well spare my tolls.'

'Meanwhile change thy dress, Father,' laughed Graziosa, 'and thou always dost as thou thinkest. I have no more to say.'

Then, as Vistarnini moved toward the house, his daughter called after him softly:

'I may tell Ambrogio, Father?'

'Thou mayst do no such thing,' returned Agnolo. 'His conscience would prick him – he is over grave and honest –'

'He is not,' said Graziosa indignantly. 'I mean – he would not tell – I am sure he will not tell!'

'And so am I – for he will never know,' said Agnolo with a smile. 'Now thy promise, Graziosa, that thou tellest no one, not even thy precious Ambrogio – and the first thing I smuggle through shall be a new silk gown for thee!'

Graziosa laughed, and seated herself on the edge of the basin.

'I promise,' she called. 'But as for the gown, thou couldst have brought me that in any case!'

Vistarnini turned into the house, and silence again fell on the sunny courtyard.

Graziosa looked musingly at the gate, then down at her bare arm and sighed.

Two pet doves whirled down from the chestnuts and strutted across the courtyard, with a show of white tails.

Graziosa noticed them suddenly, in the midst of her dreaming, and was rising to get their evening meal, when the little painter, clean and reclothed, bustled out of the house, carrying a flat dish.

'Here is thy food!' he cried to the birds. 'Are ye hungry, little ones?'

And he threw the grain in a golden shower.

'Ambrogio is not here to see you feed today,' he continued 'What makes him late, Graziosa?'

'The way is long,' she returned, 'from the convent where he works, Father, and the monks grudge him any time away from the altar-piece.'

'And the bracelet?' said Agnolo. 'He vowed thou shouldst have it back.'

'I wish he had not,' said the girl in distress. 'He will do something rash, I fear me. How can he get it back from the Visconti palace.'

'He won't get it back,' said the little painter cheerfully. 'Even a lover would not be quite so mad as to beard the Visconti for a toy.'

'Yet he swore I should have it again. It was rash of me to tell him how I lost it,' replied Graziosa.

'Then he would have thought thou hadst given it to the stone-cutter next door, and there would have been high words, flashing eyes. "Ha – ha – come out and be slain, thou varlet! Skulking dog, thou liest!" then swords out, and thou lying in a faint – or bewailing the day of thy birth. After that, thunder and lightning – gore – the brawlers driven into the street – the soldiers come up – and off we go to prison for disturbing the streets with our frays.'

'You jest too much, Father,' said Graziosa. 'It may be serious if Ambrogio try to recover the bracelet.'

But a light knock on the outer door interrupted her, and with a heightened colour she rose.

'It is he, Father!' she whispered. 'I knew he would not fail us.'

Agnolo hurried forward and drew back the bolts, and truly enough Ambrogio entered.

Graziosa's lover was of medium height, a slight man, with beautiful grey eyes. His attire was the plain garb of a student. Today his right hand was hanging in a sling, while in the other he carried a roll of drawings.

'Still alive!' said Agnolo pleasantly. 'Graziosa was fearing thou hadst spitted thyself on Visconti's sword in the recovery of her bracelet.'

Ambrogio took little heed of the painter, but closing the door softly behind him, turned with a tender glance to Graziosa.

'Wert thou grieving for me?' he said gently. 'I am safe, my beautiful, and see, I have kept my word.'

As he spoke he drew out the emerald bracelet from his robe, and handed it with a smile to the girl who stood there, blushing with pleasure and astonishment.

'Thou hast got it back,' she cried; 'from the Visconti's palace!'

Ambrogio smoothed her bright hair tenderly.

'The bracelet was thine,' he said, 'therefore I went there for It, and have brought it back to thee, even from the Visconti's palace.'

Agnolo was staring at him in amazement.

'How didst thou do it!' he exclaimed.

Ambrogio touched his bandaged arm with a smile.

'With only a small injury,' he said, 'since 'tis not the hand I paint with.'

And now Graziosa broke in with passionate exclamations of pity for his wound, of admiration for his courage, covering the injured hand with caresses.

'Thou hast recovered it – by force,' asked Agnolo again, incredulous.

'Call it by force or what thou wilt,' returned Ambrogio. 'There is no need to speak of it more. It is enough you are in no danger. No one will follow me here to regain it,'

Graziosa kissed her recovered treasure and clasped it on her arm again.

'I shall never dare to wear it save within these walls,' she said.

Ambrogio took her hand in his, and led her toward the house.

'Do not fear, sweet,' he returned, looking down at her with a smile. 'Wear it where and how thou wilt. Tisio Visconti will not annoy thee more.'

The girl glanced up, startled by the authority of his manner.

Ambrogio, noticing the questioning look, turned it aside with a pleasant laugh.

'The Duke is tired of his whims, and is putting him under a closer watch,' he said. 'From now on he will not often ride the streets.'

'I am sorry for him,' said Graziosa impulsively. 'I am very sorry for him.'

They were at the house door, and Agnolo, stepping ahead into the dark entrance, led the way up a flight of shallow wooden stairs.

'This is stirring news, Ambrogio,' he called over his shoulder. 'About the Duke of Verona's escape, I mean. Do you think there will be a war?'

'I am a man of peace,' returned Ambrogio softly, his eyes on Graziosa. 'How should I know? Still, I do not think della Scala will trouble the peace of Milan much.'

And now Agnolo, at the top of the flight of stairs, was holding open a wide door through which they passed into Agnolo's workshop, filled with the pleasant litter of his occupation. 'I do not agree with thee,' he said. 'Della Scala's is a great name. Were I Visconti, I should not feel secure.'

Graziosa and Ambrogio entered the long room, high and light, its windows opening wide on to the street.

And Ambrogio, seating himself near one of the large easels, turned to Agnolo, the while he drew Graziosa gently down beside him.

'What has the Duke of Milan to fear from della Scala?' he asked.

'Everything,' cried Vistarnini excitedly, for keenly did the little painter love to air his views. 'Everything. Mark me, Ambrogio, if the Duke of Verona do not suddenly fall on one of Visconti's towns.'

'He has no army,' said the student. 'He cannot rouse the d'Estes.'

'He will!' cried Agnolo. 'He will – he and Count Conrad. Didst thou not rejoice, Ambrogio, when Count Conrad escaped? We heard of it from the soldiers. Graziosa was glad at heart, as every man or woman or child must be. Such a fate! Didst thou not rejoice he had escaped it?'

Ambrogio was mixing colours in a china saucer, and tapped his foot a little impatiently.

'Why should we talk of della Scala – and Visconti?`' he said.

'Visconti! Who wishes to talk of him?' returned the little painter. 'Tales have come to me about him, too terrible to repeat before our Graziosa,' he added, lowering his voice.

'You gossip too much with the soldiers, Father,' said Graziosa. 'I do not love the soldiers, nor should you listen to their tales about Visconti.'

'They would seem to tell them a little too freely,' murmured her lover, and drew his brows together.

'What dost thou mean, Graziosa?' cried her father, 'as if it were only from the soldiers we hear of the Duke. Lately some fine tales have got about, and on no soldier's authority.'

'Shall we not set to work on the pictures?' interrupted Ambrogio. 'You said, methinks, these tales were not for Graziosa's ears.'

'Indeed, 'tis true,' and the little painter bustled to the second easel and drew the curtain that hung before the large panel revealing an almost completed picture of St. Catherine in scarlet robes.

'Thy work looks well, Ambrogio,' he said, and removing a similar covering from the easel by which Ambrogio sat, gazed at the companion panel on which was depicted the archangel Michael. 'But mine is better,' he added, 'as it should be; thy work will improve with thy years.'

''Tis as fine work as thy St. Michael, Father,' said Graziosa, 'and a good likeness.'

'Nay, not so fair by half as thou art,' murmured Ambrogio. 'Thou art not easy to copy, Graziosa.'

Agnolo was studying his picture intently.

''Twas an idle fancy to take thee as my model for St. Michael,' he said at length. 'Thou dost not inspire me as St. Michael, Ambrogio.'

'As what then?' asked his daughter, smiling at her father's earnestness.

Agnolo laughed.

'As no saint at all,' he said. 'He is like nothing but the wicked young man reclaimed in the legend of St. Francis, and not very reclaimed either!'

Graziosa smiled still more, but Ambrogio faintly flushed and bit his lip.

'Thou art welcome to paint me in that character another time,' he said. 'Meanwhile, I will work on my St. Catherine's robe.'

And he seated himself on a low stool before the easel, Graziosa placing herself on the floor at his feet.

Agnolo scrutinized the St. Michael once more, but finally drew the curtain again along the rod, for his day's work was over. Settling himself in the window-seat, for a while he contentedly watched the other two; but not for long could the little painter keep his tongue still, and Ambrogio's visits were a fine opportunity for voluble talk, for the young man lived in Como, and was he not now shut up in the convent of St. Joseph, five miles away, painting an altar-piece for avaricious monks who grudged him even these occasional visits into Milan? What could he know of the city's news?

'We had a fine procession this morning, Ambrogio,' he said. 'The Duke of Orleans' retinue went by, a gay sight. We hoped to see the Duke ride out to meet him, but my lord Gian Visconti keeps himself close. For all we live so near the gate, I have never seen him, or only in his helmet; and yet 'tis said he cares a good deal for sculpture and for painting, and will make a fine thing of this grand new church he's building. I would love to see what a tyrant and a painter both may look like.'

Ambrogio, bending over his painting, returned no answer; but that made small difference to the talkative little man, who continued.

'He came not, however, so we contented ourselves with the French prince, who is to marry the Lady Valentine. Graziosa did not care for him; I thought him well-looking enough.'

'His air was not a gay one, and he seems foolish,' said Graziosa; 'and since he is not marrying for love, I am sorry for the Lady Valentine.'

'Thou art always sorrowing for some one,' said her father. 'A princess never marries for love.'

'Then I am glad I am no princess,' smiled Graziosa, looking up at her betrothed.

Ambrogio raised her hand to his lips and kissed it in silence.

Agnolo continued his recitals, refreshing himself every now and again with renewed glances from the window.

'A splendid view we have here, only some processions are not so pleasant as the one that passed today. There was one in particular – some weeks ago – we stayed in the back of the house that day. The old Visconti rode to

Brescia, the soldiers said, his son behind him! Ah, for that day's work the Duke is a lost soul, Ambrogio.'

There was a silence after this; the painter kept his eyes on the darkening sky.

Ambrogio dropped his brush and rose with a pale face.

'I can paint no more,' he said. 'I am weary.'

His daughter's lover sometimes puzzled Agnolo. His history, as he had told it to them, was a very plain one, his career straightforward, but Ambrogio's manner strangely varied: sometimes authoritative, strangely cold and haughty for a poor painter; strident sometimes, curious and overawing. But to Graziosa he was always tender, and she saw nothing now but his pale face.

'No wonder thou art weary,' she said tenderly. ''Tis a long way from St. Joseph, thy hand pains thee and thou hast had no food.'

Ambrogio stooped and kissed her upon her upturned face.

'And I cannot stay for it even to take it from thy hands,' he said with a sigh. 'I meant not to stay at all, and only came to give thee thy bracelet, sweet; but soon, soon the altar-piece will be finished, and I come never to return.'

'Finished,' murmured the girl, her head against his arm. 'When?'

'By midsummer, Graziosa. Is the time so long to thee too?'

'I am so happy, Ambrogio, it does not seem possible I could be happier; still, I think I shall be when thy altar-piece is finished.'

Ambrogio looked at his painting longingly.

'If I could only stay,' he said, and kissed her again.

'Surely it is still early, even for St. Joseph?' said Agnolo.

Ambrogio glanced out into the dusky street, where several gaily attired horsemen were riding.

'The Prior begged my early return,' he said. 'And so farewell, my father, for a little while, farewell!'

'Well, if it must be, it must,' said Vistarnini cheerfully, 'thou wilt never fail for lack of industry. Still, Graziosa, even if thy lover goes, there is something left to amuse us. This evening the nobles ride in to attend the feast Visconti gives tonight to the French Duke. 'Twill be a noble feast, yet I doubt if the Lady Valentine be as happy as thou art, Graziosa.'

But his daughter returned no answer, for she was not there, but at the top of the dark stairway. She was saying farewell to her betrothed; and when Agnolo turned from the window, she was leaning on his arm across the courtyard, for a last word at the gate.

'When comest thou again?' she whispered.

'Thy father jeers me for my industry, yet heaven knows what it costs me to leave thee, sweet. In two days' time I will again be with thee.'

They were at the door, but still he lingered, gazing on her gentle face.

'Farewell,' he said at last, with a smile: 'For two days, my beautiful Graziosa,' He took her face between his hands and kissed her.

'Farewell,' she smiled, and with a sudden effort he was gone.

But once well clear of the house, Graziosa's lover paused as if undecided, then drew his hood, and wrapped himself closely in his mantle and walked rapidly into the city, keeping close to the wall. After some time he drew the bandage from his hand and flung it aside.

His left hand was as whole as his right.

Again he walked on rapidly, until, at the corner of a quiet street, a man with bent shoulders and dressed in black stepped from the shadow of a building.

It was Giannotto.

'News, Giannotto,' asked Graziosa's lover in a whisper.

'I am waiting for you, my lord, to tell you they are growing impatient. Your absence is causing surprise.'

Two horsemen passed, and Ambrogio drew his mantle closer around him.

'No one has seen thee waiting here,' he asked.

'No, my lord, I am too careful.'

''Tis well,' said the other. 'Lead on toward the palace, Giannotto. I will follow.'

XIII

Valentine Visconti's Toast

The Visconti palace was brilliant with lights and gay with the hum of voices.

Splendidly attired, in all that wealth or taste could desire, the French guests seemed to diffuse some of their own light-hearted gaiety over the sombre abode of the Visconti.

The entrance stairs of fine white marble were spread with a purple silk carpet, the golden balustrades intertwined with roses emitting their fragrance, and the long gallery opening from the stairway and lit by wide windows, deep set in the stone, showed the long, low balcony smothered in myrtles, lemons, citrons, oranges, and gorgeous flowers, scented and abundant, filling the corridors with the sense of summer and mingling their slender trails with the stiff folds of the rare and costly tapestries that covered the walls and were laid upon the floor.

At intervals stood statues, masterpieces of ancient art, faintly lit by the golden glimmer of the swinging lamps.

And all the stairs and corridors and gallery were alive and brilliant with the magnificent guests of the Visconti – lords and ladies, the finest the dismantled court of France could boast. Yet, used to splendours as they were, coming from the most refined court of Europe, the costly display made by an Italian usurper impressed them with wonder, almost with awe.

Tisio Visconti, most richly dressed and adorned with all his favourite jewels, mingled in the throng, gay and happy, forgetful of everything save the lights and the colours, the kindly respectful tones in which he was addressed, unheeding the silent page that followed him.

The wide, usually so sombre, entrance of the palace stood open upon the street, and the red flare of torches, the gleam of richly-caparisoned horses, the bustle of pages and men-at-arms, were visible to the courtiers within, and blended city and palace in one splendour.

'I would the French were always here,' cried Tisio, excitedly. 'I love the palace to be light and gay.'

The gay flutter of silk and satin, the elegant grace of the strangers, pleased him, and he smiled like a contented child. But suddenly all the light was struck out of his face.

'Gian,' he said dully.

'The Duke!' the courtiers behind him took up the word, and the tattle of voices ceased.

Gian Visconti was approaching down the gallery, followed by several pages in the Viper's silver and green livery.

He passed between the rows of bowing courtiers carelessly; there were many there of the proud nobility of France who found it hard to stand silent and respectful before this man, whose crimes alone were his passport to sovereignty.

To them this marriage was a humiliation, a disgrace to the French crown, but to Visconti it was a triumph, the successful crowning of ambition. He was in a genial mood, and as he passed Tisio stopped and smiled, telling him for tonight he might go where he pleased.

It was not too much to spare to the brother whose possessions he enjoyed.

And as Visconti passed on, more than one Frenchman raised his eyebrows and shrugged his shoulders expressively as the sweep of his scarlet train disappeared.

Among the throng the ever-ready secretary waited for Visconti's eye to fall on him, and the Duke, dismissing the pages, beckoned him forward.

'No news from Verona, or Mantua?' he asked.

'None, my lord.'

'None? The messengers are late. But after all why should they haste?' said Visconti. 'Della Scala will hardly be in the field yet,' he added with a smile.

'If ever, my lord,' replied the secretary smoothly.

The two had withdrawn into the embrasure of one of the great open windows, and Visconti, glancing through it, turned his gaze there where, clear in the blue summer night, rose the outline of an abutting building, grim and dark and silent: Isotta's prison.

'See the guards be doubled there,' he said. The secretary bowed.

'As to the Lady Valentine, my lord,' he said insinuatingly, 'she is safe and well, and at her prayers with her women. I have kept guard upon her slightest motion.'

Visconti drew a ring from his finger. He was in a generous mood tonight, a rare one enough, as Giannotto thought with bitterness.

'Take this for thy pains,' he said. 'And now I will relieve thee of thy watch; she can hardly escape under my very eyes and with her bridegroom waiting. Let the guests know I bring the bride, Giannotto.'

Visconti withdrew the length of one of the corridors, and paused there at a door before which stood two soldiers, the guard of his sister's apartments. At his soft approach they stood back, and, opening the folding doors, Visconti passed through, and quickly threaded the deserted ante-rooms until he reached the chapel that the lady used.

The place was dim, lit by red lamps that cast more shadow than light, and with high, stained windows, now scarcely showing colour. And seated on the floor under one of them, her head against a carved wall, her hands listless in her lap, was Valentine.

She wore a dress of flame-coloured satin, and her hair was elaborately dressed with rubies and pearls. She made no movement at her brother's entrance.

The air was heavy with incense and the perfume of some white roses that faded across the altar steps.

'We wait for thee, Valentine,' said Visconti.

A couple of her women moved forward from the shadows, and whispered to the Duke they could do nothing with her. He motioned to them to withdraw.

'Valentine, come! Think of the splendid life that opens before thee from today,' Visconti's tone had the gentleness of one who has gained his point. 'Thou mayst be Queen of France,' But Valentine Visconti had too much of her brother's spirit, too much of the ungovernable pride of will, not to hate this yielding to the force of power. She hated her brother's tyranny. She hated this marriage. What would life be for her, with an indifferent husband, in an idle, impoverished court, among foreigners, strangers, far from her own land? She would not be forced to it. She rose to her feet, desperate.

Visconti watched her keenly, standing waiting.

'Come,' he repeated, 'the Duke of Orleans waits. The feast is ready.'

For one moment a mad hate of him overmastered her, a wild desire to refuse to stir, to cling to the altar, dash herself against the floor, anything rather than obey. She knew his parricide; he was not the elder. She would not obey.

Words of defiance were on her lips, but glancing at his

face, the words died away, and a sense of the useless folly of resistance, the useless humiliation of refusal, surged over her. She was in his power. When she spoke, it was humbly, in a faltering voice, with tears.

'Gian,' she whispered. 'Gian – I have never asked anything of thee before. Gian – this marriage is hateful to me –' she paused, then stepped forward with appealing eyes. 'Gian – have consideration – have mercy!'

'The Duke of Orleans waits,' smiled Visconti. 'Will you not let me lead you to him?'

Valentine drew back and steadied herself against the wall.

She thought of Conrad with bitterness and shame, of his vows of devotion, how he had sworn she should never wed the French prince – and – he was free – had been so for many days, and never a word or a sign.

Visconti flung wide the chapel door, and in the adjoining room he summoned to her side his sister's page. Valentine's eyes fell on him, and she noted how the blood rushed to his face as he sprang to obey. He was a fair-haired boy with eager eyes, who worshipped her with a romantic devotion at which she had often smiled; but now –

He lifted her train, and Visconti held out his hand. Outside her doors soldiers kept their motionless guard, and beyond the gay crowd swept to and fro. Silently Valentine moved forward, but her heart was burning with rebellious hate.

'I will still try once more for freedom,' was the thought she held to; and as they traversed the great corridor and her eyes fell, as had her brother's, on the grim outline of Isotta's prison, 'I will free her too,' she added, with a swelling heart.

And Visconti thought her conquered, cowed into complete submission, and watched her pass ahead of him down the banqueting chamber with a satisfied smile to see her the fairest and the proudest there.

The brilliant courtiers streamed in, a mass of colour and jewels, and Visconti, seated at the head of the table, glanced at the effeminate faces and frivolous bearing of the guests with some contempt.

'No news?' he whispered to Giannotto behind his chair. 'No news from Ferrara yet?'

'None as yet, my lord. The messengers are expected at any moment.'

The apartment was a blaze of wax candles that threw a thousand dancing reflections on the elaborate silver and glass that covered the table.

The bright light fell too on the rubies on Valentine Visconti's throat. She sat at her brother's side, with a pale face and sparkling eyes. On Visconti's right was her bridegroom, the Duke of Orleans, an elegant young man with weak eyes and a receding chin. His scanty, fair locks were carefully arranged with grease and curling irons into stiff curls, the ends of his moustache were elaborately twisted, and his face was rouged plentifully on the cheeks.

Valentine looked at him once, then ignoring him utterly, she looked down the long, glittering table to the great entrance facing her, with a crowd and press of liveries and hurrying attendants, waiting pages. As for the French duke, he conversed with Visconti, ignoring the hardly hidden contempt that he was either too dull to see or too politic to resent.

The banqueting hall filled: and the guests in their seats, the secretary, standing back among the servitors, crept out into the antechamber. After the glare and splendour of the banquet, the room seemed dull and sombre, and Giannotto stumbled over a crouching figure.

It was Valentine's page, weeping bitterly.

'Poor fool!' muttered the secretary. 'Wouldst thou lose thy place as well as thy heart?' And he passed on with a laugh. But after a pace or two he paused. Through the palace windows floated a sound as of distant murmuring and commotion, yet so faint he could scarce be sure of it.

The page had risen, shamefaced at having been discovered. He was very young, and his grief very real to him. He choked a little, stifling his sobs.

'Silence!' said Giannotto angrily. 'Listen!' The sound grew nearer and more distinct, and the secretary went to the window nearest and leaned forward eagerly.

Several horsemen and soldiers came riding swiftly, holding flaming torches; windows were flung open, people hurried to and fro.

'Some evil news has got abroad,' said Giannotto, straining eyes and ears.

And now the noise of angry shouts and frightened cries became too plain, and the secretary could see by the flare of some horsemen's torches a throng of country folk, laden with their possessions, and some men driving herds of cattle, and soldiers torn and dusty.

'Evil news, indeed, I fear,' he muttered, and waited anxiously. A ray of brilliant light from the banquet hall beyond fell between the curtains and streamed across the room, there was laughter and clink of glasses, and a voice singing in French to a lute. The page clenched his fists and turned to go.

'Stay,' said Giannotto, 'stay. If thou wouldst end thy

days, here comes a chance, methinks, for some one will have to carry ill news to Visconti,' And even as he spoke a white-faced servant entered.

'My lord,' he cried, as Giannotto stepped before him, 'there has been some sore disaster – the country folk are trooping through the gates – there is a panic in the city.'

'The messengers!' cried Giannotto, 'the messengers!'

'The messengers have not returned – but there are plenty bringing news who were not sent for it, my lord.' And as the man spoke, a disordered group, soldiers and servants, pressed into the room behind him.

'Gently, my friends,' said Giannotto, checking their agitated outcry and pointing to the curtains that hid the banqueting hall. 'The Duke!'

A man, dusty and white-faced, forced himself out of the crowd, small, but swelling every moment.

'I bear the news the Duke must hear,' he said, 'and quickly.'

'Where hast thou come from?' asked the secretary. 'What is thy news?'

'Since daybreak I have been flying for my life – I am a servant in the garrison at Brescia – it is destroyed,' gasped the man.

'Brescia!' The echo of horror. 'Has Brescia *fallen*?'

'Aye, fallen – into della Scala's hands.'

Giannotto looked around bewildered, incredulous.

'Della Scala at Brescia,' he said. 'You dream!'

But the room was filled now with a wild-faced crowd that would not be kept back, and from every side echoed the evil tidings.

'Brescia – at dawn today della Scala whirled down on us, flushed with victory – and in two hours the town fell.'

'And Visconti thinks him idle at the d'Este's court!' broke from Giannotto.

The crowd filled the chamber with the whisper of dismay and horror, but from the banqueting room still came the song and the laughter – Visconti was in blissful ignorance of evil. Who could tell him? Who would dare?

Well Giannotto knew the fall of Brescia could be only the last of a series of incredible disasters; so swift as to seem miraculous. Victory after victory must have fallen to della Scala before he could have marched on and taken a place so near Milan; victories following too fast on one another to have reached Visconti before their culmination. The news indeed was terrible!

Who would enter the banqueting hall?

All shrank.

"Tis almost certain death,' they muttered, and Giannotto smiled.

'The Duke carries deadly weapons.'

As he spoke the curtains were pulled aside for a moment as one of the serving men stepped out, and Giannotto, bending eagerly forward, caught a glimpse of two faces at the far end of the brilliant table.

Visconti's, laughing, triumphant, insolently handsome, and Valentine's, set and white, with dangerous eyes.

The curtains fell to again, but Giannotto had a thought.

'Leave it to me, good friends,' he said, and passed into the hall.

'The Lady Valentine shall give the news!' That was the secretary's inspiration. 'The Duke dare not touch her, and it will be a pleasure to her that she may reward,' And the crowd, gathering in the ante-room, waited, bewildered and terrified, to hear the blow had fallen.

'They will stop their song and jest,' said the man from Brescia, 'let the Duke once know –' The entry of another, panting and torn, interrupted him.

'Heaven save Milan!' he gasped. 'Verona has fallen!'

* * *

The shouts and clatter from the courtyard had penetrated faintly to the banqueting hall, and Visconti paused a moment, listening.

Valentine listened too, and thought of Conrad.

But the noises died away, and Visconti turned to the Duke of Orleans with a laugh.

'My soldiers revel in your honour,' he said, 'and we will drink my sister's health, my lord,'

Valentine's breast heaved. Who was he, to dare to sacrifice her to his pride and greed? She would not suffer it. Was she not also a Visconti?

As in a dream she heard her health drunk; as in a dream she saw the Duke of Orleans' foolish look turned toward her in vacant admiration; then suddenly, with a start, she noticed Giannotto's crafty face. Valentine's eyes blazed with sudden purpose. She looked down toward the entrance, and saw, between the curtains, white faces peering and figures half-thrust forward.

'The Duke of Orleans!' cried Visconti, and the guests again rose. Valentine rose also, with inspired eyes and crimsoned cheeks.

'The Duke of Orleans!' she cried, lifting her glass, and at the first words she had spoken they stood silent in an uneasy expectation. 'Will the Duke of Orleans wait, Visconti, while I give a still nobler toast?' Her voice rose triumphant. At her words, at the mad defiance of her bearing, Visconti stood amazed.

'Here is to the one who has taken Brescia and Verona, even from thee, Visconti; here is to the brave soldier who now marches on Milan – Mastino della Scala!'

And she raised her glass high, and then turned and flung it at Visconti's feet.

'The news is true,' she said, 'and now kill me for it.'

And with a stifled cry Visconti's hand was on his dagger, but Orleans flung himself upon him, and caught him by the wrists. Visconti glanced at him, and at the startled company, not grasping what had happened, and then the cry, begun no one knew where, went in a growing volume around the hall.

'Verona has fallen!'

It circled around the table, it passed from lip to lip, from the white-faced, surging crowd to the brilliant guests, and the company broke into confusion, and looked into one another's eyes with terror.

'Verona has fallen!'

'A lie!' thundered Visconti. 'A lie! My sister has gone mad. Who says the word again shall die!'

'My lord,' said Giannotto, 'listen.' And into the sudden hush within came the wild hubbub of the panic-stricken city.

'Verona is fallen! Della Scala marches fast on Milan!'

XIV

THE TUMULT AT THE WESTERN GATE

Mastino Della Scala with his army lay at Serio, a hamlet boasting a small eminence crowned with a strongly built but insignificant castle. Some ten miles farther on Brescia was held by Julia Gonzaga's army. Only a few weeks had passed since della Scala, falling first on Verona and taking it, had marched on Milan and almost snatched it from Visconti's unsuspecting hold. But the alarm given at Valentine's wedding-feast had come in time. With almost superhuman energy, in two hours' time Visconti armed the walls and put the city in defence. To surprise a victory was impossible. Still, the Duke of Verona's army was only some fifteen miles from the walls, and day by day drew nearer.

Visconti, from the height of proud security, was suddenly, by one move, placed in a position dangerous indeed. The towns and domains behind Milan, from that city to Turin, were still his, as were Pavia and Piacenza, but from Brescia to Verona, and from Modena to Lombardy, save for a few scattered towns and forts held desperately by Visconti's men, the whole was in the hands of della Scala and his allies. Still Milan was not in a state of siege: men and supplies hurried in from Novara, Vercelli, and other towns in the Visconti's dominions, and powerful aid was coming to the Duke of Milan's assistance from the Empire.

Yet in Visconti's eyes this aid, needful as it was, was dearly bought, for Charles IV, though an ignoble ruler and laughed at by his subjects, was of an honourable, open disposition, and related by marriage to the Estes, and the one condition on which he was dispatching to Visconti's service his soldiers stationed in Switzerland and on the borders, was that Isotta d'Este should be untouched.

In the bitterness of his rage, Visconti wished he had already slain her; now, in truth, he dare not. It was no question now of gratifying an ambition, it was simple fear of losing his own throne, fear of being in his turn reduced to what he had reduced della Scala, that made him respect the wishes of the Empire, and the feeling of the French who thronged his court.

And the thought that he could not play the best card tyrant ever held was rendered doubly bitter by the fact that della Scala knew him to be helpless and Isotta safe.

Scheming in his crafty soul for means to outwit Mastino, Visconti thought of Giacomo Carrara, who held Padua, Treviso, Cremona, Vicenza. He was della Scala's ally, but a man of no upright soul.

'Could I gain him,' thought Visconti, in his musings, 'I could stand without the Empire, without France, and use my captive as I please and not as they dictate.'

To the Estes and Julia Gonzaga he gave no thought; well he knew they were not likely to desert Mastino – but Carrara —

Meanwhile, he threw his whole strength against the opposing army, keeping it at bay, gaining time – and planning.

But Mastino della Scala's object was not to lose time in idle skirmishes. Brilliant success had fallen to his share, not one reverse had marred his short campaign and it is not the policy of the victor to dally with time, rather to seize the chances each day offers, while yet fortune smiles on him.

But well della Scala knew that neither honour, nor pity, nor shame, but fear alone, would restrain Gian Maria Visconti from venting his hatred on Isotta d'Este.

Still, he kept up a stout heart. Visconti dare not! To make assurance doubly sure, he used all his influence at the court of Rome to procure the aid of the Church against the Duke of Milan.

Many a time had he rendered powerful help to the Pope, and, as his present position stood, might do so yet again; and the result of his appeal was a grave embassy from the Pope to Visconti, threatening him with excommunication and the sword of the Church should he dare to touch Isotta d'Este.

For the first, Visconti cared little; twice had the Church thrown him out, and each time had he laughed at it and emerged triumphant; but now his position was more perilous than it had ever been since he mounted the throne of Milan, and he dare not treat this mandate of the Church as he had done the others.

The Pope's temporal power too was great; were that once turned against him, even with the Empire's aid he could hardly stand; so Visconti answered them with fair words, pledging his honour for the Duchess of Verona's life.

One bright summer morning, Visconti sat at the open window of his palace, thinking.

At the other end of the room the Duke of Orleans and Tisio were playing at chess; between these two, during the Duke's enforced stay in Milan, a friendship had sprung up, and Visconti, weary of his foolish guest, was well pleased a foolish brother should take him off his hands.

The Frenchman was prepared at once to carry out the contract, marry Valentine, and depart for France, but this Visconti's pride would not permit. The Duke of Orleans had witnessed a reverse, he should behold a triumph. Valentine should leave Italy as befitted his sister, not fly from it as a fugitive; and the French prince, who in a few weeks had yielded to Gian's influence and learned both to fear and obey Visconti, assented meekly to delay, and whiled away the time as best he might.

Visconti sat so motionless and silent that the chessplayers were forgetful of his presence, and their voices rose high.

'My move,' said Tisio gleefully. 'See, the rook takes your knight.'

'Your rook could take my knight,' returned Orleans, 'if it were your move, but as it is mine –'

'You are not watching the game,' was the angry rejoinder.

'Your pardon, *my* move,' said the Frenchman calmly, and, with a smile on his vacant face, he swept up one of Tisio's men.

'My move – and – mate, M'sieu.'

With a cry of childish rage, Tisio snatched at the board, spilling the men on to the floor.

'I love not to play with you,' he cried. 'I would Count Conrad were here, he was the one to play with.'

Orleans laughed.

'Because he always let you win, M'sieu,' he said.

Tisio began to whimper with annoyance, calling loudly on Valentine.

Visconti, aroused, drew the curtains aside, and stepped forward.

Orleans was, at his appearance, a little flurried. It was impossible for his weak brain to meet those eyes and not feel flurried.

'Tisio and I are fallen out again,' he said feebly.

Visconti looked at him coldly.

'I would remind you, my lord, Tisio, though an infant, is my brother.'

'Gian!' cried Tisio, suddenly noticing him. 'Gian, it was my move!'

'Whether it was thy move or no, it does not please me thou shouldst be annoyed – remember it, my Lord Duke'; and he turned into his inner room. As he closed the door, his long brooding showed in his face. It was lined and anxious. The position was a dizzy one: a perilous one: his dark dress concealed the gleam of chain armour.

His enemies were many, and some powerful, and Visconti took no chances.

At his side hung a dagger, long and sharp, and his fingers were often on the hilt in readiness. At his old place sat Giannotto.

'I have decided,' said Visconti. 'I will attempt Carrara.'

'You think he is to be bought, my lord.'

'I think he is to be bought?' responded Visconti. 'At any rate we will try. He and his force are with della Scala.'

'And fifteen miles outside our walls,' said Giannotto; then at the look on the Duke's face, he was sorry he had spoken, and shrank together.

'Read what is on the parchment,' said Visconti; and the secretary, glad to have been let off so easily, unwrapped the roll.

Therein Visconti's bribe was plainly set forth:

The town of Cologna, near to Padua, and well fortified, the protection and close alliance of Milan, and the service of ten thousand trained mercenaries, together with the right to trade free of toll in Visconti's dominions —

'And a pair of turquoise gloves,' added Visconti, with a change of tone.

Giannotto glanced up.

'Are they not worth three hundred ducats?' said Visconti, smiling. 'Did not the Pope and Emperor both wish to buy them, and fail?'

Giannotto bowed his head over again and studied the scrip in silence.

Visconti watched him keenly.

He thought, 'I know he would betray me for a ducat – if I were not Visconti.'

He turned to the narrow window, and looked out on to the city spreading beneath him.

'The Empire,' he muttered to himself. 'The Empire and the French – I will awe them and humour them while I must – but let me once gain Carrara – as I shall – I can dispense with them and deal with della Scala as I list.'

He turned from the window to Giannotto, and his face had lost its lines.

'Well,' he asked. 'What think you?'

'This is a master-stroke of temptation, my lord. You have always found craft a good servant.'

'It would not serve me well in thee,' said Visconti with a sudden glance. 'Now, see to it that parchment is dispatched, Giannotto, by a trusty messenger, and with no delay.'

I will give it to Ricardo with my own hands, my lord,' said Giannotto. 'He is the best man we have since Filippo was wounded this morning in a skirmish by the western gate.'

'The western gate?' Visconti looked up quickly.

'It was not worth while bringing to your notice, my

lord. A band of the enemy's soldiers have been skirmishing there.'

'They were beaten off without harm to anyone within
the gates?'

'The gates were not forced, nor anyone injured – or I
should have acquainted you, my lord,' and he waited for
possibly some mark of appreciation; but the Duke
motioned curtly to the roll he held, and Giannotto crept
out with bowed shoulders. As the tapestry fell into place
behind him, Visconti approached the black bureau
between the windows, and unlocked one of the long
drawers.

In its dusky recess lay a gold box, and Visconti took it
out, handling it carefully.

The light fell in a straight shaft from the narrow window
on the delicate chasing of the casket as Visconti placed it
on the table, and as he turned the key and the lid flew
back, it gleamed on the emeralds and diamonds of an
elaborate coronet, exquisitely enamelled and pointed.

Every inch was covered with precious stones: each point
tapering into a delicate tracery of gold, as fine as lace.

Visconti drew a chair to the table, and leaned back in
it, his eyes upon the jewels; so absorbed was he, he did
not heed the opening door nor Tisio's entrance.

And Tisio scarcely saw his brother, for joy at the little
coronet, so brilliant in the sun's straight ray.

'How dost thou come here, Tisio?' asked his brother,
startled; but at sight of Tisio's vacant, foolish face, he
sank back, and noticing his joy, he smiled – for Tisio was
crazed, and remembered nothing of even the things that
gave him pleasure. 'Dost thou like it?' he continued,
gratified at the delight in his brother's eyes. 'Thy taste in
goldsmiths' work is good, Tisio.'

''Tis beautiful, Gian, wondrous beautiful!' cried Tisio in rapt admiration.

'I bought it with the price of half a city,' said Gian. 'And hold it cheap.'

The words had no meaning for Tisio, as his brother knew: he only voiced his own pride in the lovely bauble.

'And wilt thou wear it?' asked Tisio.

The Duke laughed good-humouredly.

'Not I, Tisio; still soon – when della Scala's crushed – thou shalt see it worn by some one – some one whose face will outshine these stones, Tisio.'

'Whose will it be?' asked his brother childishly.

'A lady, Tisio; and when this coronet is on her head, she will be Visconti's wife and the Duchess of Milan!'

He paused on the word, and looked at Tisio; but there was no wonder in his brother's eyes, his gaze held by the flashing stones.

'Now, by Saint Mark!' cried Visconti suddenly. 'This is no time to be maundering with a toy and an idiot.'

He put the little coronet back and locked the casket.

'How comest thou to be alone, Tisio? Where is thy page?'

As he spoke he returned the casket to the bureau. Tisio, in eager curiosity, looked over his shoulders into the open drawer. There lay the turquoise-coloured gloves.

'Oh!' cried Tisio joyously. 'The beautiful, beautiful gloves!'

And before Gian could stop him, he had caught them up.

Visconti snatched them from him; at the same moment came a clamouring upon the door. It was Giannotto knocking lustily.

'Now, who beats down the door?' cried the Duke, and

waiting for no further summons, Giannotto entered. The
Duke, starting, thrust the turquoise gloves into his doublet.

'What is it now, Giannotto? Did I not say that I was
coming?'

'My lord, it presses. De Lana would see you – there has
been fierce fighting outside the walls – the army clam-
ours for you –'

'Lead the way,' said Visconti shortly; and, preceded by
his secretary, he returned hastily towards his council
chamber.

The ante-room, brilliant in pink stone and gold, the
great hall itself, flaring in painted walls and dazzling
stained-glass windows, were full of people – courtiers,
soldiers, artists, and craftsmen.

Gian Visconti kept neither the open court nor the free
table of his father; he was neither lavish in his hospitality,
save when it suited his own ends, nor liberal in his
rewards; still he loved, encouraged, and jealously exacted
the homage of all artists. Woe be to the painter or poet
who took his painting or poetry to any other in Milan
save the Duke himself!

There were many there today, eager-eyed among the
throng, among them the German architect of the glorious new church; but today Visconti passed unheeding
through them. The city was at war.

He stepped into the council chamber unannounced,
followed solely by Giannotto.

The great gilt ornate room was full of Milanese and
foreigners, allies or guests of Visconti.

'You look grave, my lords,' cried Visconti, his grey eyes
wide, 'and fearful. I had not thought you of so poor a
courage. Yet, since you are so faint of heart, I come to tell

you from my own lips that I ride against Verona today! Have you forgotten, my lords, that a Visconti still rules Milan?'

There was no answer from the splendid throng; they had complained much of late – but not to his face. 'Have you no thanks, for so much comfort?' laughed Visconti. 'Let all those who may care to follow make them ready, and let those who care not – stay to make us welcome from a victory. Come, de Lana.'

He turned away with his hand on his favourite captain's arm.

To a man the crowded assembly flocked to follow.

'Ah!' Visconti turned again.

'A crushed foe is scarcely to be feared! Have I not set my standard in the market-place of Verona? Have I not dragged a hostage from della Scala's palace? Lords of Milan, am I not Visconti?'

With one voice they broke into loud shouts.

'To the city walls! To the city walls! Down with della Scala! To the city walls!'

And while the cry still sounded, before the enthusiasm could abate, Visconti, armed and mounted, rode at the head of some thousand mercenaries and Milanese to the farthest rampart of the city.

Orleans had not volunteered. The French duke remained in the well guarded palace, of which the Lady Valentine was left the governor during the Duke's absence, an office she had often filled before quarrels had sprung up between her and her brother, and while he held Milan against his father and she was his counsellor and ally.

For a few brief hours, power again was hers, for Visconti had not weakened her authority yet – outwardly at least. She could do nothing.

She thought of her helplessness with bitterness. All day long she set herself to revolving schemes of escape – some way whereby to avail herself of the confusion into which Milan had been thrown – some means to outwit her brother.

She could not rest for her anxious thoughts. The Visconti palace was near the walls, and Valentine, stepping on to the open balcony, looked through the clustered pillars over the flat house roofs to the distant country where the advancing army lay.

The air was heavy. From the street came the sound of tumult, noise and hurry: the walls were manned.

'There is to be some fighting,' murmured Valentine.

She shaded her eyes from the sun that, beating on the red brickwork of the palace, gave back a blinding glare.

'Oh, may God grant that victory may fall,' she murmured, 'where Count Conrad draws his sword!'

It was evening before Visconti returned, weary from his survey of his men, victorious after a fierce skirmish with some of Verona's mercenaries, led by Mastino's trusted Captain Roccia.

The palace that till then had lain so quiet was suddenly a wild confusion, a babel of noises, shouts, and trampling of horses.

Strange, flaring lights were thrown across the courtyard; the torches flung ragged, straggling rays upon the sides of the palace, falling grotesquely on the griffins that grinned either side the arched door, falling across the long rows of straight windows, and, for a second, on Valentine Visconti's pale face, looking eagerly below.

'Dogs of Veronese!' cried Visconti, turning his blazing eyes toward the prisoners. 'They have cost us a wild hour!'

And he had been in the thick of it; his rich armour was dented, the embroidered surtout torn to rags: Visconti's blood was up. In a fight, even the Torriani could not say he lacked anything save prudence.

Without alighting, he took from his head his ponderous helmet with the viper crest, and gave it to his page.

'We have given Roccia a taste of our quality!' he laughed, and pulled his gauntlets off. 'Where is Giannotto?'

'I am here, lord,' said Giannotto.

He stood at the Duke's saddle, looking around him in confusion.

'What news, Giannotto?' cried Visconti. 'Thy pallid face seems too ready to welcome me. Let me dismount.'

'Hear me first,' entreated the secretary, 'before you dismount – before anything – lord!'

'Quick with thy news then – stand back, de Lana, I must hear this rogue.'

Giannotto drew closer.

'My lord, at noon today, Rinalta, the Tuscan captain, rode in. While Roccia was engaging you, some mercenaries forced one of the gates, and before they could be driven back, a house was broken into, some prisoners made –'

The Duke fixed his widening eyes upon the speaker, and Giannotto shrank.

'What gate,' he asked. 'What house? What prisoners.'

'The western gate, lord, and Agnolo Vistarnini's house!'

With a sound of fury Visconti struck at his secretary violently, with the ends of his bridle.

'And I was not told before!'

'It was held too small a fray, lord,' said the secretary. 'Could I tell my Lady Valentine one gate was more to you than another? I besought her to send to you – I besought them all – could I tell them why?'

Even as he spoke de Lana rode up resolutely.

'More men are needed at the western gate,' he said; 'the Germans have returned. I will lead them.'

'No!' cried Visconti; 'I, de Lana,'

The soldier looked surprised. 'You, lord? There is no need –'

'It is my will,' Visconti answered fiercely. 'At once, to the western gate!'

At his cry the soldiers flung themselves again into the saddle, and those who still sat their horses gathered up their reins.

'Your helmet, lord,' cried the startled squire; but Visconti swept him aside and rushed bare headed forward, de Lana and his troop of horsemen after him in a wild riot of sound and light.

Giannotto stood bewildered in the doorway; nothing left of the wild tumult that had filled spaces save echoing shouts and trampling hoofs.

'Visconti is mad,' he thought. 'He has ridden off almost unarmed! Now – I wonder what may happen before he return from the western gate – the night is dark and dangerous,'

And with a thoughtful glance up at the cloudy sky, Giannotto slowly withdrew.

XV

A Prisoner from Milan

Mastino della Scala was proving himself. He had come to within fifteen miles of Milan.

Verona was his again; that was in itself enough to justify his allies' confidence.

Of them Julia Gonzaga's force and Ippolito d'Este's army lay at Brescia, ready at any moment to advance.

Della Scala's position lay nearer Milan, and by far the larger half of his support was Carrara, Duke of Padua's contingent, led by the Duke in person.

Between the two forces, a quarter of a mile outside della Scala's camp, was the castle of Brescia, at one time an occasional residence of Barnabas, Visconti's father, and now a gloomy fortress, with an evil reputation; for Barnabas, driven from Milan by his son, had died there – with his wife – of fever it was said. In a gorgeous tent in the midst of della Scala's camp sat Conrad von Schulembourg and the younger d'Este.

It was the slumbrous hour after noon; the air heavy with an approaching storm, and Conrad lounged languidly on a low divan, playing with his dagger. The war, although success had fallen to his leader, had already begun to weary this indolent cavalier, and even the sight of Milan in the distance, where Valentine was imprisoned, could not keep him from whining at the hardness of his fate. A parchment lay near him on the seat, and from time to time he made some pretence of looking at it: pretence only.

In della Scala's force Conrad held third command

under the Duke of Padua, who was immediately under Mastino; but Conrad's post was largely a sinecure, for though in the battle the Count's gallant courage roused della Scala's warmest praise, he recognized that his capacity for generalship was small.

None the less della Scala trusted him completely. His heart full of his one object, elated by his successes, eagerly keeping his allies together, della Scala had small leisure to notice Conrad's stifled yawns when the council of war was held, or the fact that he gave more thought to playing cards and chess with Vincenzo than to the discipline and efficiency of the men under his orders.

For the fiftieth time he put the parchment down and turned to Vincenzo, who lay along the floor, eating nuts and hurling the shells at the legs of the sentry visible through the flaps set wide back for coolness. To make the soldier jump at a telling shot was more just then to Vincenzo than the taking of Milan.

'I would there were some one else to read these despatches,' said Conrad. 'I love not this part of soldiering. When, think you, will there be another city to be taken, Vincenzo?'

'There was fighting yesterday outside Milan,' returned the boy. 'Thou shouldst have gone.'

'I asked the Prince to let me, but as usual I was bade stay at my post,' And Conrad rose with a sigh of outraged virtue and adjusted the points of his rose-coloured doublet.

'Asked the Prince!' mocked Vincenzo; 'thou shouldst have gone without asking him.'

'A dash on the walls,' said Conrad, 'that is what we need, not this idleness and skirmishing. I long to grasp my sword and fly to my Lady Valentine's rescue – but the Prince –'

'Tell me not,' said Vincenzo. 'I know Mastino always counsels prudence, and I am weary of it.'

'The Prince knows more of it than we, doubtless,' admitted Conrad. 'Nevertheless these parchments may wait while I have a game of chess with thee.'

'May they, Count Conrad? And is chess thy notion truly?' said Mastino's voice without, and unannounced he entered the tent, followed by Tomaso's father, Giorgio Ligozzi.

He was from head to foot in armour.

His eyes fell on Vincenzo, and his face darkened.

'For shame, Vincenzo,' he said, with scorn. 'Thou art no longer a child, to indulge in these page's tricks, and much I marvel Count Conrad should allow thee such licence.'

Vincenzo rose sullenly.

'Leave us,' continued della Scala with angry eyes. 'And learn from yonder soldiers to play the man, and wear a leathern jacket with more grace than a silken doublet. I am ashamed of thee, Vincenzo.'

D'Este's beautiful face flushed crimson.

''Tis not always the leathern jacket comes out best at time of need, my lord,' he said defiantly. 'Try me in it in a fight.'

Della Scala's glance softened; he laid his hand on the boy's shoulder gently.

'Thou art a d'Este and my brother, Vincenzo. I do not fear thy behaviour in battle, – only learn the harder part – to beat thyself while waiting.'

Vincenzo was melted, but not caring to show it before Conrad, left the tent without reply.

'He hath the makings of a soldier in him for all his wilfulness. I pray you pardon his present idleness, my lord, and hold him as the cause,' said Conrad. 'I should have roused him sooner.'

Mastino glanced around. It was the first time he had entered the German's abode, and the lavishness of its appointments was not to his taste.

'This is an hour of great need, Count,' he said gravely. 'The downfall of Visconti cannot mean to you what it does to me – it cannot mean so much to any man – but am I not right in thinking it means all to you to see the Lady Valentine Visconti free?'

'All! All I care for under heaven. By all the saints, Prince, I will give my right arm to serve your cause, since it serves her,' cried Conrad.

Della Scala's brown eyes observed him keenly.

'I will ask a service of you, Count,' he said; 'not thy right hand, nor any feat of knight-errantry, but something full as difficult to render.'

'Even if it be living on roots in a dungeon, I will do it!'

And, excited at the thought of some adventure, Count Conrad waited expectantly, his hand up on his sword.

The Prince smiled sadly.

'I fear it is a harder task than that, Count Conrad, and so distasteful that I would not burden you with it were there any other worthy to entrust with it,' he said. 'But all the men here are mercenaries – Captain Vanvitelli is a boor; Ligozzi goes with me to Brescia, whither I am instantly bound to confer with Ferrara.'

'Prince, I am proud to execute your commands,' interrupted Conrad eagerly.

Della Scala turned to Ligozzi, who stood silent behind him.

'See that no one listens,' he said; and as Ligozzi disappeared and Mastino drew nearer to him, the Count fell back, impressed by the eagerness of the noble face.

But the Prince took him by the hand affectionately.

'Dost thou remember the huts outside thy villa, Conrad – and Francisco who rescued thee? I am giving thee a trust. For his sake wilt thou be faithful?'

'To the death!' cried Conrad. 'Prince, I will be faithful to the death!'

'Count,' said Mastino earnestly, 'I return from Brescia tomorrow, bringing d'Este up with me to join in an assault on Milan that will make the city ours, I trust, within a week. Of necessity I leave Carrara for these hours in command – almost all the men are his providing – but,' his voice sank still lower, 'I do not completely trust him – I doubt his loyalty. I have misgivings as to the use he may make of my absence, therefore,' he paused and laid his hand on Conrad's shoulder, 'I leave you, Count von Schulembourg, privately in charge. Watch him – never leave him – out of your sight till my return.'

'Good! I understand! I swear!' cried Conrad again.

Mastino della Scala looked into his eyes.

'I trust thee,' he said simply. 'Thou knowest how my wife's safety lies on my soul – and if Carrara play false, we are well-nigh ruined. These weeks have I had him under Ligozzi's eyes, day and night, and now thou must take his place,' Conrad kissed Mastino's hand in silence, his emotional nature overcome to tears.

'Come, my lord, the time wears,' said Ligozzi, and della Scala turned to leave.

At the entrance he looked back.

'Remember, I trust thee, and thee solely, Conrad,' he

said. As he dropped the flap behind him, he turned to Ligozzi.

'Will he be worthy of it, Ligozzi?' he said. 'But I must perforce trust him when there is no other.'

Outside the Duke's tent, his escort was in readiness to start, and his white horse stood waiting, held by Tomaso.

'After all, my lord,' whispered Ligozzi, 'Carrara *may* not be false.'

Mastino shook his head. 'He only awaits the opening,' he said. 'What does console me,' he added, 'is that I shall be back tomorrow.' And he looked toward Milan as he spoke.

'Ligozzi,' he continued wistfully, 'how long the time seems since I saw her. The last words I heard her speak are for ever in my ears: "While thou livest I fear nothing"; and I live, Ligozzi. Sometimes I am ashamed of it!'

'You live to free her, my lord,' said Ligozzi softly.

Mastino mounted in silence. 'Yes, I live for that,' he said, after a pause.

He turned and saw Tomaso watching him.

'Yes, thou shalt come with us,' he smiled; 'only mount in haste The time wears on.'

At this moment, foremost among a little group of horsemen, Carrara cantered toward him, black-eyed, smiling, richly dressed, a plumed cap between his smooth white fingers.

'Farewell, Carrara,' said Mastino. 'Count von Schulembourg is second in command. I leave all to your discretion, subject to my orders already given.'

Giacomo bowed, but made no reply other than his smiling eyes. His meditated treasons were ripe for execution, and he could scarce contain himself at the good fortune of it; Visconti's messenger had reached him the same day that della Scala rode away. There remained only Conrad.

'Till tomorrow at noon,' murmured Carrara, repeating della Scala's last words, as he watched him ride away. 'An attack on Milan, in less than a week! You are mad for a woman's silly face – in less than a week I shall have joined Visconti.'

Visconti understood the art of bribery, and knew whom to bribe. Carrara, only waiting in the hope of it, had caught eagerly at the bait, and by the returning messenger had agreed to join Visconti and leave della Scala shorn of more than half his forces. And Mastino, by his absence, had made it child's play. As Carrara returned now to his own tent, thinking and scheming, a captain of mercenaries galloped up.

'The prisoners, my lord, captured by some of Count von Schulembourg's men, in the scuffle outside Milan yesterday, are being brought into the camp – is it to you or to him we bring them?'

Carrara fingered his bridle.

'Take them to the castle,' he said at last. 'I myself will see them presently.'

He glanced over his shoulder at Count Conrad's tent. The embroidered entrance was closed, the black and yellow eagles fluttered idly over it – there was no sign of the young German.

The Duke of Padua smiled.

'Are those the prisoners?' he asked, pointing to a little group of soldiers guarding a few men.

'Yes, my lord. We had almost forced the gates – when a band rushed out and there was an desperate struggle; we were driven back, and these fellows, in the heat of the victory, followed too far. Then we turned and had them, and brought them in for ransom. They seemed worth it.'

'I will go and view them,' said Carrara suddenly, and he cantered his horse toward the little group.

The noise of the prisoners' arrival was spreading, still there was no sign of Count Conrad, and again the treacherous Carrara smiled. But in a moment more the smile had faded. He noticed among the prisoners a face he surely knew.

Prudence was Giacomo Carrara's ruling quality, and helped him now to keep his wits.

'That fellow yonder,' he said, pointing, 'he with the red hair – who is he? Has he told his quality?'

''Twas he who led the chase,' was the answer, 'screaming like a madman. He is the squire of some nobleman, and gave out he thought we had his master captive.'

Carrara breathed heavily.

'I know something of him, unless I much mistake; a dangerous rogue and spy – place him apart, well guarded – in a separate compartment. Pinion him; Tonight we will put him to the question.

And again he glanced toward the German's tent. Conrad had not appeared, and the prisoners wound away out of sight into what was once Barnabas Visconti's summer residence, and where Barnabas Visconti not long since had died.

XVI

FOR A GAME OF CHESS

The day was wearing into evening when Conrad gave a last look in the little polished mirror hanging on the tapestried walls of his tent, and prepared to set out on a tour of inspection, including a visit to Carrara, who in this moment's interval, he thought, could not have gone astray.

Della Scala had been gone four hours or more, but to the light-hearted German it seemed he had only an instant ago turned from his tent.

He had employed the time in writing some verses (in imitation of the fashionable Petrarch, a production with which he was perfectly satisfied, and put aside to be fair copied by someone, a better adept in spelling than himself), in teaching Vittore to dance, and in changing his doublet.

Count Conrad was very careful of his doublets. He had a great many, and kept them carefully locked in the large coffer that stood at the head of his tent bed.

The one he donned today was elegant in the extreme; peacock purple over an under-garment of rose, curiously slashed with cream. Vittore, who had become his page, was silent at the magnificence.

Conrad sighed as he smoothed the ruffles at his wrists to think that it might not be the latest mode. He felt far from civilization, though only twice seven miles outside Milan, and secretly regretted that Valentine Visconti had ever dazzled him into the imprudence of losing her brother's favour and with it the joys of a splendid court.

Still he had exquisite leathern shoes with points a yard long, caught up and fastened by a chain to his knee; also a cap, garnished with a ruby and a curling feather, and, taking it from Vittore, he stepped out to begin his espionage of Carrara.

'Vittore, follow me,' he said. 'I have it in trust to see this black-browed duke gets into no mischief. Also,' he continued, "tis in my mind to find Vincenzo. Della Scala was severe this noon. I fear me the boy has gone to practise sword-play.'

The camp was quiet and tranquil. It struck Conrad, however, that many of Carrara's men were engaged with their horses and in packing the wagons; but carried on so openly, in broad daylight, it aroused no suspicions on the part of the easy von Schulembourg, who made toward Carrara's tent, singing gaily.

The air was heavy, the sky black about the horizon.

'There will be a storm tonight, Vittore. Let me see, art thou afraid of thunder?' and as he spoke the Count passed without ceremony into Carrara's tent.

The Duke was there, but not expecting Conrad, and as he raised his eyes at his sudden entrance, his look would have struck any save the light-hearted fop as strained and anxious; but the German had personally no doubt of Carrara, and the Duke's ready smile deceived him utterly.

'So your men move tonight, my lord,' he said. 'The Prince never mentioned it to me.'

'It was a final resolve,' answered Carrara. 'I have my orders here,' and he tapped a parchment beside him.

'Ah!' Conrad never even took the parchment up, but glanced through the opening of the tent at the threatening sky. 'You move nearer Milan, of course.'

Giacomo kept his black eyes on the floor.

'Nearer Milan,' he replied. 'Yes; but we do not break camp until the morning, Count. You and the rest remain here to join the Prince,' Carrara looked also out into the thunder-laden air, but not at the sky – at the castle, frowning black above the encampment.

'An officer of mine,' said Conrad carelessly, 'said something to me of some prisoners.'

'Yonder at the castle, Count. Will you question them with me?' asked Giacomo smoothly.

'Question them!' laughed the Count. 'You may have that task, my lord! – and I shall know then where you are,' he added under his breath.

Carrara kept his eyes down, lest even Conrad should see the excitement in them.

'Possibly even I may not question them tonight, Count,' he returned with a smile. 'I intend to rest now, as we march at dawn.'

Conrad rose, with a pleasant feeling of having done his duty, though in his heart a little annoyed that della Scala had not trusted him with the movement of the army.

'The thought of his wife has made him crazy,' he said to himself. 'Giving Giacomo credit for treachery, still he entrusts him with orders he withholds even the knowledge of from me,' And leaving Carrara, he went in search of Vincenzo.

Giacomo sat silent till the Count 's laughter had died away in the distance, then rose with a passionate exclamation at his own luck and Mastino's blindness.

Without a question the Count (left in trust, Carrara knew as plainly as if he had been told) had swallowed his lies, and left him to do as he pleased while he revelled with Vincenzo d'Este. Seeking the entrance once more, Carrara looked out into the heavy evening.

In that great castle Visconti was a prisoner.

Though with his own eyes he had seen Gian Visconti bound between the soldiers, he could not rest for his impatience to see him again and have it confirmed before any other eyes should recognize this rare prize.

Tonight Carrara's army was to desert to Milan. That had been already arranged with Visconti's disguised messenger. It should still desert, but Visconti was now a prisoner, his life in Carrara's hands – there must be slightly other terms between them.

To be in a position to dictate to such a man! Giacomo stood in the gathering dusk, waiting for the dark, his eyes on the castle that held Gian Galeazzo Maria Visconti, Duke of Milan – a prisoner.

* * *

'The storm nears: how hot, good St. Hubert, how hot!' And Conrad tossed the damp curls back from his forehead. The entrance of his tent was flung open to admit what little air there might be, showing to the soldiers without Conrad and Vincenzo bending over a game of chess; on a table near were flasks of wine and elegant glasses; along the floor Vittore lay, half in a heavy sleep.

The tent was lit by jewelled lamps, and by their dull light Vincenzo's beauty shone with an almost unearthly brilliancy. He was clothed in white, his thick black hair falling about his shoulders.

Evidently Mastino's reproof was already forgotten. He leaned forward with flushed cheeks and parted lips, eager and intent on a victory at chess; war and the price of it far from his thoughts.

'Hark!' said Conrad. 'Thunder!'

A low rumble filled the tent, d'Este took no heed.

'I take thy knight,' he said, 'it ruins thee.'

Conrad laughed, he did not take the game so seriously.

'I will visit Carrara,' he said, rising, 'and go the rounds.'

'Thou wilt finish the game,' said Vincenzo angrily. 'Does it pall the moment thou failest to win?'

'My faith, I fail when it palls. But doubtless thou wilt win yet, if thou dost not grow too hot,' and Conrad fanned the boy with the points of his sleeves.

Vincenzo's lustrous eyes flashed.

'Doubtless I shall, Count,' he drew from his finger an emerald ring, 'and I will stake this on it.'

He dropped it on the table with a rattle, and Conrad was animated at once.

'And I this,' he cried, 'my forfeit if the game is not mine in four moves!'

He placed his pearl thumb-ring beside Vincenzo's emerald.

'Four moves!' cried Vincenzo scornfully, and leaned back with shining eyes. Conrad reached for the glasses with a glance of good humour at the dozing page.

'A night from the infernal regions!' he said, as he poured out the wine. 'How does Visconti feel tonight? Methinks some kinsfolk of his from below are abroad.'

Vincenzo emptied his glass and moved.

Conrad emptied his and counter-moved. 'I hope thy emerald was not a lady's gift,' he laughed.

Vincenzo bit his lip, reflected long, and moved again. Conrad turned to the slender flasks and lifted them, one after the other; empty all.

'Vittore!' he called. 'Vittore!'

The boy rose, rubbing his eyes, half-dazed.

'Bring us more wine, Vittore,' Conrad turned to the board again and laughed at Vincenzo's intent face. 'My move,' he said; his plump hand hesitated scarcely a breath. 'Check, Messer Vincenzo.'

'This is no light to play by,' cried Vincenzo, and in annoyance he moved with too little thought.

Conrad waited provokingly till fresh wine had been brought and drunk, patted Vittore's head, and turned to the game again.

'Mate, Messer Vincenzo, in three moves,' And he leaned back with the calm air of a conqueror.

Vincenzo rose in a passion, dashing his glass to the ground.

'I question thy fair play,' he cried.

'And I thy discretion,' returned the Count, and his eyes were suddenly wrathful. 'Thou art a child, and canst not play; and so like a child cry out: "You cheat."'

'I said no word of cheating,' returned Vincenzo. 'Is the accusation one you are accustomed to, Count Conrad?'

Conrad crimsoned. 'Play another time with thy equals, boy, and take better care not to insult thy betters!'

'Betters!' And Vincenzo laughed in reckless scorn, his hand on his toy-like dagger. 'A d'Este demeans himself to play with thee – thou German upstart!'

But Conrad was to be moved no more. With a smile more provoking than any reply he picked up the rings and slipped them on his finger.

But Vincenzo, hot-tempered and passionate, sprang forward with boyish passion.

'Thou shalt not have the emerald,' he cried.

'Must I fight for it?' smiled Conrad, and glanced at Vincenzo's little dagger. 'The emerald seems worth it – only I should be afraid of hurting thee,' And as he spoke he poured out more wine, drinking it gracefully.

'I will fight only with an equal,' said Vincenzo.

Conrad turned on him, and for all his smile, his blue eyes were dark. 'Thou reckless boy!' he said. 'The Germans are the lords of Italy. What is thy family but a fief to the Emperor?'

Vittore had watched the scene in terror. Tomaso had let him know della Scala had left von Schulembourg in trust, and he felt his master was hardly acting as the Duke had meant. In child-like fashion, eager to stop the quarrel, he spoke his thoughts.

'My lord,' he said, 'shall I not accompany you to the Duke of Padua's tent, as the Prince commanded.'

'Commanded!' cried Vincenzo, catching at the words. 'Aye, Count Conrad, remember my brother's commands!'

'I remember none,' returned the Count haughtily. 'What dost thou mean, boy.'

But Vittore lost his courage under the angry glance.

'Only, my lord, what you said,' he stammered, 'about keeping watch upon the Duke of Padua.'

'So you were left as a spy?' sneered Vincenzo, 'is that it? Make haste, Count Conrad, hurry to Carrara's tent as you were told, and see what he is doing.'

Conrad, flushed with wine, allowed the boyish sneer to goad him into fury.

'I play the spy at no one's bidding,' he said. 'I do not leave my tent tonight,' And he flung himself on the couch.

'But what did the Duke order? It will go ill with you when he hears of disobedience,' sneered Vincenzo.

'Let it go well or ill, I will not leave my tent tonight on any errand, save I choose,' And Count Conrad's words were heard by another than Vincenzo and Vittore, Giacomo Carrara, who listened outside.

The storm-wind was beginning to howl and the rain to fall in heavy drops, but the Duke of Padua only thanked his good fortune for such propitious weather, as he turned away and made rapidly toward the castle to question the prisoners.

XVII

THE TERRORS OF THE NIGHT

The storm had risen, the low whispering of the wind, the distant rumbles of the thunder, gathering unheeded, burst suddenly into a tempest.

Its very fury spoke it brief, yet many cowered and shrank before it, as if its termination must be the termination of the world. And to no one did it strike more fear than to the solitary prisoner in the castle of Brescia – Gian Visconti. In obedience to Carrara's orders, he had been placed in a separate chamber, as far from the other prisoners as space allowed. His chamber was a circular, vault-like space, once serving as antechamber to a gloomy suite of rooms beyond, in which Barnabas Visconti had chosen to beguile the summer heat. The doors of this suite were locked; Gian Visconti himself had locked them, when he and his father last came there together. This vault-like room was high and ill-lit, and, in the blackness of the storm, pitch dark. Visconti sat underneath one of the windows, whither he had dragged the wooden stool, the sole furniture the place contained; his face was buried in his hands, and he writhed in horror.

The wind howled and tore at the locked doors, making them creak and groan; the thunder shook the building; and at every fresh convulsion Visconti shrieked aloud in unison.

The lightning, flashing blue through the crevices, seemed to play about that inner door, and he cowered from the sight, and bit at his fingers in a fierce endeavour to resist the madness seizing him.

It was not so very long ago that he had turned the great key behind him in that ponderous door, and ridden from the deed he had done, shouting through the midnight. He thought then never to return, and here he was, thrust in alone, and his madness on him. Visconti staggered from his seat, groping blindly.

The blackness seemed to whirl with faces and clutching, tearing fingers; he knew not where he was – he could see nothing – blackness and space – seemingly unbounded.

Another flash revealed to him that he had drawn near that inner door – in the instant it was visible; it seemed to open and shut – quickly.

Visconti fell back against the wall, and wrestled with his terrors as if they were some living thing, and again with savage teeth he bit into his flesh.

But the floor was opening beneath him, opening into gulfs deep and still deeper, bottomless.

'I am mad!' said Visconti, and shrieked and howled with the storm. It did not help him; he heard hurrying feet through all the alarm of the tempest, hurrying to him behind that locked door. Let him not look, for what he feared to see the dark could not conceal – and now they were at the door, and now they were fitting a key.

'Keep away!' he yelled.

Then he stood, hushed, with bated breath, eyes staring into the blackness, listening. And through the dark he heard the creaking and twisting of the key, the slow opening of a heavy door, the groaning of the hinges as it opened, slowly.

The wind howled in a wild gust, and suddenly through the narrow window there showed the black sky torn in two by the lightning flash. As it circled the chamber,

Visconti raised his head – the door was open. And through the opening two faces peered – they were not human faces – Visconti knew them whence they were.

Utter blackness followed upon the vivid flash, and the thunder crashed and rolled, and at last the rain came with a mighty roar.

'I am in hell!' yelled Visconti. 'I am dead, and in hell!' And maniac shrieks rose. He dragged himself to the narrow slit that made the window, and some of the heavy rain-drops were dashed in upon his face.

'I am alive!' he cried, 'alive! It does not rain in hell!' He dropped, and lay prone along the ground. After a while he rose, and began groping for the outer door.

The walls seemed to rock and twist, but on his face and hand was the cold splash of the rain, and Visconti kept a hold upon his self-control, saying between his teeth: 'A light; if I can get a light.'

He found the door, and struck upon it with the fury of madness.

There was no response: again he struck and shouted. The worst had gone by, but only to leave his thoughts centred on one idea: to see a human face and in the light.

Suddenly, in the midst of his blows, the door opened showing a glimmering light, and in the entrance the figure of a soldier, who looked fearfully around the chamber.

'I thought it was the fiend himself who called!' he said, and crossed himself.

Visconti clutched his arm. 'It was the fiend,' he said. 'Legions of them – the place is haunted! Give me a light!'

The soldier shrank back in horror at his words, at his hardly human eyes.

'Santa Maria!' he muttered. 'I have heard evil tales of this castle, the storm too is fearful –'

'Give me a light,' said Visconti; 'give me a light!'

'None of the prisoners have lights – it is forbidden –' began the man, but Gian Maria cut him short.

'A light, I say!' and he put his blood-marked hand upon the other's shoulder.

'Thou heardst the fiend scream – and it *was* the fiend. Wilt thou give me a light?'

The frightened soldier shrank from him anew.

'Thou art distraught,' he cried with a paling face.

Visconti laughed wildly. 'Do I not say so? Give me the lantern!' and he held out his finger, on which there blazed a splendid ring.

'Would any ordinary prisoner wear a ring like this? I tell thee it is a coal from hell, and I will give it thee – for thy lantern. See how it shines; try if it will burn thee to the bone,' and he stripped it from his finger, dropping it on the pavement at the soldier's feet.

'Truly,' gasped the soldier, looking at him, 'thou art no ordinary man, and as for thy gems – whether they be coals or no, thou shalt have the lantern.'

He stepped across the threshold as he spoke, a little fearfully, and placed the lantern in the niche cut to receive it in the wall.

'Thou wilt be getting it down and firing thyself with it,' he remarked. 'For thou art clean distraught, methinks.'

Visconti made no reply, he had noticed that *both* the inner doors were shut.

'And as I must answer for thee,' continued the soldier, 'I will secure thee with this,' and stepping back into the passage, he returned with a rope and advanced toward the prisoner.

The Duke rose with flashing eyes.

'Remember thou art the devil, messer,' said the soldier soothingly, 'and naught can really hold thee.'

Visconti felt for the dagger that no longer hung by his side, then showed the soldier his fingers, red and still bleeding.

'The teeth that met there can meet in thine,' he snarled, and his eyes were like a wolf's.

The soldier stepped back, then with a sudden thought pointed to the light.

'Stay unbound then, and I will take that away again,' he said, and again advanced.

Visconti suffered his arms to be bound together at the elbows, nor did he seem to heed when the soldier left him, and the great door fell to once more in silence.

The storm had sobbed itself away, leaving only the steady patter of the rain. The chamber had light, and the sight of a human face had restored Visconti.

Once more he felt his hold on life and on reality, and he turned from that closed door with its superstitious horror to face real terror and a staggering mischance.

Milan! He had left Milan in an hour of need – and with no one to check Valentine. Only within the last few weeks had he known what she was capable of. What might she not attempt once she realized his absence? Giannotto too, and the Duke of Orleans! What of their sincerity? He had left not one man within the city whom he could trust implicitly.

Then he considered his own plight. Clearly they did not know him; none the less they had him. He ground his teeth at the thought of della Scala's triumph.

His art of bribery occurred to him, and he remembered with a savage vexation how he had flung a jewel to his jailer for a light. A jewel that might have purchased freedom. Still, it was in his madness; he might be thankful he had not shouted his name – and his crimes. Suddenly, with a start of recollection, it occurred to him anew that he had been placed apart. Then Carrara *had* recognized him. The cords around Visconti's arms began now to torture him: he was weak from lack of food and mad excitement. Thoughts of Carrara vanished. He saw the face of the girl on whose account he had risked his dukedom.

'Graziosa!' he cried, but the face looked at him unseemingly. 'You know me!' as if in appeal. 'Graziosa, you know me!' The face suddenly distorted, as if with horror. Visconti shrank from it – and she was gone.

'What frightened her? Those other faces,' Visconti whispered to himself, then roused himself with a harsh laugh. 'Will Carrara come?' He fixed his eyes on the lamp, then on the door. And presently he heard the subdued bustle of arrival, the great door clang; the ringing answers of the soldiers; then outside his own door hushed and respectful voices – the door opened, shut, and Visconti saw his visitor.

A man, black-eyed, florid, richly dressed in velvet, well armed, unattended, and carrying the castle keys – Giacomo Carrara. He stood in amazement, and shrank back half-afraid, though the guard had warned him.

'Visconti!' he cried. 'What has happened?'

The sickly light of the lantern showed him a white, haggard face, with wild, bloodshot eyes, the hair hanging lank and damp about its forehead, the plain doublet gashed and torn, hands and face smeared with blood.

But, at sight of the man he hoped to buy, Visconti's face took on a more human look.

'You have seen my messenger?'

'Hush!' and Giacomo looked around cautiously. 'Yes, I have seen him, and dispatched my answer.'

'My offer suits you?' said Visconti grimly.

'It suited me, Visconti, till just now,' returned the other. 'It suited me to such purpose that my men even now await my orders to desert to Milan.'

'Ah!' Visconti said. 'And what of it now,' he added, looking around again, the old subduing spirit in his glance.

'What of it? It shall still be done, only,' Carrara smiled, 'there is an unforeseen addition to the bargain. Not only do you need my men, Visconti; I think, as well, you need your liberty.'

'And so the price is higher. Is that what you would say? Unloose my arm. It shall not be forgotten in the bribe,' he sneered.

Carrara advanced and undid the rope in silence. He knew Visconti was unarmed.

Visconti gasped with relief as the torture was removed.

'And now,' he said, taking at once the mastery, 'how do matters stand between us? Be wary; be brief.'

Rapidly Giacomo told him how, with the desertion, half Mastino's army would be gone; how Padua was to be given into the hands of Visconti's generals, and how Count Conrad played at chess.

Visconti hated the smooth traitor who was waiting to drive a hard bargain with his necessity – and his freed hand went to his doublet: the turquoise gloves had not been lost.

'And now, your terms?' he said.

The Duke of Padua hesitated a moment – even with Visconti in his power he hesitated.

'Those you refused two years ago,' he said. 'When we warred with Pavia.'

Visconti remembered. Two years ago, when he had been by half not so great as he stood now, he had refused them in scorn – they meant half his dominions – they would place Carrara on a level with himself.

'Well,' he said, 'and if I refuse?'

'A prisoner does not refuse – his liberty,' smiled Giacomo. He could afford to smile.

Visconti controlled himself.

'And if I accept – you take my word, all I have to give – a prisoner's word?'

'A Visconti's word,' corrected Carrara. 'Nay, lord, I think I shall need more than that.'

'What more can I give?' he asked. 'You waste the time, Carrara.'

Giacomo was playing with the keys in his hand.

'Yourself, Visconti,' he returned calmly. 'The army only waits for me to march on Milan, leaving della Scala stripped of half his force. You will go with it, Visconti, as my prisoner. My army will conduct you into Milan – where I shall not leave you till the terms I offer are fulfilled. Then, Visconti, but not till then, we will together ruin della Scala.'

Visconti was silent.

'Come,' continued Carrara, 'shall it be so – or will you wait and meet della Scala and Count Conrad?'

'I accept your terms,' said Gian, and rose to his feet. 'I accept, Carrara.'

Giacomo's eyes shone. With trembling fingers he unbuttoned his long black velvet cloak and flung it on Visconti's shoulders.

'We must hasten; even now the tipsy German may

think to visit the castle,' And he selected a key from the bunch in his hand, and advanced toward the inner door. Visconti started forward, with staring eyes.

'Not that way!' he cried.

Carrara turned in surprise, the key in the lock.

''Tis the only way, Visconti. Are you thinking we could pass unnoticed, you and I together?'

Gian, deathly white, sank back obstinately against the wall.

'I will not go that way,' he said. 'I will not go that way.'

'He is in his mad fit again,' thought Giacomo; aloud he said soothingly: 'Come, lord, this is the only way; will you rather wait to see Verona's face when he discovers you? What is wrong with this way,' he added in vexation as Visconti made no movement. 'Quick! the moments fly!'

Gian stepped forward with an effort.

''Tis my fancy,' he said. 'Idle, truly, at such a moment. Open the door, Carrara.'

The key ground in the lock – as Visconti had heard it once before that night, turned on the other side.

Carrara paused, however, and having taken the lamp from the niche, put it down with a smile, and drew a parchment from his belt.

'I had forgotten,' he said. 'I will leave this, else Verona will miss the point of the jest; we will tell him what a brave catch his lieutenant hath allowed to escape the snare?' And with the end of his dagger he drove the paper into the crevice of the stone. 'I never loved Verona,' he added with an evil smile.

But Visconti had not heard, nor was he heeding him; his eyes were riveted upon the door.

Again Padua raised the lantern above his head.

The glimmering light fell faintly on a dark chamber,

and dimly lit a large black couch from which the tapestry coverlet was half dragged off. Visconti peered an instant over his rescuer's shoulder eagerly, then fell back.

'I cannot,' he said sullenly. 'I will stay and face della Scala – I cannot pass that way.'

Carrara turned and looked at him keenly.

'What do you know of these chambers, that you are afraid to pass them, Visconti'" he asked.

"'Tis no matter what I know – I will not pass them,' cried Visconti, fiercely, and clutched at the rough wall as if to keep himself from being made to enter them even by force. Giacomo looked into the chamber curiously; the lantern showed only parts of it, and that dimly – an empty audience chamber, stiff chairs against the wall, the couch, dust on the floor and shadows in the arras – nothing more; and Carrara turned impatiently.

'I risk my life for this,' he said. 'What do you think it will mean, Visconti, if I am found helping you to escape?'

He stepped across the threshold, and flashed the lantern around.

'Nothing!' he laughed over his shoulder. 'Nothing,' but as he advanced he paused a moment, and lifted up a corner of the dragged coverlet, 'save that this coverlet is riddled as if with dagger-thrusts,' he added, 'and the floor seems stained' – he sank his voice – 'with blood.'

He looked back at Visconti, standing in the doorway, and with a sudden fear of him his hand sought his sword.

'Whom did you murder here, Visconti?' he asked, awestruck.

'Whoever it was,' he added presently, 'I would not lose my life for fear of them, seeing they are dead.'

In a second Visconti was by his side, gripping his arm, and Carrara, startled, shrank, and kept his hand upon his dagger.

'I do not fear them,' whispered Visconti, in his ear. 'Nor you.'

And he hurried across the chamber, Carrara at his heels.

Room after room they traversed, deserted, gloomy, and unopened since that night.

'Hurry!' breathed Visconti. 'Shall we never see the blessed sky again?'

And snatching the keys, he pushed on, taking every door and turning with a certainty that showed he knew them well.

'At last!' he cried, as they stepped out into the air.

They were at the back of the castle, on a ledge overhung with ivy, and overlooking a narrow flight of steps, the masonry half-ruined and overgrown with flowers.

The storm was over, a few great clouds tore across the sky, but the moon was clear and serene, the night calm and peaceful.

The cool air blew around Visconti's damp hair, and stirred the dark ivy leaves, glistening with the rain. Beneath them lay the tents, a large body of men, half the army, silently and swiftly preparing for flight.

'Some have gone already,' said Giacomo. 'These wait for me and you, Visconti: come,' and stepping past him he led the way.

There was no one to observe them save Giacomo's men, that he had been careful to station there; but when they had gained the bottom, and Carrara would have passed on, Visconti caught at his sleeve and drew him behind a clump of elder.

'The German!' he whispered, and they waited, breathless.

A soft voice was gaily singing, and the words of the song came clearly through the night.

'Heinrich was my bosom friend,
White feather and purple cloak:
Now that folly's at an end,
His the flame and mine the smoke!'

'He comes this way,' said Carrara. 'If he takes to questioning where I am –'

'If he takes to coming nearer,' smiled Visconti, 'I shall be obliged to – kill him.'

'We parted for a silken knot,
White feather and purple cloak:
Whose fault it was I have forgot,
His the flame and mine the smoke!'

The last words were lost in a burst of laughter, as Conrad and Vincenzo, each mounted on a white horse, and attended by an escort with torches, rode past, back too their tents.

So close they came, that Visconti, with gleaming eyes, leaned forward, longing to strangle the singer with one of those long curls that hung around his laughing, careless face.

But Carrara was relieved.

'As long as he does not inquire for me,' he said. 'But even then my officers understand.'

Visconti smiled grimly; he was to pay for that.

'Now!' he said, and as Conrad's German song and

Vincenzo's wild laughter passed, Visconti and Giacomo stepped out from behind the bushes and looked after them, the freedom of one secured, the treachery of the other well-nigh accomplished.

XVIII

GIACOMO CARRARA'S REWARD

The dawn was breaking, the sky streaked and barred with cold grey light, and along the winding road to Milan rode the Visconti and Carrara, the army before them.

It had been accomplished, without demur, openly and completely; behind them they left the Veronese and Mantuan troops, over whom Giacomo had no command – and Count Conrad, laughing in his folly.

Quite near to them lay Milan – and Visconti rode in silence, wondering what had befallen in the city; wondering, and fearing Valentine had revealed too much of his own spirit; he was afraid of her.

Along the distant horizon the grey walls of the city began to be visible across the flat plain, and Visconti's eyes lit at sight of his city, and he turned to Carrara impulsively.

'Give me a sword, Carrara,' he said. ''Tis not fitting I should enter Milan weaponless.'

'The Milanese will so rejoice to see you, my lord,' returned Padua, 'they will never notice –'

'That I come as a prisoner,' flashed Visconti, but the next moment he laughed and urged on his horse. 'But what care I how, so long as I do re-enter Milan? Now, with you as my ally, Carrara, I can crush della Scala without France or the Empire; and together, as ye say, we will rule Lombardy.'

Carrara rode abreast of him, glancing at him keenly.

'Even now he will try to outwit me,' he thought, and resolved he would not be outdone in cunning for the lack of care.

'How came it you were captured,' he added, 'and in this guise.'

'The chances of war,' laughed Visconti. 'Foolishly I went myself to defend the gates, and pursued della Scala's men too far.'

But this candour did not deceive Carrara. 'Foolish indeed!' he smiled. 'Your hurry excelled your prudence, lord.' And he wondered what was the truth.

'You have cause to thank heaven no one knew you,' he continued.

'They were German boors,' answered Visconti, 'Count Conrad's men, and there was nothing to tell my degree. Yet, had they looked a little closer, they might have found one thing that would have told them I was different from what I seemed – these.'

And he drew out of his doublet the turquoise gloves.

Even in that cold, faint light they showed brilliant and beautiful, and Carrara gazed at them in wonder.

'As I was summoned,' continued Visconti, dreamily, 'I was looking at them. Are they not beautiful, Carrara? Two years they took to make, and cost more than I care to tell. Each turquoise is flawless, and set by Antonio Fressi himself.'

'And is this a gift for someone,' asked Carrara, and he looked keenly into Visconti's face.

'It was one of my bridal gifts to the Duke of Orleans. I must honour him, Carrara, although I love him not,' said Visconti simply. 'But now I will offer it to one to whom I owe my life. Take the gloves, a gift from me, Giacomo.' And he turned in the saddle and held them with a winning smile to Carrara, who, mistrustful, looked at him doubtingly and keenly.

'Thou wilt not refuse my gift,' and Visconti looked at

him proudly. 'Let it seal our bargain, Carrara. Take it, for the sake of the goodwill with which it is offered.'

Carrara's ruling quality was prudence, and all Visconti's seeming guilelessness did not deceive him; still, he hesitated, considering where the trap lay.

Then, as he glanced down at the gloves, his eyes caught the gleam on the hilt of his dagger, and a thought struck him.

'He means to make me put them on,' he thought, 'and snatch the sword meanwhile'; and he smiled to think Visconti could be so simple.

'I thank thee for thy gift, Visconti, and for the goodwill that offers it,' he said, with an ingenuousness equal to Visconti's, and reaching out his hand, he took the gloves, meaning to have the gift and outwit Visconti also.

Gian's manner had lost its gloom and wildness, he seemed light of heart and in a pleasant mood.

'They are riding-gloves,' he cried. 'Wear them into Milan, Carrara.'

'Ah,' thought Giacomo, 'I see the plot. Thou wouldst snatch a weapon while my hands were busy,' and, priding himself on his cunning, he deftly slipped them on his hands, keeping his elbow on his sword-hilt and his watchful eyes upon Visconti.

'A beautiful dawn,' said Gian softly, seeming to take no heed of Carrara's clever manoeuvring; his eyes were fixed on the sunrise behind Milan. 'All pearl and silver, blushing into life anon; about the time when I shall enter Milan.'

And he fixed his eyes on Giacomo with a strange expression.

'When *we* shall enter Milan,' corrected Carrara. 'The sun will be fairly high: these marches are toilsome.' And he glanced down proudly at the beautiful gauntlets on his hands, calculating what the pearls and turquoises might be worth, picked off, and vain at having outwitted Visconti.

'The promise of the day!' said Visconti, dreamily and sadly. 'Hath it never struck thee how that promise never is fulfilled? Day after day, since the world began, something in the mystery of the dawn is promised – something the sunset smiles to see unfulfilled – something men have been ever cheated of – something men will never know – the promise of the dawn!'

The road began now to be fringed with poplars, and in the faint light the colours of the wayside flowers were visible.

They rode awhile in silence. Carrara looked back at the small rearguard in the distance, and before him along the road to his army blackening the plain, and then again at Visconti.

'Either he is always mad or –'

With a sharp exclamation he fell forward on his horse's neck, but recovered himself instantly. Visconti turned to him, still with that far-away look in his eyes.

'The road is stony,' he said. 'Thy horse stumbled.'

'Fool or devil,' Carrara was still wondering, and, looking at Visconti's face, he almost thought him a fool.

'You and I,' cried Visconti, with a sudden change, 'together, Carrara! Lords of Lombardy!'

And he struck his horse into a gallop so unexpectedly that Carrara had difficulty to keep abreast with him.

'I have been so long away!' he cried. 'Haste! I long to be in my city again. Valentine – and others – will be grieving. Haste!'

And he still urged his horse.

Carrara, galloping at his side, suddenly reeled in the saddle, with a cry of anguish.

'Faster!' cried Visconti. 'Faster!'

With an effort Carrara kept his horse to the pace, but his face was deathly, his lips set. Visconti never looked at him; his gaze was toward Milan and the sunrise.

Suddenly Carrara cried aloud. 'Not so fast, Visconti, not so fast!'

But Gian flew along the level road.

'Milan!' he cried, 'on to Milan!'

Carrara swayed forward to grasp Visconti's cloak, but he shook him off with a laugh.

'What ails you, Carrara? The army waits, you must ride faster still if you mean to ride into Milan today with me.'

But Carrara was clutching at the neck of his doublet with staring eyes.

'My heart!' he gasped. 'I suffocate – ah –!'

And he rode on blindly.

'Your heart,' laughed Visconti, drawing rein a little. 'Do your treacheries stop its beating? You suffocate? Do your lies choke you?'

A cry of mortal agony broke from the unhappy Carrara.

'Stop!' he gasped; 'I am – dying – stop –'

Then his glazing eyes fell on the brilliant blue gloves he wore, and he sat upright with a scream of rage.

'The gloves! the gloves!' And with his remaining strength he tried to tear them off. '0 fool! A Visconti!... I might – have known –'

Frantically he pulled at them, while Visconti, now moving almost at a walk, looked dreamily ahead at the fast nearing city.

'Fiend!' cried Carrara wildly. 'Fiend!'

And he lurched forward, falling heavily on to the road, where he lay, convulsed, the turquoise gloves still on his hands.

Gian Maria drew rein now, and looked down at him, his face no longer indifferent, as he gazed into the white and contorted countenance of the dying man.

'"Whom did you murder here, Visconti?"' he quoted. '"Whoever it be, do not fear him now, since he is dead"; and I answered, did I not, that I feared neither him nor you? And now, Carrara, thou mayst tell him what I said, him whom I murdered in that room we passed.'

Giacomo, writhing on the ground, looked up at him with hate equal to his own, and feebly still tried to pull off the turquoise gloves.

Visconti, leaning low from the saddle, gripped his sword and thrust it through his belt.

'I shall not ride into Milan swordless,' he said; 'thou might'st have spared thy caution, Carrara: I shall ride into Milan with thy army, thy towns, and thy sword; and I have bought them – with a pair of turquoise gloves.'

He looked curiously at Carrara, who suddenly sat upright; the cold light fell on his face, his starting eyes looking straight into Visconti's.

'Thou art not human, Visconti,' he whispered. 'Yet, remember, even devils meet their punishment, and there will be the bitterest of all for such as thou art – failure.' And he fell back again among the flowers, where he lay, white and still.

Visconti looked back at the advancing rearguard, waved to it, pointing downward, and then before him to Milan, brilliant in the sunrise.

From its turrets still floated the banner of the Viper.

XIX

A Sign from Heaven

The day had dawned fair and clear after the storm, and the early sunlight struck across the dark chamber that had held Visconti.

The stamped leather hung before the high window had been torn away and lay along the ground, but the room was unchanged save that the inner door was open, and near it, stuck into a crevice of the stone, a parchment hung.

Before this stood Count Conrad, with a face dazed.

Vincenzo, when he learned the news, had flown like a madman along the road to Milan, in a fury of rage, with some half-frenzied project of overtaking the traitor.

Outside the door was a group of soldiers, who peeped through with curiosity at the motionless figure within.

At last he moved dizzily to a seat. 'St. Hubert, when the Duke returns!' he gasped, and wiped the perspiration from his forehead with a groan of woe.

He looked a somewhat sorry figure, his peacock doublet crumpled, his hair uncurled, his hands shaking.

Last night, only last night, Visconti had been in this very room, a prisoner in his power, and he had revelled with a boy and quarrelled over a game! One of the soldiers pushed the door open softly and entered.

'The Prince has returned, my lord,' he said.

'So soon!' gasped Conrad. 'So soon!'

'The army is moving from Brescia; the intention is to march on Milan –'

'With the men who are not here!' groaned Conrad.

'The Duke met my lord d'Este. He knows,' said the soldier gruffly, and left the room. It would have pleased him to strangle the foppish foreigner who had well-nigh ruined them.

Conrad felt half relieved, half sorry; whether Vincenzo's relation had been as kind to him as his own would have been he doubted – he felt a wild desire to hide himself till della Scala's rage had blown a little over.

As he stood there, miserable, undecided, he heard the salutations of the soldiers and a heavy tread outside.

He remembered that Mastino was a giant – he had once found it to his advantage, he might now find it to his peril; but it was not fear, but bitter shame, that brought Conrad almost to his knees.

He knew that della Scala was there, though he did not raise his head.

'Conrad,' said Mastino, and his voice was strangely altered. 'Conrad.'

The Count, with an effort, looked at Mastino, who stood in front of the door he had closed, with a face from which all colour had been struck.

'When did you discover – this?' continued della Scala, and pointed to the parchment. All elaborate excuses and appeals for pardon Conrad had prepared died away on his tongue.

'An hour ago,' he replied lamely.

'An hour ago!' Mastino walked across to the parchment hanging on the wall.

Conrad's eyes followed him; he could find no words to break the silence.

Della Scala first read, then tore the writing down, and crushed it in his hand; then he looked at the door, standing ajar.

'How many have deserted?' he asked in a hard voice. 'Vincenzo said half the army.'

Conrad could not answer the truth.

'How many?' and Mastino turned toward him.

'Carrara has taken all his force,' faltered the wretched man.

Mastino crushed the parchment yet tighter in his hand, and walked up to Conrad, who shrank before his face.

'Your sword, Count,' he said. Conrad hesitated, bewildered.

'You are no longer in my service; as my officer you wear that sword; as what you are, I demand it from you.'

And he held out his hand.

In silence Conrad drew the weapon.

Mastino took it, broke it, threw it on the floor.

'And now go,' he said.

At last Conrad found his voice.

'Lord!' he cried, 'let me stay.'

'Go,' said Mastino.

'I will stay,' faltered Conrad, 'and amend my fault.'

But della Scala turned his back on him.

'Go to Visconti,' he flashed. 'Tisio plays chess almost as well as Vincenzo.'

The taunt made speech come more easily. 'No man can ask more than another's humiliation, that other suing humbly for pardon –'

'I did not ask so much,' said Mastino, his back still to him. 'You are unhurt.'

And the Count glanced at della Scala's face, and saw a little of what he had done; that speech was useless.

He moved to go, murmuring something with bent head; at the door he turned again. 'Della Scala,' he began, 'I –'

'I will never willingly see your face again,' interrupted Mastino. 'Go and join my other allies – in Milan.'

Conrad drew himself up.

'God helping me, I *will* go to Milan,' he said. 'I will further your cause in Milan itself – even though I leave with you my sword.'

Still Mastino stood motionless, and slowly Conrad passed through the doors, and down the stairs, through the soldiery that turned their backs – cast out. As the door clashed to behind the Count, Mastino turned passionately and strode into the inner room, not knowing what he did, so great the agony of his helpless fury and despair.

A gloomy window gave a view upon the open country.

Della Scala strode to it; little he heeded the gloomy couch and the stained floor. He saw only the green plain of Lombardy, and his own diminished tents, lessened by the better half. He struck his hand against the window-frame violently – Visconti had triumphed!

This evening had he meant to seize Milan – the evening of this very day; and, behold, now it was all to be done again, the weary, weary waiting, the watching, the planning, the soothing his allies, the making good Carrara's treachery; and meanwhile – Isotta!

Della Scala dropped his head into his hands with a cry wrung from his heart. 'Isotta! Isotta!'

The sunlight fell too on the crumpled parchment on the floor, and Mastino, raising his head, saw it lying there and ground it beneath his heel.

'Am I to be for ever laughed at and betrayed?' he cried. 'Ever served by traitors and leagued with fools? Shall I never learn I trust too much?' He looked around the chamber, and thought, with a bitterness beyond expression, that only a few hours before Visconti had passed through it.

Della Scala leaned against the wall; the very sunlight seemed black, the very sky hopeless. Yet his spirit rose against his fate.

He drew out and kissed the little locket he wore around his neck, the pearl locket that always hung there. Then suddenly rousing himself and walking blindly forward, opening one door in mistake for another, he found himself at the top of two steps, looking down into a chapel. For a moment, his brain reeling and sick, he stepped back, bewildered, doubting what he saw.

The place was high and dome-shaped, with plain stone walls, lit by two windows facing each other, but shrouded in dark hangings that admitted only a faint, cold light.

The air was damp and vault-like, and the room itself bare of any furniture or adornment save a purple hassock, and two lamps of rusty gold that hung by long, blackened chains from the ceiling. Opposite the entrance hung against the stone wall a purple curtain, and before it a large crucifix, crudely painted. The dim light just struck its dismal colouring, and to Mastino's fevered fancy the dead Christ seemed to twist and writhe along his contorted body.

The lamps were out, and the trace of incense in the air faint.

Della Scala entered softly, catching his breath painfully, the terror of religion strong within him.

On the purple hassock he knelt, with clasped hands, before the disfigured Christ, his heart rising to his lips in passionate prayer.

'Lord, thou understandest! Because I cannot deck thy altars with the gold of victory, thou wilt not forsake me, thou wilt have mercy on me and on her!'

And he stretched out his arms to the figure in an exaltation of trust and hope. 'Even as I spare those who betray, so wilt thou spare her, O Christ!' He flung himself from his knees, face downward on the stones, in a tumult of hope and trust. Around the folds of Mastino's cloak lay the leaves of some dead roses that had fluttered at his movement, from forgotten wreaths, hanging brown against the wall.

Mastino rose, eager for some answer – some assent. But the dead Christ was silent. Mastino could see the cracking paint on the ribs, the tawdry gold of the halo, and he came still nearer in a strange desperation.

Half-hidden in shadow, two faces looked down on him – expressionless, stone, the angels on the wall.

Mastino looked from them to the crucifix, and his fervent faith sank, chilled.

'Stone,' he murmured in his heart. 'Stone and paint,' and he noticed the empty lamps that should be blazing with eternal fire, and he cried aloud in bitterness. 'Men keep those alight, and without them the eternal fire dies! Stone angels and a painted God! What help in them?' And he dropped again upon the floor. 'The lamps burn bright on Visconti's altars, and his saints smile – for the painter limned them so.'

He turned from the dismantled chapel and rushed up the two steps, half distraught.

In the outer chamber the sunlight dropped strong and golden, and Mastino shut the door of the dark and gloomy chapel behind him with a shudder.

'Lord!' cried an eager voice. 'Lord!'

It was Tomaso and his father.

'Did ye fear for me, Ligozzi?' said della Scala kindly. 'I have been praying for a patient heart,' And the two who loved him looked at him awhile and could say nothing.

'My lord,' began Tomaso again with a timid eagerness, 'there is news –'

'Tomaso,' said his father, 'thy news can wait.'

Mastino picked up his gauntlet from the deep window-seat where he laid it down, and fastening it on, looked at Ligozzi.

'What hast thou to say, Ligozzi? Have any of the men returned?'

Ligozzi stood fidgeting with his cap, looking uneasily at the ground.

'Come,' and Mastino smiled sadly, 'I am used to bad news, Ligozzi.'

'Some few men have indeed returned from Giacomo's army, my lord, some four score –'

'Some four score!' repeated della Scala. 'Are there so many as four score that will not serve Visconti?'

'They have strange tales, my lord. They say Carrara himself is dead.'

'Carrara dead!' cried Mastino with a sudden fierceness, savage as a bite. 'Now, I had promised myself to kill Carrara. Who has forestalled me?'

'It is said – Visconti himself – they do not know.'

'And the traitor dead,' broke in della Scala, 'was there not one – not one to lead the men back to me again? Visconti, single-handed and unarmed, was allowed to take an army into Milan.'

'Alas, my lord, not only Carrara, his captains too, as it appears, have all been bought.'

'Tell me no more,' cried Mastino. 'I am alone to blame. I cannot learn to deal with traitors.'

'As for Count von Schulembourg, the wretched

German,' continued Ligozzi, 'he has left the camp.' As he spoke, Ligozzi glanced through the window at the tents. 'He took no one with him, but, ordering his Germans to fight as one man to the death for you, he rode along the road to Milan.'

'Oh!' cried Mastino, with a great cry wrung from his soul. He rested his hand a moment on Ligozzi's shoulder. 'I am well-nigh sick, Ligozzi,' he said. 'The empty-headed and the villain prosper, and I – and mine – go to the wall.'

Tomaso stole forward. Della Scala noticed him and turned kindly.

'Something to tell me, sayest thou?' he asked.

Tomaso's eyes were full of tears. For some moments he could not find his voice.

'He hath discovered some secret passage; useless, I fear me,' said his father.

'Nay, Father, I tell thee it leadeth to the city! Today, lord, as I explored it, I found stored there some rolls of silk, new and clean; together with some earths such as I have heard say painters use.'

Della Scala started. He found the news not so unimportant as Ligozzi had.

'Go on, Tomaso,' he said, and kept his half-closed eyes upon the ground.

'Indeed, my lord, it must be some old subway into Milan. 'Tis wide enough to admit six abreast, and recently used, as it opens some mile and a half outside the city. I have not yet penetrated to the extremity. Lord, think of it – it must open into Milan!'

Della Scala's worn face flushed involuntarily, his eyes turned to the closed door of the chapel. Had he belied the stone angels – the extinguished lamps?

'This seems great news, Tomaso,' he said slowly. 'I will see into it,' He moved as he spoke. 'My other gauntlet, Ligozzi.'

'I cannot see it, lord.'

'Ah!' said Mastino suddenly. 'I left it in the chapel!'

Tomaso had already departed for the gauntlet. Mastino, following to the door, saw him stoop and lift it from the ground.

Tomaso handed him the ponderous glove, and, as Mastino took it, he stifled the cry on his lips, and turned away to clasp it to his heart.

For inside his glove, almost hidden in the velvet lining, lay a soft white rose: a sign from heaven.

XX

IN THE DUKE'S ABSENCE

'My chance has come,' said Valentine.

A day had passed since Visconti had ridden so wildly to the western gate, and as yet he had not returned.

The soldiers, weary and wounded, had reeled that night into the palace courtyards, de Lana at their head, expecting to find Visconti there before them. They had missed him in the wild fray – the Germans had been driven back from the walls without their prisoners – had not the Duke returned?

Neither then nor as yet, near a day after the sortie. Doubtless he, victorious as ever, was reconnoitring some stronghold of the enemy, or their encampments outside Milan.

Still, in the palace some were getting anxious; there was no word, no message. Who, in the Duke's absence, ruled Milan?

The question suggested itself among others to Valentine Visconti.

She put it to herself.

'I rule Milan, and I will give myself my freedom by it, whether Gian be alive or dead, returning now or never.'

It was late afternoon, and Valentine had formed her plan; with courage and skill she made no doubt of success. To enter her brother's private room was the first step.

All day Valentine had plotted some means of accomplishing this.

The rooms were locked, and Gian wore the key around his neck.

The Visconti palace was part old, part new; the great circular tower in which Isotta was confined, the low heavy stone buildings that surrounded it were the only remaining portions of the ancient gothic castle.

The new building, bright in yellow and pink tiles, was supported on low, horse-shoe arches, and gave straightly on the courtyard in front and the gardens at the rear – the whole encircled by a great wall.

Detached from the palace, standing alone in the grounds, was a high, square brick tower, the highest building in Milan, and from the summit there floated night and day the banner of the Viper.

Along the second storey of the palace ran the open arcade or corridor, a wide and pleasant walk, paved with black and white stone, looking on the garden through the clustered columns that supported it, richly ornate with carvings.

A private entrance to Visconti's rooms opened on to this corridor.

The banqueting hall gave upon it also, and to Valentine Visconti, standing between the arches looking from the fair garden back to the closed doors, a thought occurred.

In her wild intention to escape, she had only one ally, Adrian, her page, feeble and powerless at best, but devoted to her with an utter devotion that might be worth much.

Valentine had confided in him, since she must have help, if only the help of speech; and now, of a sudden, his use appeared.

She had withdrawn from the observation of her women and the court, in pretence of praying for her brother's safety, and no one was with her.

'Adrian!' she called softly, 'Adrian!' She had privately bidden him follow her, and well she knew he was not far away.

The boy came forward eagerly.

'Hush!' said Valentine. 'Do not speak – listen – I have need of thee; wilt thou serve me even to the death, for it may be that.'

'You know I do not heed death, lady,' replied the page with glad pride. 'Anything that may serve you will make me for ever happy.'

"Follow me,' said Valentine, and stepped on to the balcony. 'Now walk behind, and as if I were not speaking to thee. There may be sharp eyes upon us in the garden.'

The sun, late as it was, fell between the pillars in strong bars of gold, and Valentine raised her ivory fan as if to shield her from the heat, but in reality to conceal the movement of her lips, in case there might be watchers.

'I must procure an entrance to my brother's rooms,' she said, speaking low over her shoulder: 'They are locked. No key will fit them. I cannot force the entrance in the palace. Still I *must* enter. You are listening, Adrian.'

'With all my soul, lady!'

Valentine kept her eyes upon the garden; there was no one there to see. The tower was not as yet finished, and so uninhabited; the garden itself was empty; still Valentine kept her gaze before her and spoke without turning her head.

'At any moment the Duke may return; or, if he does not, there will be sore confusion I cannot cope with; it must be done.'

They had traversed almost the whole length of the corridor, and Valentine suddenly stopped.

'There, this door,' said Valentine, 'into the Duke's rooms, Adrian,' and she rested her hand against it as she spoke.

It was a folding door, opening in the middle, firmly bolted from the inside, and appeared as hopeless as the great entrance to the suite within the palace, though unguarded.

Either side of it were deep-set, circular windows, ringed round and round with carving and ornamentation, placed too high to reach and too small to gain admission by.

The door itself was of wood, as firm and heavy as iron, clamped with gilded metal, and immovable to the touch.

'Does it look hopeless,' whispered Valentine.

Adrian would not have said so for his life.

'You would force it,' he asked eagerly.

'Yes, hush!' Valentine leaned through the low arch and looked into the garden; as before, all was quiet; the life and bustle of the palace came through the front today, awaiting news of the absent Duke.

She turned again with glistening eyes.

'Yes, I would force it – and I will show you how, Adrian.'

Half-way up the door, deep set in the thin and delicate foliage of the carving, were two circular windows, one in each panel.

'Can you reach them?' asked Valentine. 'I am a hand too short.'

By means of standing on the base of one of the side pillars of the door, Adrian could easily touch the whole span of the glass.

'Now, do I break it,' whispered the page.

'Yes,' returned Visconti's sister. 'But wait, there may be some soldier on hidden guard.'

She looked around cautiously.

'I see no one,' she continued. 'Now, only through this one arch canst thou be noticed from the garden, and there I will stand, with my open fan; now quick – thy dagger handle.'

She turned her back to him and raised her hand against the stonework of the arch, her mantle so falling over her arm that anyone, looking thither, could have seen nothing save her figure.

Adrian leaned forward and struck the glass a violent blow with the handle of his dagger; it was hard, and resisted, but at a second blow shivered. The page tore away the metal framework, and slipping his arm through, thrust back the first bolt. But it was fastened in three places, and the other two were not so easy. Straining up to his full height, the page forced half his body through the broken window and succeeded in slipping back the second bolt; the third was almost at the bottom of the tall door, nor was the opening he had forced large enough for him to do more than admit his arm and shoulder through. He still held his dagger in his hand, and grasping it at the end of the blade, struck violently downward at the bolt head with the handle. It did not move the first time, nor the second, nor the third; but at the fourth blow it suddenly shot back and the door was open. Adrian struggled through the window, backward, on to his feet, his hand and arm torn in several places, dizzy with the strain.

Valentine turned with a glad cry.

'Now stand thou in the archway,' she said; 'and.close the door behind me and keep watch; our one need is haste!'

The page pushed the despoiled door open and

Valentine sped through, closing it carefully after her; the broken window would not be noticed from the garden, but an open door might. The space she entered seemed so dark after the bright glare outside that at first she could see nothing.

But soon the light sufficed to show Valentine this was not the room she wanted.

It was gorgeously decorated, frescoes covered the walls, the ceiling was richly gilt and painted, the floor glass mosaic, the furniture florid and ornate.

Valentine glanced around hurriedly: at one end was a door, and trying it, she found it opened easily, leading into another splendid apartment – still not containing what she sought.

Hastening on through a door, not only unlocked, but standing ajar, she found herself in a small, sombre room, hung with purple and gold; its principal furniture the secretary's table, Visconti's chair, and the imposing black carved bureau.

This was the room she wanted; and on the bureau, flung down in haste, a bunch of keys.

Valentine seized them with trembling hands; they were the keys of the drawers, and one by one she flung them open, so possessed with excitement she could hardly stand. Gian was not in the palace, yet she seemed to feel his eyes upon her; to hear his step; catch his low whisper of her name; feel his touch upon her shoulder.

In one drawer were the parchment passports, some of them, for convenience, already signed with Visconti's name. Hastily Valentine thrust three into the bosom of her dress. But where were the palace keys?

She turned over the drawers in reckless haste; she found Visconti's seal and one of his signet rings, and slipped them both into her gown – still she could not find the keys. The Duke's pass-keys that unlocked every door.

The seal and the parchment were much – but the keys would be everything. They were not within the bureau; she rifled it once again – no, they were not there.

She turned away in vexation, and stood a second irresolute.

These rooms, deserted, yet so full of their owner, were terrifying. Valentine was sick with fear – still, she must have those keys.

Hastily she turned over every article in the room, left as Visconti had left them – books, papers, ornaments.

There were no keys there.

She looked into the antechamber, that was bare and empty; she knew it too well to suppose what she sought could be hidden there.

In desperation she retraced her steps and stood again within the second room. An impulse made her lift the arras, and she beheld another door; and another still; they were either aside Visconti's empty seat. She tried one: it opened immediately on a black marble stairway, and she closed it again with a thrill.

Frantically, she opened the other door; held to her courage desperately, and crossed the threshold. The room was panelled in black and scarlet, floor and ceiling inlaid with gold and black.

A great mirror hung opposite the door; either side a table, covered with a collection of articles left in utter confusion.

Valentine turned them over in frantic haste; there were laces and rings, jewels and curios, gloves, and strangely carved bottles. She handled the last carefully – she knew not what they might contain.

Still there were no keys.

Valentine, fast losing nerve, felt that she had been in these rooms for hours, the silence and suggestion oppressed her till she could have screamed – but she had risked too much to retreat.

There was an inlaid bureau, and a coffer beneath it; she opened the bureau and sought again; rings, daggers, treasures from della Scala's collections, uncut gems, powders, scents, rosaries, charms, missals – only no hint of what she looked for.

On top of the coffer was a roll of drawings, the plans of the new church, several parchments, petitions, specimens of marble from the new quarries, carvings, mail gauntlets – Valentine swept them off on to the floor, and then threw the coffer open.

It was full of clothes – upon the velvet of the topmost mantle lay the small bunch of master-keys.

Valentine grasped it, and hid it in the little pocket at her side.

She had all she needed now, and was turning in relief to go, when, struck by another thought, she bent again over the coffer, lifted the contents out on to the floor.

Visconti's doubtlets were mostly too splendid for her purpose, but she seized the plainest, wrapped it in her mantle, snatched one of his daggers from the table. Then making rapidly through the rifled room, with a breathless prayer of gratitude for safety, she stealthily pushed open the door on to the balcony, and saw the sunlight and her page's eager face.

'Shut the door,' she whispered. 'Climb up and shut the top bolt.'

The boy obeyed.

'No one has been.'

'No, lady; you have been quick.'

'Quick!' gasped Valentine. 'I thought I had been years.'

She unclasped her mantle and gave it to the boy. 'Take that back to my room – say I was too hot – give it to Costanza – she alone is in my confidence, as thou knowest; let no one stop thee – and listen – by tomorrow we shall be outside the gates.'

The page turned away with her mantle on his arm, and Valentine leaned against the wall, and with her hand upon her heart, took a moment to steady herself; then with excited eyes, but even steps, she too walked slowly along the balcony toward the banqueting hall.

* * *

'The Duke has not returned,' said de Lana.

He spoke a little anxiously, and looked around at the others who filled the council chamber, a few nobles, and the principal captains of the army and the mercenaries who defended Milan.

'Meanwhile, from whom do I take my orders? Who commands in Milan?'

'I cannot answer you, my lord,' said Giannotto. 'The Duke left no orders, at least with me.'

'The Duke expected not to be gone so long,' said Martin della Torre. 'And ill it will be for him if he stays *too* long.'

'Meanwhile,' cried de Lana again, 'to whom are we to look?'

The two pages announced the Lady Valentine.

The men glanced at one another.

'The Lady Valentine,' repeated Giannotto to de Lana. 'She may tell us what to do.'

Not that he did not well know what terms of jeopardy

she stood on with the Duke – but it was a shifting of responsibility that he welcomed.

All in the room rose to their feet to greet Valentine.

She was leaning on Orleans' arm, Adrian and her women following.

She looked regal, glorious. There was a fine colour in her cheeks.

De Lana kissed her hand. She did not wait for him to speak, her eyes wandered over the assembled faces.

'I have not come before, my lords,' she said, 'because I thought the Duke might at any moment be again among us; but now, hearing you were gathered here and that there was some question of the Duke's pleasure in his absence as to who should issue orders for him, I am come to answer it in person.'

She drew nearer the head of the table, Orleans dropping a step behind.

'My lords, the Duke left me in power; in any absence he may make, enforced or at his pleasure, I rule Milan.'

'You, lady!' cried Giannotto, the words forced from him in his great surprise.

'I,' answered Valentine. 'Though I am no man – I am a Visconti. Has not the Duke left me in charge before, de Lana?'

She turned to the captain as she spoke.

'In the late war with Florence – yes, lady,' Valentine smiled.

'Still, I need not ask you to believe me on that only – lest any should be doubtful, I have proofs.'

'Methinks they are needed before we take the law from thee, lady,' said Martin della Torre, roughly.

Valentine looked at him. 'What is this, Lord della Torre?' she replied.

And she laid Visconti's signet ring and seal upon the table.

Giannotto choked his wonder back.

'Does the Duke give these to any save those he trusts – and these?' She showed the keys lying on her open hand: the key of the armoury, the treasury, the prisons: the master-keys of the whole palace.

'He gave them to me – when, Adrian?'

'Yesterday morning, lady.'

'Yesterday morning. Had he not left too hastily even for speech, he would have made it public; doubtless he thought you would accept my word – and these proofs.'

There was silence.

'Are you convinced, lords?' asked Valentine.

'I am,' said Giannotto, bowing to hide the twinkle in his ugly eyes; and the others, each according to his fashion, murmured an assent.

'And now I will take upon me my brother's duties,' continued Valentine. 'For you, de Lana, I have no commands; only look well to the arming of the walls, let not my brother say we were idle in his absence; I would have the soldiers in readiness to guard against a surprise – and meanwhile I ask your company.'

De Lana bowed.

'On a visit to della Scala's wife. She is a priceless hostage, and ill would it suit with our safety even if aught befell her.'

'You would visit her yourself, lady?'

'Aye, myself, since with me lies the power and so the responsibility, and I would not shirk it. Lords,' she continued generally, 'we can do little else but wait – only hold yourselves in readiness – for the Duke's sake and the honour and security of Milan!'

She put her hand on Orleans' arm again and left the room, followed by de Lana and Giannotto.

'Now, I had almost forgot, my lord,' she said, pausing with a smile. 'My page, his sister and his brother, would leave Milan tomorrow for Brescia – what for, Adrian? Indeed, I have forgot – but I have the Duke's permission, and would only ask your countersign upon this passport.'

She spread before the captain a parchment bearing Visconti's signature.

'This is no time to be leaving Milan, boy,' said de Lana.

'Our father is sore sick at Brescia,' returned Adrian. 'Dying, my lord.'

De Lana smiled.

'A long and dangerous journey to make for a sick father.'

'There is money in the matter for these children, and it is my pleasure,' said Valentine.

De Lana bent over the parchment, and affixed his name, and in that second, Valentine glancing at Giannotto, their eyes met, and the secretary understood. He had meant to hasten to Visconti's rooms; he meant not to now. De Lana gave the parchment back, and Valentine handed it to Adrian.

'And now, Lord Orleans, will you come with us to Isotta's prison?'

'Truly,' said de Lana, 'the lady is as firmly guarded as at any time. I have looked to that.'

'Desperation is a great sharpener of the wits, my lord,' smiled Valentine Visconti. 'When life and liberty are at stake, the weakest will venture – and accomplish much.'

'Indeed, I think with the lady,' put in Giannotto, 'that too much zeal cannot be shown for anything so near to the Duke's heart as this.'

De Lana shrugged.

'We will go, lady.'

Half an hour later Giannotto and the captain waited in the guard-room of Isotta's prison.

Valentine, one of her women and the page, had entered the prison itself. The Duke's signet had passed through all the formidable barriers. It was late, almost dark.

'This shows a malice in the lady I do not like,' said de Lana.

'What need she to triumph over her brother's victim?'

'She is a Visconti,' returned the secretary. 'She has something of the Duke's temper and his strangeness – there may be in it curiosity also.'

'Curiosity?'

'To behold for herself if Isotta d'Este be as fair as she is – to spy into her brother's treatment of his prisoners.'

'Have you seen the lady, my lord?'

'I? Never,' replied de Lana. 'Nor do I greatly care to,'

Giannotto made no reply; he felt unusually placid and content. He saw plainly enough that Valentine was out-witting her brother, and as he hated the Duke and admired his sister, he would help her with all his power as long as he ran no risks. Visconti had not left *him* in charge – and for asking no untimely questions, Valentine would reward him well.

With some excitement he awaited her return.

'She is a long time,' said de Lana impatiently.

'She has her brother's daring,' thought Giannotto. 'And yet – she would hardly dare that – hardly.'

The door of Isotta's prison was opened and Valentine came out, followed by her attendants – dark-cloaked fig-ures keeping in the shadow. Adrian closed and bolted the door behind them as she slowly stepped down into the room.

'The prisoner is sick,' said Valentine. 'Not dangerously so, I hope; we would not have her die in my brother's absence. She has fallen asleep and must not be disturbed. Where is her woman?'

Luisa shuffled forward.

'You will not rouse your prisoner until my return with a physician,' she continued. 'She sleeps. I will return or send; till then let no one pass those doors, nor you yourself.'

The page and Valentine's two women still stood on the steps in the shadow.

'Come,' said Valentine suddenly. 'Much as I am relieved to see my brother's hostage in such security, this is gloomy, dark – come, Costanza.'

The two ladies moved forward, one weeping sadly, keeping her hands to her face.

'The poor lady hath unnerved her,' said Valentine with a sharp word of reproof, and she crossed to Orleans.

'Now it seems to me,' said de Lana to Giannotto, 'that only one lady entered with the Princess.'

'Your eyes deceived you,' smiled Giannotto. 'I am trained to watch; I saw two enter.' De Lana was silent. The two ladies had joined the few others left by the outer door, the soldier kept his eyes upon the one who wept.

Valentine was talking gaily to Orleans, and led the way across the garden. 'On your life I charge you to guard the prisoner,' she said to the captain and the soldiers. 'She means more to the Duke than his own life almost – more certainly than any other,' she added meaningly.

De Lana, watching keenly, still kept his eyes, as they crossed the garden, upon that second lady, who puzzled him, and with a soldier's indiscretion he whispered his fears to Giannotto.

'My Lady Valentine,' said the secretary smiling, 'my lord here thinks you entered the prison with one lady and came out with two!'

Valentine laughed.

'And who, think you, was my second woman, then, lord? Isotta d'Este? Nay, I will satisfy you.'

'Indeed, lady,' began de Lana hastily, but Valentine cut him short.

'Come here, Costanza.'

The girl came forward.

'Now hold the torch higher, Adrian,' laughed Valentine.

The light fell on Costanza's face.

'Is that Isotta d'Este, Giannotto,' she asked.

'Nay,' smiled the secretary.

'Now, Giulietta, come hither thou,' said Valentine.

The other lady stepped forward and threw back her hood.

'Now, my lord, Giannotto shall satisfy you – is this Isotta d'Este.'

The secretary did not flinch.

'My lord,' he said, 'you must know della Scala's wife well enough, if by hearsay only. Look yourself. This is not she.'

They moved on again, de Lana uneasily convinced.

'*Ma foi*,' said the silent Orleans suddenly. 'It is growing very damp. These Italian nights are most unhealthy.' And so they passed into the palace.

That night a light tap was heard by Giannotto, sitting in his room, and Adrian entered and put two emerald earrings and a bag of ducats on the table.

'For a lapse of memory,' he whispered, and went as softly and as swiftly as he had come.

XXI

THE DUKE'S RETURN

Having succeeded so far, Valentine had little fear; it was now an almost easy matter for her to accomplish the remainder of her plan.

She had the palace keys in her possession, and they unlocked secret doors, and more than one hidden entry and private way, entries and ways she knew well, and yet otherwise could not have used.

Soon after that dawn that saw Carrara fall by the wayside, Isotta d'Este and Valentine slipped from the palace; aided by Costanza, and joined by Adrian in the long gallery, they passed through the secret door that led through winding passages to the old part of the building, and thence by another entrance almost beneath the walls themselves.

Valentine wore a page's suit, her upper lip darkened, a heavy cloak, with a hood such as was worn in travelling, drawn about her, and by her side Visconti's dagger.

Despite her anxiety, her passionate desire to frustrate her brother's tyranny, her wild eagerness to be free and outside Milan, Valentine almost enjoyed the part that she was playing; she swaggered more than Adrian, and looked with some scorn on the weakness of Mastino's wife, who wept with her happiness.

The thought of Gian's rage and discomfiture was very sweet to Valentine, almost as sweet as the thought of Conrad in della Scala's camp, and the happy life of freedom coming.

Rapidly they traversed the narrow street that led to

the gate, Valentine erect and joyful, Isotta leaning on her arm, happy too, with a deeper happiness, but faint and bewildered from her long imprisonment, nervous and fearful of every sound.

Behind them strode Adrian, with eager eyes and swelling heart – the Lady Valentine had smiled on him!

But the lady's thoughts were not on the page. With every step to freedom, Count Conrad's blue eyes and merry laugh rose before her the more clearly, and she remembered that last time she had essayed escape, and he had near given her, for all he knew, his life. He was in della Scala's camp.

But, hasten as she might, Isotta dragged her on yet faster. Her eagerness was pitiful to see; Valentine looked down at her white face and trembling lips, and with a sudden impulse stooped and kissed her.

It was still so early that the streets were empty, save at the gate where the soldiers clustered, but they took small heed, for the three looked no unusual figures.

'Now the passports,' whispered Valentine. 'Adrian must show them, but do ye stand ready, Isotta, to answer if they question. I dare not, lest they know my face. Remember, Adrian, an escort meets us half a league away, and 'tis a quiet village that we travel to.'

Isotta d'Este steadied herself against the wall, and grasping Valentine's hand, followed Adrian toward the soldiers on guard.

'Stand to thy part now, Adrian,' said Valentine; 'remember 'tis our lives.'

A growing knot of men stood outside the guard-room; there seemed to be some great excitement; ringing orders, loud talk, increasing bustle. No one took heed of the three, nor even noticed them, and only after a delay at which Isotta's heart sickened could Adrian find an officer to whom to show the passports.

He glanced them over hastily. 'They seem to be in order,' he said, then suddenly turned to the woman of the three:

'What do ye do leaving Milan, mistress, when the country is in arms, with no escort save two boys?'

She hesitated, and Valentine stepped forward quietly.

'Our father is sick,' she said, 'and 'tis a pressing question of inheritance. Our kinsfolk promise us an escort.'

The officer shrugged his shoulders.

''Tis your own lives,' he said. 'Later in the day ye can go. Not now. There is an army coming, and the Duke in front of it.'

Valentine stood still and calm.

'Our father is very ill,' she said; 'if we are not in time, we may be beggared. Our passports were signed by the Duke himself. We demand to go.'

But the officer had hardly heard her. A fresh detachment of soldiers had ridden up, and the man's thoughts and eyes were engaged in half a dozen places.

Half mad, Isotta sprang forward, shaking off Valentine's restraining hand.

'We must pass, we must through this moment,' she cried. 'Let us through, and we'll make it worth thy while.'

At the eagerness of her tone the officer turned, surprised.

'Ye are very anxious,' he said.

'For the love of Heaven, a matter of life or death!' said Isotta, and in her despair she would have knelt, only Valentine dragged her back beside her.

'It is very serious,' she said. 'After the Duke has

entered, we may leave,' she asked. 'Indeed, ye cannot stay us.'

'Aye, leave after the Duke has entered, but now, clear yourself away; my lord comes apace, some allies with him –' and with a wave of his halberd he swept them back.

Valentine flushed at his tone, yet drew back, her hand on the page's shoulder.

But Isotta struggled free and again rushed forward.

'I will pass!' she cried wildly. 'I will! I have not got so far to be stopped now!'

'Oh! thy madness!' murmured Valentine.

But Isotta had rushed to the very gate itself; and was only forced back by the pikes at her breast.

The officer looked at the group with mistrust.

'What is this?' he said. 'What means this passion?'

'She is half distraught,' said Valentine. 'Beggary is no small matter, messer. We will be quiet, though, I promise you, until the Duke is past –' And to Isotta at her side she whispered, holding her hand tight, 'Thou wilt ruin all; control thyself.'

But the unfortunate Isotta was calm enough now; she followed Valentine without resistance.

And now Carrara's army had reached the gates, and fell back to await Visconti. The whole city was in tumult, the streets filling with excited people; there was mad shouting, the clash of arms. 'A Visconti! A Visconti!'

'We shall be crushed to death,' said Adrian. 'I must find you shelter, lady,' and he looked around eagerly.

'The Duke – the Duke!' and the great gates began to open.

'It is useless!' cried Valentine, 'and as well die this way as another.'

'There is a door here,' said Isotta; and turning with difficulty, they saw indeed a door, deep set in the wall and closely shut.

In desperation, Adrian knocked loudly. 'A Visconti!' shouted the soldiers. 'A Visconti!'

They were fast being hemmed in by the crowd, soldiers were pouring through the gates in companies, strange soldiers, the new allies; and as Valentine beheld them in strength and numbers, and heard them shout her brother's name, she felt her last desperate throw was lost.

'A Visconti!'

'Knock on the door again,' cried Isotta, 'knock again.'

Cavalry was passing, going at a trot, so close the hoofs were almost in their faces, the foam flew over their mantles.

Then in wild confusion they pressed back against the door; passing close, a host of pennons waved from glittering spears, the tossing of horses' heads, the champing of their bits, a clamour of noises, deafening shouts, a hurry of the cavalcade, and then – suddenly a horse drawn up close to the shrinking group in the shadow of the doorway, and a rider looking down at them.

Wild with terror, Isotta flung herself against the door, which yielded. Valentine looked up at the man who had stopped – saw her brother's face.

'Ah, my sister,' he said between his teeth; and Valentine, scarce knowing what she did, fled after Isotta, the page behind, closing the door upon Visconti.

In the pleasant courtyard was a girl, dressed in scarlet, who rose, surprised at their disordered aspect.

''Tis only a moment gained,' cried Valentine, hoarsely. 'He will follow!'

Isotta turned to Graziosa in an agony. 'For the love of Heaven hide us – for the love of Heaven, from Visconti!'

'Hide us!' said Valentine bitterly. 'Hide us from Visconti!'

And Graziosa thought of the secret passage.

'I will help you,' she said. 'I and my father do not love Visconti –'

'Quick, maiden,' cried the page. 'I see the spears are motionless outside. I will guard the door.'

'They will kill thee,' cried Isotta. 'Thou art too young,'

But Valentine turned to the boy and gave him her beautiful hand. 'Guard the door, gain us a moment, Adrian – for me,' she said, and hurried across the sunny courtyard, followed by Graziosa and Isotta.

'For me!' repeated Adrian, and set himself before the door proudly, with flashing eyes and dagger drawn. He was only a boy, a page, she a princess, but he could set his life against her smile, and think himself well paid.

Graziosa, panting with excitement, hurried them into the house, and into the lower room from which the secret passage opened. The pleasant little home was still half dismantled from the recent attack of the Germans, the neat trimness of the cool chambers gone.

At their entrance Agnolo came forward in alarm, but at his daughter's hurried explanation, turned willingly to the secret door he kept well concealed. For the little painter took no thought of what it must mean to shelter any from Visconti's wrath.

'Quick!' cried Valentine imperiously. 'How long can one page keep that door?'

'The poor boy!' moaned Isotta, hanging half lifeless upon Valentine's arm. 'Unhappy boy – they will kill him!'

Valentine looked at her with scorn.

'Canst thou think of a page now?' she cried. 'Think of della Scala. Quick!'

But the door would not yield, and while Agnolo struggled with the spring, a crash was heard, a cry, the ring of armour and the tramp of feet.

'The door is down,' said Valentine. 'We are lost.'

'I cannot move the spring,' cried Agnolo.

'Quick! quick!' shrieked Graziosa, but even as she spoke, the chamber door burst open and a man stepped in; there were others at his heels, but he entered alone.

Agnolo, starting back, dropped his concealments into place and trembled for his secret and these poor folk who had not escaped Visconti.

The man who entered was in black, it was all that could be seen in the dark, disordered chamber, but Valentine needed no light to tell her who it was. Isotta sank to the ground, shrieking wildly.

'Oh, Father, Father!' cried Graziosa, agonized, 'save them!'

The newcomer laid his hand on Valentine's shoulder, she standing calm and erect, and turned his face to Graziosa.

'From me,' he said, and his voice was very sweet. 'From me, Graziosa.'

'Ambrogio! Ambrogio!' cried the girl. 'What do *you* here?'

Valentine would have spoken scornfully, but Visconti turned his eyes on her, and she dared not. The courtyard was full of armed men.

'Ambrogio!' repeated the painter in dismay. 'What does this mean?'

Visconti laughed pleasantly, but his hand tightened on his sister's shoulder.

'It means thy daughter hath found a lover worthy of her in Visconti.'

Visconti! As in a flash the little painter saw explained a thousand things that had perplexed him. Visconti! His quickly working brain had grasped it and summed it up before Graziosa could even realize she heard aright. She stared there silent, with a piteous look upon her face. Visconti turned to his prisoners.

'Take Isotta d'Este back to her prison,' he said, curtly, and a group of soldiers advanced.

Isotta clung to Valentine in an agony.

'At last!' said Visconti, in her ear, 'at last thy calm fails thee!'

And then he stood aside watching, while she implored in turn Valentine and Agnolo to save her, in incoherent words of anguish.

'I cannot bear it!' she cried. 'I have borne it too long! O God, have pity on me! Have pity on me, I have not the courage to face it again. I have not the courage!'

Visconti turned to her in a savage triumph of hate he scarcely troubled to conceal.

'Find thy courage again, where thou found'st it before,' he said. 'Thy husband is not dead, although he leaves thee to pine in prison. He may remember thee even yet.'

Isotta sprang up at the taunt, wild-eyed.

'Keep thy face away from me!' she shrieked. 'Ye have slain him! Kill me too!'

Then, seeing resistance useless, and those who would have saved her helpless, della Scala's unhappy wife surrendered quietly; only as she crossed the courtyard with her guard, and saw the tree-tops wave above the walls and the sky that was outside Milan, a cry rose that made the hardened soldiers wince.

'Mastino! Oh, Mastino!'

Visconti watched her out of sight, then turned again to Graziosa, his hand still on his sister's shoulder.

'Graziosa,' he murmured.

But the girl made no answer; she was huddled on the bench that ran along the wall, looking out with frightened eyes.

As he spoke she shuddered, and crouched closer to the wall.

But Agnolo answered, and Visconti, serene in his pride, did not notice the painter's tone.

'My daughter is dazed with her surprise, lord, as who would not be? Graziosa, speak to the Duke, speak to thy Ambrogio,' and he gripped her hand fiercely. But Graziosa rose at his touch, and snatching her hand away, fled from the room, with one wild look toward Visconti.

'Ye see, my lord, she is bewildered, she can scarce believe it true –'

'It matters not for now,' said Visconti. 'Thy daughter loves *me*, painter, and none the less, I doubt not, that I am Duke of Milan; and she shall be my duchess, as I have vowed.'

'Truly the honour is more, I think, than she can bear,' and Agnolo bowed to the ground.

'I have won a wife for myself – a wife who loves me for myself alone.'

'And she loves thee for what thou art not,' cried Valentine aloud.

But Visconti took no heed of her.

'Think of thy daughter as a precious charge, Agnolo,' he continued. 'Meanwhile I leave one of my captains here on guard. That last attack on thee and thine came near costing me too dear.'

'My daughter –' began the painter, but Visconti interrupted him:

'Thy daughter will be my wife, painter; remember it, and heed her safety. And thou, Valentine, come with me, and I will tell thee in private how Count Conrad's folly lost della Scala thy dear brother, and gave me the day – and an army,' He turned to go; Agnolo made an impulsive movement forward, but checked himself.

'Tell Graziosa,' said Visconti, 'she is my duchess on the day my sister weds the Duke of Orleans.'

Visconti crossed the courtyard; the soldiers closed around him and his captive; Agnolo sprang forward, and drawing the little dagger he wore, hurled it after him.

It fell unheard, unseen, amid the trampling feet.

'Your hand – hurts me,' gasped Valentine, suddenly very white and trembling.

A soldier was pulling Adrian's dead body from the gate to allow of the Duke's passing, and she, dragged in his grasp, had almost stepped on him. This was what it had ended in – Adrian had flung away his life for nothing.

Visconti's voice broke upon her.

'Take this cloak to hide thy garb; I could not have Milan see thee thus – even if thou hast lost all shame.'

A ring of soldiers kept the crowd back, all the crowd the narrow streets permitted. The high morning sun sparkled on their halberds, spears, and armour; the dazzle of scarlet and gold from their trappings was blinding in its confusion, and Valentine hid her eyes – from that and the dead boy's face.

'A Visconti! A Visconti!' came the shout. The horses of the Paduans were champing impatiently, Visconti's charger reared between its holders-in.

'Now, where is my lord?' cried de Lana, riding up

breathless through the noise and glitter. 'I have been outwitted –'

'Hush!' said Visconti softly. 'I am here, de Lana – and so is she who outwitted thee,' and he pointed to the cloaked figure beside him. 'Take her ahead in secrecy, and swiftly, to the palace.'

The command and the movement were lost in the confusion. The horsemen were forming up behind Visconti, the walls and street crowded; from every distant window and housetop shouting spectators gazed on the gorgeous scene below.

Visconti drew his sword, and held its glittering cross high up against the sapphire sky.

'Now glory be to God, His angels, and Sant' Apollinare, my patron saint, that I am entered into my city again; and for my most miraculous escape, there shall be an altar of jasper and serpentine in the Lord's new church – and therein hear my vow!'

He lowered his sword and kissed the hilt, then turning in his saddle to the men who had followed him as their new leader: 'Have I not led you well, Paduans,' he cried, 'safe into the fairest city of Lombardy? Do you repent you of following a Visconti through the proud gates of Milan – Milan that I have made more beautiful than Ravenna, and stronger than Rome? I am your leader now, knights of Padua, and Gian Visconti never yet led to aught but victory or turned against a foe he did not crush! Once already have I trampled della Scala to the dust, and ridden through nine wide cities of his, and spoiled his palaces to pay my soldiers, with pay that men would die to win!

'I do not pay with ducats, Paduans, or measure my rewards with coin; follow me, and I will give you cities for your plunder, and nobles to hold for ransom. Like to the thunder will I circle Lombardy, and city after city shall surrender me its keys, and the meanest soldier in my train shall gain him fame and riches from my spreading greatness such as kings might envy! Now, who but a faint heart would follow della Scala, who lost into my hands his very wife? So long as there is a Visconti, he rules in Italy!'

Shout after shout, deafening, triumphant, greeted his words, the very air filled with the spirit of victory, the madness of triumph, the glamour of gold, the flash of scarlet, the high glitter of spears, that waved to and fro, the mad plunging of a thousand horses blinded with the dazzle of the sun; and from the throats of the thronging army, from the throats of the thronging citizens, one wild cry arose: 'Visconti! Visconti! Sant' Apollinare! Visconti and Milan! The Duke rides the city!'

XXII

THE SECRET PASSAGE

Standing on the steps of the old castle, della Scala looked down on his diminished army; at least they were purged of traitors, he thought grimly; what remained were Veronese, and true.

At the news of Carrara's treachery, d'Este had marched aside to Mantua, whither Vincenzo had been sent.

The sun was dazzling down, a glory of gold, sparkling on the still wet leaves, and the brilliant colours of the pennons and banners that floated above the tents.

Della Scala greeted Ligozzi and his son.

Tomaso would have spoken eagerly, but his father hushed him.

'The news is most important, my lord,' he said, 'best tell it you in private,' Then, unable to restrain himself, he added in a whisper: 'Oh, the saints and angels be praised, I think we have Milan!'

Mastino della Scala, as he led the way back to the castle, trembled, almost with awe. It was a sign from heaven.

As they gained the chamber, and Ligozzi closed the door, Tomaso burst out into his tale, half-crazy with delight.

'It seems you have success,' said Mastino quietly.

But he seated himself at the extemporized table, and with his hand shaded his face; it was almost more than he could bear.

'The passage leads into Milan,' said Ligozzi breathlessly. 'It is large enough to admit an army, and opens into the house of one who is our friend. That, my lord, is why we have been so long. The good fortune is miraculous, for we were brought out into the house of a man mad against Visconti, and thinking of nothing but revenge. He alone knows of this passage, and through it will admit your men.'

'Ah!' Mastino drew a deep breath and raised his eyes. 'God hath heard me, Ligozzi.'

'It was true,' cried Ligozzi. 'Oh, lord, he was indeed here. Only this morning he re-entered Milan, Carrara's army behind him; returned in time to stay his sister, who loathes her enforced marriage, and – and –' he suddenly faltered in his recital as Tomaso laid his hand upon his shoulder.

Mastino looked at them keenly.

'And what?' he asked.

'I was going to say, lord, that in his absence, Valentine Visconti, trying to escape, was recaptured by the Duke himself in this Agnolo's house.'

'Is it for that he hates Visconti?' asked della Scala.

'Nay, my lord, he hath other wrongs,' and Ligozzi proceeded to relate the tale the little painter had poured into his ears that morning.

'"Not for naught did I conceal that passage!" he cried to me. My lord, truly it was not for naught, seeing we shall thereby slay Visconti!'

'This man, Agnolo, he is to be trusted?' said Mastino.

'If ever man was! He would see Milan in ashes, and Visconti were among them.'

'And the girl?'

'I did not see the girl, but methinks she has the same cause to hate Visconti.'

'And that no one should know of this passage, it is

strange,' mused della Scala. 'Thou art sure there is no trap, Ligozzi? Much disappointment makes me wary.'

'I will stake my life there is no trap, my lord, and that this man, Agnolo Vistarnini, is dealing with the truth.'

'Vistarnini,' repeated Mastino. 'Methinks I know the name – a painter, didst thou say.'

'A painter, my lord; the house is near the western gate.'

'The western gate! I remember. It was the day I found von Schulembourg. Truly I think we may trust the man that I remember,' and Mastino faintly smiled. 'There is no guile in him – nor in his daughter, poor lady. She was happy then!'

'Visconti has left a guard of soldiers to protect the house; but not so many that they will not be easily disposed of. Vistarnini speaks them fair, they have no suspicion.'

Mastino rose and held out his hand. 'So thou hast done it, my friend, thou and thy son. I owe thee much, Ligozzi. A poor man's thanks are but a halting gift; some day, however, the Duke of Verona shall tell thee what his gratitude is worth, my friend. I thank God, Ligozzi, for one friend!'

* * *

In a thick wood near Milan, a man on a white horse was slowly picking his way through the dense undergrowth. The trees were close, and in their dark shadow the place was nigh as black as night.

Great tufts of flowers grew in the cool shadows. There were no signs of life, save the birds whirring through the leaves, the plants nodding in the breeze.

The rider dismounted, and tied his horse to the low bough of a large beech, flinging himself on the space of cleared ground beneath with a sigh. He wore a dress of peacock-coloured velvet, tumbled and torn, and, save for a richly jewelled dagger, more for ornament than use, was unarmed; but in the fight from which Count Conrad had just emerged, though a fight with two, weapons had not been needed; persuasion had done the work, and he had come out victorious.

In a bundle on his saddle hung his spoils, and as he discontentedly sucked the scratches on his wrist, he looked at them with interest and triumph.

Presently he fell to fingering his hair, then, sitting suddenly upright, drew his dagger with fine resolution. He seized the first of his long curls and severed it.

Grimly, not giving himself time to pause, he proceeded to the next, and one by one hacked them from his head, his beautiful blond, perfumed curls.

Conrad sighed as he saw them lying on the grass, and felt his shorn head. He longed for a mirror in which to see the extent of his disfigurement, but there was not even a pool near.

Disconsolately he arose, and detaching the bundle from the saddle, he laid it upon the ground and opened it.

It contained a monk's robe, a rosary, a book, a wallet, and a girdle.

Conrad opened the wallet, and found food therein, and he was growing hungry; but when he came to consider it, he sickened at its coarseness.

Scraps of fat, sour, hard cakes, mostly soaked in stale wine – the refuse of farmhouses.

'Have I parleyed with and robbed a begging friar?' cried the Count in high disgust, and flung the wallet far into the bushes.

'Food for hogs!'

Then with many sighs he removed the peacock-coloured doublet and hose, and donned the monk's garb, drawing the hood over his shorn head, tying the girdle around his waist.

The robe was rather short, and Conrad noticed with dismay that his laced white shoes showed beneath.

'Saint Dominick, curse him, but I forgot to take his sandals!' he cried in a passion.

But passion did not avail him; he must go barefoot.

'Bleeding feet will complete the disguise,' he thought bitterly, and flung off his shoes and stockings.

The robe was rather dirty; Count Conrad's fastidious nostrils fancied it smelled of the roadside, 'where the old wretch has often slept, I warrant,' he said, then crossed himself in contrition at the sacrilege.

Next he hung the rosary and crucifix about his neck – it was hatefully heavy – and the wallet about his shoulder. The strap galled him, and the wretched Count moaned at his fate.

He was bound to admit he had brought it on himself; he would carry it through; and with a truly heroic air he strapped the velvet doublet on the horse, and taking the bridle, made his way back toward the road.

On reaching it he flung the reins over the steed's back, and turned him adrift toward Brescia; then, with resolution in his heart and tears in his eyes, Count Conrad von Schulembourg, with feet bare on the stony road, made painful progress toward Milan.

XXIII

FOR LOVE OF AMBROGIO

It was early morning of the second day since Ligozzi had discovered the secret passage, and Milan lay peaceful, for in those two days there had been no fighting; but the calm was the lull before the storm.

Agnolo Vistarnini stood in front of the secret door, with shining eyes. The spring had just slipped back behind Tomaso, the last arrangements had been made; tonight della Scala should enter Milan – and he, Agnolo, would be the means.

Agnolo looked across the courtyard now in shadow to where a soldier kept his guard. The guard was the Duke's orders, and to the painter's face the soldiery showed all respect; yet well Agnolo knew they laughed at Visconti's whim, and shrugged their shoulders at the pale-faced girl who was to be Duchess of Milan. And the painter had heard their talk among themselves.

'It was likely enough for the Duke to amuse himself in disguise,' they said, 'but to marry a painter's daughter!'

'It were more reasonable had he dowered her to wed another, and yet 'tis of a piece with all his madness!'

'I would sooner see her dead,' thought the little painter, 'than Duchess of Milan, the Visconti's wife.'

The white agonized face of Isotta rose before him, the fierce rebellious hate that marred Valentine Visconti's beauty, and Visconti's own expression as he stooped to mock a woman in his power; the gallant heart of the little painter throbbed with wrath and honest fury against the tyrant who played with hearts, who thought the offer of a crown he had usurped atoned for crimes as black as hell.

'Tonight, tonight!' he murmured to himself as he mounted the stair to seek for his daughter. 'Tonight we shall both avenge the use of us to please a whim.'

He entered his studio; it was empty, the two pictures stood with their backs to the room. Agnolo looked at them grimly. How often had Visconti sat painting that St. Catherine, unarmed! How easy then to have struck him low! What would Lombardy have said!

'Graziosa!' he called. He was eager to tell her Tomaso had been again.

He never doubted for a moment that her love had turned, as his had done, to a passion of outraged pride.

'Graziosa!'

But no answer came, and Agnolo mounted the stair and entered her little chamber in the turret. It was circular, lit by three long windows, and now ablaze with the morning sun.

The walls were hung with painted linen, faded browns, and in each window stood a rough stone jar of lilies, drooping neglected in the sun.

Seated on the floor near one of them was Graziosa, her face buried in her hands, but at her father's entrance she raised her head and looked out of the window.

'Graziosa,' said Agnolo, and there, was a boyish triumph in his voice, 'Visconti dies tonight.'

She did not move.

'Tonight della Scala enters Milan; there is no chance of failure.'

'None,' she asked. Her voice was dull.

'None! Ah, Graziosa, Visconti roused more dangerous foes than he reckoned on when he played with me and thee.'

The girl moved impatiently; her father's words jarred on her senses.

'Father, I am tired,' she said wearily, 'and my heart is very sore –'

'Never fear, my daughter; tonight, tonight!'

Graziosa turned to him; her face was white and strained.

'But if – he – the Duke – should not be – be slain?' she said. 'He has a new army here in Milan.'

'Aye, but a surprise at dead of night is worth two armies to the others. The palace is near; Visconti will be in their hands even while he sleeps –'

'In della Scala's hands –' she breathed. 'That means, indeed – he – O God, it means Ambrogio dies!'

The last words were breathed so low Agnolo did not hear them, but he saw the pain on his daughter's face and came gently to her side.

'Forgive me if I pain thee, my dearest. God knows, if I speak lightly 'tis but to hide a bitter grief –'

But Graziosa interrupted him with a passionate cry and seizing his hands covered them with kisses.

'Take no heed of me!' she cried. 'I am half distraught – soon I shall be better.'

'After tonight there will be a shadow gone from off us, Graziosa, and not from off us alone.'

'There is no chance of failure?' asked the girl again.

'Comfort thyself – none.'

Graziosa said no more, and Agnolo turned to leave, for there were the soldiers still to hoodwink, but at the door his daughter called him.

'At what hour do della Scala's men enter?' she asked, in a low voice, her head still turned away.

'One hour after midnight,' returned the little painter.

'Della Scala leads them?'

'Della Scala himself,' said Agnolo, proudly. 'He is a noble prince.'

His daughter made no answer; long after the little painter had left her alone again she sat there listless in the sunny, silent chamber, listless, with her white face, leaning back against the window frame.

'There is no possibility of failure,' The words beat upon her heart till she thought it would break.

'Tomorrow he will be dead!'

She sprang to her feet with sudden energy; the sun was rising high – the time was short.

It was silent, maddeningly silent; Graziosa grew afraid of it – the silence and the sun; she wished she were dead; it came to her to kill herself, yet full well she knew that she had not the courage.

She twisted her damp, cold hands together; she wondered if she shut her eyes and leaped from the window she might die without knowing it, and nerving herself looked out.

But the stone courtyard seemed far away, hard and cruel, and she winced back again.

In her own heart she knew she was a coward, and wept to think it was so – wept to think she could not rise to act, in any way to act.

There was no tinge of greatness in Graziosa's soul; she would have gone through life, if unmolested, merry, gentle, sweetness and happiness itself, content always to stand aside for others, eager to do little kindnesses that came within her compass, never tempted because never seeing the temptation, happy in utter simplicity and ignorance; but a great moment found her wanting, a crisis she could not face; as she tried to think, right and wrong grew strangely confused. She only knew she loved Visconti, and that he was in danger.

She was too weak to kill herself, although she did not shrink from the cowardice of it, only from the pain; she was too weak to tell her father she still loved Visconti; she could not bear to see his face should she confess it; he would never understand.

'I will lock the door,' she said, with wild eyes, 'lock the door, and let no one enter till it is all over – and perhaps my heart will break,' she added pitifully.

Then she stood a long time, still with hands locked tight. Suddenly she turned and her robe caught the jar of lilies, throwing them into the room.

There they lay, faded by the heat, amid the broken jar, and Graziosa looked with unseeing eyes, and picked them up mechanically.

Opposite hung a mirror, and as she raised her head she saw herself reflected there.

The lilies dropped from her hands as they had dropped before in the street, the day Tisio took her bracelet.

'He would have made me Duchess of Milan!'

She drew nearer and surveyed her pale face closely.

'Duchess of Milan! And he had all Italy to choose from!'

The thought brought a flush to her cheek.

'His sister is very, very beautiful. I am not so fair as she, nor as della Scala's wife, and yet he thought me fit to share his throne –'

She moved toward the door with faltering steps.

'I must not think,' she moaned. 'I will lock the door – I will lock the door –'

But another thought struck her, and she quivered with her agony.

'He trusted me – he trusted us – he never questioned our faith!'

Then her heart rose in rebellion at her own weakness. Let Visconti be betrayed: why? What did she know of his crimes?

She could hear her father feasting the soldiers below, and thought of him restless and impatient for nightfall. He had never loved Ambrogio.

She listened and heard his voice in pleasant laughter with a triumphant ring in it, and a sort of rage rose in her heart.

'Who are we to save Milan from a tyrant?' she thought. 'Ambrogio is more to me than all the Milanese.'

She put her hand on the door handle.

'When would he have sent for me?' she wondered dully. 'He smiled. His voice was gentle; Ambrogio's voice! And he is Ambrogio, and – tonight, tonight –'

Her eyes fell on the long blue hooded cloak hanging on the wall near. She took it down and paused with it in her hand, looking at it with fixed eyes.

A bird flew past the window, sending a swift shadow across the floor.

Graziosa opened the door slowly and stepped out on to the stair. It was almost dark there; silently she closed the door behind her and wrapped the cloak about her, drawing the hood over her head and face.

Leaning over the stair rail, she saw that the door of the room below was open, her father's voice was silent: the soldiers had gone elsewhere. Softly she crept down into that pleasant chamber where Visconti had sat so often; the sunlight came in from the open door in a great band across the dark floor, falling on her white face as she moved through it and out into the yard. She saw there was no soldier by the door into the street. She opened it, she could see her father and the guard chatting over winecups by the sundial in the garden, they were not looking; she crossed like the shadow of the bird upon the floor. Her pet doves flew away at her guilty steps as if they did not know her, and Graziosa knew herself indeed changed from the one who had last fed them.

The bolt of the door would at first not move for her trembling fingers, but she did not stay here; in a second more she stood in the street, a closed door behind her. Graziosa would never see it open more.

The houses stood clear against a brilliant sapphire sky, and above them moved a silver banner, the banner of the Viper. It floated from the Visconti palace, and Graziosa, with no glance back, bent her steps in its direction.

XXIV

TREACHERY

The day that was to place Milan in the enemy's hands was wearing to a close; the sun had almost set in a wide sky, a flare of orange and purple, against which the chestnuts stood in rich dark.

Mastino della Scala and some few of his officers were standing in the little wood into which the secret passage opened.

Behind them the army was in readiness.

'I have wrenched success from the hands of failure!' cried Mastino, his eyes brilliant, a different man. He could have laughed aloud for joy; he would see Isotta tonight, he would keep his word; Visconti's palace was near the western gate, they would be upon him before he knew.

'There is no possibility of failure, Ligozzi; no possibility of treachery?' he said, eagerly, and pressed his friend's hands in his.

'None, lord; Vistarnini is to be trusted to the death.'

'Von Schulembourg's horse returned to camp this morning,' said Ligozzi. 'I know not where the Count is.'

'When I am in Milan I will find him; he shall wed the Lady Valentine; I bear him no bitterness. Ah, Ligozzi, the world will be a different place tomorrow.'

And Mastino leaned forward eagerly, waiting for the first sign of the return of Tomaso, who had been sent ahead to reconnoitre.

The sky flared and blazed through the trees till the whole world seemed on fire; the red clouds were reflected in della Scala's polished armour till it glowed in one bright flame, above which the plumes on his steel cap floated long and white.

The next second the glory faded and was gone, leaving the world cold and grey.

The sun had set.

A cold breeze stirred the leaves against the pale sky, but to Mastino, leaning against the tree trunk, waiting, no foreboding came. It was success, success – at last!

'Tomaso is long,' said Ligozzi.

'The way is long,' smiled Mastino. 'But not so long that we shall not enter Milan before dawn!'

The passage opened into the undergrowth from the wide mouth of a cave, and della Scala, in his eagerness, stepped forward into the shadow of its blackness, listening intently.

No sound broke the stillness save the little murmur of the wind, the occasional clank of the bridles of the idle horses.

'Hark!' cried Mastino. 'I hear him!'

He turned with shining eyes to Ligozzi.

'My friend, at last Heaven has heard!'

'He carries no torch,' said Ligozzi, wonderingly, for though footsteps ascended, no ray of light fell across the dark.

'He stayed not for torch,' cried della Scala. 'Bring up the men, Ligozzi!'

As he spoke, a figure forced itself out of the dark, a wild figure, and yet Tomaso's; his white face was smeared with blood which trickled from a great gash on his forehead, his doublet was rent and torn, and he reeled as hurt and spent.

'0 Mother of God!' muttered Mastino. 'Mother of God!'

Tomaso sank at his feet with a bitter cry.

'All is over!' he cried. 'We are betrayed. Oh, would I were dead before I had to tell thee!'

'Betrayed?' echoed della Scala. All the life was struck out of him, he steadied himself against the cavern wall and looked at the boy dully. 'Betrayed?'

'Betrayed? By whom,' cried Ligozzi. 'Ah, thou art hurt!'

'Nothing, nothing. I am in time – Visconti – his men guard the other entrance – with difficulty I escaped to warn thee,' gasped Tomaso.

'Who betrayed us?' demanded his father, his face dark with passion.

'The girl,' said Tomaso, bitterly; 'the girl who loved Visconti.'

'And Heaven favours her love and not mine!' The cry was wrung from Mastino. 'We are betrayed for a girl's love of Visconti. And my wife waits for me!' He laughed wildly, and drew a faded rose from the folds of his sash, flinging it on to the ground.

'Look, Ligozzi, a sign from Heaven – a sign I thought had been fulfilled. But a girl prayed for Visconti, doubtless, and her prayers are heard. Isotta must perish, but Visconti is saved! To mock, Heaven sends me a sign.'

He ground the rose to powder beneath his heel, and Ligozzi quailed at the wild anguish of his face.

'I should have known,' he cried. 'I should have known. I called on God and this is His answer. I will fight Visconti alone!'

He turned from the cavern to the open, and stepped out among the waiting officers.

'Back to camp!' he cried wildly. 'We are betrayed again, by a woman who loves Visconti! The Duke of Milan is fortunate; who would do the like for me?' And he flung himself down upon the bank, and sank to the ground.

'Leave us,' whispered Ligozzi. 'Leave us, all is over for tonight, the Prince and I will follow.'

'He is much moved,' returned one of the officers.

'All his hopes were on it,' said Ligozzi bitterly. 'His wife, his God.'

In disappointed groups the men moved off, to spread the evil news.

It was now fully dark, but not so dark that the three left by the cave could not see each other in the faint starlight.

Mastino called to Tomaso. His voice was hoarse and strained.

'Tell me all, boy; tell how it happened.'

'My lord,' faltered Tomaso, 'it is too painful.'

'Painful!' And della Scala laughed harshly. 'I am well used to that; tell me how it happened.'

He had risen, and standing in the shadow of the trees, only the outline of his great figure was visible to Tomaso and Ligozzi, standing a few paces before him.

'There is not much to tell,' said the boy uneasily; he was sick with disappointment and the pain of his wound and leaned heavily against his father.

'Agnolo opened the door to me – as had been arranged; he told me, with a wild face, his daughter was gone. Visconti had carried her off, he vowed. He was half-crazed, and ah, my lord, even as he spoke, the court-yard filled with soldiers, Visconti's soldiers. The girl had fled to the palace, and told the Duke all! We were betrayed!

'They laughed to see me there; vowed I should die a merry death, trusted you would follow and let them give you a warm welcome. Agnolo, they mocked with talk of pardon, for his daughter's sake, his daughter the

Duchess to be, whom Visconti had proclaimed to all his court, if he would tell them a little more of what you meant to do. But Vistarnini met them with defiance.

'"At least Visconti shall not claim us both!" he cried, and then they laughed and killed him. *That* was the Duke's word, they said, not pardon.'

Tomaso paused.

'And his daughter lives to be Duchess of Milan!' said della Scala. 'It is the will of Heaven!' He laughed again, harshly.

'I escaped while they argued over the poor painter's body, and they dared not follow, being in terror of an ambush. If it had not been for saving thee, I would I might have died!' And he sank his head upon his father's shoulder with heart-wrung sobs.

'Take him to the camp,' said Mastino, rising. 'How can I comfort him or thee, wanting it so much myself?' And he turned away through the trees.

The air was perfumed and soft, it fanned the heavy hair back from his face and rustled the flowers around his feet.

He walked fast, in a fury of hate. It came to him to rush into Milan, and die upon the soldiers' spears, if he might only get his hands upon Visconti. 'I will challenge him to fight, to single combat,' he thought madly. Then his mood changed, he stopped and felt for the locket at his neck.

'Isotta! Oh, my dear, my dear!' and his voice was full of tears.

XXV

In Cloth of Gold

Graziosa Vistanini, the saviour of Milan, and the Duke's betrothed, was lodged with regal state in the magnificent new tower that stood in the grounds of the Visconti palace. Visconti could be liberal to a fault where it suited his vanity or his purpose, and Graziosa's new residence was decorated with a lavishness that made the French stare.

For not only had she saved Milan, but she had done it solely for love of him, and it gratified Visconti's pride as much as it pleased his ambition. Save for this girl he had been now even as had been della Scala, and Milan humbled as Verona.

She had been the means of his once more outwitting a foe; she had assured his safety and the safety of his city; and Visconti's proud gratitude showed in the state and splendour with which he surrounded his chosen wife.

This glorious summer morning she was seated on the side terrace that surrounded the tower, a terrace of black marble and alabaster, the delicate balustrade smothered in lemon and myrtle trees and clusters of white roses.

Graziosa was in the midst of a brilliant company; the best-born dames in Italy were among her women, and more knights and pages composed her train than had ever waited on Visconti's sister.

Beneath them the garden, reached by a shallow flight of steps, spread in perfect loveliness to the palace, above whose pink brick walls and rugged grey fortifications floated the banner of the Viper.

The air was golden with the brightness of the sun, there was not a cloud in the purple sky, and Graziosa's heart was singing in pure happiness.

She rose from her chair impulsively, and walked to the edge of the terrace, leaning over the balustrade, the ladies behind her.

''Tis sad to think there should be fighting on such a day as this,' said one, handing Graziosa her fan. 'God grant it may soon be peace!'

'God grant it!' repeated the painter's daughter fervently.

'They say the Veronese cannot hold out much longer,' said another. 'This very morn there was news. Bassano has fallen —'

Graziosa picked a cluster of roses and buried her face in them.

'How beautiful they are!' she said. 'See, they have little hearts all gold, never showing till they die; a pretty fancy, is it not?' And she stroked them tenderly.

'Bassano has fallen?' she repeated idly.

'Yes, and 'tis said they cannot fail in getting Reggio.'

'Then my lord's arms are everywhere victorious!' cried Graziosa with sparkling eyes.

'As ever, lady,' was the answer.

'And we can hope for peace,' continued Graziosa softly.

'And when peace is proclaimed you will be Duchess — almost Queen — of Lombardy, Gian Visconti's wife!'

There was a note of envy in the speaker's voice at such a splendid destiny, but Graziosa did not notice it. She even shuddered faintly at Visconti's name; it had been associated with awe and terror too long for her to be able easily to shake the fear away.

'Meanwhile, the sun is shining hot, lady,' said a third attendant. 'Will you not come into the shelter?'

Graziosa moved away; the white roses at her bosom were not more pure than her face. Two pages lifted her rich train, and as she crossed the terrace a third came and spoke to her on bended knee.

'My Lord Giannotto awaits your pleasure, lady.'

'Tell him I am here,' and the colour rose in Graziosa's face at so much honour.

She turned to the steps where Giannotto waited, cap in hand, and advanced toward him.

'Lady,' said the secretary, bowing low, 'my lord sent me to say he will wait on you himself; and meanwhile, if you have any commands –'

Graziosa interrupted him.

'Indeed, my lord is too good; what commands should I have? Tell him so, with my deepest thanks, sir.'

Giannotto looked at her curiously, with a mixture of pity and wonder.

'He comes himself, lady, to hear your thanks, and learn your will.'

And he stepped aside, joining the group that had been gathered about Graziosa.

Gian Visconti was coming through the garden, a grave-looking man by his side, a white hound at his heels, and two boys following, one bearing a wooden case, the other carrying a roll of drawings.

Visconti was talking to his companion; he was in the best of humours, at the height of triumph and success, his enemies well under his heel, his ambitions on the point of being gratified.

Graziosa came to the head of the steps, and Visconti took his gold cap off and waved it, coming up them gaily.

She stood silent in the glory of the sunshine and held out her hands, and he kissed them, and looked at her and laughed pleasantly.

'Now art thou happy, *donna mia*?' he said. 'Hast thou all that thou couldst wish?'

'More than I ever dreamed of my lord,' she answered softly. 'I did not know the world could be so beautiful – or so happy,'

''Tis but a small return, Graziosa, my beloved, for what thou hast done for me,' returned Visconti. 'And I will make it more – this is but an earnest of the future. Visconti's wife shall live in such splendour that men shall not see her for its dazzle.'

'What am I, that thou shouldst give me so much joy!' cried Graziosa, with swimming eyes.

Visconti smiled.

'Thou art thyself – it is enough!'

He turned to his companion, who stood respectfully at some little distance.

'Come hither, Messer Gambera. Here is a lady who shall often pray within your church – my betrothed, who saved us Milan.'

Messer Gambera bowed low, and kissed the hem of her gown.

Visconti watched his homage with pleased pride, and turned again to Graziosa.

'Now I have somewhat to show thee. This is the architect of my new church, which shall be the wonder of Italy. Follow me, messer,' And he led the way into the entrance hall.

It was low and wide, the walls covered with frescoes, the floor red sandstone, the windows opening on to the terrace.

In the middle stood a gilt stucco table, and to this Visconti drew a chair and bade Graziosa seat herself.

'Here is what I will make of Milan, sweet, when the war is ended!' he said, as the architect unrolled and arranged his drawings.

'And will that be soon?' she asked, looking up at him.

'Aye, I hope so,' laughed the Duke. 'Mastino della Scala grows weaker day by day – I have Bassano, and shall have Reggio. He has lost his wits as well as his fortresses, for he bids me to a single combat: all to stand or fall by our own swords. He has his answer, and I have his wife. Now, look at these, Graziosa –' and he took the drawings from the architect and spread them on the table.

'My new church,' he said. 'The plans, my well-beloved.'

And he looked eagerly at Graziosa.

'Indeed, my lord, I do not understand them – it is no church, surely?' And she raised a sweet, bewildered face.

''Tis the plan of one. Messer Gambera will explain it,' and he motioned eagerly to the architect. 'Here, messer, this is the porch?' and he laid his finger on the drawing, absorbed in contemplation.

'Yes, my lord.'

'Set on three steps?'

''Tis so, my lord.'

'I do not care for that, messer, and I will have more carving – would you not, Graziosa?'

'You must not ask me; indeed I do not know,' she smiled.

Visconti's face for an instant darkened. 'You must learn,' he said. 'My duchess must know architecture. Take away the plans, messer; I will look at them alone.'

'Perchance the lady might care for the model, my lord?' returned the architect. He spoke bad Italian, and was shaking with nervousness.

'Bring the model,' replied Visconti, and the page placed the box upon the table.

Messer Gambera touched a spring and it flew apart, showing an exquisite little model of white marble, some twelve inches high.

'Oh! it is beautiful!' said Graziosa, and Visconti looked at her with sparkling eyes.

'You think so? Yes, it will be beautiful – the church of all Lombardy.'

'It will be like this, of marble?' she asked, breathless.

'Every inch – from the porch to the pinnacles, and the floor shall be precious mosaic, and the altars crystal and serpentine, jasper and amethyst; men shall spend their lives in carving one pillar, and the price of cities shall pay for the gold that shall be lavished on it. Not in our life will this be done, nor in the lives of those that reign after us – or even them that follow, but finished it shall be, and one of the wonders of the world – and I shall be remembered as he who planned it – to the glory of God and the house of Visconti!'

He turned with shining eyes to the architect, who gazed on him with admiration, with a face that reflected the speaker's own fervour.

'Yes, mine will be the glory, though I shall never see the pinnacles kiss the sky, or hear the Mass beneath that marble roof – mine will be the glory – even though I am not buried there, it will be my monument to all eternity!'

Graziosa gazed at him in silence: she could not understand. Gian glanced down at her with a smile.

'Would it not be a worthy tomb, even for a king, Graziosa?'

'For an emperor – but we will not talk of tombs, my lord,' she answered, 'but of pleasant things, and – and – of something that I have to ask you?'

'What?' smiled Visconti.

The pages had gathered up the drawings, and the architect had removed his precious model and withdrawn.

They were alone, and Graziosa rose and looked at Visconti a little timidly.

'I – I mean – there will be peace soon – you think, my lord?'

'I think so – but peace or war, it shall not touch thee, Graziosa.'

'Indeed, I do not fear it – but –'

She hesitated a moment, and glanced anxiously at Visconti's smiling face.

'Prince Mastino's wife – my lord –'

'What of her,' asked Gian, lightly. 'How does she trouble thee?'

'I fear she is in sad woe,' said Graziosa, encouraged by his tone. 'She will return to della Scala when the war is ended.'

Visconti laughed.

'The war will not be ended till she does, methinks; yet be comforted, Graziosa; before our wedding day she shall be in della Scala's camp – and the war over now think of it no more.'

'Indeed I am satisfied; and my father, my lord?'

'Now, can I help it and he will not come to the palace? My word on it, he is safe; think no more of that Graziosa. Now are you content?'

'My dear, dear lord, I am content: I will trouble you no more with questions. I am content to leave my father's safety in your hands – content.'

She laid her arms about his neck, and Visconti kissed the roses on the breast that crushed them against his golden doublet, and then her upturned face.

Through the open window came the distant sound of singing; someone was singing in French, and then a woman's laugh. Graziosa drew herself away, and Visconti's face darkened.

'Please Heaven, she will not annoy me long,' he muttered.

He took Graziosa's hand in silence and stepped out on to the terrace.

Seated on the steps was Orleans, playing with the red ribbons of his lute, and standing among the cluster of ladies at the foot of them was Valentine Visconti.

She looked very brilliant and beautiful, and angry and scornful; her laughter was bitter, and the veiled bright-ness of her eyes not pleasant.

The shade of Visconti's face deepened as he looked at her: compared to his sister, Graziosa was a candle beside the sun; the contrast did not please Gian.

Orleans rose and bowed low to the lady, yet in a way that was not respectful.

'So there has been a challenge from the enemy,' he lisped. 'Now I shall love to see a single meeting of brave swords again.'

'Who said so?' asked Visconti. He came slowly down the steps; his manner had quite changed, and his eyes were on his sister.

'The Lady Valentine,' said the Frenchman. 'She –'

'The Lady Valentine,' interrupted the Duke sternly, 'had best remember – what I have often remembered to her advantage – that she is a woman, and these affairs are none of hers.'

And he gave her a glance that made her wince, as that glance always did, for all her boldness.

Graziosa, her hand held lightly by the Duke, was following him down the steps, her pages behind, and Visconti kept his eyes upon his sister.

There was a meaning pause, and Orleans grew restless in the silence and moved away.

Valentine sent after him a look of bitter scorn, then walked slowly up to Graziosa and saluted her humbly, though her eyes were burning brightly.

Visconti watched them keenly, and noticed with displeasure how crushed and silent Graziosa showed before his brilliant sister: she shrank into herself; as if she divined the scorn Valentine concealed, and could scarce stammer a few words of greeting in reply.

'I must go back to the palace, Graziosa,' said Visconti, as they reached the garden, and his eyes roved over the crowd of attendants for Giannotto's figure. 'Remember these are all at thy commands – and, for the present, then farewell.'

To Valentine he said nothing, but turned away toward the palace with the secretary.

Graziosa looked after him, a little pained; she had noticed he was always different when his sister was there. Valentine had noticed it too, and guessed the cause, and the knowledge gave a triumph to her beauty that made it dazzling indeed.

'I fear I interrupted your discourse,' she said with another curtsey.

'Indeed no, lady,' replied Graziosa, timidly. 'Will you not come within with me from the sun?'

'Nay, that were too much of an honour,' said Valentine. 'Are you not my brother's promised wife – and the saviour of Milan.'

'I pray you, do not speak of it – I – I –' answered Graziosa hurriedly.

Valentine lifted her brows and opened her grey eyes wide. 'Do not speak of it? Why, 'tis a deed to be proud of – even when so well rewarded, lady.'

Graziosa flushed under the mock in her tone, and turned to one of her ladies.

'We will go in – alone – since the Princess will not come,' she said.

'Come and walk in the garden, madama,' said Valentine. 'At least it seems like liberty – there will be little enough of that when you are Duchess of Milan.'

Graziosa, looking at her with frightened eyes, joined her meekly, having not the spirit to refuse.

'Now, bid your ladies back a pace – at least Gian will allow us that,' and Valentine motioned them away.

'What do you mean?' faltered Graziosa, with a pang of something like envy, as she noticed the grace and dignity of Valentine's bearing, and the superb carriage of her queenly head.

Valentine shrugged her white shoulders and laughed bitterly.

'Many things – among them this – get yourself a better tirewoman and you will keep Visconti longer – learn a little spirit and you will keep him longer still.'

Graziosa glanced down at her dress, the richer of the two, but worn with no such grace.

''Tis no question of my dress, lady,' she answered, with some dignity, 'nor of beauty – but of love alone.'

Valentine looked at her curiously, scornfully. They

were passing between rich bushes of roses and lilies, the air was heavy with scent, and from the ladies following came gentle laughter.

'You think he loves you?' asked Valentine.

'I know it,' answered Graziosa, proudly.

Valentine smiled and looked away. The smile and glance stung Visconti's betrothed like a whip-stroke. 'What do you mean?' she cried. 'You insult me – you insult him!'

'Do you know Gian Visconti so very well?' asked his sister. 'Have you seen him torturing his prisoners with the slow torture of the mind – worse than any rack? Have you seen him lying and betraying, stealing and murdering?'

Graziosa looked at her wildly; Valentine looked strangely, as her brother could look, her voice was very like his.

'You know how his father died? How his mother's heart was broken?'

'I know you never raised a hand to save them – I know I love him!' cried Graziosa.

'Doubtless,' smiled Valentine with scorn. 'But does he love you? Why, he is so stained with crime I do not care to touch his hand. Would such a man love – you?'

'Some tales I have heard, but now I know them false,' said Graziosa, white and trembling. 'And I will hear no more.'

'She thinks he loves her!' murmured Valentine. 'She thinks Gian Visconti loves her!'

Graziosa was as near hate as was possible for her; her heart was too full for a reply, she called to her ladies and turned away. But Valentine followed, and laid her hand on her shoulder with what seemed a loving gesture.

'Tell Gian what I have said,' she whispered. 'It will be

an office to suit you, traitress!' and with a smile she turned away.

Graziosa walked slowly toward her tower; somehow the garden had grown dim, the sky was not so bright, nor the sun so brilliant; she was looking at them through a veil of tears, unshed and bitter.

'The Lady Valentine is not a gay companion today,' remarked one of her attendants, looking at her.

'No,' said Graziosa dully. Valentine's words were rankling in her heart; all the past came before her, all the tales she had heard of Visconti, all her father's tenderness, the old, happy time. What if it had all been a mistake? What if Visconti still played with her and he was what Valentine had said? The idea was too awful, she crushed it back, she would not believe.

She thought of her father with a sudden yearning; she had always turned to him in her little troubles. She felt uneasy about him with a sudden wave of homesickness. 'Can I forget?' she cried in her heart. 'Can I live this life and forget?'

But the next moment she calmed herself. She thought of Visconti leaning over his cathedral, of his hand in hers, of his earnest voice – and she had his word for her father's safety.

Smiling to herself, she mounted the steps to her gorgeous dwelling, made splendid by Visconti's love.

'My father! We shall be happy together again yet!' And she laughed and kissed the roses Gian had kissed, and the sun seemed bright again.

But Agnolo Vistarnini lay in the little chapel of Santa Maria Nuova, near to the western gate, with tapers burning at his head and feet, and five sword-thrusts through his heart.

XXVI

IN VISCONTI'S HANDS

Valentine Visconti was praying in the Church of Sant' Apollinare. It stood some way from the Visconti palace, a magnificent building, rich with the Duke's gifts.

That morning thanksgiving rose from every church in Milan; from the palace to the hut, all showed some sign of rejoicing. The Duke had ordered public processions and thanksgiving, and none dared disobey.

His Holiness Pope Boniface had deserted the failing cause of Verona; there was nothing to be feared and little to be gained from Mastino della Scala; the Duke of Milan had offered his aid against the rebellious Florentines, and many bribes besides, and today had seen the new league between the powerful tyrant of Lombardy and His Holiness publicly ratified.

From Rome Visconti had nothing more to fear, Mastino nothing more to hope.

The country around Padua was Visconti's too; Bologna, which he had always held, the great seaport of Chioggia, Mestre and Lovigo, betrayed by Carrara.

Bassano had fallen, and now Reggio; there was cause for thanksgiving in Milan.

As a last triumph, Valentine had been sent to offer up prayers and gifts for her brother's success. She was guarded on her errand, practically a prisoner. Soldiers stood at every door of the church, and a mounted escort waited to conduct her back. She was on her knees before the blazing altar, her head low over her missal, but she was not offering thanks to heaven for Gian's victories.

She thought of Graziosa with angry hate. But for that girl, della Scala had been in Milan, and Count Conrad with him – and in reward for her treachery Graziosa was to queen it over her! Visconti delighted to flaunt her with her at every turn.

That morning Visconti had told her the war was drawing to a close – said it with much meaning, and promised her, smiling, Count Conrad's head as a wedding gift. He had been closeted long with Giannotto; strangely elated he had seemed, and Valentine shudderingly wondered what was in the air.

That there was something she knew full well; Visconti was hatching some stroke that would complete della Scala's ruin. For some days she had seen his purpose in his face, and today the alliance with the Pope confirmed it.

She did not greatly care, she was too crushed with her own failures to care much for the failure of another. She felt sorry for Isotta d'Este, and bitter toward Count Conrad.

'But were I either of them, Prince Mastino or Count Conrad,' she thought in hot anger, 'I would not *live* to grace Visconti's triumph.'

The sound of bells penetrated even into the hushed interior of the church. As the service ended and Valentine rose to her feet, she heard them burst into wild music; the dim, incensed air seemed troubled by their triumphant throb, the gold tapestry to shake with it.

'Is it another victory?' murmured Valentine. The church had emptied, she was alone in it save for two ladies kneeling motionless.

The monks swept out, with a swinging of censer and a low chanting. Only one remained, putting out candles about the altar.

Valentine closed her missal and turned to leave. The sun was streaming through the gold and opal windows in a dazzling shaft of light, it fell over her face and blinded her for a second. The next, she looked round to see the solitary monk behind her. His head was hidden in his cowl, his arms folded, he passed her without looking up.

'Count Conrad is in Milan,' he said, under his breath, and silently and swiftly he was gone.

Valentine, hardly believing she had heard aright, gazed after him wildly, then collecting herself, walked down the aisle, her brain on fire.

Her ladies-in-waiting rose, and under no excuse could she prolong her stay.

'Count Conrad is in Milan!'

Did that mean that he would rescue her yet – was it Conrad himself who spoke?

The thought was grateful to her sore, angry heart. She had not much confidence in Count Conrad's skill nor his chances of success – still, he was in Milan, he cared enough to have risked that, and she could wait.

After the dim church the sun was blinding, the crash of the bells deafening. Valentine mounted her horse with a throbbing heart; that whisper in the church had given her new life.

The soldiers formed up either side, behind and before; it would not have been possible for her to drop even her glove unnoticed. She was riding the streets of Milan as her brother's trophy, as his prisoner; every one of those who bowed so humbly to her as she passed, every peasant her guards thrust back from her path, was freer than she.

Sant' Apollinare was far from the palace, and for that

reason Visconti had chosen it. All Milan should see her ride to offer thanksgiving for his victories.

'Surely there is more good news,' said Costanza, as they crossed the bridge that spanned the canal; 'the air is full of rejoicing, and I have seen many messengers spur past.'

Valentine set her teeth, and looked between the spears of her escort at the bright blue water beneath them. All the craft that covered its surface were gay with flags, its depth reflected buildings hung with the banners of the Viper.

'It fills the very air we breathe,' shuddered Valentine, 'the shadow of the Viper.'

Costanza glanced at her.

'I must confess,' she replied, 'I should be proud if it were my bearing. To be a Visconti on such a day as this would please me well; and though I am your friend, madama, I must say it.'

'As do all the others,' said Valentine, bitterly. 'You are blinded by splendour and power – you see no deeper than the skin!'

'Maybe,' said the other lightly. 'Yet am I glad the Duke hath triumphed, and not Mastino della Scala, who is as sullen as a peasant, and a foe to all display.'

'And his wife?' asked Valentine in a low tone. 'Have you no thought for her?'

Costanza shrugged her shoulders.

'Methinks I have done much to show I have! But she is a prisoner of war, and must take her chances like another. Were it the Visconti's wife in such a case – she would not be a prisoner long! Let Mastino della Scala tear her from his foe himself – let him do as Visconti did when the Lady Graziosa was in danger.'

'Hold thy tongue,' returned Valentine angrily. 'You talk as a child – you know not what you say.'

'I only know this,' retorted the other, 'I would I were the Lady Graziosa,' and she looked defiantly at Visconti's angry sister.

'For shame, Costanza,' said Valentine. 'Remember yourself.'

They rode in silence till, at the turn of the street, another splendid cavalcade crossed theirs. It was the Lady Graziosa and her suite. Tisio Visconti and Orleans were in attendance; she rode a white palfrey.

The sun lay tenderly in her soft hair; her green dress was covered with pearls, and round her throat she wore the emeralds Visconti had promised his sister, the first jewels in Italy, robbed from della Scala.

Valentine noticed them, she noticed Graziosa's happy face, the joy she took in the homage paid her, in Visconti's success that so galled her, Visconti's sister, and a sudden purpose rose in her eyes.

She smiled sweetly on Graziosa, and rode up to Orleans; the Frenchman remarked with pleasure how she outshone the Duke's betrothed. The deep blue of her velvet robe made her skin appear of dazzling fairness, her hair was like burnished gold, her mouth like a red flower, but her eyes, for all her smile, as dangerous as Gian Maria's could be, as mad, almost as wicked.

'We are well met, my lord,' she said, smiling. 'Have there been even greater victories?'

'I know not, lady; they say something of Lucca's having fallen,' returned Orleans. 'I have been escorting the Lady Graziosa to view the new church – by the Duke's orders'; he added in a lower tone, 'could I have chosen my companion, it had not been she.'

Valentine listened with downcast eyes, playing with the rubies at her wrist. Her escort was grouped about her, and Costanza glanced aside at her curling lips with some mistrust.

'The Lady Graziosa is happier and fair today,' she whispered to her companion, and Valentine overheard and smiled the more.

'And my brother, the Duke?' she asked.

'I have not seen the Duke all day,' replied the Frenchman. 'There is talk of an embassy to the enemy – confusion and crowds –'

'You have been riding Milan to see the rejoicings?' interrupted Valentine, and she raised her eyes to Graziosa once – the glance was not pleasant – then she fell to playing with her bracelet again.

'Yes,' said Graziosa innocently. 'My lord bade me ride to the new church.'

She was very happy, and affection welled up in her tender heart, even for the woman who had used her so cruelly – for she was Gian's sister.

With a timid gesture she held out her little hand to Valentine.

'Will you not ride back beside me?' she asked, pleadingly.

But Valentine ignored her hand and her request.

'Have you visited any other churches in your ride?' she asked.

'What other church in Milan should interest the Lady Graziosa?' asked Orleans wearily, fearing to be sent back on some distasteful journey.

'I did not know – I thought there might be one – Santa Maria, close to the western gate.'

And Valentine looked straight at Graziosa, who paled beneath her tone.

'How should that interest me?' she faltered.

Costanza put her hand on Valentine's sleeve.

'Have a care,' she whispered. 'Not before them all, madama, for pity's sake!'

But Visconti's sister took no heed; she gathered up her reins and signed to her escort to move on.

'Of course,' she said, 'why should it interest thee? There is nothing there – it is only a small, mean church, where a poor, obscure traitor lies on his bier.' She looked around the startled faces with a bitter scorn on her own. 'Who has heard of him? – one Agnolo Vistarnini – killed by the Duke's orders, killed by thy lover's orders, in the very hour that thou betrayedst him to him, Graziosa Vistarnini!'

She flung the words at her as if they had been knives, and if they had been they could not have been more deadly. Without a word, her hand catching at her throat, Graziosa sank from her horse, the scene in an instant one of confusion.

'Dieu! What have you done!' cried Orleans, springing from the saddle and raising Graziosa. 'Who will answer for this?'

'She will not die of it,' said Valentine, scornfully. 'She will take care to live – to be Duchess of Milan.'

'Oh, shame! Shame!' cried Costanza, and several echoed the cry.

''Twas no gentle act,' said Orleans, lifting Graziosa, 'and Heaven save you now, Princess!'

'And our heads may have to pay for it,' grumbled the officer who led Graziosa's escort. 'Men, see the Princess does not escape, or there will no one of us live to save himself.'

'Shame! Shame!' said the Duke again, as Graziosa, white as death, was laid in a litter. 'You have done a mad thing!' And the whole fluttering cavalcade whirled in startled confusion toward the palace.

Valentine looked after them, and there was no remorse in her face.

'You must answer to the Duke for this, madama,' said the officer, 'and at once.'

She turned her horse slowly, and at a quiet pace rode toward the Visconti palace. Costanza began to weep.

'Nothing can save you now, mistress – why did you do it? Oh, why!'

'Count Conrad is in Milan!' was Valentine's answer to herself; and to Costanza she said, coldly, 'Do not fear for me. I am too valuable to be meddled with. Even a Visconti would not dare to slay his sister before the Frenchman's eyes.'

They entered the courtyard in silence, the soldiers forming up close around her. The cavalcade had ridden slowly, and there was no trace of Graziosa's arrival. The palace seemed quiet. Valentine dismounted as usual, and was mounting the entrance steps when de Lana advanced.

'I have a painful duty to discharge, Princess,' he said. 'You are my prisoner.'

Valentine went white: she had not expected this so swiftly.

'The Lady Graziosa is in danger of her life,' continued de Lana.

'Tis no fault of mine,' said Valentine. 'What do you want with me?'

Costanza clung to her, weeping loudly.

'Have done!' said the soldier, sternly. 'Follow behind your lady. You will follow me, Princess.'

'Seeing I cannot help it,' retorted Valentine, with flaming cheeks. 'Where is my brother? Where is the Duke of

Orleans?' She looked round once; from somewhere there stepped forward two of de Lana's men and took their places at her side. She moved up the stair, Costanza with her, weeping with fear.

The corridors were empty, save for the soldiers at their posts. De Lana opened the door of the Duke's apartments and stood aside for her to enter, but Valentine shrank back.

''Tis the Duke's orders,' said de Lana, and he moved Costanza back. 'You will enter alone.'

Then Valentine summoned up her courage, and when she had passed the door, de Lana followed and stood beside it.

Visconti was at the table, behind him Giannotto, and at her entrance he raised such a white, distorted face of fury, that Valentine quailed and sank back against the wall.

'Ah!' said Visconti, 'I have it in my mind to kill you, my sister. I have it in my mind to give myself that pleasure – to kill you.'

He rose as he spoke, and Giannotto drew farther away from him, glancing at Valentine with a white amazement; the Duke was bordering on frenzy.

'Oh,' cried Visconti again, 'so you have no more wits than Tisio: you think, because it suited me that you should wed with Orleans, that you are free to flout me at your will!'

'Now be silent,' breathed de Lana to Valentine, who leaned against the wall beside him.

'You!' said Visconti, stopping before her. 'You! – to meddle with me – let me lift my finger and I can bring you lower than any slave in Milan!'

'Silence!' breathed de Lana again. But Valentine had too much of her brother's own spirit. The madness of

the Visconti rose into her eyes; she straightened herself
and moved forward defiantly.

'Aye, or you can kill me,' she said, 'as you have the others; but you cannot make me humble before your wife
out of the streets.'

Visconti stood stock still, and Giannotto, glancing at
de Lana, wondered if she were to be murdered before
their eyes.

Under the look in her brother's face Valentine stepped
back again and huddled against the wall: she saw
Visconti draw his dagger – and she hid her eyes – but
motionless and without a sound.

'I have had enough of you,' said Visconti, and strode
down upon her in a white madness of fury, forgetful of all
else. 'I will clear you from my path – yes, as I did the others.' Then he looked at de Lana, and something in the
soldier's face told him he would have to kill him first.

'And as I will any who oppose me,' he cried, furiously.
'Am I not the Duke of Milan? Take thy hand from thy
sword, de Lana. Now we will settle scores, Valentine.'
His hand was lifted, Giannotto turned his face away, and
de Lana had thrown himself forward, when a light knock
on the door close by broke the moment's silence, and
Visconti's hand sank to his side.

'Open!' he cried. 'It is the messenger from the Lady
Graziosa,' and de Lana, eagerly seizing the interruption,
flung wide the door.

Visconti looked up and met Valentine's eyes, and she
knew how near she was to death.

'My lord,' said de Lana, returning, 'the Lady Graziosa
hath recovered – there is no fear of her life, my lord.'

'Ah!' Visconti returned his dagger to its sheath, and
Giannotto gave a gasp of relief.

'Take my sister to her apartments, de Lana, and guard her well there – and if any ask for her, say she is under my displeasure –'

The captain turned, glad to take her from the room alive.

'Will you see the messenger, my lord?'

'No,' said Visconti, fiercely. 'As long as she lives, what care I for the messenger?'

The soldier seized Valentine's wrist and forced her, still reluctant, from the room. She was conquered, not subdued.

'If Graziosa dies,' said Visconti, turning to Giannotto, 'she does not live either. You have heard me say it. She and her woman's venom!' he continued, pacing the room furiously. 'I should have swept her away sooner – I would now but for the French, and the French shall not save her next time. He is a fool, Giannotto, who thinks that because a woman is a prisoner she is powerless – let him remember her tongue.'

'My lord, she may have thought the lady knew,' faltered Giannotto.

'Silence!' cried Visconti. 'She may have thought I wanted to give Isotta d'Este her liberty! Ah, let her beware! Graziosa, too; why did she not tell her that she lied? Had I not said he lived? Has she no spirit – no dignity – to shame me by her silence and her moans.'

The secretary ventured on no reply. He fumbled with the parchments on the table and drew one forward. Visconti's glance fell on it and his rage calmed instantly; his eyes flashed with a changed expression.

'These are the terms we sent to della Scala.' he asked, with a sudden smile.

'Yes, my lord; terms I think that cannot fail.'

The Duke sat silent a while, and the smile deepened to a laugh.

'I disturb myself for a woman's quarrels,' he said at last, 'and am on the eve of winning Lombardy!'

'The Estes may already have detached themselves from della Scala, my lord,' said the secretary.

'We will hope not. They will cling to the losing cause, and Mastino della Scala, the stainless knight, himself shall betray them!' smiled Visconti, with such cruel wickedness that Giannotto shrank.

'You stand so strong after your victories, my lord,' he said, 'you might well crush them all by force.'

'Only I do not choose that way of doing it,' replied the Duke, still smiling. 'I will accomplish a bloodless victory, I will spend no treasure, no time, and no men on this conquest, but I will win from it, not alone della Scala's towns, but his honour and his fame.'

XXVII

UNEQUAL ODDS

For days the sun had risen and set in cloudless splendour, hanging through the long summer day in a sapphire sky, flooding the beautiful country with gold, making the air heavy with perfume and sense of summer.

Mastino della Scala, standing at the door of his tent, hardly saw the glory and the brightness, the splendour of the great chestnuts, all deep green and snowy white, the proud beauty of the heaped-up flowers, the vivid richness of the foliage; for his heart was too sore for the finest sun that ever shone to ease it.

He had waited long, and waited hopelessly.

In the tent behind him, Tomaso and a page polished his armour. For once Mastino was without it – yesterday he had donned it, and waited expectant for the answer to the challenge he could not believe Visconti would refuse. It was his fault to think the best of men, a fault that had cost him dear when he had trusted Count Conrad, a fault that had cost him the insult now of Visconti's answer to his message.

'I have tried everything, and in everything I have been outwitted or betrayed. I am helpless, powerless. Will it last unto the end?'

The thought burned across Mastino's heart like fire.

Would it last unto the end?

The dazzling sun blinded him, the waving of the green made him giddy; he lifted the flap of the tent and entered.

After the glare the dark and gloom were welcome.

The tent was large and bare, only the two boys in their quiet dresses and the bright armour strewn over the worn grass, only these and Ligozzi seated near the entrance watching Mastino with anxious eyes.

Della Scala could not speak to him. He avoided his eyes, he had talked to him so often on this one theme. He could not meet his friend's eyes, so often humiliated with failure, with nothing but fresh disaster to speak of.

In silence he paced up and down the tent, Ligozzi's eyes following him wistfully. He also did not care to speak.

Mastino had left the entrance half open, and a great shaft of sunlight fell across the ground like a branch of yellow flowers.

And as della Scala passed it fell upon him, showing clearly his erect figure in its leathern doublet, his fine worn face and the unhappiness in his eyes, his hands locked behind his back.

The next instant he had passed into the shadow again, and Ligozzi leaned from where he sat and shook the covering into place. Twice Mastino had passed, twice he had seen the look on his face, and he did not care to see it again.

The tent was hot.

Tomaso and the page laid the armour down in silence, overawed by the silent figure pacing to and fro.

Outside it was quiet too, only now and then the gallop past of horses or the tramp of men as they moved from one part of the field to another.

At last Mastino spoke, stopping before Ligozzi suddenly.

'I have not told thee yet,' he said, 'but a messenger has arrived from d'Este. There have been some slight successes with his army, and he thinks that I should join him.'

'And leave Milan?'

'And leave Milan. He thinks it is hopeless, now Rome leagues with Visconti – he thinks it better to hold what we have nor risk it all by careless daring – but I – I shall stay here, Ligozzi.'

Ligozzi was silent; he knew d'Este's words were true; he knew Mastino knew it also. There was nothing to be said.

'I shall advance on Milan,' continued della Scala. 'If the d'Estes' troops care not to join me, I will advance alone with my Veronese.'

He sat down on the wooden bench, fingering with nervous hands his gold belt and the dagger that hung there.

'Why dost thou not speak?' he said, after a moment's pause, suddenly turning to Ligozzi. 'Dost thou too think it hopeless?'

There was a wistful eagerness in his voice that struck to Ligozzi's heart; he could not utter his thought.

'With waiting, my lord,' he replied. 'With new allies –'

But della Scala cut him short.

'I see, Ligozzi, I see. I am a man wanting to be persuaded against himself; yet do I still hope – against myself –'

'To rescue –'

'To rescue my wife, wouldst thou say?' flashed Mastino. 'No, I do not *hope* that: that I *will* do – in my soul I know it; but I still hope to conquer in fair fight. What did the attempt at guile avail us? We were betrayed; open force were better.'

Ligozzi's anger rose at the thought of that betrayal.

'I would I had the slaying of the traitoress!' he cried.
Mastino smiled sadly.

'What were we to her? She loved, perchance. I should
have done the same – for Isotta.'

'Thou wert ever too gentle, my lord,' returned Ligozzi.
'Could woman love *Visconti*?'

'She loved someone of her own creating, I trow,' said
della Scala. 'Poor lady! The awakening will be her punishment.'

Ligozzi made no reply. Mastino's point of view was not
his: in his eyes Graziosa was a hussy he would have liked
to have the hanging of.

'In two days or a little more, when I have had my
answer from the Estes,' said Mastino, rising, 'I march on
Milan.'

'But in those two days?' questioned Ligozzi.

'Visconti seems to have ceased all sallies,' said della
Scala; 'and yet I know not what this quiet means.'

'It means his policy was ever caution,' returned
Ligozzi. 'Of a sudden he may –'

'He may do anything,' cried Mastino; 'he hath Milan
and Rome and the Empire to back him. Still do I hold
many towns. Verona is strongly fortified; I lie between
him and Mantua. He cannot fall on those.'

'He has Padua, Bassano, Mestre, and Chioggia,' said
Ligozzi.

Mastino struck his hand against the tent impatiently.

'I know!' he cried. 'I know the odds are not equal!
When I seek to comfort myself why wilt thou remind me,
Ligozzi? What can I do? Nothing but what I say: march
on Milan. And mark me, Ligozzi; whatever befall, if all
desert me to a man, if d'Este fail me, I will not leave the
walls of Milan – alive – without my wife.'

'I will not desert thee,' said Ligozzi simply. 'I will never desert thee, my lord.'

'I never doubted thee,' returned Mastino impulsively. 'Ah, forgive me if I am harsh, for in truth my heart is very heavy; when I think of her – in Visconti's power – it is terrible! Terrible!'

He shuddered and put his hand on Ligozzi's shoulder, speaking eagerly.

'Such things cannot happen, Ligozzi, can they? It cannot be I shall never see her again! God cannot mean that – though He take all from me, though He humiliate me before my enemy, He cannot mean that! No! Visconti is not leagued with Heaven: it cannot be! It cannot be!'

'No,' said Ligozzi; 'even Visconti would not dare to harm the Duchess. Ye will see her again, my lord.'

Della Scala turned away to the other end of the tent; it was plain to him Ligozzi's heart was not in the comfort that he gave, that he thought with the others that they would do well to fall back from Milan, join the Estes, and hold the towns they had.

'But they do not understand,' said Mastino in his heart. 'I will never go back alive – without my wife.'

XXVIII

THE VIPER

The Duke of Milan had sent a secret embassy to Mastino della Scala, lying crushed outside Milan – a secret embassy he had long been meditating. The master-stroke of his policy should be the Duke of Verona's ruin, and his complete triumph.

And the moment of his sending was well chosen. The two days of which Mastino spoke had passed. The answer from d'Este at Novara had been unfavourable. His plans, he said, were to march back to Modena and Ferrara, protecting that part of Lombardy, held now by Julia Gonzaga's men alone, against Visconti; he would wait for his army to come up; he would wait for Mastino, but not long; his duty lay inside Modena and Ferrara, not outside the hopeless walls of Milan.

And Mastino had set his teeth, and taken his answer in silence.

That night there was a wild attack on the walls of Milan, so sudden, so fierce, that it almost seemed as if the ramparts must fall before the furious onslaught.

For five hours the Veronese and the defenders had struggled on the walls. Twice Mastino had wrenched the towers of the western gate from the enemy's hand; twice he had been driven back, leaving his dead piled high. A third desperate attempt had also been lost, and della Scala fell back toward Brescia with frightfully diminished numbers, and mad with the agony of final defeat. His cause seemed hopeless. And in the moment of his hopelessness Visconti's embassy arrived.

'Give della Scala one day to consider,' Visconti said to Giannotto, who accompanied de Lana on this mission. 'And if he mislikes the terms, say thou art to carry them to Ippolito d'Este.'

It was evening, and very still. Visconti stepped on to the balcony, and looked through the clustered pillars of its arcade into the garden.

The setting sun blended all flowers alike with soft gold; a little breeze shook the leaves, and stirred the jasmine that clung to the carved sandstone, fluttering its white stars delicately; the sky was very clear; as pure as a shell, and tinted like a wild rose.

Visconti was busy with his thoughts. His eyes rested on Isotta's dark prison with an utter satisfaction in gazing on this evidence of his power over della Scala. And then he looked to Graziosa's dwelling, and a shade crossed his face. Even to himself he would not yet admit it – but with her it was not perfect success.

Since Valentine's cruel stab, Graziosa had faded, grown silent and dull; and her beauty had gone with her happiness. She looked no wife for a Visconti. Torn from its setting, her fresh face lost its charm; the simplicity that had pleased him in her father's house annoyed the Duke in his own palace; the meekness and devotion that had flattered his vanity now angered it – in his eyes she had no more presence than a serving-maid; she was making his choice a mock before all Milan, with her white face and timid voice.

Visconti frowned to himself as he thought of her. She had said no word, she had uttered no reproach; she had remained passive and dull; but she was grown a mere shadow, a reflection of her former self.

'Maybe her folly will wear away,' mused Visconti

moodily. 'But if no – if she prefers her father before me – she may follow him.'

Today he had not as yet seen her. This was the first thought he had spared her; now he had a free moment and he would visit her – see for himself if her humour should promise of changing – the humour of:

'My Lady Graziosa Vistarnini, who hath not spirit for her destiny, who hath not the greatness to be proud to be a Duchess of Milan.'

Visconti sneered at her scruples, and was inclined to be angry with his own folly in choosing his wife for a soft heart and true affection; and with more even than anger he thought of Valentine. He took his way alone through the sumptuous gardens.

Graziosa was not in her gorgeous residence. 'She had gone to the little summer-house in the garden,' he was told, 'to see the sun set, and pray to Santa Teresa, whose name-day it is.'

Visconti turned on his heel with an impatient shrug of the shoulders. He was not attuned to passive virtue or to saintly prayers, nor was his palace their best background.

He saw Tisio and his pages in the distance – behind them, the white marble summer-house, standing on a gentle eminence, half hidden in laurel; and as he advanced through the clustering flowers he saw Tisio enter the low door, the scarlet liveries of the pages flashing through the deep green.

The perfect evening was like music in its calm loveliness. Visconti felt its charm; he was ever alive to obvious beauty, and none of his artist's perception could have walked this glorious summer garden, at such an hour, unmoved. His heart softened toward Graziosa: she had saved Milan – for his sake: in his great triumph he could afford to remember it, and the affection that prompted it, and set to her credit much else she might seem to lack.

He picked up a white rose from the bush that crossed his patch, and stuck it in his belt; he remembered she had often worn them – there was a bush in Agnolo's bower, and they reminded him of her. He looked up at the white summer-house, a square tower, distinct against the sky: the top window was open wide, then suddenly blew to – and Visconti started at it curiously and so suddenly that a pang shot through his heart. Then he advanced with a quicker step toward the marble summer-house.

Graziosa stood in its upper chamber, a circular room, broken by three large windows – the walls a marvel of serpentine and jasper, the casements a glory of stained glass, through which there poured the last rays of the setting sun, flooding everything with a thousand dazzling colours.

A carved marble bench ran around the wall, and above it shallow niches, in one of which stood a gilt lamp. On the floor lay a forgotten lute, tied with a knot of cherry-coloured ribbons.

Graziosa unlatched one of the windows; it opened centre-wise, and the girl stood, one hand on either leaf; the sun making her golden bright from head to foot. Before her lay Milan, the beautiful, with its trees and gardens, clear in the setting sun that sank, a fiery ball, behind the distant purple hills. Graziosa breathed heavily. The tower looked toward the western gate; the sun caught the roof of a little house beside it, the roof of a house and a flock of white doves that flew around it, as if looking for something they could not find. Near rose the square tower of a little church, Santa Maria Nuova.

Graziosa stepped back into the room, letting the window fall too with a clang. Some one must come soon. With a piteous little gesture she pulled at the jewelled fastening of her stiff satin robe. For some moments her trembling fingers could not undo the great pearl clasp. At last it opened, and the yellow robe fell apart.

A rope of pearls bound her waist: with a hasty movement she undid them, and let slip the gorgeous dress, that fell stiff and gemmed on to the marble floor. Beneath was the blue robe she had worn when she first came to the palace.

With hasty fingers she pulled the ornaments from her hair, throwing them to the ground. Her long curls fell about her shoulders; a little sob shook her throat; she looked wistfully around, and sank into the chair. For a little while she sat silent with closed eyes, panting.

Suddenly the sun sank, leaving the room dull, all the light and colour gone.

Graziosa opened her eyes with a little cry.

'I am so lonely!' she whispered to herself – 'so lonely. I want someone – to kiss me – good-bye.'

She rose and fumbled among the folds of her fallen gown; she found something small she grasped tight in her cold fingers.

'I am not brave – ah, I fear I am not brave!'

She rested her head against the arm of the chair, as if collecting herself; then, with a little smile, lifted it with a pitiful show of courage.

The wind blew the unlatched window open, showing the city roofs and the wall distant and grey; then it fell to again, leaving the chamber dull, almost dark, when a little later a footstep fell on the stair and the door was pushed open.

Tisio stepped in, peering around with vacant eyes. Orleans had lost his lute. Tisio remembered it left here. A heap of shimmering yellow satin caught his eye – yellow satin and a great rope of pearls. He marked it with vacant surprise, then, seeing the lute he sought for, made for it eagerly. He was proud to do these things. It pleased him to be so useful. He would not risk the page should find it. The lute lay near the bench against the wall, and, picking it up, Tisio noticed that someone sat there, someone very still and silent, against the cold white marble. He dropped the lute and came nearer. The chamber was utterly silent in the cold light, and the window was blowing to and fro with a dismal, sullen sound; but Tisio knew no ghostly terrors, he was not fearful of the dark.

He leaned over the figure eagerly, and when he knew it for Graziosa he was pleased. He liked her. That morning she had met him and seized his hands, and talked to him wildly, telling him with sobs something he could not understand. He thought it had to do with Gian.

Her head lay back against the purple cushion, and Tisio stroked it tenderly, fondling the beautiful bright curls that fell over the plain blue dress.

'Pretty thing!' he said gently. 'Pretty thing!'

He had no remembrance how he had stroked that hair before, in the streets of Milan, in the sunshine.

She never moved under his touch, and something in the droop of her attitude struck him.

'She is sad,' he thought, and with a change of tone he lifted one of her limp hands.

'Poor thing!' he said again. 'Poor, pretty thing! Art thou sad, poor, pretty thing.'

She made no answer, and he laid her hand back on her lap tenderly, smoothing her dress, and whispering comfort in her unhearing ears.

Suddenly the door swung under an impetuous hand. It was the Duke, but Tisio was not startled.

'Gian!' he said, 'be kind to her; talk to her, poor thing!'

Visconti stepped into the room, looking at Tisio keenly.

'Where is she?' he asked, for in the gloom he could not at once see the silent figure in the corner. 'Where is she, Tisio?'

'The girl with the pretty hair –' began his brother; but Visconti grasped him by the arm with a cry.

'Bring me a light!' he cried, 'a light –'

With trembling hands Tisio lit the lamp and brought it near. Its yellow light fell over Visconti's green dress and Graziosa's bright hair.

'If it should be so!' muttered Visconti. 'If it should be so!' The light was faint, but it showed him enough. He looked into her face, and his own changed darkly.

'Tisio,' he said, 'she's dead! Graziosa! Graziosa!'

He bent closer, eagerly.

'Get help, Tisio! Help!'

And Tisio, eager, alert, put the lamp in the window, where it flung long, ghostly shadows, and sped calling down the stairs.

Visconti had sent for help, yet even while he sent he knew it useless: she was dead! He stood looking at her. Poison! – she had poisoned herself! Something was tightly locked in her right hand! He forced the fingers apart, and looked at it – poison.

'How dared she do it?' he muttered, with an ever-darkening face. 'How dared she? Who gave it her? Who dared to give it her?'

He would never have thought it lay in her to do this. All Milan must know she had preferred to die rather than be his bride. He had failed in this, though he had sworn he could not, though he had sworn she should share his throne before them all – the woman who loved him for himself alone. He remembered Valentine. Valentine had done this.

At his feet lay the satin garments and the jewels Graziosa had flung aside: she would not wear them. Not all his power could do that; not all his pride, all his ambition, could make her wear the crown, without the love. Gian Visconti stamped his foot. How dared she! How dared she!

Her eyes would never sparkle at his coming nor sadden at his good bye. And Visconti, coming back to look at her again, was awed; affection stirred anew, and something like respect at the sight of her still dignity.

He looked around to find the door full of anxious faces, and Tisio behind him.

'Finely I am served!' he cried in a transport. 'Do you let the Lady Graziosa go unattended? She hath been murdered, and those who should have been with her shall die for it!'

Weeping ladies and frightened pages crept in and stood aghast, silent at what they saw – more silent at his face.

Visconti stood before Graziosa's body and looked at them with mad eyes; he held a white rose in his fingers. The flickering lamp was just over his head; its light fell on his face and on hers – her sweet face that told its own tale.

For some moments Visconti was silent, gazing at them wildly, and it seemed to more than one of those who crowded there appalled that there came a new expression to his face, a new look into his widely opened eyes – not madness and not rage – but fear.

'In a week I would have made her Duchess of Milan,' he said at last, with a sudden break in his voice; and he dropped his white rose at her dead feet with a shudder, and turned away, through the crowd that fell away from him, down the stairs in silence.

It was two hours later, in the hushed, awe-struck, half-expectant palace, when Visconti opened the door of his inner room and stepped into the ante-chamber, where one page kept watch.

To him the Duke beckoned, handing him a glass with milk-white lines circling it – a slender, flower-like glass with a long stem.

'Fill up with wine,' he said.

The page obeyed.

'Now bring the glass and follow me,' said Visconti, and left the room, the boy behind him.

Before his sister's door he paused. Soldiers guarded it: within could be heard footsteps and anxious frightened voices, the whispers of the tragedy. The key was turned: he entered, opening the door quietly, admitting himself and the page, the guard closing it behind him.

The room was lofty, and, like all Visconti's rooms, ill-lit. A great crucifix hung at the far end, and before it knelt Valentine. When she heard the door she turned and started to her feet.

'Put the wine down and go,' said Visconti to the page.

'Ah, no!' cried Valentine. 'Let the page stay, Gian!'

She stepped forward with imploring eyes upon the boy.

'Go,' said Visconti again.

'In the name of mercy, stay!' cried Valentine, in sudden desperate fear, seeing her brother's face. 'Stay!'

The wretched page hesitated, but not for long. Visconti turned once more, and he tapped on the door to be let out, making no more ado.

Visconti watched him go, then stepped to the inner door and locked it on the women whispering and quaking within.

Valentine tried to speak; the words died away on her tongue; she fell back against the tapestry, grasping it in stiff fingers, her eyes on his face.

Visconti seated himself at the table on which the page had stood the glass, and, resting his face on his hands, looked at her. The Viper on his doubtlet seemed to writhe, alive.

'Graziosa is dead,' he said.

Valentine's eyes grew wild with fear.

'I did not kill her!' she cried. 'I did not kill her, Gian!'

'I found her dead,' said Visconti, still looking at her.

Valentine writhed against the wall, wringing her hands. 'She slew herself,' she moaned, 'I did not kill her!'

'I shall not kill thee,' said Gian.

He looked down at the wine as he spoke, with a smile.

Valentine threw herself on her knees.

'I did not touch her!' she screamed wildly. 'I did not lay a hand on her!'

'I shall not touch thee; I shall not lay a hand on thee,' smiled Visconti.

'Then I shall not die? I shall not die?'

She staggered to her feet, with an effort to be calm.

'Thou wilt not die.' said Visconti, softly, his eyes on her. 'Thou wilt drink – this,' And he touched the glass beside him.

'Thou canst not be so cruel,' pleaded Valentine. 'I am thy sister, Gian –'

'Do I think so much of family affection,' said Visconti. 'Still, she was to be my wife! Thou wilt drink this.'

Valentine flung herself on her knees again, and dragged herself along the floor toward him.

'Have pity!' she cried. 'Have pity, I am so helpless! Spare me, and I will never offend thee again – never!'

'Thou hast strangely lost thy courage,' returned her brother. 'What is there in drinking this wine?'

She was at his feet, clinging to him, imploring.

'Let me live till morning!' she pleaded. 'Do not kill me here – in this dark chamber. Oh! I cannot die here, I cannot!'

Visconti looked at her calmly.

'Graziosa died not in a fairer place, she died lonely and alone,' he said. 'Thou wilt drink this,' He put out his hand and drew the glass nearer. 'Come, thou wilt drink this.'

'I am so young,' sobbed Valentine. 'Think, Gian; I am so young, Gian!'

'Graziosa was no older,' he said.

She clung to his hand in agony, beseeching him, calling on him, wildly trying to move him to let her live until the morning – only until morning!

'Graziosa died after the sun had set,' said Visconti. 'Drink the wine, nor keep me here so long. Thou hast often wished to escape – where is thy courage gone, not to take this chance?'

'But not to die like this – not like this – give me a priest!'

'Had Graziosa one?'

She cowered down on the floor, her beautiful hair

falling over her shoulders, her face hidden; then suddenly uplifted it again to Visconti, who sat looking at her, motionless.

'Gian, I loved thee once, when we were little children.'

'I have forgotten it, and so hadst thou until this moment – drink!'

Valentine sprang up in a paroxysm of uncontrollable terror.

'I cannot! I cannot! Kill me thyself!'

'With this,' and Visconti touched his dagger. 'No; a smoother death for one so fair.'

Valentine flew to the dcor and clung to it.

'Philippe! Philippe!' she shrieked. 'Conrad! Costanza!'

Visconti rose suddenly, with such force as to fling over the chair. 'Cease!' he cried. 'Wilt thou drink this? Or who dost thou think will dare to interrupt me now?'

Valentine's wild eyes looked at him in silence a moment, then her glance dropped.

'Give it me,' she whispered.

Visconti did not move.

'Come and take it,' he said.

She came slowly, one hand against the wall, her long shadow flickering before her.

Visconti watched her, motionless. 'Make haste,' he said. 'Make haste.'

She came to the table, her eyes down, her breast heaving, past tears or entreaties.

'Drink!' said Visconti, leaning with narrowing eyes across the space between them. 'Drink in it della Scala's health, as thou didst once before.'

Valentine raised her head and looked at him, and grew fascinated with terror. She crouched away from him, and lifted the glass to her lips.

Visconti bent nearer and she drank, putting it down half empty with a shudder and staring eyes.

Visconti smiled, and brought the evil of his face still nearer.

'Drink the rest,' he said. 'Drink it, Valentine.'

Still in silence she obeyed him.

When the empty glass stood before him, Visconti turned away, taking his eyes from her with a laugh, and walked toward the door.

Valentine's gaze followed him with a look of utter woe; still she said nothing, from her parted lips there came no sound. He looked back over his shoulder at her, standing there with her face toward him, with all expression gone, with unseeing eyes.

'I will leave thee,' he said savagely, 'to await – the morning.'

She seemed roused by the sound of his voice, and stepped forward with a cry on her white lips.

But the door closed heavily – the room was in darkness, or was it her sight failed her? Everything swam before her in a blackening mist; she grasped at the table and fell across it, senseless.

The dawn was breaking, filling the room with a grey and ghostly light; the great curtains looked black and gloomy, and the corners of the room were filled with strange and moving shadows. Through an open window a cool breeze blew across Valentine's sick forehead: she opened her eyes. The empty glass met her gaze, the fallen chair was beside her: she looked at them strangely. She was still alive.

'Gian's poison is slow,' she said, and smiled to herself.

After a time she rose and stumbled to the window.

'When the sun rises I shall be dead, or perhaps I shall live till noon,' she said to herself.

She mounted the estrade and sat beside the open window, resting her head against the woodwork, singing to herself.

Suddenly the whole grey sky flushed purple: the sun rose above the horizon.

Valentine looked down into the garden, the sight seemed to awaken memories.

'Hush!' She laid her finger on her mouth. 'Hush, Conrad – if Gian hears us – hast thou velvet shoes on – hush! He treads warily – ah, but it is no use – he poisoned me! He poisoned me!'

She rocked herself to and fro.

'In a tall glass with white lines – it was not Gian – it was the Viper from the Standard – all green and silver – all green and silver – a coiling viper.'

She dropped her head forward, then raised it with trembling lips.

'Conrad, come and save me!' Then she fell to laughing, whispering under her breath, counting on her fingers the hours she might have to live. 'If to noon – how many?'

The door opened, and she stopped her muttering, turning lacklustre eyes toward it.

'Goodmorrow,' said Visconti, standing with his back against it and looking at her keenly. 'Goodmorrow, Valentine.'

She looked at him and put the hair back from her face.

'I thought I saw Count Conrad walking in the garden: I would have called him up to see me die – how long will it be?'

Visconti advanced with a bitter smile. 'Has the lesson tamed thee? It would have been reality, but ye are pledged to France. I would that I dare poison thee, thou tiger-cat, but thou art tamed!'

Valentine's face did not change. 'Hush!' she said, leaning from the window. 'He is back on the tower now –'
she pointed to where the silver banner hung idle against
the brightening sky. 'What dost thou think? Shall I sit
and watch, lest he spy on us, Conrad?'

Visconti looked at her.

'Thou art tamed indeed,' he said. 'I am not ill-
avenged.'

Valentine stepped down into the room, her tangled
hair hanging about her, and grasped him by the arm. 'I
was waiting –' she whispered. 'I feared he would come
back before I was dead. Ah, and he did! Count Conrad
could not keep him off; the Viper, green and silver; the
Viper, he has poisoned me.' And she sank on to the floor
with a sudden scream, her hands before her eyes.

'Thou art neither poisoned nor dying,' said Visconti,
roughly. 'Call thy women, and – remember.'

She looked at him with vacant eyes.

Visconti turned away. 'She is not likely to forget, it
seems,' he thought. 'Her spirit will not trouble my path
more.'

Neither his nor anyone's. The brilliant, witty, and daring Valentine Visconti was to dare, to mock, to laugh no
more; her high spirit was broken, her proud courage
gone. From that fearful night she was timorous, shrinking, like a child, wandering and vacant – like Tisio, half-
crazed.

XXIX

The Ordeal of Mastino della Scaka

'A secret embassy from Milan!'

Mastino repeated the words slowly, and looked at Ligozzi who had brought them. 'And to see me alone?'

'With terms from Visconti – so they said,' answered Ligozzi. 'Terms of peace.'

'From Visconti!'

Mastino looked out through the open entrance into the blinding summer day, and then back at Ligozzi. 'I fear they come with no honourable terms – from Visconti victorious.'

'They would never dare come with dishonourable ones – to thee, my lord,' returned Ligozzi.

Mastino laughed bitterly.

'Dare! He is Visconti – with near all Italy at his back – he knows no such words as shame or honour. And I must see his messengers,' he added, after a pause. 'I know no such words now as pride or refusal.'

Ligozzi turned, but hesitated at the entrance.

'And – alone,' he asked. 'They are from Visconti.'

'And may be skilful in dagger thrusts and poison,' said Mastino. 'Nay, that is not what I fear, Ligozzi,' But he unstrapped his sword and laid it on the table in front of him. 'All the same, I will have thee with me, Ligozzi. I see not why I should humour them too far – I shall have naught to say thou mayst not hear.'

Ligozzi left, and Mastino sat alone, his head in his hands, his elbows resting on the table.

It was blazing hot, the very crown of summer, languid

and golden, with a haze of purple sky beating down on the swooning trees; noon, the sun at its height, the stillness of great heat in the air.

Mastino raised his head and looked out on it. What was Gian Visconti planning now?

He had some faint foreboding – a secret embassy from Milan – and following so swiftly on that last crushing blow; following so swiftly as to come upon him helpless from it – what had it to say, and to his ears alone? He had some premonition as he sat there. But it was not long. Ligozzi, exercising due precaution, returned with the two Milanese.

Giannotto stepped forward with a smooth obeisance, but stopped, a little surprised at the one occupant of the tent – the tall man with the proud dark face.

'My lord – the Prince,' he asked.

'I am della Scala,' said Mastino, and he turned to de Lana who looked an obvious soldier, and the worthier of the two. 'Your errand, sir? I would hear you quickly.'

'We have greetings from our lord, the Duke of Milan,' replied de Lana, his speech and bearing uneasy, like one trying to gain time. He had always disliked his mission, and never more so than now, standing face to face with della Scala.

Here was someone very different from the man he had expected, and it tended to confuse him.

Della Scala's dignity was his own, not that of pomp and splendour, the terror of crime, or the dazzle of power, that made Visconti feared and obeyed. As plainly attired as any of his soldiers, Mastino overawed the Milanese with something new to them – the sense of worth.

They were not trained to dealings with it.

'Greetings from Gian Visconti, Duke of Milan,' took up the secretary. 'Moreover, we bring terms of peace for your acceptance, my lord.'

Mastino was silent a space, and Ligozzi, standing behind his chair, looked at them with an ill-concealed abomination that Giannotto's quick eyes noticed keenly.

'My lord, is the one with you to be trusted even as yourself?' he asked, submissively. 'For our mission, Prince, is secret.'

'He is my friend,' said Mastino, shortly. 'And now these terms of peace.'

'The Duke is weary of the war,' said de Lana. 'He hath powerful allies, my lord.'

'And the choice of means to crush me,' interposed Mastino, his bright eyes full on the speaker, 'are in his hands, you would say? Perhaps; and yet, messer, I ask for no quarter from Gian Visconti.' De Lana bowed.

'Nor could he offer it, my noble lord; only terms as between equals.'

Mastino smiled bitterly.

'That is generous in Gian Visconti, seeing we are not – equals.'

Giannotto wished the Duke could have heard both words and tone. Visconti's birth was a sore point with him. The secretary wondered if there might be found a safe way of repeating them. De Lana flushed a little under Mastino's steady gaze and quiet scorn of the master who had sent him.

'The Duke of Milan sends by us this,' he said, and laid the parchment before Mastino. 'These are his terms, my lord.'

But della Scala did not drop his eyes to it.

'What are these terms?' he said.

'They are set forth there, my lord,' began Giannotto.

'So you have forgotten what they are, or did Visconti not tell you?' and della Scala handed the roll to the secretary. 'When you have read it, tell me what Gian Visconti says.'

He leaned back, his eyes still on them.

Giannotto bit his lips in vexation.

'Spare Visconti's loving greetings. To the point, in a few words,' continued della Scala, as the secretary still hesitated.

'Then, my lord, this: the Duke of Milan will leave you Verona, where you may rule under his protection, provided you now put into his hands every other town you or your allies now, singly or together, hold.'

Mastino flushed and half rose.

'Gian Visconti might have spared these insults,' he said sternly, 'and you yourself the relating of them. When have I shown myself such that your master should think I could betray Lombardy to keep one town? Get back, I have no answer save I have left you your lives.'

De Lana fingered the parchment nervously.

'That is not all, my lord,' he began, and stopped suddenly. 'I cannot say it,' he murmured to Giannotto.

Della Scala beat his feet upon the floor impatiently.

'Do you think I am afraid to hear.' he said. 'Still, it may be spared. I see, Gian Visconti's spirit is not peace but insult. On no terms will I treat him.'

'On no terms.' repeated Giannotto.

'On no terms of insult,' said Mastino coldly. 'I favour Visconti too much in listening so long. Leave me and take your lives back for answer.'

'Better listen, perchance, my lord, before refusing,' said Giannotto. 'It is the Duke's interest to offer you these terms; methinks it will be no less yours at least to consider them.'

De Lana stood silent, his eyes upon the ground. After this, give him plain soldiering.

'What plot has Visconti hatched now?' asked della Scala. 'What more has he to say?'

Giannotto's pale eyes twinkled unpleasantly.

'Only this: Visconti bids me tell della Scala, Duke of Verona, that if he refuse his terms we take them instantly to my Lord of Este; also he bids me remind my Lord della Scala that he holds the Duchess of Verona, my lord's dear wife.'

Ligozzi drew a deep breath and looked at della Scala; he had not quite expected this.

But della Scala rose with a white face and stared at the two ambassadors, incredulous.

'Surely even Visconti will not use that against me?' he said.

'Visconti must have the towns; Visconti holds your wife. The rest is for you to reflect upon, my lord: or, since you refuse all terms, we will take them to my Lord of Este. Perhaps he will give up the towns and save his daughter?' And Giannotto turned toward the entrance.

'Stay!' cried Mastino, in an agony. 'Stay! Your terms again –'

He dropped back into his seat with wild eyes on Giannotto. All his calm had fled, his pride was cowed: the secretary noted it, well pleased, but de Lana shrank from his changed look.

'This is what Visconti offers, my lord,' repeated the secretary smoothly: 'Give up all the cities, forts, and soldiers under your command, and the Duke forthwith makes an honourable return to you of the Duchess he holds captive, giving you leave to hold Verona under fief to him, doing yearly homage for it – he garrisoning it. If, however, my lord, you refuse –'

'If I refuse?' cried della Scala, leaning forward. 'If I refuse?'

'Visconti's prisons are unwholesome; for some weeks the Duchess has pined; it is feared, without instant liberty –'

Giannotto paused a moment, and lightly shrugged his shoulders.

'In a word, my lord, if you refuse – the Duchess dies,'

A terrible silence fell, no one moved or spoke, the lazy flapping of the tent struggling on its cords was the only sound. Della Scala sat rigid, looking at Giannotto, all power of thought struck out of him.

'Shall we take these terms to d'Este – shall we offer him his daughter for his towns?' said Giannotto softly.

D'Este! D'Este was not the man to place his daughter before states – Mastino knew it; Visconti knew it.

'No! No!' he cried, with sudden vehemence, 'I will.'

He put his hand to his forehead with a dazed expression and whispered something to himself.

Ligozzi, standing erect behind his chair, touched him gently on the shoulder.

'Send them away, my lord,' he whispered. 'Let them not remain here – send them away,'

'With a refusal?'

Della Scala lifted his white face. 'With a refusal?' he muttered stupidly.

'With what else?' said Giorgio firmly. 'With what else?'

Giannotto moved a little nearer and spoke with a sickly smile.

'Our answer may wait. The Duke of Milan gives a day in which my Lord of Verona may decide upon his answer.'

'Give them their answer now,' whispered Ligozzi, eagerly. 'Do not let them imagine for one moment that you hesitate.'

Mastino did not heed him; he sat as if frozen.

'Leave me to –' the words died on his lips. 'Leave me – to answer – I will give you my answer – anon.'

De Lana and Giannotto moved in silence to the far end of the tent.

'Visconti is a fiend,' said de Lana, with a gesture of revolt. 'Santa Maria, I wish I had never seen this della Scala. His face will haunt me.'

Giannotto smiled.

'Thou hast not been in Visconti's service long,' he said, 'and what have these things to do with us?'

'But this is inhuman,' returned de Lana. 'Della Scala hath a winning face. I might have been a better man if I had sold my sword to him.'

'This way, messers,' said Ligozzi. 'I will come to you presently.' And the flap of the tent fell to behind Visconti's messengers. Mastino sat, his head dropped into his hands.

'My lord –'

Ligozzi put his hand upon his master's arm.

'My lord –'

Mastino raised his head and looked at him; his face was distorted, his eyes unnaturally bright.

'Give them their answer, my lord,' said Ligozzi. 'Every moment gives them a triumph. Send it now.'

'Now,' cried Mastino, hoarsely. 'They gave me till tonight – surely, Ligozzi, they gave me till tonight.'

'Thou dost not need until tonight, my lord. Visconti asked thy honour.'

'And offered me,' said della Scala slowly, 'Isotta,'

Ligozzi looked at him horror-struck; an awful thought was breaking on him.

The eyes of the two men met; Ligozzi's were steady, but Mastino's flinched.

Neither spoke for some moments, Ligozzi at last incredulously.

'You cannot mean – to accept?' Mastino was silent. 'Oh, no,' cried Ligozzi, passionately. 'You are not yourself. For the love of Heaven let me go and tell them to depart.'

And he started forward, but Mastino caught him by the arm.

'Stay, Ligozzi; I command it.'

'Then you yourself will tell them? Oh, it is impossible that *thou* couldst fall!'

'Impossible,' Mastino rose with clenched hands. 'I think it is impossible that I could let her die.'

Ligozzi looked at his changed face.

'The cities are not yours, my lord; the soldiers are not yours – would you be a traitor, della Scala?'

Mastino winced.

'I would save my wife,' he muttered, his face turned aside.

'Your wife! A woman!' cried Ligozzi. 'Gian Visconti will burn in hell for tempting you, but, by all the saints, so will you, my lord, if you accept such terms.'

Mastino was roused. The energy of Ligozzi broke the bonds of his dull agony. He turned, also passionately.

'Have I not prayed and implored for this – only this – her life and return? Have I not sworn and vowed I would recover her – at *any* cost? Have I not warned them of it – and she shall not die! She shall not die! What care I for the cities! Did I not warn them? She shall not die!'

He fell to pacing the tent wildly, but Ligozzi stood in his place, bitter sorrow, deep anger in his face.

'Think what it means,' he said sternly.

'I will not,' cried Mastino. 'I will be baited and hounded no more. What has their grudging help done for me? I tell thee I warned them, I would hold them as nothing when it came to saving her.'

'Still they trust you,' returned Ligozzi. 'Listen, della Scala; I speak in the cause of honour – you *shall* hear, you *shall* know what it means, before you lend yourself to such a thing for love of a woman! It will give all Lombardy to Visconti, it and hundreds to the sword; it will mean the burning of cities to the ground; it will mean the misery of half Italy! It will give a mad tyrant to rule over thousands who are at present free – it will send d'Este and Vincenzo to prison – to shame, misery, death perchance – it will strip Julia Gonzaga of everything – and is she not as young and fair and good as Isotta d'Este – and did she not trust you with her all? And yourself? What will it make of you? What triumph will it not give Visconti to see you fall? Have you kept your name high so long to make it a by-word now? Beyond redemption will you be dishonoured, della Scala – an outcast, a traitor – to hold a little fief at Visconti's pleasure, the mirth of your enemies, the scorn of your one-time friends.'

Mastino broke into a wild exclamation. 'I will hear no more! I will hear no more!'

'I must wound you to save you,' continued Ligozzi. 'Against yourself I will persuade you; my love cannot see you do this thing. Oh, remember yourself! A man, a prince; no hothead of a boy. This black offer will be the turning-point and strengthen you. No man's cause is bettered by such means as this. All Italy will rise to cry shame on Visconti – heaven itself will turn against him and make you firm to overthrow him!'

'And Isotta!' said Mastino fiercely. 'Isotta will be slain!'

'She is one woman – how many as fair and good as she will perish if della Scala betrays Lombardy! She is one woman against the fate of half Italy.'

'She is my wife!' cried della Scala desperately; 'that one woman is my wife! Thou haste forgotten!'

'Forget it too, my lord; for your own honour's sake, forget it too.'

'Ligozzi, Ligozzi,' whispered Mastino, 'thou canst not mean it: deliver up to die by *Visconti's hands* the woman I – love!'

'If they hanged her from the ramparts where I must watch her die, they should not move me,' said Ligozzi grimly. 'But – all the saints, I would take my revenge.'

'Aye!' said della Scala bitterly. 'But perchance it would not be given thee to take revenge – perchance thou wouldst fall lower and lower, and be crushed after all and have gained nothing! Ah, Ligozzi, is this the beginning? Have I not pitted courage and high purpose, and honourable dealing and a righteous cause, against craft and cruelty and force? And to what end? Visconti triumphs. Always Visconti! What availed honour and faith when Visconti's cunning and Count Conrad's folly made the plans of weeks naught! Again, undaunted, I said I will succeed in the face of failure, I will succeed! What happened? Visconti had a handsome face; what mattered if his cause was bad? Again we failed! And what since? Half my men are dead against the walls of Milan! And now, am I to choose again what thou callest honour, am I to leave Isotta to die by his dishonouring hands –

oh, canst thou think of it! – and then be crushed at his leisure for all my reward? Am I so tied by tradition as that? Does not Visconti fling all laws, all humanity, all honour to the winds – can I fight him within the bounds of a boy's code of honour? The time comes, Ligozzi, when such things hold one no longer – the soul thrusts them asunder and does what it must, regardless of the laws of men! I must save her. Here is my chance and, fair or foul, I take it. I cannot think of the welfare of unknown thousands; what are they to me? Cities pass under Visconti's rule and cities are snatched from him – am I responsible for the fate of Lombardy? Men fight, betray, deceive and lie for wealth, ambition, and revenge – and common folk pay the price – shall I consider it too closely if they suffer once in a cause like mine? I tell thee, Ligozzi, I would hold it cheap to have her from Visconti with the misery of all Italy.'

Ligozzi's eyes did not move from della Scala's face.

'Thou art striving to blind thyself, della Scala. Oh, my lord,' he resumed, 'because others are dishonourable will ye be so also? And what do ye say of common folk? – not common folk alone will ye sacrifice, but d'Este –'

'He has helped me half-heartedly – and is she not his daughter? Yet at a word from Visconti he would league with him behind my back,' cried della Scala.

'I do not think so,' said Ligozzi, firmly. 'But Julia Gonzaga, who trusted you – what have you to say to her?'

'Naught!' cried Mastino, distracted. 'Naught! save that I do not love her – let him who does look to her – as I will to Isotta!'

'And she!' said Ligozzi, resorting desperately to his last argument, 'will she not turn from the liberty bought at such a price? Is she not the daughter of a noble house? Has she not been taught to consider death preferable to dishonour – if she was asked, what would she choose?'

Mastino's breast heaved.

'Ah – but I cannot ask her. If I could – Ligozzi, if I could go to her and look into her eyes, and say, "I promised, give me back my promise, for only on terms thou wouldst spurn can I save thee," she would understand – she would die with a smile, as I should – and that I could do. But to let her die a slow death – a dishonoured death! Wilt thou remember it is Visconti! His lies in her ears – knowing nothing of my struggles! Thinking herself forsaken, yet hoping against hope, and ever coming to her belief I would not let it be, till one day it was! Ah! I cannot do it! I cannot do it!'

He threw himself on the chair again and hid his face. 'She loves me,' he said brokenly. 'It seems strange, Ligozzi – that she should – care – for me. God knows, I have no charm such as Visconti has. I cannot please, I am clumsy and uncouth compared to those she had around her – and yet she chose me. "While thou art alive I fear nothing," were the last words I heard her say, and I shall leave her to curse the day she met and trusted me to save her from a villain. What commonest foot-soldier I have would leave the woman that he loves to die Visconti's way? Ah, Heaven have mercy! For what crime is this a punishment!'

'Then you will accept these terms for her release?' said Ligozzi. 'I will plead with you no more, my lord – only, if you do this thing, I, who am your faithful servant, I, who ever loved and worshipped you, can serve you no longer – it is too terrible a thing – I cannot stay and see it done!'

Mastino's head was bent forward, his hands clenched so tightly that the flesh was broken, his whole attitude so hopeless in its agony that Ligozzi feared for his reason.

'Oh, my lord!' he cried passionately, and flung himself on his knees by Mastino's side. 'Oh, my dear, dear lord! Thou wilt choose the noble part, I know! Thou wilt not let Visconti triumph, for this is all a devilish plot to make thee dishonoured, to make thee betray thy trust – foil him – say no!'

Mastino made no answer, and Ligozzi too lapsed into silence, rising from his knees softly…

How hot it was, how hot! Ligozzi felt dizzy – he wished the sun would cease blazing down – he wished della Scala would move – had he persuaded him? Mastino raised his head.

'Bring them back,' he said slowly, 'I will see them now.'

Ligozzi's heart beat high. 'He has won – over himself at least he has a victory!' he thought – but looking on della Scala's haggard face, he ventured no speech.

Mastino sat erect – his hands on the table in front of him, his eyes on the floor. Visconti's envoys entered.

Giannotto, glancing at Mastino and then at Ligozzi keenly, saw that there Visconti had an adverse advocate. But the strained silence on them all was hard to break. They were uneasy, like men before a great grief, or in the presence of one about to die – it was difficult to treat the matter as an ordinary one, or to ask a decision from that tortured man before them.

Even Giannotto's heart failed him, and he stayed near the entrance, abashed and afraid, but with a fear different from that with which he fawned upon Visconti. Visconti's moods and motives he could understand – to some extent they were his own, on his own level – but this man – some things were beyond the Duke of Milan's secretary, and for the first time in his life he felt it. Mastino himself broke that hideous silence. He raised his head, and with a little affectionate movement Ligozzi laid his hand on his master's arm as if to strengthen him.

'I have considered,' said della Scala, in a hard voice. He paused a moment, but a moment only. 'I have considered, and my answer is: I will accept Visconti's terms – my wife against the towns.'

'Oh, dear lord!' breathed Ligozzi. It was the only sound; the Milanese were silent, almost as if they too winced to hear the words.

Mastino rose, with defiance in his burning eyes.

'I accept – every city in my hands, every soldier – all – against my wife – I accept Visconti's terms,'

Ligozzi's hand had dropped from his shoulder, the clink of metal was heard through the heavy silence, without a word he stepped forward and laid his sword on the table before the Prince, then turned toward the entrance.

'Ligozzi!' cried Mastino, incredulous. 'Not thou, Ligozzi – not thou, my friend!'

He held out his hand imploringly, regardless of the eyes upon him. Ligozzi stopped and turned, answering della Scala's wistful look by one of bitter scorn and pain.

'I had that sword from an honourable prince – I go to weep that I should have to return it to a traitor!'

'Ligozzi!' Mastino staggered back, his extended, rejected hand fell against his side. 'Thou might'st have spared me that before *these* – for the sake of the old days – Ligozzi –' he said, steadying himself. Ligozzi did not turn; with a hard face he walked across the tent – without a look back, without a word or a sign, he was gone.

Mastino watched his only friend depart with straining eyes, that then he covered for a moment as if to shut out what they had seen. But the next moment he turned proudly to the messengers.

Giannotto was alone. The soldier, de Lana, had vanished.

Mastino started forward with a cry, but the secretary interposed: 'My lord,' he said smoothly, 'our duty is our duty. There is no harm intended, there shall no harm be done; but of what value is your consent to my Lord Visconti's terms, if your *friend* should speak of it?'

Mastino fell back. A swift beginning.

'Your lady's safety, my lord,' said Giannotto, 'depends on your friend's silence. He has left his sword. There will be no bloodshed.'

There was a silence, then Mastino looked up and spoke hoarsely.

'Begone! And take my answer to Visconti. I accept and will carry out his terms; my wife against the towns.'

'Only remember, my lord,' and the secretary smoothed his hands together nervously, 'any attempt on Milan, any movement on your part, and the offer is null and void and the Duchess dies.'

'Begone!' screamed Mastino, 'take my answer and begone!'

Giannotto turned and went softly out of the tent.

It was done – it was done – beyond redemption had he fallen; he had chosen – there was no turning back.

Mastino della Scala sat alone and stared in the face of what he had done. These few moments were his; then he must go and lie to his officers, deceive his men, weaken his towns, destroy his forts – prepare to place them in Visconti's hands. He must send false messages to the

Estes and to Julia Gonezaga – lie and deceive and betray! But he had saved his wife from Visconti – his wife – Isotta.

Outside he heard familiar voices, officers and men; his Veronese, still glad to trust his leadership; and he was to betray and trick them into shame.

'Can I carry it through, can I go forth with a calm face and lie to them – my soldiers!' he cried in agony. 'But her life – her dear life – her more than life – hangs upon my falsity!'

He thought of the beautiful free towns of Italy: his Verona he had rescued once; proud Ferrara; Mantua that had never felt any yoke but that of the Gonezaga; Pavia; all the haughty fair towns that had scorned Visconti. What would Visconti's vengeance on them be? Mastino could hardly believe he had done this thing. Yet were the choice given again, he would choose the same – he would choose the same!

The sultry breeze blew back the opening, showing the deep blue sky and near-lying tents; a company of soldiers galloped by carrying the standard of Verona – the ladder of the Scaligeri.

How soon would that banner be torn from the walls of Verona and the Viper take its place?

'My city!' cried Mastino, 'my city!' and his head sank forward on his out-thrown arms, while his shoulders heaved with sobs.

XXX

The Wedding

Seven days had passed.

In Milan there was much rejoicing, in its streets and palaces much splendour; it was the Lady Valentine's wedding-day.

Among the throng outside the church of Sant' Apollinare, the eager crowd that fought and battled for a better chance of seeing the splendid procession, was a monk, seemingly a wandering friar, who pressed his face against the cold marble walls in the silent vexation of an utter disappointment. It was Conrad.

He had failed in his mad mission; success from the first had been hopeless; he had not redeemed himself. He had not helped della Scala, he had not rescued Valentine – he had failed.

A dozen different plans had been formed – equally futile and impossible to carry out. Who could outwit Visconti in his own city? Bitterly Conrad regretted the false hopes conveyed in that whisper in this very church. Perhaps she had trusted to them, and here was her wedding day and he was standing outside, helpless!

He knew it pure folly, this risking his life for nothing; and what had brought him there he could scarcely tell; but under his monk's habit he had a concealed dagger.

He felt desperate, wounded badly in both heart and pride. It was not so much for love of Valentine Visconti – that had ever been more fancy than aught else – it was the sense of failure – of self-humiliation; a bitter sense of how Visconti laughed at him. Far better a fine, romantic death than disgrace one side, defeat the other. In fact a fine, romantic death in a lady's cause would be decidedly gratifying. With this new thought of it struggling in his mind, Count Conrad suddenly turned from the wall and forced lustily through the crowd to the church steps.

He was there none too soon. A sudden wild shout from the crowd, a movement of the soldiers keeping guard, told him they were leaving the church. The pushing, struggling people were well kept back by the stout halberds; but Conrad, partly by virtue of his dress, but rather by the strength of his squared arms, managed to force to the front, where he stood close behind the stalwart figure of a German mercenary.

Conrad glanced at the blond hair and mild blue eyes. 'Friend,' he whispered in German, leaning forward, 'have consideration for a German father who will say many prayers for thee – in his native tongue.'

The soldier turned.

'Quick,' said Conrad, 'a place next thee, my friend.'

The soldier smiled at the friar's curiosity, and allowed him vantage; and Conrad, stationed near the foot of the steps, looked up them eagerly to the brilliant group issuing from the church doors.

His roving eyes sought Gian Visconti. It was only four months since he had seen him, talked to him freely, face to face, his friend and favourite, but it seemed years. Visconti had grown in greatness since then, and Conrad, when his gaze caught the once familiar figure, felt far away from knowledge of him.

Visconti was standing, his cap in his hand, surveying the crowd. He looked much older, Conrad thought, his face was dark and sombre, hardly like the face of a man at the summit of his ambition. He came down the steps slowly, on one side his sister, her bridegroom on the other, and taking no further notice of the shouting people, gazed down moodily.

Conrad hardly looked at Valentine, whiter than her white dress, gazing vacantly before her; he did not notice the utter change from her former brilliancy, he had no eyes for the overdressed, foppish bridegroom – he was looking at Visconti.

The steps were thickly strewn with flowers; the train of lords and ladies was one of colour and gems still flowing from the church as Visconti came to within three steps of the Count, and Conrad sprang forward before the startled soldier could throw out a hand.

Visconti stopped, and the procession behind him, arrested, stood a flaming band of movement and colour. Conrad threw back his hood with a sweeping gesture, thrilled by the excitement of the moment to dare anything. What his motive he could not have told, but it was a fine moment. He caught one glimpse of Valentine's suddenly illumined face, and drew the dagger.

'Another wedding gift!' he cried in ringing tones, and struck Visconti full upon the breast.

Then an utter confusion fell upon Count Conrad. He was seized and pinioned tight amid wild yells, while the dagger, glancing off the armour beneath the soft rose-coloured velvet, fell on the steps unheeded.

'Count Conrad?' said Visconti clearly through the babble of voices. 'Conrad von Schulembourg.'

'Aye,' said Conrad wildly, struggling between the two soldiers who held him. 'Complete your triumph, Visconti. I would have killed you; kill me – kill me! You tried before and failed. I have tried and I fail. End it.'

He would have added more defiances, but the soldiers

hauled him roughly back, and choked the words back into his throat.

'Count Conrad?' asked Valentine, in a clear tone. 'Did he say Count Conrad?'

Visconti motioned to Orleans.

'Take the Duchess on, my lord. I will remain and deal with this crazy friar.'

'Surely he needs but little dealing with!' said the Frenchman. 'An assassin! There is the gallows ready!'

'There is also your wedding procession waiting,' returned Visconti quietly, and he motioned the train onward, and Conrad forward, the eager people in the street all straining every nerve to know what might have happened; appeased by the oncoming train, they gave only half a thought to the little knot pressed round the steps, and what the Duke had paused for.

Conrad stood between his guards, with a flushed face and a proud bearing. He would have liked to kiss his hand to Valentine, stepping into her gorgeous litter, looking back with half-awakened eyes; but his hands were held firmly, and his feet lashed together.

'Well, Visconti,' he said, with a still higher carriage of his head, 'what is it this time – starvation or the rack?'

Visconti made no answer: he was looking down at the flowers on the steps.

'Take those away,' he said to a page, and pointed to a spray of white roses.

The boy obeyed, and glanced at his companions, wondering.

'Saint Hubert!' cried Conrad, with a sudden laugh. 'You are full of whims as of old! How long must I wait for my death, at your good pleasure, my lord?'

The Duke turned his eyes on him.

'You are strangely foolish,' he said, and hesitated, looking at Conrad with a moody face.

'Foolish indeed, or I had never been Visconti's friend!' retorted Conrad. 'Foolish – or I had never trusted to his friendship. But call me also bold, my lord, to be here now, buying with my life the pleasure of saying so!'

'The impudent German!' murmured a lady in Visconti's ear. 'Heaven has given your lordship even this – to crown your perfect triumph.'

The Duke was still silent: he looked from Conrad to the crowd, shouting, throwing up their hats to see the procession pass, and then to the soldiers, wondering at this strange hesitation.

'Why did you come to Milan?' he asked at last, fingering the gold tassels on his sleeve, and speaking slowly.

'To save your unhappy sister,' cried Conrad. 'To try and kill you, Visconti!' And he struggled fiercely in the grip of his captors.

'Take him away,' said Visconti. 'Take him –' He paused a moment.

'To the gibbet, my lord?'

'No – outside the gates. Give him a safe-conduct that will take him out of my soldiers' lines. And so farewell, Count Conrad; I can waste no more time on you.'

'I will not go!' shrieked Conrad furiously. 'I will not have your mercy, Visconti – I will not accept from you my life!'

Visconti passed on.

'I say I will die!' cried Conrad after him. 'Do you quail at another murder, Visconti? Dare you not kill one more?'

The Duke looked back at him.

'I owe you somewhat, Count. You may remember a certain game of chess you played in della Scala's camp.

It served me well – it saved my life – and gave me – della Scala. Now take yours – as a most unequal recompense.' He smiled unpleasantly, and Conrad was silent, struck, chilled.

'Put him outside the gates,' continued Visconti; 'and give him money for his journey. Maybe he left della Scala too hastily to bear much away; maybe della Scala did not in any case pay well; and we would not have the noble Count beg his way to Germany.'

'Visconti—' Conrad choked on the word. 'Visconti –'

'I will spare thy thanks,' smiled the Duke. 'Farewell.'

'Give me a dagger – someone!' yelled Conrad. 'That villain shall see I do not live to profit by his scorn. Give me a dagger – I – you truckling knaves! You shaveling cowards!'

'When your blood is a little cooler,' said the soldier calmly, tying his hands the tighter, 'you'll be giving us a ducat apiece for not taking you at your word.'

'Silence, churl! I will not leave Milan; I will not be put outside the gates!'

'Just whatever the Duke says, messer, you'll do – just whatever the Duke says; and thank your guardian saint he was not himself today, or you'd have had your death – but not quite so pleasant as you seem to think it.'

And for all he could shriek and threaten and pray, struggle and fight, Count Conrad was escorted through the crowded streets, between soldiers with immovable faces, and amid a crowd that laughed in huge enjoyment of his angry threats and bitter entreaties. A good mile outside the gates they led him, a fine rabble at his heels. And then they left him, with a good horse, a sword, and a bag of ducats.

'Now, Count, take those and ride to Germany – or if

you must die, try and get back into Milan,' And they rode away, laughing heartily.

Count Conrad seated himself on the roadside, and was silent a long while. Then he rose, and rubbed his stiff arms, bruised by the soldiers' grip, looked back toward Milan, looked at the horse and sword, gave one sigh to the past, mounted and rode away out of the shadow of Milan toward Novara, the first town on the route to Germany.

There was a great coming and going of brilliant company in the Visconti palace, at constant spurring of horses through its gates, the riding in of messengers and soldiers, the riding out of officers and nobles.

The Duke of Orleans and his wife had left for France, with a splendid cavalcade of knights and ladies, escorted by the flower and chivalry of Milan.

All Valentine's struggles and proud resistance and scorn had come to this: she left for France, as Visconti had ever said she should – left Milan dull to craziness, forgetful, with no sign of either joy or regret.

Visconti thought of this consummation with some satisfaction, then banished his sister from his mind. There were other matters more important to Visconti than the subdual of his sister – Mastino della Scala and his wife for one.

Mastino had kept his pact: in one week, Pavia, Treviso, Cremona, Vincenza, and Verona had fallen; company after company of Mastino's soldiers had passed into the hands of the Milanese. Modena and Ferrara were left, but so weakened that a few days must see their end, though the deserted garrisons were fighting desperately, and sending wild messages to della Scala, imploring aid.

Julia Gonzaga in Mantua was sore beset. At an urgent appeal from Mastino, almost every trained man holding the city had been sent to his assistance, to find themselves surrounded and cut to pieces by the Milanese, and Mantua left defenceless.

In Novara the Estes were shut up, waiting anxiously for news from Mastino – waiting in vain. Isotta d'Este had been removed from Milan, and was lodged in a strong fort some miles outside Brescia, guarded still by Visconti's soldiers, but also by some of della Scala's trusted but still unwitting Veronese – men who kept watch over her night and day, inspected all she ate, and allowed no emissary from Visconti to see her alone.

Such were the terms.

The thing had been done secretly. Vague rumours that the Duchess's release was being negotiated were the utmost that got abroad. The soldiers guarding her for Mastino thought the privilege bought, or that the Emperor had wrung it from Visconti. There were none who suspected the truth. Though for those ten days had been disaster on disaster, though town after town had fallen, squadron after squadron been ambushed, and though some whispered treachery and pointed to this captain and to that, none thought of staining the loftiest name in Lombardy with even a doubt – Mastino della Scala, the son of Can' Gran' della Scala, of a race that had never lied or betrayed, the one race in Lombardy of a lofty honour. Men would have as soon thought the stars would fall as Mastino della Scala.

Visconti, pacing his palace in a fever of triumph, thought of all this; thought of the d'Estes in Novara, still trusting – thought of Mastino's Veronese, their devotion, their sympathy – thought of Mastino's feelings. It was almost enough to satisfy his hate – but not quite – not quite.

'Tomorrow,' he said, stopping before de Lana – 'tomorrow I shall march from Milan, and I shall lay in ashes every village, every town that has favoured della Scala. I will let loose my soldiers to pay themselves from the wealth of Lombardy, and I will make the Estes take their proud banner down from the walls of Novara, and hoist with their own hands the Viper!'

'Mastino della Scala lies at Brescia,' said de Lana, with an uplifting of his dark eyes. 'His army has dwindled almost to a handful of picked Veronese; so a deserter who rode in tells me. He waits there for his wife.'

'And I,' said Visconti, leaning against the table, 'have given orders she is to be sent, de Lana. He has kept his word; I will keep mine. He has paid dearly enough – he shall have his wife. And tomorrow I march on Novara.'

'I have my orders, my lord.'

'I have nothing more to say, de Lana. Tomorrow we leave Milan.'

The captain was turning in silence, when Visconti spoke again.

'Della Scala is at Brescia, ye say? Then his wife will reach him tomorrow about the time we reach Novara.' He paused and looked at de Lana steadily. 'I have sent orders for her release and forwarding in all due privacy, but with sufficient state, and I have sent her back her wedding ring.'

De Lana only half understood him, but Visconti had small care for that.

'The Estes – in Novara, de Lana – they are unsuspecting.'

'How can they be otherwise, my lord? They are isolated –'

'Waiting for succours from della Scala doubtless! How many could their numbers be?'

'Some thousand – no more. Della Scala called his Veronese out, my lord.'

''Twill he almost too easy a victory,' said Visconti, smiling. 'And then, from Piedmont to the Apennines, Italy will be under my rule: and della Scala – I wonder what will happen to della Scala, de Lana?'

'There is nothing but death for della Scala,' returned the soldier, standing at the door as if anxious to be gone. 'Nothing is left for him but that, my lord.'

'Ah – you forget,' said Visconti softly. 'There is his price – his wife; there is always his wife.' And repeating the words, as if to himself, Visconti motioned de Lana away, and entered the inner room.

Giannotto was looking out of the window, and at Visconti's sudden entrance turned with a start.

'Giannotto,' said the Duke smoothly, 'you will come with me on the march tomorrow – not for love of your company, my friend, but because I do not trust you. Still, I keep you.'

'There is now no Lady Valentine to outwit me in your absence with some of her brother's skill, my lord,' replied the secretary meekly.

Visconti made no reply, but viewed the secretary sullenly.

His words had brought up unpleasant memories: his palace was free of his rebel sister, but it was free also of another one who should have been his wife.

All his brilliant, his magical successes could not quite obliterate the sting of that one failure. Graziosa's name was a forbidden one; the splendid dwelling where she had shone so brief a while, shut to moulder. She was a thing of the past, though only ten days dead; but Visconti could not quite forget.

She had been buried quietly, in the same church as her father, at dead of night, with no mourners. And was she not gone – forgotten? Yet, disguise it as he might, it was failure.

'Yet she loved me,' thought Visconti; and it roused his wrath that he must think of her – the house by the western gate – the sweet face, the white roses.

'Giannotto,' he said moodily, 'had she lived, I would not have done it – on my soul I would not have done it!'

'Done what, my lord,' asked the startled secretary, looking up at his dark, musing face.

'Ah, I forgot,' said Visconti. 'You do not know.'

XXXI

The Pride of the d'Estes

'No news! So many days, and still no news!'

Ippolito d'Este spoke in an anxious voice, leaning in the wide-cut window of the watch-tower that rose above the gates of Novara.

'I would we had not sent those last men,' said Vincenzo gloomily.

He was seated at the table, his head resting in his hands. The chamber was large and dark, built of rough stone for strength and defence, fixed with narrow windows, and set with three doors – one into the narrow stairs, standing open, one on either side of it, shut. The walls were bare of arras. Vincenzo's armour lay piled in a corner, and a great crucifix, a red praying hassock beneath, hung near one of the windows.

'How many have we, my father?' asked Vincenzo, rising.

'Six hundred trained soldiers,' was the brief answer.

'And the townsfolk?'

'Are the townsfolk,' replied d'Este, 'and useless.'

Novara had been stormed and taken from Visconti some months ago, and the Estes, fixing their headquarters there, had foraged the country around as far as the ramparts of Magenta, a large town held by Visconti's men.

For these last fatal ten days, disaster after disaster had reduced the Modenese soldiers to a mere handful; and when Mastino, sending word he was in desperate straits, had called out all of the Veronese that manned the town, they were left practically defenceless, in the midst of a country where Visconti's arms were everywhere triumphant.

They dared not leave the town; behind its walls was the only chance of safety. They knew not what positions Visconti held, nor what positions della Scala. Since that last appeal for aid, they had had no message, no sign from him. Scouts sent out had not returned; one company, advancing from the walls, to find no sign or trace of Mastino, was surrounded and cut to pieces – the few who escaped returning to Novara with ghastly tales. Visconti's arms seemed everywhere victorious. The country was laid waste – and not by their allies.

But the d'Estes' hope was still in della Scala. Urgent messages were sent to his camp outside Milan, and when neither answer nor messengers returned, the Duke of Modena grew sick at heart indeed.

He had not mentioned all his fears to his son, though Vincenzo could not but know their strait desperate.

'If we hear not today,' said d'Este slowly, 'I shall think there is treachery; not one messenger has returned – treachery, or some misfortune to della Scala.'

'Then are we lost indeed!' cried Vincenzo. 'So far from Modena – so near Milan – only, what of the army that is with della Scala – our army, his and ours?'

'What army we had with us,' replied Ippolito, still looking with anxious eyes on the level country, 'I sent to della Scala – he was in sore need. What men we had outside the town have melted away like snow.'

Vincenzo began to pace the room impulsively – a slender figure in a scarlet velvet doublet, his great black eyes bright and angry.

'Shall we not make a sortie, my father? Shall we not

dash out and fight, seeing for ourselves what has become of della Scala?'

Ippolito turned and looked at him, with a yearning love lighting his dark face.

'I am waiting, Vincenzo. I have sent trusty scouts to Brescia. This silence cannot last long now; either Mastino or Visconti march this way – and in either case we shall be ready to receive them, Vincenzo.'

The younger d'Este lapsed into silence. Ippolito, too, was quiet, and the pause was broken by an officer entering.

'The Count von Schulembourg,' he began.

'Conrad!' cried Vincenzo, springing up.

'Has he news?' asked his father, eagerly.

'I know not, my lord,' replied the soldier. 'He is riding unattended, and craves a passage through the town.'

'He is riding away!' said Vincenzo, 'away from Milan!'

'I must see him,' said d'Este, with a darkening face, 'at once.'

As the soldier left, Vincenzo looked at his father eagerly.

'What may this mean, that Count Conrad rides away?'

'We lie on the route to the Empire. The German maybe rides home from a losing cause.'

'I never thought such of Conrad,' began Vincenzo, when the door opened and the Count himself stepped into the room, brilliant, gay as ever, well armed, the double-headed eagle on his breastplate, and the black and yellow of the Empire floating from his helm.

'Now well met, my good lords,' he cried, 'and fair fortune smile on you! I would ask the favour of a good horse – I am on my way to Germany.'

'You leave the fight?' asked d'Este.

Conrad nodded.

'For better men – i'faith, I've tried all I know – no man is asked to break his head against a brick wall for nothing – not while the sun shines, and there is such a place as his own land to see again!'

'You used not to hold such language, Conrad,' said Vincenzo, with some reproach.

'I have tried everything,' cried Conrad, gaily. 'I tried to rescue the Lady Valentine, I tried to kill Visconti, I tried to make him kill me – I have failed. My Lady Valentine is married, and is set out for France.'

'For France!' interrupted d'Este. 'Then must the country indeed be in Visconti's hands if his sister and a wedding-train set out for France! What news, Count? Surely there is some news.'

'Not much I care to repeat,' replied Conrad. 'Only rumours – all the country I rode through, from here to Milan, seems to swarm with Visconti's men – I saw no sign of della Scala – there were wild tales abroad, and wild sights.'

'On my honour, Count, you might have come with better information than this – days have we been waiting with no sign nor word –'

'From Mastino, would you say?' asked Conrad, eagerly.

'From Mastino. Have you not heard or seen aught of him,' cried Ippolito.

Conrad looked at d'Este's intent face, and from him to Vincenzo, waiting expectantly for his answer.

'I – I cannot say I have,' he answered. 'But as I tell you, I heard nothing save rumours –'

'And they –?'

Conrad fingered his yellow sash uneasily.

'One said Modena had fallen –'

Ippolito gave a sudden cry.

'Modena!'

'Aye,' said Conrad, regretfully. 'And Ferrara and Verona – so I heard –'

'Mastino is dead!' cried d'Este, and Vincenzo echoed the cry wildly.

'Mastino is dead!'

'I know not,' said the Count. 'I cannot tell – only this, that Visconti marches this way – and once more – a good horse. Vincenzo, Saint Hubert has saved me once – I dare not ask him again!'

'Modena fallen,' murmured d'Este, unheeding Conrad's words. 'And Verona – Mastino dead – Visconti marches on Novara!'

'My father, we are lost indeed!' cried Vincenzo, with a white face. 'If Mastino be dead –'

'*If*!' said the elder d'Este, sternly. 'There is no if, Vincenzo,'

The boy looked round bewildered, and his eye fell on Conrad, waiting by the door.

'I will give orders for thy horse,' he said. 'Come with me –' and he led the way from the room. Conrad paused in the door, but Ippolito waved him aside sternly.

'Fare you well, Count, Vincenzo will see to your needs; meanwhile I have other things to think of –' and he strode past them, swiftly ascending the stairs to the soldiers in the higher chamber of the watch-tower.

Vincenzo, leaning on the stair-rail, with very bright eyes, looked after his father, and then toward Conrad with a sudden wistful smile. 'I almost would I were to be riding gaily across a summer plain, away – away – this castle has grown gloomy of late – there is horror in the air.' He shook the feeling off, speaking gaily. 'Well, be glad thou art on thy way, Count Conrad, and in exchange for the horse, take, for my sake, with thee the little page Vittore. He is very young, and not of Lombardy.'

'Gladly will I,' replied Conrad, as they descended the narrow stairs. 'And always shall I keep him for thy sake.'

'Aye, do,' said Vincenzo wistfully again, 'otherwise thou wouldst forget – of a surety, forget.'

'Not I – I shall always remember.'

Horses were brought to the courtyard, and Vincenzo called his little page and put him on one.

The sight of him brought memories to both of a certain game of chess – how fatal it had been: how long ago it seemed!

'I tried to make atonement,' Conrad murmured.

'My atonement, methinks, is to come,' said Vincenzo. 'But Mastino will never hear of it – Mastino is dead.'

Conrad winced. He knew Mastino was not dead, but he would as soon have stabbed Vincenzo d'Este as told him.

'Fare thee well.' he said, holding out his hand.

'Fare thee well,'

Vincenzo took his hand, smiled up at him gravely, and re-entered the castle, mounting to the room he had left.

Visconti was on the march.

Vincenzo caught his breath sharply and went to the window to see the last of Conrad. Again he wished he was riding away into the sunshine, away from the dark walls that seemed closing round him for ever.

'Farewell!' called back Conrad, gaily waving his mailed hand, and Vittore, excited at the sudden journey, drew off his cap and waved it gaily too. 'I go to my own land,' cried the Count. Vincenzo's lips trembled, but his words sounded as cheerily as Conrad's.

'And we stay here in ours,' he called back.

And in after days in peaceful times in Germany, when that brilliant, bloodstained Lombard summer seemed far away and strange as a wild dream, Conrad remembered; a memory he shared only with the dead.

The spurs jingled, with a trampling of hoofs the horses turned, the strong sun caught Conrad's plumes and Vittore's bright hair, he looked back with a laugh, and at a swift trot they passed through the castle gate.

Down the long paved street they clattered, till that sound too was gone.

Count Conrad had ridden away. Vincenzo stood silent in the great patch of sunlight that lay along the floor till Conrad's bridle bells were quite lost in the distance; then he turned, with something like a sigh.

He was not alone long – Ippolito re-entered with a calm face, and yet one his son was startled by.

'Count Conrad's news has been confirmed,' he said; 'a messenger has returned,' He paused a moment. 'All the country is in Visconti's hands.'

'The saints save us!' cried Vincenzo.

'Aye, the saints, for there is no hope in man!'

'We must get arms – and succour into the city –'

Ippolito looked at him with a proud affection.

'Follow me, Vincenzo.'

He opened one of the small doors; it led to a twisting flight of steps, and the two mounted in silence.

At the head of the stairway was a chamber used as an outlook toward – Milan.

'Gaze yonder,' said Ippolito, pointing through the narrow arched window.

Vincenzo obeyed, and looking out over the great wide plain, with its white campaniles dazzling in the sunlight, at first saw nothing.

But on the horizon was a silver light, a light that danced and quivered, flecked here and there with red, and dotted about with curious faint smoke wreaths, fires in broad day.

'Visconti's army!' said d'Este. 'And those fires the forts and villages della Scala held – held but yesterday!'

Their doom was in those words and in what they saw; there was no need for more.

'Santa Maria save us!' murmured Vincenzo, with a blanched face. It was all he said – words were poor, there was little enough time for action, none for comment.

Outside could be heard the steady tramp of the sentries, and the hurry of more soldiers to the walls.

'Do they know?' asked Vincenzo, as they descended. 'The soldiers – yes – they are Modenese. The townsfolk – poor wretches – why tell them.'

They watched the other chamber, and after a silence Vincenzo spoke incredulously.

'Conrad said Modena had fallen.'

'It is true,' said his father, in a low voice. 'And Ferrara – oh! – my cities!'

Vincenzo gave a little gasp of pain.

'And Verona?'

'That too.'

The younger d'Este looked out blankly at the sunshine, all hope faded from his face.

'And Mastino, Father?'

Ippolito was silent, a silence worse than speech. Vincenzo was awed.

'So we are abandoned – defenceless, resistance hopeless! Oh, my lord! My father! We cannot fall into Visconti's hands! We – the d'Estes!'

'Hush!' said his father, sternly, yet with sparkling eyes. 'I have been considering all – the Viper shall never fly in triumph from the walls from which a living d'Este is turned. Oh, had I never left Modena! See, Vincenzo – as soon as Visconti is within two miles of the gate – this!' He touched the door beside him, pushing it open, and Vincenzo's startled gaze followed the direction of his hand.

In the dark recess were the stone steps leading to the store beneath; the powder, the rude engines of war, and a vast quantity of wood, stored for winter use, and piled high even to the door. Vincenzo felt his heart grow cold; he looked from his father's proud face to what the steps beyond conveyed, and understood.

He raised his eyes steadily and smiled. He, too, was a d'Este, and in this moment the proud glory in his birth was plain.

'My son!' cried Ippolito, suddenly, passionately. 'My son!'

Vincenzo could not trust his voice to answer; he sat very still, the smile on his lips, his hand on his toy-like dagger.

D'Este turned his head away. From without came the sound of voices and footsteps – sounds of alarm, commands, shouts.

Ippolito turned to the door.

'I go to give the last orders,' he said, and left Vincenzo alone with his approaching fate.

He sat very silent.

This, then, was the end, the end of it all!

That one thought beat strongest on his brain – this was the end. What had he not meant life to give him – all he had seen others enjoy, all he had ever dreamed of, honour and fame, power and love, visions there were no words for – the future for him had held all these – and now, a burst bubble!

In the very richness of his youth he had flung away his days and hours, laughing at time, if he ever thought of it, and at life – then were life and time and an unending world before him.

Life! And even while he sported with it as endless, it could have been measured by hours.

A great wave of homesickness rushed over him, homesickness for the world, for the past he had never treasured, for Modena, the leaves and roses outside his father's palace, and Conrad riding away into the sunshine – away from this dark chamber he would never leave. Yet he did not for a moment flinch, such a thought never entered his mind, only he could not bear to have to wait; he wished it were done and over – now.

From the street below rose a great uproar; there was some panic among the people; the country folk were pressing through the gates, fire and sword behind them – Visconti was on the march! Wild frightened screams, and the hurry of feet, rose to the gloomy room, and Vincenzo sprang up; he wished his father had not left him, he wished he were not alone.

For his thoughts were bitter, and hard to bear alone. His life would be different, he thought, if he lived it again: not wasted, flung away. For the first time he felt he loved his father dearly, for the first time he realized how Mastino loved his wife – he understood. Was all knowledge coming to him so late, things to be made clear only to be darkened for ever?

Ah, well, it was all over now; there were only a few moments to – what? He shuddered a little – to what? He wished his father would return, passionately he wished it; he did not want to think – for the first time and the last. He stood there with tight-clasped hands, his eyes on the door, holding desperately on to his control.

And at last Ippolito entered, quietly, closing it behind him.

He held a missal in his hand, and a parchment. As he laid them on the table, Vincenzo noticed the last was sealed with the seal of Verona, the ladder of the Scaligeri.

'Mastino?' he whispered.

'Mastino is dead,' said d'Este, in a calm voice, and he crumpled the parchment in his hand.

On it was written: 'I have betrayed you for Isotta's life,' and it was signed with the proudest name in Lombardy – 'Mastino Orazio della Scala.'

'That shall not destroy the glory of Vincenzo's death,' thought d'Este sternly, and he flung it from him, into the room beyond, among the powder – something only fit to be consumed.

The castle within was built largely of wood, and Vincenzo, looking into the darkness with a painful eagerness, watched the powder laid carefully about the walls, extending in a long train to tanks of oil, while fire boughs, dry and leafless, lay scattered thickly. D'Este had not been taken unprepared. Vincenzo's flesh stirred and shrank; he remembered snatching a bat once from the camp fire, and how the pain on his hurt hand had tortured him.

''Tis a fearful death!' he murmured.

Ippolito turned a drawn face toward him.

'What didst thou say, my son.'

'Naught, Father,' answered Vincenzo bravely, though

his heart was beating hot and thick. 'Naught, save that *that* cannot fail us.'

'No, Vincenzo; the wind blows eastward across the town,' said d'Este, with a calmness that was almost brutal. 'There will be none for Visconti to take back to Milan.'

'We shall light the sky bravely tonight,' said Vincenzo, and bit his lip to keep it steady.

His father's dark face lit with a sudden proud smile that transfigured it.

'Some scouts say Visconti sends men to treat with us, Vincenzo – with us – d'Estes! This will be what he never reckoned on: the flames blowing from the walls shall be our flags of truce!'

The streets, the whole town, were in a panic. The wild terror of the whole countryside had found its voice inside the gates of Novara; there were six hundred men to defend the walls – and God! How Visconti sacked a town!

The sunlight that had rested along the walls when Conrad said farewell, lay along the floor now, a great square of gold that just tipped the table where Vincenzo's hand rested, and lay lovingly on his scarlet doublet, with its little foolish vanity of ribbons, and that other hand among them, clutched nervously, almost desperately, in the poor crumpled finery.

D'Este took the crucifix from the wall and laid it on the table. Under it burned a candle, and he moved that too, standing it beside him, as he took his seat opposite his son.

Behind him was the open door, in front the symbol of his religion – both meaning one thing, that the crucifix lying there baldly on the rough wood table told more plainly even than the powder kegs.

Vincenzo's eyes were on the missal, but not his thoughts: his ears on the strain for that sound he set his teeth in readiness to hear – the call to the gates.

In the silence of the chamber, the noises from the street sounded distinct, painfully distinct – shrieks and cries. Poor souls! So near eternity, and fighting over a handful of goods! Presently all noises died away into faint murmuring – or had he lost his power to hear? Then all at once it came – the beat of the drums, the summons to the walls! Louder, louder, wild, inspiring, the beat of the drums; and Vincenzo's heart bore them company.

They rose to their feet, the two d'Estes, and clasped hands across the table, the crucifix between them.

'God have mercy on our souls!' said Ippolito, and raised the pale, flaming candle.

'Amen,' said Vincenzo, kissing the missal with cold lips.

The drums beat wildly, intoxicatingly, then suddenly stopped.

D'Este pushed back his chair; for a moment there was perfect stillness, then he laid the candle to the powder.... And Vincenzo d'Este was on his knees in the patch of sunlight, its glory full on his beautiful, upturned face.

XXXII

The Price of Dishonour

He who was once the great Lord of Verona and a proud and stainless knight stood without Brescia, awaiting the price of his dishonour. It was midday, of a swooning heat, and great purple clouds lay heavily about the horizon, with a sombreness that foretold a storm.

Mastino della Scala stood alone on a group of rocks scattered upon the plain, that sent his tall figure up against the deep sky, erect and motionless.

All that was left of his army was behind him in the chestnut wood: half had been betrayed, half had been cut to pieces rather than yield. Some few – the lowest dregs of his camp, the men who cared not where or when they drew their swords, so they had food and drink – remained, to try their luck with him, now no better than one of themselves. Through all the miseries of that weary week his gallant band of Veronese, some two hundred, had stood by him, watching the others ambushed, attacked, surrounded, and destroyed, hearing of town after town that fell, and smiling scornfully at talk of treachery, accepting without question Mastino's silence. Was he not the son of Can' Gran' della Scala, and his name one with honour, the proudest name in Lombardy, the proudest badge in Italy, the ladder of the Scaligeri!

So had they stayed with scorn at thoughts of betrayal whispered among the baser residue, until that morning, when he had summoned their leaders and told them, with a strange calmness, he had sold them, Verona and

Veronese, for his wife's release – sold Lombardy for Isotta d'Este.

Then leaving them, standing silent and bewildered, della Scala mounted to these rocks to await his wife – alone. His eyes were on the fields before him; he hardly noticed a slight figure that crept timidly to his feet – Tomaso.

'My lord,' – the boy's voice faltered, and he kept his eyes turned away – 'the Duchess hath started safely; I saw her mount her litter with glad eyes; they bade me hasten forward and tell thee so.'

'Ah!'

Della Scala stepped on to a higher rock and shaded his eyes with his hand. He was in armour, and bore on his arm his shield, across the boss, the ladder, the ladder on which the Scaligeri had climbed so high, and from which they had fallen – to this!

Tomaso crouched beside him, silent and dismayed. He had clung to della Scala in spite of his father's loss (that he could not understand), and spite of what was happening now, that began to make plain that and many things.

Tomaso glanced up at the sombre figure standing alone above him. Mastino wore no mantle, and the golden circlet was gone from his helmet. Mastino della Scala was no longer Duke of Verona.

No pages or footmen followed; save for this one boy, he was alone, carrying his own shield, holding his own horse, despised of those he once had thought of as beneath even his scorn.

A gallop of horses broke the summer quiet, and spears gleamed through the ruddy chestnuts behind them. The Veronese, thought Tomaso, the Veronese soldiers.

Della Scala neither turned his head nor moved, but stood there with his shield hanging on his arm, his sword hand listless by his side.

Tomaso was right. The riders were a band of Veronese. At a full gallop they flew out of the shade into the sun, in face and movement, fury.

Tomaso shrank back at sight of them, roused from their bewilderment, riding full tilt toward Mastino in a silence that was more deadly than shouts of hate; and Mastino turned at last and faced them with wild eyes.

The foremost man was swiftly on them, his furious face brought close to theirs. As he swept up he drew the dagger at his waist and hurled it full on Mastino's shield.

'That from me!' he cried, and rose in his stirrups with a shout. 'That and my scorn, della Scala!'

But Mastino was prepared; he stood erect and did not flinch. Another rode by; bending his face close to him, he spat at him; both shattered their daggers on to his shield, those daggers mounted with his arms that they carried as his soldiers. One tore from his neck the collar Mastino had hung there, and flung it at his feet with curses.

'Traitor, where is Ligozzi?' cried one, hurling an imprecation, and della Scala took a step back with a cry wrung from him; but the man was gone, and the face of another Veronese was looking into his with utter loathing. Without a pause they dashed by, each hurling his dagger, and many some order or sign of Mastino's friendship, full upon that shield that hung on della Scala's arm.

'That to cheer thee in thy shame!'

'That to make a necklet for Isotta d'Este!'

'This from me, who would have died for thee!'

The taunts were bitter and savage, and hurled in a fury

of scorn and hate; but Mastino della Scala, save for that one movement, neither flinched nor stepped out of the way of the onward rush, but bore for a long hour of that summer day that wild ride past of the Veronese and the batter on his shield of the daggers that disdained to slay him.

'Stop! in the name of Heaven, stop!' shrieked Tomaso, and held his hands against his ears.

They took no heed of him, in their mad fury did not even see the boy. But to Tomaso it was most terrible that della Scala made no movement to defend himself; his calm face was awful. 'Stop!' Tomaso shrieked again. 'Stop!'

How many more, how many more! How many times more that rattle as the daggers struck the shield and then fell to lie bright in the sun? How many more furious faces, how many more bitter curses? How long would della Scala stand there turned to stone? Tomaso crouched and hid his eyes. At last they came to an end! The last rode by, the standard-bearer, tearing the standard to rags with furious hands.

'Verona is no more!' he yelled. 'The Scaligeri are no more, the standard is no more, the standard of Verona!'

He threw the twist of red and gold at Mastino's feet with a sudden wail in his voice. He was an old man, one who had served Mastino and Mastino's father well. He stopped his horse; the first who had done so.

'Mastino della Scala! Oh, why didst thou do this thing? Tell me thou repentest!' he cried.

Mastino looked into the old man's wistful face.

'Verona is no more, the Scaligeri are no more. Ride thou to the others, old man,' he said.

The standard-bearer wrung his hands.

'I loved thee!' he pleaded. 'Save thy soul and say thou dost repent!'

Mastino's proud head was erect.

'And do I live to save my soul? Get thee to the others, I do not repent.'

The old man rode away sorrowfully. Della Scala watched him disappear behind the rocks and trees.

He was the last, and silence fell.

'They are gone!' breathed Mastino. 'They are gone!'

His eyes fell to his shield; from rim to rim it was defaced and dented and the ladder of the Scaligeri was beaten from its boss. The ground around was piled with arms, and Mastino put his hand up to his eyes, staggering. The ladder of the Scaligeri was beaten from his shield!

'Some men remain, my lord,' said Tomaso timidly, at last, with a boyish effort at some consolation.

But Mastino winced; that they remained was a sorer shame even than the desertion of the others: for they were men, scum of camps, who fought solely for pay and plunder, and laughed dishonour and admired treachery – they were the men who stayed.

'Isotta!' cried Mastino, with a sudden wild movement. 'Why does she not come – have I not waited long – have I not paid enough?'

'I think I see her escort coming across the fields,' said Tomaso timorously.

Mastino turned and grasped his arm with a sudden change of manner.

'Tomaso,' he faltered, 'methinks I am changed since last I saw her; perhaps she will – not know me – or will startle at me if she does. Tomaso, she is very fair and I have nothing to offer now – Tomaso, am I very changed?'

He was changed, so changed the boy would scarce have known him; his soft, brown hair was streaked with grey, his fine face drawn and white, his eyes, once soft and kind, unnaturally bright, and, like his mouth, strained and hard.

Mastino laughed pitifully as he read the answer in Tomaso's frightened eyes.

'She will not care – she will not care,' he said. But his voice was unsteady, and he supported himself against the saddle of his horse.

'The Duchess comes!' said Tomaso, and clutched Mastino's hand.

Out of a little wood of delicate trees, in front of them, the cavalcade was winding: Visconti's soldiers, Veronese soldiers, and a white, curtained litter in the midst.

Mastino's gaze flew to that, and to that only.

'Oh, my heart's desire!' he murmured. 'I do not repent!' And he forgot the ladder of the Scaligeri battered from his shield.

The soldiers cantered up and lowered their halberds in a salute to the magnificent figure standing there alone, while the officer read in a high voice from the parchment, that stated that Isotta d'Este, Duchess of Verona, prisoner of war of Gian Galeazzo Maria Visconti, Duke of Milan, was returned to her husband in fulfilment of the league and treaty between them.

'Into your hands we deliver her in safety, my lord, and my Lord of Milan offers three months in which either to quit Lombardy or choose some post in his service in Verona,'

'My choice is made: I quit Lombardy,' said Mastino. 'Leave me.'

The soldier slightly shrugged his shoulders and gave the word, and, cantering off, Visconti's guards wheeled and followed swift behind him. They had fulfilled their duty: Isotta d'Este's safety was no affair of theirs now.

The Veronese footmen bearing the litter had set their burden down; the white curtains fluttered – was it the breeze, or Isotta's hand, that stirred them so?

'Tomaso, Tomaso, I have borne much; can I bear this?'

His eyes were sparkling, his tone joyful; he had thrown all his shame from his heart; the miserable past, the miserable future, were alike forgotten; the world had narrowed to this – her welcoming face.

He laid his shield on the ground gently, and walked across the grass softly. The curtains, white in the still blazing sun, dazzled him; his heart was beating so, he thought it must choke him.

'Isotta!'

He called her name so low she could not hear.

'Isotta!'

Still she made no answer.

'Perchance she is very weary,' said Mastino to himself, tenderly, and drew the white curtains' back. She lay back among silk cushions.

'Isotta, my dear!'

There was a tremor in his voice. Had she fainted?

She lay back, her head away from him, and, bending over her, he saw through her long curls that her eyes were closed, her lips parted, and one hand at her throat – the hand that bore his wedding ring. Oh, heaven! –

He caught her head in his hands and looked at her. She was dead, quite dead. The silk curtains fell to again, and at Mastino's cry the bearers shrank, appalled. Isotta d'Este was dead.

And Mastino lay along the ground, senseless, his defaced shield near him, bare to the bright glare of the sinking sun.

XXXIII

THE STORM

The storm had gathered and burst; rain fell in great drops that did not allay the heat; the sky was covered with clouds that dragged across the moon in a slow procession, dark and mysterious.

In one or two tents, thrown open to catch the breeze that stirred the chestnuts, sat the little handful of soldiers left to Mastino. Rude and coarse, still were they awed, by the horror that had befallen, to a whispering quiet.

Like a patch of white showing dimly through the gloom, the curtains of a litter were to be seen. At thought of who sat within alone there in the rain and dark, the men shuddered and drew nearer together.

'The Prince?' one whispered.

'I have been to the tent, but further than the door I dare not.'

'What was there to see?'

'The boy – alone, weeping like a woman. Santa Maria! I should not like the watch he keeps!'

'The Prince is mad, think you?'

'The Prince is mad, or – hush! – possessed.'

The men fell again to a silence, broken only by the patter of the rain. At last another spoke, one drawn further back into the tent.

'How came it about, think you?'

'Visconti –'

'Ah, yes, Visconti, of a surety; but how?'

'The wedding ring, Petio – it was handed to her as she

entered the litter – it was poisoned! She put it on, poor soul – kissed it, no doubt – well, it was poisoned, Petio.'

'And so she started alive, and now lies there dead – poor soul!'

The men muttered and crossed themselves; a few sat in moody thought.

'The sun – we need the sun,' said one at last.

'And a little wind, not these stifling puffs – a little wind from heaven. 'Tis hot as hell!'

'Hush!'

How it rained! And a wind rose, but it scarcely seemed from heaven. The chestnuts moaned, tossing their branches.

'Hush!' said some one suddenly. 'The dear Lord forgive my sins! Who comes?'

They heard a footstep; a hand was fumbling at the entrance of their tent.

'The Prince!'

And the next instant the men sprang to their feet in affright at what was before them, at the livid face looking at them – Mastino della Scala.

'My wife!' he cried hoarsely. 'Give me my wife!'

They looked on one another, helpless, and made no answer. But Mastino, striding forward, seized the foremost by the throat and shook him like a rag.

'Where is she? What have you done with her? Is she not bought and paid for? Where is she?'

Tomaso sprang into the tent, a piteous young figure, wet to the skin.

'Oh, my lord! I will take thee to her. Come away! Come with me!'

His voice broke into a passion of sobs, and Mastino dropped his hands and paused.

'Your lady lies still in her litter,' said a soldier.

'Out yonder in the rain, you rascal!' cried della Scala. 'What is she doing there?'

He flung from the tent, and Tomaso after him, the bitter sobs catching at his throat.

'I cannot bear it,' he cried. 'It is doom itself. Oh, my master! My dear master!'

The soldiers crowded together and watched.

'Look!' gasped one, pointing through the dark. 'He hath got her – he hath got her!'

And they huddled back, half falling over one another, as Mastino came into view – a slender thing in white and purple in his arms. Close by, he paused, and laid it tenderly across the saddle of his white horse, whinnying low and waiting.

'Jesu, protect us!' cried the men. 'Where is he going?'

'Stop him! stop him!' shrieked Tomaso, running to them. 'He goes to find – Visconti!'

'Then no one of us had best dare meddle,' was the answer. 'Keep away from him, boy; he is mad, possessed – maybe by the devil!'

'I care not!' cried Tomaso in an agony of sorrow. 'He shall not ride so; he has no armour on – it will be to his death. He shall not go – my lord! My dear lord!' He sprang forward to the white horse, which Mastino had mounted, and clung to the stirrup.

'Not tonight, my lord; wait till the morn – till the storm is over; thou art unarmed!'

Mastino drew Isotta close to him, till her head rested on his shoulder, and looked down wildly at Tomaso.

'Visconti lies outside Novara – I know the way!' he said.

'Take some of us with thee!' implored Tomaso. 'Oh, my lord –'

But della Scala spurred the horse into a sudden leap, that threw Tomaso to the ground.

'I know the way!' he said.

The white horse plunged forward into the storm, and the dark closed round the rider and his burden.

* * *

For hours had della Scala ridden with his wife across his horse and against his breast, but riding always toward Novara; and now he had ridden suddenly into a wild red glare that lit the sky.

Mastino's thoughts were centred on one thing – Visconti. There was no reflection in them; neither the past nor present had meaning. He was riding in a nightmare: he knew he carried Isotta, and that she was dead; he knew too he was riding to find Visconti – nothing more.

The red glare rose into the sky in pointed flames.

''Tis a burning city,' said Mastino; but the words had no meaning. Here was light, however, had he needed it whereby to find Visconti.

That blinding flare, though still a mile away, lit up the great posterns of a gate near, and a long wall adjoining was glowering red in it, the trails of the flowers showing like blood as they hung over it, spectral and strange. It was a noble's summer palace, lit by Novara burning yonder.

Mastino stopped his horse, that needed no checking, worn out by that wild ride, and gazed before him at the flames, and slowly something of reasoning power returned. He had ridden to meet Visconti, and Visconti was here. He knew it – either of God or devil – knew it surely; and he rode his horse on slowly, with the double burden, through the unguarded gates, and came to a flight of steps unguarded too, leading up to a wide balcony, overlooked by high, open, lighted windows. Here was the place – unguarded. Here was Visconti, and the soul of Mastino suddenly blazed into a white heat that for a moment blinded him.

Then he dismounted, and laid Isotta down, speaking the while to his horse. The glow from the burning city wrapped them both and made the fair dead face rosy. The tempest was over, and only a soft rain fell, ceasing gradually. Mastino found a sheltered spot beneath the bushes, and with a pitiful gentleness laid Isotta down and drew the hood about her head.

'I will come back,' he murmured, kissing her: Then he turned to the steps with his naked dagger in his hand. He wore no armour; he was bare-headed – he gave it no thought. He was here to slay Visconti. That was God's fact.

Along the steps a soldier came lazily, and Mastino sprang on him and strangled him before he could cry out, bearing the body noiselessly to the ground. Then, listening, he heard from within the palace a laugh and a voice – Visconti's. Della Scala looked round. How was he to get him? He must feel Visconti's blood run warm over his hands, and quickly.

'How it blazes! The soldiers will have poor spoil,' said Visconti. 'But we will build another town; de Lana: we are rich enough.'

'Outside the walls just now we found a ghastly thing,' said a second voice: 'a human hand grasping tight a knot of scarlet ribbons – just the hand, a beautiful hand.'

'Your tales sicken me – I have always hated horrors,' said Visconti.

Mastino crept along and found a door.

'I will get in there,' he said within himself; and then within himself he laughed, for it was opened.

The tapestry within was moved aside, and there was a glimpse of a white sleeve and a delicate, ringed hand. The next moment the curtain was torn, in a giant's grip, from its fastening, and Mastino, trampling it under him, was upon them – in his madness staying to reckon on no odds.

Where was Visconti? Not far, for he himself, with his own hand, had opened the door.

But from the red glare outside, the blaze within blinded della Scala. He looked round him for Visconti. Then a voice screamed: 'Keep him off!' and suddenly his eyes met the Duke's and he strode forward. It seemed almost done. Visconti, in wild fear fell back before that terrible face, staggering against the wall his hand fumbling for his dagger, and the men in the room scattered to right and left, as before an apparition.

'Gentlemen!' shrieked Visconti, 'you are ten to one: stop him! A fortune for the one who slays him!'

But Mastino had him in his grip – almost: another moment –

But Visconti fell, and crouched along the wall, those reaching hands above him; and a dozen swords leaped out: the soldiers flocked in from the ante-room; there was a wild confusion.

'Slay him!' shrieked Visconti. But from della Scala, as they closed on him, came a yell that froze the marrow.

Ten to one! They needed to be. The place began to run with blood.

'Gian Visconti! Gian Visconti!'

Visconti rose by the wall again. 'Kill him!' he gasped. 'Kill him!' and cowered away. He was not sure if that face or that figure, struggling ever toward him, could be killed; that they were earthly, or that that was the voice of a man which, with no sound of the human left in it, called his name.

'Let them kill him!' screamed Visconti.

But de Lana did not move, he did not look round; neither did Visconti.

'Visconti! Visconti!' gasped the voice... Ah!... There was a great scuffling of feet, the dragging of a heavy body, and Mastino, an inert mass upon the soldiers' arms, was forced back upon the balcony.

They let him fall there, and one heard him moan; but he was bleeding from twenty wounds. They left him and closed the door.

Visconti looked round fearfully.

'Is he gone?' he asked.

The great candelabra had been overturned and the room was in a semi-gloom, broken only by the dim candles in their sconces and the fitful flare from the city.

No one answered Visconti. The men drew breath in silence and looked at their wounds. How he had fought! A horror fell upon them.

'Is he dead?' asked Visconti, shaking like a leaf.

'There were fifteen men to kill him,' said de Lana, and he wiped some blood from his hand with a shiver.

No one else broke the silence, all stood still as if spellbound; it was a horrible, horrible thing, and they drew back from the door – afraid.

'Hush! What was that?'

Visconti leaned forward fearfully.

'What was it?'

The sound of some one on the balcony. Visconti's face went livid.

'He is alive –'

A horrid shudder ran through them all. De Lana strove to speak and could not.

'The door is not fastened,' whispered Visconti, hoarsely. 'Fasten the door – some one!'

But no one moved, no one dared, for superstitious horror.

Something fell back from the door, then the sound of something that dragged itself against it painfully, then a rattle at the unbolted door.

'He is not dead!' half screamed Visconti. 'A town to the man who will go out and slay him!'

No one moved.

'A half-dead man!' cried the Duke, 'and no one will end his misery?'

They dared not.

'Hark! He will have the door open. De Lana, I command you –' He pointed with a shaking hand, but de Lana only shook his head.

'There has too much been done already,' he said, shudderingly.

The Duke looked round wildly.

'A town, a fortune to the one who will have compassion; and with a shrug and a grimace, a rough soldier stepped forward, his drawn sword in his hand, and opening the door, pushed something back before him and went out.

Gian breathed heavily, listening, but the next second the soldier was in the room again, with altered face, and the door ajar behind him.

'I cannot,' he gasped – 'it's blind, struggling – it – does not look like a man – I –'

'Shut the door!' yelled Visconti, and then fell back

against de Lana, shaking, for a livid face appeared, with dim eyes and a bare throat streaked with blood. For one moment the ghastly apparition showed there, then fell into the dark again.

There was a sickening pause. Visconti spoke first, looking around.

'Are we fools or women? He came to murder me, and he is slain – what is there in that? Go and see *now* if he be dead.'

Someone went, fearfully.

'He lies very still, my lord; he is dead –'

The trembling pages had brought more lights, and light was life to Visconti. He came forward and looked, a little nearer, on the figure in the doorway, but very slowly, with de Lana between.

Mastino lay out straight, in a sudden up-flare from the burning city, his arm flung over his face.

'He was a giant,' whispered Visconti, fearfully. 'And how dark! I do not remember him so dark –'

He looked over de Lana's shoulder at him.

The soldiers peered behind him. That man was Mastino della Scala once! It was strange even to their cold hearts.

He was dead – *dead*! Visconti's fear, the superstitious fear of a righteous, God-sent vengeance, turned to a savage joy; still he was afraid, still afraid.

He touched the body with the point of his gold shoe.

'Throw him into the garden,' he said to the soldiers, showing his teeth.

Giannotto and de Lana exchanged a curious glance; the soldier set his lips.

'Are you all traitors or cowards, that you do not heed me?' cried Visconti in a fury. 'Throw, thrust, kick this thing into the garden – let him lie there till the morning.'

'My lord,' said de Lana, with a dangerous look in his eyes, 'he was a prince and a Scaligeri!'

'He was my enemy – scorn for scorn! Throw Mastino della Scala from the balcony – or –'

And half a dozen men came forward and lifted the prostrate body.

'Haste,' said Visconti, his eyes on de Lana. 'Throw him out of my sight.'

'Let them carry him down the steps, my lord,' cried de Lana.

But Visconti turned on him, his face and hair glowing in the light of the flames from Novara, his face fiendish.

'They shall do as I bid, or hang from the nearest tree! Now haste!' he said again, as if he feared the dead might yet arise.

They carried the body to the edge of the steps and pushed it over, crashing dully down the foliage that half overspread the marble.

Visconti stepped to the parapet and looked over.

'He said something as he fell,' he whispered to himself. 'I heard him – but he must be dead now –'

He turned back into the room, breathing more freely.

'Now close the door again,' he said, and watched while it was done.

XXXIV

An Instrument of God

'How many, de Lana – how many?'

'Five – six or seven –'

'Hundreds!'

'Thousands, my lord!'

Visconti leaned forward in his chair in his excitement. 'Thousands?'

'The men from Magenta are come in, laden with plunder,' Visconti laughed.

'I said I would give them Lombardy to sack – and there are thousands of prisoners.'

The scene was the summer palace, that same night. Visconti sat at the head of a table in a room adjoining the one in which the tapestry was torn and the floor still sticky with blood. It was a small apartment, beautifully inlaid with mosaic, and now blazing with lights, and full of a fine company of officers and nobles.

'Thousands – men, women, and children – some men of note, too, my lord; the ransacking of palaces for miles –'

'And Novara?'

'Some beat the flames out still – they say half the place is saved.'

'Let them plunder it!' cried Visconti. 'Let them pick Novara bare! The palace was burned.'

'To a cinder.'

'To a heap of ashes!' said another. 'There is nothing but the bastion, red hot –'

'As you should know, da Ribera,' laughed the officer next him, 'seeing you tried to ride over it.'

'And killed his horse,' said another.

'And saved myself!' shouted da Ribera. 'I look for a reward for that, my lord – the saving of a valiant officer of yours –'

'Shall not be forgotten!' laughed Visconti. 'Be paid by this advice. Remember burning towns are dangerous, as to his mortal cost a certain great Frenchman found at Rouen, and several great Germans more recently at Milan –'

'When they lay along the ramparts like flies, I have heard my grandfather say, striving to loot in the midst of the very flames,' said de Lana, 'like da Ribera here.'

'Had *I* been in Milan, Barbarossa himself would have burned in the midst of it,' said Visconti, sweeping back the glass and silver before him. 'The town had weeks to prepare.'

'Had you been there, Milan would not have burned at all, my lord!' said a flattering voice.

'Maybe it would not. It was certainly before the Visconti's rule began,' and he looked down the table with a smile at the dark face of Martin della Torre.

'And now the plans, de Lana – Novara to Magenta, Magenta to Vercelli.'

He swept the glasses still further back, and spread the parchment de Lana handed him on the coloured marble table.

'Vercelli – we hold Vercelli, de Lana?' The officers moved up closer, leaning over the table.

'We hold Vercelli – and Magenta.'

Visconti placed a silver goblet to keep the parchment down, and traced the route with the point of his dagger.

'To Turin – to Cuneo – as near as we dare to the stiff-necked Genoese, and we have circled Piedmont.'

'And these same Genoese?'

'Let them keep quiet,' said Visconti, sheathing his dagger and leaning back, 'and they may keep Genoa; we have larger game in view – the Empire. From the walls of Novara the Alps are to be seen, from the walls of Magenta they hide half the sky, from Turin one may touch them, and so we go closer –'

'And hold the Empire in check,' said de Lana, with excited eyes. 'Ah, my lord, it was almost worth it –'

Visconti turned to him sharply.

'What do you say, de Lana?'

There was a second's pause. This was the first, even vague, reference to what had happened earlier that same night; it seemed weeks since, and yet the sun had not risen on it.

Visconti looked at de Lana and laughed.

'Almost worth it – almost worth *what*, de Lana?'

The soldier, recovering himself, returned his glance.

'The extinction of four noble families, my lord.'

'Did my lord do it?' cried another.

'Did he ask the d'Estes to burn Novara.'

'No,' smiled Visconti. 'But had they not, I had done it for them, as I will burn Mantua, and the Gonzagas in it. We will have no seditious spots in the Lombardy *I* rule. There will be one capital and one ruler,' he added sternly 'The d'Estes knew enough to anticipate it.'

De Lana was silent.

'And these prisoners, my lord?' asked da Ribera. 'What of them?'

'They choke the camp,' said another.

'They are partisans of Mastino della Scala, naturally,' said Visconti. It was the first time the name had been mentioned, and Visconti's eyes flared to see that there was silence at it.

'Mastino della Scala, I said – they favoured him.'

'Yes, my lord; him, or the Estes.'

'You will put them to the sword.'

'All?'

'All!' shouted Visconti, half rising. 'I will have no rebellious slaves to groan over della Scala's grave, and hatch me plots from the ashes of their bones – we will raze the cities to the ground, and put them to the sword. My triumph will need no prisoners to prove it – and see it done, de Lana.'

They quailed; their attitude acknowledged him the master.

'Spare the churches,' said Visconti, 'and see that all relics are brought with due honour to Milan. Da Ribera, you ventured furthest into Novara; saw you any churches?'

'One, my lord, is saved: the church of Santa Chiara.'

'We tried to rescue the monks,' struck in Martin della Torre. 'They refused our succour, and returned into the flames – screaming –'

He paused.

'What?' demanded Visconti.

'Somewhat about God's curse,' answered della Torre. 'Their execration was not pleasant.'

'Had you not been there, you had not heard it,' said de Lana. 'And a few crazy – hark!'

There came a great noise from without, and the trampling of crowding feet.

'Another company is joining us,' remarked Visconti.

'The soldiers from Novara,' said della Torre, and put his goblet down, and de Lana turned expectantly to the door. Visconti, facing it, rose in his seat as it was flung wide and a couple of scorched and bleeding soldiers entered followed by a trampling guard.

'From Novara?' asked the Duke.

They stopped short, saluting.

'From Novara! We have saved the library and the college, my lord, and some three palaces.'

'They would have burned the library,' cried Visconti, 'sooner than it should enrich Milan – the jealous fools!'

'Now, hark you,' he added to the soldiers, 'every man bringing a book or a gem or a picture, I reward; every man destroying one, I hang. Now, which is he who saved the library?'

An officer pushed forward.

'This is he, my lord; one of my company.'

'Take this from me,' and Visconti handed the man his neck-chain.

'And the prisoners, my lord?'

'What care I for the prisoners! You will give no quarter, I say!'

The officer bowed, and drew a little book from his doublet, laying it on the table.

'A monk gave me this for his life,' he said. 'And all Lombardy knows your taste in books, my lord.'

'Remember we league with the Pope,' said Visconti, taking it up. 'The monk should have had his life without a bribe; now go, and heed what I have said,' He turned to de Lana: 'Follow, and see if the flames be out; 'tis daylight.'

The curtains were drawn away from the window, and the early light, fast glowing into sunlight, and the fresh morning air, filled the heated chamber.

The lamps flared pale, the gorgeous dresses and flushed, eager faces of the men round the table, the glimmer of the gold and silver vessels before them, showed in a garish contrast with the soft light.

'Seneca,' said Visconti, turning over the volume the

soldier had brought. 'Where is that knave Giannotto? Seneca, spoiled by interlining, but still Seneca. Giannott – I say!'

The secretary was not in the room, but the page dispatched soon brought him. He stood in the doorway, blinking at the daylight, looking around confused, and the company broke into laughter.

'Take this!' cried Visconti. 'A Seneca on vellum, with some dolt's comments; take it, Giannotto.'

'There is a library being brought in below,' said the secretary.

'Because we spared the church of Santa Chiara, who must have been the patron saint of poets – eh, de Lana?'

'Messer Francesco Petrarca found her so,' said a noble laughing. 'A lucky day for him when he stepped inside the church of Santa Chiara!'

'He had cause to thank her, doubtless –'

'If Messer Hugues had not,' smiled Visconti.

'I know not, my lord; for a dull boor like that, he gathered some fame else never his.'

'And the poet turned it to good account,' said Visconti. 'Methinks he used his love for money-making; he coined the Lady Laura into good gold pieces!'

'Now, my lord, is not that spite because Messer Petrarca left his library to Venice?'

Visconti laughed.

'Let him leave his library where he pleased, he was a fine man of business, say I.'

'And a wearisome poet,' said de Lana.

'0 Fiametta!' said Visconti laughing. 'Joanna! Naples and the blue sea! These are thy patron saints, de Lana.'

'Nay, I like not that book of feeble love-making – any better,' replied de Lana; 'a Florentine dallying!'

'I doubt me if thou hast ever read it,' said the Duke gaily.

'Alighieri is more to de Lana's mind,' remarked da Ribera, pouring wine, 'and the fair daughter of old Folco. I myself used to sing Alighieri's verses till I tired.'

'Yourself or your audience, my friend?'

But Visconti looked at the speaker, frowning.

'You have mentioned Alighieri, forgetting who was his patron,' whispered della Torre.

'The court of Verona and Can' Gran' della Scala –'

'He recanted, my good lord; he died a Ghibelline,' said da Ribera, acting on the whisper.

'Mastino della Scala was a Ghibelline; we never quarrelled over that,' said Visconti easily. 'But Mastino was no patron of poets like his father,' He leaned back in his chair and looked out of the window, where above the beautiful fresh green of the garden faint smoke-wreaths showed the last of Novara.

'De Lana, you stood next; "What did he say – as he went over?'

At the sudden brutal question, they started, and de Lana suppressed a shudder.

'I did not hear – I thought – he was dead.'

'I think you are still afraid of him,' smiled Visconti. 'I should like to know what he said.' And he looked round for Giannotto, who had shrunk into a corner, and sat there gazing dully at the company.

'Did you hear, Giannotto.'

'I? How should I, my lord,' and the secretary shuffled uneasily.

'Ho! a sullen knave!' cried Visconti, then leaned forward and touched de Lana on the arm.

'I hear more arrivals – hark!'

'What should this be?' asked da Ribera in surprise. 'Not my Lord Arezzo from Modena.'

'From Modena!' cried Visconti with sparkling eyes. 'Is there success there too?'

'Your arms cease to meet with aught else, Lord Visconti,' said della Torre. 'I drink to your perfect triumph!' He raised his glass, red as a huge ruby in the light, and Visconti, triumphant indeed when the leader of a faction admitted it and deemed it politic to say so, drank to della Torre standing.

There was a clatter of footsteps and the noise of a great entry.

'Silence!' said Visconti. ''Tis Arezzo, I hear his voice.'

The door was again thrown wide, this time upon a splendid cavalier, clad in magnificent armour, shining beneath his travel-stained scarlet cloak.

'Success rest upon your helm, Visconti, for Lombardy to Belluno is yours!' He swept his cap off, and stood, flushed and panting, before the eager, excited company, who rose to a man.

'Modena?' asked Visconti. 'And Mantua?'

'Yours,' said Guido d'Arezzo. 'And of Ferrara, I myself received the keys, and rode post-haste to Milan, through a country that dared not raise a finger, where even the nobles came uncovered to my stirrup; and so from thence I followed you here – with these as proof of my success.' He stepped aside, showing a glimpse of the disordered room beyond, and beckoned to one of the men behind him, taking two great standards from him.

'This as a proof – the banner of the Gonzagas, the standard of the d'Estes!' He dropped to one knee and laid them at Visconti's feet, both bloodstained, torn to rags, the bearings beaten from their surface; still, the flags that had floated from Modena and Mantua. The company burst into wild shouts, mad with the intoxication of success, and Visconti raised Arezio and placed him beside him at the table, the banners at his feet.

'Thou hast done splendidly,' he cried. 'On our side too there is fortune – Mastino della Scala will trouble us no more!'

'Dead!' cried the general. 'Dead!'

'He lies yonder in the garden.' With smiling lips Visconti pointed through the open window. 'He was killed last night!'

'The last of the Scaligeri! Then Lombardy is yours indeed!'

'From Vercelli to Belluno!' cried de Lana.

'I shall not forget those who helped me,' said Visconti, and called for wine and himself served Arezzo. 'I will prove I am no niggard to my friends – your health, Arezzo!'

The name of the victorious captain was shouted down the table; only Giannotto was silent, seated in the window-seat, and the Duke's eyes fell on him.

'Give the rogue there some wine,' he laughed. 'Have no fears, Giannotto, I will remember thee, there are palaces enough to loot. Thou shalt have the pickings of one. Drink!' he added in a sterner tone, as the secretary refused the wine with muttered excuses. 'Take it, and warm thy frozen blood, or we will find somewhat will do it better.'

The secretary took the goblet, but so gripping the glass that the slender stem snapped, and the liquid ran red over the black and white floor, like a trail of fresh blood.

'The cellars are not so full that we can spare good wine,' said da Ribera.

But Visconti laughed, and pulling the map again toward him, pointed out the march to Arezzo; and the secretary was forgotten, cowering in gloomy aloofness.

Giannotto watched the scene with a dull interest, as if it were far away and in no way belonging to him; he had had no sleep that night, and felt dizzy and confused. He could not forget Mastino, slain last night, and yet an eternity ago, and lying now out in the garden, marring the perfect morning with the horror of his face.

Giannotto turned his back to the garden and fixed his eyes on the group round the table.

They made a brilliant picture.

The background was mosaic, black and silver, gold and white, saints with glittering haloes, warriors in shining armour, placid and dignified – a splendid decoration; and against these the moving figures, brilliant in colour, scarlet mantles, doublets, purple and orange, glittering with jewels, and laughter and talk – a riot of life and colour. Slashed sleeves and gorgeous tassels were laid on or swept across the many-tinted marble table, on which there stood gold and silver goblets of curious shape, and glasses, milk-white, azure, or painted, some delicate as flower-bells, others with twisted stems clasped by a snake with emerald eyes. And the centre of it all was Visconti, leaning eagerly over the map, with brocaded mantle thrown back.

'And so to Turin!' Giannotto heard him say through the confusion of voices. 'We march next to Magenta.'

A dozen voices caught up the word. Giannotto watched them idly. The sun, flooding the room, made the gold on the wall twinkle and glint, and caught Arezzo's inlaid armour in points of light.

Visconti overturned one of the glasses, and drew on

the table the plan of Turin in spilled wine, de Lana leaning over eagerly.

Giannotto closed his eyes and leaned back. To his fevered senses the scene seemed unreal, and the two torn banners resting against the wall to add a touch of the horrible to the brilliancy and the triumph.

From Mantua and Modena – how much that meant! How many lives had been flung aside in wild agony and despair to make way for those banners to stand there!

'Mantua resisted desperately,' Arezzo was saying. 'But della Scala had left them so weakened.'

'Della Scala!' cried Visconti. 'I remember, he is in yonder garden; see he be brought in, da Ribera; out of all Lombardy I can spare him a tomb!'

The soldier left the room, and the talk went on with little heed of the interruption; Visconti still busy with the ramparts of Turin and the defences of Modena, de Lana disputing the route to Vercelli; but the secretary was not interested. His head pained him, and he fixed his eyes on Visconti's triumphant race with a strange fascination. It seemed a long time before da Ribera returned, and when he did, at something in his face, a sudden silence fell.

'What is it?' asked Visconti, and, half-reeling, Giannotto leaned forward to listen for the answer.

Da Ribera did not at once reply.

'What is it?' repeated the Duke angrily.

'We have found della Scala,' returned da Ribera, finding voice, 'but not only his body.'

'Ah!' cried Visconti as if a sudden thought had struck him, 'whom else then, da Ribera?'

'I cannot tell, only there is a dead lady in the garden; she is laid as if sleeping on the grass, quite dead.'

Visconti rose so suddenly that the sweep of his long sleeve sent the glasses crashing to the ground, and made Arezzo start.

'It is Isotta d'Este!' he cried. 'Mastino's wife!'

'Isotta dead?' cried de Lana, and the words echoed around the room. 'How should she be here, and dead?'

'The dead only can answer you,' said Visconti. 'Now I can recall what 'twas Mastino said – something about her! Still, it may not be his duchess. As you say, how should she be dead, and here?'

'How should she be dead?' asked de Lana again. 'Yet truly what else –' he paused, keeping back his words, and his glance met the secretary's.

Giannotto was remembering something: the figure of Visconti standing sullen, with a moody face, thinking on another dead woman; 'Had she lived I would not have done it!' he had said. The secretary rose; now he understood.

In this triumphant Visconti there was no sign of the spirit that had prompted that murmur, but the secretary understood.

Close behind Giannotto was a fresco painting, a panel between the windows – St. Sebastian in a glory, smiling, transfixed with arrows, brilliant against a background of blue.

Giannotto, standing there half-dazed with his new thought, noticed it, and clutched the wooden ribbing underneath with something like a prayer on his lips. Might the saints and martyrs remember to him he had had no share in this!

Visconti turned to leave the table, and with a clinking of armour and a dazzling display of scarlet and blue the nobles moved back; the sunshine was now golden and filling the room.

'Can he be going to look at her?' thought the secretary, dully; then, stumbling over something as he moved forward, he glanced down and started. The next moment he looked round sharply to see if any eye was upon him, stooped quickly, and picked it up.

It was a little stiletto, a thing dropped, perhaps last night, and overlooked, a tiny thing with a long, glittering blade. Giannotto slipped it into his dress, he hardly knew why – it gave him a feeling of security; it was a long time since Visconti's secretary had been armed, even by so much as this.

'With good horses,' said Visconti, drawing on his gloves, 'we reach Magenta – when, de Lana?'

'In two days, my lord.'

'And Turin?'

'If there's no resistance –' began de Lana.

Visconti laughed.

'Resistance? Lombardy is ours, my good de Lana! Resistance –'

'Is hardly wise,' put in da Ribera.

'And quite useless,' said della Torre, with a low bow.

The splendid group was passing Giannotto, standing dully beneath St. Sebastian, when the Duke stopped.

'Come, I may have need of you, Giannotto.'

The secretary's hand stole to his breast. He felt the handle of the stiletto, and wondered why he had picked it up.

The doors were thrown open for the Duke to pass, and as they passed out into the stairs, Giannotto slunk into his place behind Visconti.

Here were also noise and crowds; the coming and going of soldiers and courtiers, excited talk and laughter, and in the distance the sound of the drums, for the army was preparing to march. The front of the palace was alive with them, the rattle of the new-fashioned artillery, the shouted commands, the sunshine upon the standards and the armour, and the fluttering, coloured plumes.

But Visconti turned aside to the back of the palace, and descended the steps that led to the garden. It was quiet here, all sounds subdued and distant.

The balustrade of the steps and terrace was smothered in roses, white, pink, and crimson, past their full summer pride, and many lying crushed across the marble while tangled trails of leaves and creepers lay torn from the stone where they had clung.

Visconti noticed it, and looked with a smile at da Ribera, who in his turn smiled also and passed a light word on at which the laugh was general.

They were great nobles, princes some of them, yet not one dared to look grave when Visconti smiled, or was not eager to fawn upon his notice.

At the foot of the steps the grass was crushed and blood-stained, and from beside the oleanders and olives, drooping in the sun, a little procession of men was engaged lifting something from the ground.

Visconti stopped.

'Della Scala' said de Lana. 'They are moving him according to your orders my lord.'

Visconti stroked his chin thoughtfully.

'Bid them set him down again.' And he stepped softly down the steps.

Giannotto looked at his smiling face with a cold strange horror and glanced round to see if it were not in the others' faces too, but he did not see it.

The soldiers, at de Lana's peremptory order, stopped and laid the burden they were lifting at Visconti's feet.

'Mastino della Scala!'

Visconti repeated the name and grasped his dagger.

Mastino della Scala, the man who had checked him, scorned him, foiled him all his life, the proudest race, the most stainless name in Lombardy, ended here and in this!

Visconti stepped close and looked down into his enemy's uncovered face.

'He was not beautiful, this della Scala,' he said.

Then he glanced up and round with a wordless, an unutterable exultation. All he had asked had been given him and more! He, Visconti, Duke of Milan, could ask for nothing more than this moment gave him – a perfect triumph.

Da Ribera peered forward curiously. 'He is torn to rags,' he said. 'He must have fought like a madman –'

'He *was* mad,' said Visconti.

'And the lady?' said de Lana, suddenly, to Visconti. 'Where is she, my lord?'

Visconti, lacing his gold gloves, paused a moment, and answered over his shoulder, lightly:

'She seems to fill thy thoughts, de Lana!'

'Only, can it be the Duchess,' said da Ribera. 'I have never seen Isotta d'Este, so cannot tell. I left her where I found her – on the grass, beneath those laurels. But that it is a lady –'

He pointed as he spoke to a distant bush, round which tall lilies grew.

'It is the Duchess!' cried another.

'How should she be dead?' asked de Lana, and his glance again sought the secretary's.

'How, indeed?' said Visconti, with a curious smile. 'And yet there are enough ways of dying abroad. I will see for myself – so that if it indeed be Isotta d'Este she may have fitting honour –'

The group moved forward. The advance of the army was already marching past the walls of the garden, past the gate through which Mastino had ridden; the pennons from their lances showed above the yellow jasmine that covered the stonework, and the drums beat loud as Visconti and his company reached the laurel clump and stood looking down at the silent figure in the crushed and bedraggled white and purple.

'Isotta d'Este!' said Visconti, under his breath, and yet with an unmoved face, that showed no surprise.

'Dead!' said de Lana, after a pause, and looked at him.

Visconti laughed softly, and turned with shining eyes.

'Did I not tell you della Scala was mad – did we not see it for ourselves last night?' he said.

'So it *is* the Duchess,' whispered da Ribera. 'She was very beautiful, they say.'

She lay where they had drawn her from her shelter underneath the laurels, her dress clinging close, her head turned away. Mastino had wrapped her round carefully, with a clumsy tenderness; wrapped her veil about her face, and laid his own cloak over her to shield her from the night and rain. And his last whisper was for her – an appeal to someone's humanity to see that Visconti should not look upon his victim's face, should not defile her with his touch.

It rushed on Giannotto with the certainty of conviction – he had caught only the ghostly whisper, but he was sure in this moment of the sense of it; and the music the colours and sunshine, and splendour and pomp of triumph, and Gian Visconti's cold, mocking face began to dance before Giannotto's vision like figures and fancies of a dream. He heard Visconti speak to Arezzo, saw Arezzo stoop and lift the mantle, and he moved back a step and put his hand to his breast.

'Isotta d'Este!' said Visconti, turning to the others, and pointing down to the dead uncovered face. 'Now what was she to lose everything for?'

'His wife ' said de Lana, and turned his head away.

'Yes, my friend – do not forget it: *della Scala's* wife!' and Visconti touched him on the shoulder warningly.

The group turned to go, and the secretary saw it with a feeling of relief, when by some sudden impulse Visconti stepped back, and stood looking down once at the poor white face.

His own showed neither fear, nor remorse, nor wonder, only triumph, and the secretary felt the blood rise slowly from his heart toward his brain, and he drew the stiletto half from his breast.

'*Donna mia*,' said Visconti, speaking to her with a smile, 'we must not part so coldly, you and I – I will give you a fair tomb in Verona – in red Verona, *donna mia*.'

He dropped on one knee beside her, holding the laurels back and the lilies that hung above her head.

'This as in earnest,' he said, and bent over her and kissed her – kissed the cold cheek of Mastino's wife.

The group watching stirred among themselves; no smiling faces now; each eye averted, but still no one spoke.

And Visconti stooped and kissed her again, where the dark hair lay about her forehead.

Then something gave in Giannotto's brain; a voice seemed to thunder in his ears – 'Judgment!' His hand flew from his breast and up and down upon the kneeling figure, while he cried out terribly with a white, inspired face, and Visconti fell forward stabbed through the back.

'Treachery,' cried da Ribera, scarcely seeing who had done it. 'The Duke is stabbed!'

Visconti clutched at the flowers and fell without a word.

'Killed!' screamed de Lana. 'Now God is just!'

'Killed – the Duke is killed!'

Guido d'Arezzo bent over him with a white face, but della Torre stamped in a passion of excitement and dragged at his shoulder.

'Killed! – come away – there are ourselves to think of – come away! –'

Arezzo sprang to his feet.

'To Milan!' cried della Torre. 'He leaves no heirs.'

Visconti was still breathing: he struggled, and Giannotto pushed to his side and stood above him, bursting into wild words.

'I did it – Visconti! I did it – do you hear – do you hear! I knew, and I did it!'

'Keep away!' yelled della Torre, and pulled him back.

Then he dropped to his knee and tore the signet ring from the hand of the dying man.

'To Milan!' he cried, springing up. 'Haste! To Milan!'

'To Milan!' echoed Arezzo; 'To Milan and the army –'

'Back – all of you!' said de Lana, and he raised Visconti. 'He is not dead –'

'He is past life. To Milan!'

The garden was one wild, yelling confusion; the news was spreading like fire; each thought and acted for himself; and Giannotto, instrument of vengeance, whimpered on his knees.

The rush to the gate came by so close, the flying feet almost touched Visconti's face; and as della Torre passed, he struck his glove across him.

De Lana lifted Visconti from the grass, but with a last effort he struggled from him and dropped back.

'Milan!' he sobbed.

De Lana bent down eagerly to catch a muttered prayer, but there was nothing more.

'Milan!'

The voices and shouts rose to a deafening pitch of confusion, the very air seemed fevered with excitement; a flock of startled doves flew past in panic, a rainbow of colour; flew so low and so close to de Lana as to blind him for a moment with the whirr of their wings, and in that moment was a terrible cry.

They passed, beating the lilies down.

'My lord!' cried de Lana. 'My lord!'

But even as he spoke, he knew Gian Visconti was dead.

YOUNG SPITFIRE'S

Bows Against the Barons by Geoffrey Trease

The tale of young Dickon – made an outlaw for killing one of the king's deer – and his fight against injustice. This classic work captures the struggle between rich and poor, and above all, the story of the great leader, Robin Hood of Sherwood Forest – presented as the author felt he really might have been.

ISBN 1 904027 26 1   156pp   Paperback   £6.99

The White Camel by Eden Phillpotts

Set in the Arabian desert, this tale of physical and spiritual growth stirringly captures the adventures of Ali, a Bedouin chieftain's son.

from Joanne Harris's Introduction:
'I can't tell you how happy I am that this magical book is finally going to be made available once again… It is a wonderful book for adults and children alike, with a style which manages to be both intensely poetic and excitingly muscular at the same time. It is good to see a children's book written without a hint of condescension or any taint of political correctness.

…It is also a terrific adventure story in a kind of Arabian Nights tradition.'

ISBN 1 904027 25 3   192pp   Paperback   £9.99

John Diamond by Leon Garfield

Narrated with verve and pace by a master story-teller, *John Diamond* follows the quest of William Jones and his heart-stopping adventures through the streets of a richly-imagined eighteenth-century London. With a cast of characters worthy of Charles Dickens, *John Diamond* was the winner of the Whitbread Award and the Boston Globe–Horn Book Award.

ISBN 1 904027 32 6   208pp   Paperback   £7.99

A selection from Geoffrey Trease's

BOWS AGAINST THE BARONS

Crack!

The long whip curled round his shoulders, burning the flesh under his ragged tunic. Dickon swayed sickly, but did not cry out. His hands tightened on the woollen cap he held, and he bit his lip to still the pain.

'I'll have no idlers,' said the bailiff.

He glared down at the boy, a mountainous man on a mountainous horse, his hard face dark with passion.

'That'll teach you to fail in your duties, my lad. You know what they are well enough. Repeat them.'

Dickon looked up sullenly. His blood boiled within him. He longed to leap on the bailiff's saddle-bow and drive his dagger into that fat belly, but he knew how impossible it was. The man would shake him off like a rat, and the long sword would flash down to finish him for ever....

It was no good. The masters were the masters. The peasants must obey and be whipped and work again, till death brought time for resting.

'Yes, sir,' he answered between clenched teeth. 'I must work on my lord's land every other day; I must plough four acres of his land in the springtime and furnish two oxen for the work; I must –'

'That'll do,' interrupted Master William harshly. 'Why weren't you at work this morning?'

'It was the pig, sir. It had strayed into the forest. If I

hadn't gone to look for it –' He broke off with an appealing look. 'It is the only pig we have, sir.'

'Pigs? What the devil do I care about your pigs?' The horseman raised his whip again menacingly. 'You are all pigs, you labourers. Next week you will work on the lord's land every day as a punishment.' He wheeled his horse in the sandy track. Once more Dickon longed to plunge his knife into that fleshy body. 'Mind you're there,' the bailiff shouted over his shoulder, 'or I'll have you flogged.' He cantered away to inspect the work at the mill.

Miserably, Dickon walked on towards the mud-and-straw hovel which he called home. It had been a long, tiring day, toiling on the miserable strips of land held by his father, and he had not yet a man's strength.

If only his father would return! But he had been gone for years now, along with Sir Rolf…

A selection from Eden Phillpotts'

THE WHITE CAMEL

Sheikh Abbas was a mighty man of valour who lived in Arabia and reigned over a clan of the Bedouin Arabs, leading them from place to place with their herds and flocks. His people feared him, but they always obeyed him because he was not a person you could say 'No' to very easily.

Now, when I speak of Arabia and tell you that the White Camel lived all his wonderful life there, you will say, 'Which Arabia?' Because there are three. Arabia the Stony is a land of mountains and fierce wadis, or river-valleys, where the great streams roar down in the rainy seasons and dry up again when the sun comes out to roast the world; Arabia the Blessed is the land of cities and farms and fruit and oil and honey and corn and sweet scents that make the air delicious to breathe; and Arabia the Sandy is a vast and burning desert, where strange things happen and strange folk dwell. Mountains thrust up out of the great ocean of sand, and scattered upon it sparingly are oases and wadis, where the precious water rises from far below and gives the trees and shrubs and grass a chance to live and prosper in the midst of that thirsty world.

Now Sheikh Abbas dwelt upon Arabia the Sandy; but he had a beautiful oasis of his very own in the midst of it. When he and his people were tired of wandering upon the great Red Desert of Dahna – to find the browse that their sheep and camels needed – he would break up his camp and take everybody back to his oasis, that the men and women and children and flocks might see the green of living things again, and drink sweet water from the wells, and eat fresh fruits and enjoy themselves, before they set out once more upon their restless wanderings. For the roaming Bedouins cannot stop in one place very long: they must be on the move and they would hate to be like the townsfolk and settle down in one house for evermore. They better love to dwell under their tents and wander amid the adventures and dangers of the eternal sand.

And now you meet the little clan of Sheikh Abbas, encamped two days' march from the oasis, under a low ridge of hills that ran between them and the eastern sky. It is the middle of the night, and the moon shines above the desert and makes the sandy wilderness all grey. Far out in the desert hyenas are laughing together and making a faint but horrid noise. What they are laughing about nobody can tell you, but they are rude fellows, with rather nasty manners, and I don't suppose their jokes would amuse us very much. The desert jackals are also breaking the great silence. They howl in rather a mournful fashion and don't sound as if they had much to laugh about; but they annoy the dogs of the camp, and the dogs bark back at them and tell them to shut up and run away.

Where is the camp itself? But for an accident you would hardly see it, for it is crouching under the low, dark hills, and there beneath their little tents, woven of goats' hair all dyed pitch black, dwell a large company of men and women; while round about the horses, camels and sheep are herded. At this time, in the dead of night,

A selection from Leon Garfield's

JOHN DIAMOND

My father made his fortune in London. He'd been in coffee – not like a spoon, but in the way of buying and selling it, in barrels and sacks. He never talked about his years in trade, which consequently gave them an air of mystery and romance, with a strong sensation of ships.

He never really talked much at all; or at least, not to me, except to remark on my dirty fingernails and to ask me if I intended to grow up to be a sorrow to my mother and a disgrace to my sisters, who always nodded as if they fully expected that to be the case.

Yet, like everybody else, I couldn't help liking and admiring him, and would have done anything to earn his praise. I would lie awake at nights, dreaming of distinguishing myself in every possible way – except, of course, the one that would have pleased him most, which was to be clean, neat and studious, to follow in his footsteps and be a pillar of the community.

His footsteps! Now I've come to them. I hated and dreaded them. Every night I heard them, back and forth, back and forth across his room, which was directly under mine.

They started when the house was quiet, at about midnight, and went on and on until I fell asleep. Sometimes I tried to count them, like sheep, and then to work out how far they would have reached if they'd been laid end to end. I think it was to Edinburgh; but later I discovered that his journey was a good deal longer.

At first I thought he might have had the toothache; but, as his face was never swollen, and he had no trouble with eating, it was plain that the reason lay deeper than that.

I knew he was unwell. Dr Fisher from Hertford had called to see him several times, and had gone away looking glum; so it occurred to me that, just as some people have the sleeping sickness, some the falling sickness, my father had the walking sickness, and that was the cause of it.

If so, it was a very strange malady, for it only attacked him by night and drove him from his bed, to walk and walk, as if he would wear out a grave in the floorboards with his feet.

That he was as ill as that – to bring graves to mind, I mean – I first learned from Mrs Alice one Saturday afternoon in September, when the rain had kept me in.

Mrs Alice was our cook and housekeeper rolled tightly into one, and secured by an enormous white apron and a crusty white cap, so that she looked like a wrinkled old baby who had been left waiting at the font.

I was in the scullery, helping myself to raisin wine, which was kept in a stone jug covered with a bit of beaded muslin to prevent the flies.

She came in so suddenly that I had no chance to escape and could only stand, with the jug up to my face and the muslin veil on my head, waiting for her to shout loud enough for my father to hear.

Instead, she gazed at me mournfully and said it was high time I stopped thinking only about myself and began to think of being a support to my mother and sisters as my father could not live for ever.

Published in Great Britain by

Elliott & Thompson Ltd
27 John Street
London WC1N 2BX

First published in 1904
This edition © Hilary Long 2004

Introduction © the Estate of Graham Greene

ISBN   1 904027 24 5

First edition

Book design by Brad Thompson
Printed and bound in Malta by Interprint